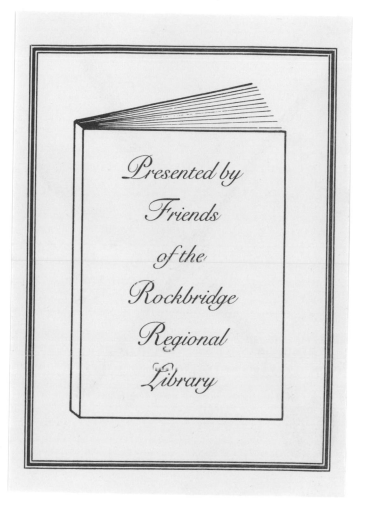

Presented by

Friends

of the

Rockbridge

Regional

Library

CIRCLES

OF

STONE

CIRCLES

OF

STONE

JOAN DAHR LAMBERT

POCKET BOOKS
New York   London   Toronto   Sydney   Tokyo   Singapore

This book is a work of fiction. Names, characters, places and incidents are products of the author's imagination or are used fictitiously. Any resemblance to actual events or locales or persons, living or dead, is entirely coincidental.

POCKET BOOKS, a division of Simon & Schuster Inc.
1230 Avenue of the Americas, New York, NY 10020

Library of Congress Cataloging-in-Publication Data

Lambert, Joan Dahr.
    Circles of stone / Joan Dahr Lambert.
        p.   cm.
    ISBN: 0-671-55285-6
    1. Man, Prehistoric—Fiction. 2. Goddess religion—Fiction.
I. Title.
PS3562.A452C57   1997
813'.54—dc20   96-30904
                                                                    CIP

First Pocket Books hardcover printing April 1997

10 9 8 7 6 5 4 3 2 1

POCKET and colophon are registered trademarks of
Simon & Schuster Inc.

Printed in the U.S.A.

To my father, whose love of intellectual pursuits
and regard for the natural world are gifts I cherish, and
to my husband for his unfailing support as the
book evolved.

CIRCLES
OF
STONE

PROLOGUE

Zena took her daughter's hand to help her up the steep path. She was hardly aware of making an effort, so familiar was the way. Hundreds of times, she had come to the sacred ledge where she spoke to the Goddess, the Mother of all that lived. But for the young Zena, the way was new and strange.

They came to the opening high on the cliffs. Zena led her daughter out upon the ledge and stood, arms upraised, to greet the Goddess. The young Zena watched, still and silent.

"Great Goddess, I bring you my daughter, who is destined to serve You, for she, too, bears the name of Zena. Help her as she learns Your ways; walk within her as she journeys through her life. Send her Your knowledge, Your wisdom; guide her heart and mind as she leads our people in the years to come. Blessed Mother, we reach now for Your strength."

Zena waited until she felt the Goddess within her, deep and secure, before she turned to speak to her daughter. The young Zena listened carefully, for she knew she must never forget what she learned this day in the sacred place.

"For many years, more than any can remember," Zena told her, "we have lived in harmony with each other and with the life around us. That is because we have followed the ways of the Mother, the ways of peace and caring. In each tribe, there was a wise woman who taught the Mother's ways to her daughter, or her sister's

1

daughter; she, too, passed on her knowledge. And so it has been, until now, for all the years of our existence.

"Some of these wise ones were called Zena, like ourselves. To us, the Mother entrusts Her most arduous tasks. The first one lived long ago, before the time of our people's memory. Still, her love for her people, her suffering when they were hungry or in pain, was no different than our own. The next Zena could see far more with her mind than any other, and she changed our world in many ways. Because of her, all people came to know the Mother, so that all could live in peace.

"The one who came after her was myself, and already you know something of my story. But now you must know all; you must journey into my heart and mind, into the hearts and minds of the others who bore the name of Zena, for we are one even as we are separate. Here, as we wait on the cliff, the Goddess will bring you our lives, in Her visions. You will feel our joy and suffering, know our thoughts, our fear and wonder, see and hear all that we have seen and heard, until you have become us. Only in this way can you fulfill the destiny entrusted to you by the Goddess: to keep the Mother's ways alive in the time of trial to come.

"Come with me now, child; come with me to greet the Goddess, for She calls us. Pull Her wisdom into your mind, Her strength into your body, Her love into your heart. Feel Her deep within you as She takes you back to the beginning, to the one who was first called Zena. She will teach you, as each of us will teach you. Fill yourself with our lives, our knowledge and visions, all that we have experienced, until we have become a part of you, a part of all the Zenas yet to come, so that the ways of the Mother will never be forgotten."

PART I

The Great Rift Valley of
Africa—one to one and a half
million years ago

CHAPTER

1

The scream exploded across the empty savannah. Zena flinched and huddled closer to the base of the ancient acacia, trying to make herself invisible against its gray bark. Her hands betrayed her; they rubbed ceaselessly across the swollen curve of her empty belly in a futile gesture of comfort. She had not eaten for many days.

The shrill cry of alarm had come from her mother, Tope, above her in the tree. She screamed again, and this time the piercing sound broke through Zena's lethargy. Grabbing a low limb, she scrambled into the gnarled tree. Only when she had reached the safety of Tope's side did she look down. The hyena stared hungrily up at her. Its massive jaws were still wide open in readiness, and drool spilled from its grinning lips. She shuddered and moved closer to her mother.

The hyena stretched its forelegs up the tree and lunged toward them. Tope shook her stick at it, screaming all the while. When it leaped again, she struck it hard in the nose. The animal retreated, whining, and loped slowly away. Tope watched intently until it had disappeared from sight.

Zena watched with her until exhaustion made her eyelids droop. She forced them open again, afraid to sleep, and stared listlessly toward a horizon turned pale with dust. Waves of heat shimmered against her vision, but she saw no other movement, no sign of life anywhere on the expanse of cracked brown earth before her. Once, huge herds of animals and miles of undulating grasses had deco-

rated the plains, but this Zena did not know. All she had ever seen
was an occasional tree thrusting its bare branches upward as if in
supplication, and piles of sun-bleached bones, mute testimony to
the power of the drought.

A twig snapped beside her, and she jumped in alarm. But it was
only her mother, climbing slowly from the tree. An infant, its round
eyes enormous in a nearly fleshless face, was clutched tightly
against her bony chest.

Calling to Zena to follow, Tope headed toward an old stream
bed she had spotted in the distance. The pebble-lined fissure was
all that remained of a stream that had once thrust its way, bubbling,
through the grasses. Now it looked dry as bone, but water sometimes lingered beneath the surface of such places. Without water,
Tope knew they would not last much longer.

Too drained to move, Zena did not respond. Tope looked back
and called to her. Every few yards, she stopped and repeated the
calls. Finally, when Zena still had not stirred, she uttered an imperative hoot of alarm. The harsh sound, familiar to Zena since her
birth six years before, triggered an automatic response. Whimpering
softly, she lowered herself from the tree and floundered after her
mother.

A tiny pool of water slowly formed as Tope dug deeply into the
old stream bed. Imitating her mother, Zena finally managed to ob-
tain a few slurps of tepid, earth-laden liquid. But it was enough to
ease her thirst a little.

All the rest of that day, Tope headed west, following an instinct
she did not question. Her deep-set eyes, protected from the glaring
sun by a jutting ridge of brow, swept the barren landscape constantly as she walked, and her sensitive nostrils twitched, testing
the air for scents. Zena tried to imitate her mother, but there was
nothing to see but the haze, nothing to smell but dryness. She licked
her forearms, seeking a few precious drops of sweat. Dust coated
her tongue instead.

Tope lunged suddenly at a small lizard that had crossed her path.
She caught it deftly and crammed it into her mouth. Dislodged by
the abrupt movement, the infant began to whimper. Tope pulled it
close to her breast, which hung low and pendulous so the baby
could suckle as she walked. But little milk was left to comfort it,
and the thin wailing did not stop.

A sound made Tope whirl. The big male had crept up behind
them, his footsteps muffled by the powdery earth and the baby's
crying. Tope eyed him warily. She did not trust strange males.

Once, she had seen one grab an infant and smash its head against the ground. The image was indelibly printed on her memory.

Zena ducked behind her mother's back and peered nervously at the intruder. She seldom saw others like herself. Her troop had dispersed long ago, for nowhere in the drought-ravaged land was there enough food and water to support a group. The stranger frightened her. Almost twice the size of her mother, he had massive shoulders, and his jaw and chest were matted with dark hair.

The male reached out as if to grab the infant, then lunged unexpectedly at Zena. She shrieked and ran back a few steps, but Tope stood her ground. Holding the baby tightly against her chest, she turned and presented her rump. The male sniffed her, then grabbed once more at the infant with a heavily muscled arm. Tope screamed at him and clutched it closer. Again, she presented her rump. This time, the male mounted her and thrust eagerly. He groaned with pleasure, and so did she. When he had finished, he ambled off in the direction from which he had come.

Tope waited until she was certain he would not follow them again, then she hurried on. Streaks of brilliance on the western horizon told her that darkness would soon come, and she wanted to find a secure place to spend the night. But no tree or pile of rocks that might offer refuge was visible on the pale and dessicated land that lay ahead. All she could see was a clump of stunted bushes, branches stripped of the withered berries that had been the only remnants of a once sumptuous annual feast. But the branches had thorns and would offer at least minimal safety from predators during the dark hours.

Zena followed her mother into the meager protection of the bushes and watched fearfully as darkness gathered around them. Soon, the air was so black she could not even see the shape of her hand. She listened instead, straining her ears for the stealthy sound of padded claws so she would be ready to run. But no lion or tiger appeared, and finally the light came again.

As soon as she could see, Tope crawled out of the bushes and started to walk. Zena stumbled after her. Her legs felt heavy and useless, and her throat was so dry she could hardly breathe. She gasped, and sank to her knees. Tope grabbed her arm to pull her up again, but Zena was too heavy for her, so Tope went on by herself. She struggled over a low embankment, holding tightly to the infant.

At the top of the rise, Tope turned suddenly and called. Zena could hear the excitement in her voice. Wearily, she raised her head. Her mother was gesturing wildly, urging her forward. With the last remnants of her strength, Zena staggered over the embankment. Her eyes widened in hope. Before her was an old lake bed, and in its center was a small puddle of water.

Mother and daughter hesitated despite their terrible thirst. Once, the lakes of the savannah had gleamed blue in the sunlight and sustained all manner of life. But neither Tope nor Zena had any memory of such beneficence. To them, lake beds held only death. Vast, sunken depressions in the earth, their cracked surfaces were littered with the bones of animals that had died in a last, desperate attempt to slake their thirst. The urge to drink could be perilous. Predators lurked nearby, ready always to spring upon those who chose water over safety. But even they were not safe. Lured by the promise of an easy meal, hunter as well as hunted often flailed helplessly in the treacherous muck near the center of the lake.

Tope walked cautiously toward the water. Zena followed, eager to drink. But when the thick mud oozed over her feet, sucked at her legs, she grabbed her mother's arm, whimpering in fear. Tope stepped back a few paces, pulling Zena with her. Her dark eyes darted between the clear water in the center and the damp blackness at her feet, then she handed the infant to Zena and dug into the muck with her strong fingers. Brown water bubbled to the surface, and mother and daughter knelt to drink.

When her thirst was satisfied, Tope dug still deeper, first in one place, then another, using her stick as well as her hands. A vague memory had returned, from a time when her own mother had dug deep in the mud. Grimacing, she stuck a hand into one of the holes and pulled out a clump of hard objects. She struck at them with a sharp stone until the soft flesh inside was revealed, then she stuffed the contents voraciously into her mouth.

Zena sniffed cautiously when her mother handed her a few of the strange objects. Their smell was unfamiliar but good. Her stomach rumbled in anticipation. Passing the infant back, she pulled eagerly at the mussels and ate until her hunger had begun to abate. Then she found a stick for herself and dug for more. Finally, their bellies full and their thirst appeased for the first time in many months, the pair moved on.

In the weeks that followed, they were not so lucky. Each day they struggled simply to survive, to find enough food to keep their legs from buckling beneath them, enough moisture to prevent the delirium of dehydration. Nights were an even more terrifying ordeal. Often, the long, dark hours were spent in a shallow hole in the parched earth, without even a bush to cover them. Mother and daughter slept uneasily, wincing at each noise, shrinking toward each other as the blackness deepened.

Gradually, the terrain changed as they continued to travel west. Rocks littered the dry ground, and the flat plains gave way to occasional low hills. Desperate now to find a place that still offered at least the promise of life, the possibility of a secure shelter at night, Tope struggled up each of them to survey the landscape. Late one afternoon, her perseverance was finally rewarded. A tumbled pile of boulders, big enough to offer shelter, lay ahead. Beyond them a long, rocky slope led to an old river bed, where there would be food. Still further in the distance, she saw the faint outlines of mountains. They drew her forward, for instinct told her that where there were mountains, there could also be water. And where there was water, there was life.

Excited by the discovery, Tope broke into a run. But when she came near the boulders, her demeanor changed. Keeping Zena behind her, she approached with caution, watching for movement. Predators often made their homes in these rocky outcroppings. When she was sure there was no immediate danger, she moved closer and sniffed carefully at each boulder. Without conscious thought, her sense of smell told her what animal had left a particular scent, whether it signified danger, whether it was old or new.

A strong, musty smell permeated the air near a wide crack between two of the largest rocks, and she leaped away. The scent was not new, but still it alarmed her, for it told her a tiger had once lived in this place. She called nervously to Zena and began to investigate a smaller opening at the other end of the rock pile. No smells assaulted her, so she squeezed into it, gesturing to her daughter to follow. Zena sniffed the rocks as her mother had, so she would remember the predator's scent. Then she followed her mother through the other narrow opening.

The space beyond was cavelike and dark, and a welcome coolness radiated from the rock walls. Zena crept into a corner and watched as her mother fingered a few bones that were scattered across the floor of the enclosure. They were old and brittle, with no remaining scent. Mother and daughter dropped wearily to the ground. No other creature lived here, and no animal larger than themselves could enter their refuge. Here they could sleep, finally, without fear.

II

Zena was awakened by a drumming sound on the boulders above her head. The air had a strange smell, faintly acrid, and moisture had collected on the rock walls during the night. Its presence surprised her. Never before had she known wetness on rock. Still, she was grateful. Water could be found in the river bed, but they had to dig deep to reach it. She licked the damp places eagerly, her tongue describing a wide arc against the rough surface.

Abruptly, she realized she was alone. But the scent of her mother and baby brother remained, reassuring her, so she began to explore the crevices where rocks met ground with her sensitive fingers, looking for food. They had been here for almost a year now, and she knew all the places where plump worms hid or beetles scurried for cover. This time, she discovered a cache of moist seeds. She chewed them quickly, making smacking sounds of pleasure.

A slender snake, disturbed by her probing hands, slithered toward her, and she jumped away with a cry. It hissed at her and disappeared beneath the rocks.

Frightened by the snake, she thrust her head out of the enclosure to look for her mother, but withdrew it quickly. The unfamiliar smell was stronger outside. Even more disturbing were the cool drops of moisture that had landed unexpectedly on her face. She mewed apprehensively, bewildered by these strange events. But the need to find her mother was stronger than her fear, and she soon pushed herself out again.

Immediately, she was wet. Drops of water landed on her face, her arms, her back. She shook them off, but more returned. Puzzled, she looked at the sky. The drops seemed to come from up there. She had never seen drops fall from the sky before, and they alarmed her. Even more terrifying was the absence of sun. Never before in her life had the sun failed to rise and spread its harsh glare into every corner of the landscape. Now it had disappeared completely, and the day was gray and muted instead of blindingly bright.

Zena mewed again, this time a louder call of distress. An answering call came from the dry river bed below. Wide and deep, with high banks, it carved a winding gash through the land. Her mother was standing inside it, holding the baby with one arm. The other arm she stretched toward the sleeping place on the hill, as if in invitation. She uttered another low call, then bent down to resume her search for grubs and snails.

Zena hesitated. Still the sun had not returned, and the peculiar, acrid smell was stronger than ever. A loud rumbling noise suddenly came from the sky. She looked up fearfully, but she could see nothing, for the drops of water came hard and fast into her eyes and blinded her. The whole world seemed filled with them now. They splashed with loud plunking sounds on the rocks all around her and gathered in puddles on the pale earth, making dark lines as they raced toward the river bed.

She watched them, frozen into immobility; then, with a sharp cry, she retreated into the shelter. Just as she moved, a blinding flash of light tore across the clouds, and a terrifying crack seemed to split the air into pieces. The sound drove Zena into the farthest corner of the refuge. Wetness came with her; it trickled down her back, making her shiver, and cascaded down the sides of the rocks. Clutching her arms to her chest for protection, she huddled there, listening, afraid.

A scrabbling sound made her jump, but as she caught the familiar scent, Zena relaxed. Her mother's head, water streaming from it, appeared at the entrance to the cave. In her free hand, she held a limp rodent. It was covered with light fur and had a short, stubby tail. Washed out of its burrow by the rains, it had been easy to catch.

Tope responded with a comforting grunt to her daughter's squeal of greeting. Then she probed deftly at the animal's skin with a sharp rock. Tearing at the exposed flesh with her strong, blunt teeth, she chewed industriously, spitting out the fur in disgust. Zena held out her hand, and after a while her mother handed her part of the carcass.

Zena gagged at the strong taste, and chewed with difficulty. Her teeth were better adapted for grinding tubers and grains and nuts than meat. But the flesh of rodents filled a place in her belly that had been empty for so long she had forgotten it was there. Satisfied, and reassured by her mother's presence, she drank from a puddle near the entrance to their refuge, and curled up to sleep again.

All that day, and for many days after, the rains continued to fall. Flashes of light tore through the sky, followed by deafening crashes. Zena huddled in her corner, occasionally gnawing on the rodent's bones and other scraps left by her mother. Fearful of the unfamiliar sights and sounds, she had not wanted to venture outside. But now her hunger was too great to ignore, and the drumming of rain had slowed. She poked her head out to sniff the air, then emerged into muted daylight.

The world that greeted her was unlike anything she had seen before. Water was everywhere, in puddles on the ground, in crevices in the rocks, in rivulets that bounded down the slope toward the river bed. Light drops fell on her forehead and dripped into her eyes, but she was too astonished by the strange sights even to wipe them away. The sheen of the rocks, the glitter of puddles, and especially the perplexing ripples that spread outward each time a drop of rain fell, fascinated her. She stooped to examine the ripples more closely in a nearby puddle. Quickly, her hand lashed out. A large insect floated on the water, struggling to fly. She crunched it between her teeth even as she spotted others. Grabbing as many as she could fit into her hands, she crammed them into her mouth.

Her mother called from farther down the slope, and Zena started toward her. A larger puddle distracted her. Wriggling just under its surface were small black creatures with long tails. Zena reached out to catch one, but it slid from her grasp. Again she tried, and this time she caught the tadpole. For all the years of the drought, they had lain dormant in clusters of eggs. As soon as they were wet, they sprang again to life.

The rains had begun to transform the landscape as well. A light sprinkling of emerald showed at the roots of long-dead grasses, and clumps of feathery leaves were already thrusting up between the rocks. On the plains behind her, Zena saw spots of red and white and deep blue, waving at the ends of their short stalks. She ran to see, and tasted some of them. The purple was bitter, and she spat it out. But the white ones were sweet, and when she dug beneath them with a nearby stick, their bulbs were succulent and tender.

The sun burst unexpectedly through the clouds. Bits of light were everywhere, on each leaf, each rock, on the ripples in the water. Zena dropped to her knees to examine them, but when she touched them they disappeared. She blinked and looked again. They reappeared, but then a huge shadow spread across the ground and they vanished once more. She looked up, startled. The clouds had suddenly darkened. Thick and bulbous, they loomed menacingly above her, blotting out the light.

She stood abruptly, mewing in fear. The air had become almost as dark as night, and she heard a strange noise, a subdued roar, different than any sound she had heard before. It seemed to come from the mountains, not from the sky. She stared toward the peaks, but clouds blocked her view. The rain began again, making it even harder to see through the gloom. First, a few large drops fell, then water began to come at her in torrents, battering her upturned face. She ran toward the entrance to the cave, but she did not enter. Even more than the security of the shelter, she wanted her mother. Darkness when the sun should be high in the sky and the ominous new roar terrified her.

Squinting against the downpour, she spotted Tope still standing in the river bed. Water swirled around her ankles, and as Zena watched, she took a few steps toward the hillside. Then she stopped and turned a questioning face upstream, toward the river's source in the mountains that loomed against the southern horizon.

Zena listened to the sound that had attracted her mother's attention, and her terror grew. It was another new noise, a rushing, pounding racket. The sound grew louder and louder, more and more fierce, until it was a deafening clamor. There was wind now as well, furious, tearing wind. She clung desperately to the rocks, calling frantically. Her cries were lost in the howling around her.

Then, as she watched, a massive wall of water rounded the curve of the river bed far upstream, and came crashing toward her mother. She saw Tope clutch the baby under one arm and start to scramble up the steep bank. But the wall of water was almost upon her; it rose far above her head, filling the width and depth of the river bed. Tope raised a hand to her face, as if to fend off the approaching onslaught. Then it hit her, knocking her backward, and she disappeared beneath the roiling fury.

Zena uttered a howl of absolute helplessness and despair. Squeezing her body between two boulders so the wind would not tear her away, she stared frantically at the place where her mother had disappeared. But she could see nothing beyond the rain that slashed mercilessly into her eyes.

Mewing piteously, she slithered into the protection of the cave and huddled in its darkest corner. Deep inside herself, she knew that her mother would not return. She was alone in this harsh new world where the sun did not rise, where wetness and deafening crashes came from the mountains and the sky.

CHAPTER
2

Night fell in total blackness. Mountainous clouds scudded heavily across the sky, obscuring the sliver of moon. Only once did it escape, and its appearance was so quick, so ghostly, that it seemed a mirage.

Numb with shock and grief, Zena barely moved as the hours passed. Below her, the raging current tore at the banks of the river, pulling bushes, animals, even trees into its widening grasp. Water crept relentlessly up the hillside, erasing the life that had grown there since the rains came. It slapped at the boulders by her entrance, sending cold trickles toward her feet. She shivered and drew them closer to her body.

Toward dawn, the deluge lessened. The lashing of heavy rain became a soft patter, and wind no longer screamed through crevices in the rocks. Now Zena could hear other noises besides the savagery of the storm. A rhythmic swishing accompanied the passage of pebble-laden water up and down the hill, and there were soft, scrabbling noises, as if an animal with padded claws was prowling above her refuge.

She stiffened. The musty smell that had alarmed her mother that first day had returned. Then, directly overhead, she heard a low, ferocious growl. The menacing sound had meaning for her. Though she had forgotten her former troopmates, she would never forget the piercing screams one of them had uttered when a tiger had sprung upon her and dragged her away. A picture of the great cat, with its huge curved teeth, appeared in her mind, and she shrank back against the protecting rocks.

The tiger was pacing; she could hear it moving restlessly, back and forth across the top of the rock pile. The pacing stopped and the footsteps came closer. Hardly daring to breathe, Zena crept noiselessly into the farthest corner of her refuge. Just as she moved, a massive paw thrust through the entrance, and tearing claws scraped the earth where she had been sitting. The paw retreated, and the tiger began to dig energetically, hurling its strength first at one side of the boulders that framed her enclosure, then another. The torrential rains that had driven it back to its high lair had made hunting difficult, and it was hungry. But her mother had chosen well, and the huge predator could not find a way to enter.

The digging stopped and Zena heard the tiger pad over her head in the direction of its cave. For a long time she dared not move, even to relax her cramped legs, lest it hear her and try once more to enter. Finally, she gathered her courage and crept warily toward the entrance. She should try to escape now, before the huge cat began to prowl again.

Stiff with caution, she thrust her head out and scanned the area, muscles tensed to pull her back at the slightest sign of danger. But she could see nothing except the ravages of the storm. All around her lay devastation. The clumps of green between the rocks, the emerging grasses and flowers had been swept away, the puddles drained of life. Sticks and branches, even trees, torn from their roots in the mountains to the west, littered the hillside. And still the water was rising, even though the rains had stopped. It lapped loudly at the boulders, and with each wave it crept higher.

The musty smell was strong, and she saw the tiger's scat on a nearby rock. Zena whimpered anxiously. Without her mother to guide her, she did not know what to do. She could not live near the huge cat, but she was afraid to run, lest it hear her and attack. It could be returning from the hunt already, or perhaps it was waiting nearby, hidden in its lair, behind a rock. . . .

Fear sent her scurrying back to her corner. All that day and the following night, she cowered in the cave, shivering with cold as water crept around her legs. Hunger gnawed at her belly, but the anguish of being alone was even harder to bear. She wanted desperately to feel her mother's warm body, to smell her comforting scent and the fresh, milky odor of the baby. But they were gone, and they would not return.

She dozed fitfully. Hunger and cold and dreams would not let her rest for long. Over and over again, she was jerked awake as images of her mother, arms raised against the deluge, vied with pictures of the fierce predator above. But she did not hear it again, and finally she fell into a deep and dreamless sleep.

She was awakened by sunlight streaming into her eyes from a crack in the rocks above. Reassured by the return of the sun, and prompted by hunger, she dared to poke her head out of the shelter again. There was no sign of the tiger, and its smell seemed fainter, so she emerged. The water had retreated, leaving enormous puddles filled with litter from the storm. Below her, the river ran swollen and fast, its waters muddy. But it did not rage as harshly as it had the day before, and sun sparkled on the crests of its ripples.

She began to investigate the debris-filled puddles on the hillside below the cave. No tadpoles were visible in the muddied water, but there were a few uprooted plants, their bulbs shining white, and many insects, as well as a dead rodent. The bulbs and insects she ate immediately, but she was reluctant to smash at the rodent and alert the tiger. Instead, she found a sharp rock and turned back toward her enclosure to eat it.

As she turned, her eye caught a stealthy movement on the boulders. Instantly, her muscles were rigid with fear. A sharp cry froze in her throat as she watched the tiger emerge from its lair. It pulled itself out and stretched, lifting its muscular haunches and massive head high in the air, while its long, tawny back curved toward the rocks. Then it padded slowly toward her cave. It sniffed the area carefully, turned a few times and lay down facing her. Its great paws hung over the entrance to her shelter, obscuring it completely.

Resting its muzzle on its paws, the tiger yawned. Zena stared, mesmerized by the long, curved teeth that framed its mouth, the gaping cavern between them. The blinding sun made her eyes water, but she dared not look away or even blink, for the huge predator still had not seen her. Then a lizard that had been sunning itself on the rocks scuttled away from the big animal's shadow. The tiger lifted its head lazily to watch the retreating reptile. Zena saw its yellow eyes scan the area toward the river and come slowly to rest on her face. For a long moment, it stared fixedly at her, its tail twitching. Then it pulled itself up and began to lope toward her.

Zena screamed. There was no escape. The river, with its wild and swollen current, lay behind her. In front, between her and her refuge, was the tiger. Terror paralyzed her body; only her eyes moved, darting frantically between the cave and the river. But then the great cat roared, and the horror of the sound released her. Down the hill she charged, legs clumsy with fear. Rocks and sticks tripped her, and she stumbled in the deep puddles. She ran on, straining to breathe against the pounding in her chest.

The rushing torrent came closer. Zena stopped, terrified by its angry clamor. Growling ferociously, the tiger broke into a run. In three great strides, it was beside her. Screaming, she plunged into the river.

Immediately, the turbulent current pulled her legs out from under her. She struggled to regain a footing, then gasped for breath as the river sucked her down and tossed her mercilessly as it tore through the high banks. Her head popped up for a moment, and she drew in a great gulp of air. Then, helpless, she went down again. Branches dragged at her, pulling her under until her lungs screamed with pain. She wrenched herself free and lurched forward, tossing and bumping.

A large stick knocked her shoulder. She grabbed it and hauled herself up to the surface, managed to take a meager breath before the limb was torn from her grasp. Down she went again; water filled her eyes, her ears, her nose. Flailing and kicking, she tried to right herself, but she could not fight the tempestuous river. Her body went limp, and she barely noticed when the raging water tossed her up to the surface, then buried her again, sent her careening into rocks and sunken branches. Then, more than a mile from the place where she had plunged in, it pummeled her into a boulder on the far bank. The impact pulled at her consciousness, and she clutched the rock with desperate strength. With a final heave, the current sent her sprawling toward the sand. Her head hit the boulder, and she lay still.

Almost an hour later, she moved. Her body was tightly wedged between two rocks. Water pulled harshly at her feet, but her face lay safely on the sand. She retched violently, and felt a ringing pain in her head. After a time it subsided, and she hauled herself determinedly up the bank, away from the clutching water. There she stayed for many hours, while the sun poured its restoring warmth onto her bruised body.

When she stirred again, the light was fading. She struggled to her knees, then tried to get to her feet, vaguely aware that she must find shelter. Dizziness and nausea overcame her, and she fell back heavily. She gave up the effort to rise and crawled instead, dragging herself tenaciously away from the water. Her eyes were clouded with the tears of her retching, and she did not know she had reached some low bushes until thorns scratched at her face. She pulled herself into them, oblivious to the pain. When it seemed that the bushes were all around her, protecting her with their barbs, she collapsed against the hard earth.

II

Zena groaned. Every part of her body ached, and she was cold, numbingly, agonizingly cold. The wet chill of the ground seemed to have penetrated her bones as she slept. She could not stop shivering, and the compulsive movements tortured her bruised flesh.

She made an effort to rise, but thorns tore at her, and she could not bear this further pain. So she lay still, mewing softly to herself. The sounds comforted her, almost as if another of her kind had uttered them.

Finally, the sun rose over the ridge of mountains to the east. Its warmth, still tentative in the early morning air, touched her shoulder as she lay curled in a tight ball. It gave her the strength to crawl forward a few yards. Panting, and nauseated again with the effort, she rested again until the sun was high and had sent its heat coursing through her body. Then, with a final push forward, she emerged into open savannah.

The first thing she saw were legs, many long slender legs, scattered across the plain. Her eyes followed the legs up to rounded bellies, and on to the graceful necks and tossing horns of a herd of antelopes. She stared at them; in the seven short years of her existence, she had seen them only once before, and this she had forgotten. Before the drought, they had come each year to graze on the lush grasses that appeared almost overnight when the rains came. Since the year of her birth, they had not come at all. Now, following ancient instincts telling them greenness had returned to this part of the savannah, they had returned.

She did not fear them, sensing intuitively that these long-legged creatures meant her no harm. Her instincts also told her to watch them carefully. If they jumped suddenly in alarm, a predator could be near. But they were feeding peacefully, so she pulled herself painfully upright and ventured onto the plain.

A triangle of verdant grasses stretched before her, framed on one side by the river, on the other by towering mountains, purple in the distance. Directly ahead, across the plain, were a series of low hills sprinkled with boulders. Toward these she headed, for she knew from her mother that boulders meant possible safety.

She moved slowly, looking for tubers and other edibles as she walked, stopping often to rest. Once, she came across some termite mounds. As her mother had taught her, she poked a stick carefully

into one of the nests. When she pulled it out again, it was covered
with scurrying insects. She grimaced as they crawled up her fingers
and tickled her lips, but she licked them up and ate them with
relish.

The sparkle of water caught her eye as she neared the hills at the
edge of the plain. She approached it cautiously. The sucking mud
she had encountered with her mother and the violence of the river
had made her wary. But this water lay still and placid in its bowl-
shaped depression, and grasses grew right up to its edge. Near its
center was a large, flat rock. As she approached, a small, dark
green creature she had never seen before jumped from the rock and
plopped into the water. Ripples rose around the place where it had
landed. Zena stared at them, waiting for the animal to reappear,
but there was no further movement. Finally, satisfied that no danger
was present, she knelt to drink.

Shelter was foremost on her mind as her shadow lengthened. She
went first to the boulders she had seen from the far side of the
plain, but they were widely scattered and none had a suitable enclosure. She looked on all the other hillsides where there were rocks,
but still found nothing. Discouraged and weary, she sat down to
rest near the crest of a long ridge that ran along the eastern side of
the pond.

The shadow of a huge pair of wings darkened the ground in
front of her, and she ducked into some bushes to escape detection.
She was not fast enough. The shadow passed slowly across her
body twice again. She could hear the rush of wings as the vulture
swooped, turned, and swooped once more.

Zena whimpered with terror. Vultures had always frightened her.
Almost every day of her childhood, she had watched them yank
savagely at carcasses bleeding into the dry earth, had felt her stomach turn at the scent of death and rot. The ugly, naked heads with
the fearsome beaks that jabbed and tore at defenseless flesh, the
piercing talons that grabbed any creature too weak to crawl away,
were imprinted deeply in her memory. Now that she was alone,
the images were more terrifying than ever.

Another vulture swept down to look at her, then another. Panic
drove Zena deep into the vine-entangled bushes. There was no
space to stand, or even crawl, so she wriggled doggedly on her
stomach along a vague track that became narrower and narrower
until she could barely squeeze through. Frightened by the confining
space, she tried to retreat, but the vines were thickly entwined
above her and she could not turn. So she went on.

Gradually, the ground rose under her belly, and the vine-covered dirt gave way to a surface of small rocks. They pressed against her bruised flesh, but at least the bushes were beginning to thin, so she could see what lay before her. Directly ahead was a narrow patch of bare ground, and beyond that rose a short, rocky cliff. A thick, overhanging ledge jutted out near the top of the cliff. Beneath it she saw a deep crevice, just wide enough for her to enter.

Hesitantly, she stretched one arm into the blackness, to test its depth, then maneuvered the upper half of her thin frame into the hole. Powdery dust rose in thick swirls, and she sneezed violently. Immediately she was afraid, lest the vulture hear her and attack. But at the same time she hesitated to go farther. A sour odor she had not detected before emanated from the back of the cave. Sharp-toothed rodents or a nest of snakes, even a small hyena, might live there. In the darkness, she could not tell.

Suddenly more fearful of an unknown danger than the vulture above, she began to back out. A sudden rush of wings startled her, and a shower of pebbles landed on her exposed legs. Zena peered up and saw the fierce bird settling its chunky body on the ledge just above her. It leaned toward her and stared, its black eyes unblinking.

A scream rose in her throat, but the muscles contracted and only a gurgle emerged. Quickly, she squeezed her whole body into the cavelike space, drawing her legs close to her chest so the vulture could not reach them. Thick dust coated her throat, making her gasp and choke, and the sour smell grew so strong she could hardly breathe. Desperate, near hysteria, she shoved her shoulders against the constricting ledge, pressed her knees against the hard earth, trying to force more space. Over and over, she arched her back, pushed at the ground. Suddenly, to her astonishment, it gave way. Her mouth gaped open in surprise, and her arms lunged forward protectively. The earth under her body had dropped away, and she was falling.

She landed with a thud on the dirt floor of another enclosure. For a moment she could see nothing, as dust swirled through the air. But it settled quickly this time, and she knew immediately that there was more light here, more space. The terrible blackness had given way to a murky gray glow that emanated from two narrow shafts of brilliance behind her head. Lingering motes of dust danced and shimmered in their beams. She stared at them, entranced, then terror and her aching body pulled her back into awareness.

She lay perfectly still, alert and wary, but no sounds came to her, from the world outside or from the cave into which she had fallen. It was silent, almost odorless. Slowly, her panic subsided. There was no sign that any other animal lived here, and she was certain the vulture would not come through the dark space after her. For the moment at least, she was safe.

Tired now almost beyond endurance, she began to mew softly to herself for comfort, as she had before. For a long time, she just lay there, listening to her own small noises. Gradually, the deep well of loneliness that stayed always within her diminished, and she slept, relaxed and free of fear for the first time since her mother's death.

III

Light filtered gently into the cave. Zena opened her eyes and frowned, momentarily puzzled by her surroundings. Then the memory of her fall returned, and she sat quickly. She was about two feet below the dark space where the earth had given way, on a hard-packed earthen floor that stretched for more than twice her length in every direction. She tried to stand, to explore the new space, but she bumped her head. She crawled instead, searching each corner of the refuge with her sensitive fingers. There were droppings, but they were very old and crumbled at her touch. She sniffed them delicately and then ignored them.

Behind her, opposite the place where she had fallen, were the two openings through which light entered. One was only a crack, but the other was a long narrow passage, just big enough to accommodate her small body. Zena wriggled into it, pulling herself upward with her elbows. It led her to a gap in the cliff above. She scrambled out and studied the area, so she would be able to find this entrance again. Like the hole through which she had fallen, it was well concealed behind dark slabs of rock, and was almost impossible to spot from above. Both entrances were too narrow for a predator to use, but if a snake or smaller animal should threaten her, she had a second exit through which to escape. Few such refuges existed on the African savannah, but because the ground had given way beneath her, she had found a perfect one.

Remembering the vulture, she listened carefully before she moved toward the ledge. No sounds disturbed her, so she clambered on top of the rocky outcropping and stared down at the scene below.

The pond lay motionless, pale gray in the early morning light. All around it, luxuriant grasses and flowers swayed gently in the light breeze. Leafy, wide-crowned trees decorated the banks of the river to the north, and the ridge on which she stood was covered with bushes and vines, thickly clumped with berries. To her drought-accustomed eyes, the land looked infinitely welcoming, rich with potential food and water. She glanced behind her, as if to call her mother, urge her forward to appreciate the abundance below. Even after many days, the habit of constant communication was hard to break.

A glimmer of brilliance caught her eye, distracting her from the sadness that had abruptly spoiled her pleasure in the scene. The ribbon of river had begun to glitter, its gray turned to sparkling silver. Then the sun rose over the ridge behind her and touched the dark bulk of the mountains to the south. She stared, entranced. The nearest peaks shimmered in pink and rosy orange; the others withdrew toward the horizon in a succession of sunlit mounds, each more richly colored than the one before.

Another sight intruded, and she frowned. A thin plume of smoke rose lazily from a mountain with a bowl-like summit. The smoke seemed out of place, not quite right.

A herd of antelopes, golden-haired in the sunlight, appeared between two low hills north of the pond and stepped gingerly down to the water. They were skittish; their delicate hoofs dug at the grasses, and they raised their heads continuously to sniff the air, so Zena stayed where she was, watching.

Presently, the cause of their nervousness became apparent. A noisy band of pigs trotted past the ridge that had concealed them. Snorting and prancing, they proceeded toward the pond. Water flew into the air as they splashed in the shallows and slurped up great mouthfuls made muddy by their trampling hooves. When their thirst was quenched, they rolled vigorously in the mud, then jumped up, stiff-legged, to shake themselves.

Zena did not move until the pigs had finished their raucous visit and headed back into the hills. Then she continued her exploration. Farther along the ledge, she found four spotted eggs in a nest made of thick twigs. Her memory of eggs was dim, but she knew at once they were good to eat. She was less certain about how to eat them. She bit into one, but the shell broke. Not wanting to lose the contents, she shoved the whole egg into her mouth. The liquid was delicious, but bits of shell caught in her throat when she tried to swallow. Sputtering helplessly, she spat the whole mess out onto the rocks. Then she picked out the larger pieces of shell with deft fingers and licked up the rest of the egg. Grit from the rocks accompanied it, but still the taste was wonderfully satisfying.

She peered at the remaining eggs, considering whether to take them. A noisy pair of birds dissuaded her. Screeching furiously, they flapped their wings in her face and dived at her hunched shoulders. Zena wrapped her arms protectively around her head and fled downhill as their raucous complaints died away. The birds were not big enough to frighten her, but she did not want to provoke another attack. She would remember the eggs, though. Perhaps later she would return.

Now she was thirsty. She had no desire to maneuver her way through the prickly bushes on her stomach again, so she began to search for an easier way down to the pond. Soon she came across a narrow path, just on the other side of her ledge. She followed it down and was quickly buried in thorny shrubs. They pressed in on her, but there was space to stand upright, so she continued. The track smelled strongly of an animal she could not identify. Nervously, she scanned the area ahead. If another creature came up toward her, escape would be difficult.

She rounded a bend in the path and came face to face with a pair of horns. They were long and twisted, and rose straight up. The animal before her started violently. Bushes cracked sharply as it struggled to turn in the confined space. Another animal was behind it, and still another behind that one. All of them twisted around and ran back the way they had come, their hooves thudding on the packed earth of the trail. Still shaking with the suddenness of the encounter, Zena crouched silently at the edge of the path, in case more animals came. But nothing happened, and after a while she continued on her way.

The bushes ended abruptly. Immediately below her was the pond, still and sparkling. Many antelopes, and a small herd of the animals she had encountered on the path, grazed on its far side. They raised their heads and stared at her, then resumed their feeding. Reassured by their calm, she ran eagerly toward the water and knelt to drink.

Splashing sounds near the center of the pond made her look up in alarm. Tiny creatures, slender and silvery in the sun, were leaping in and out of the water. Curious, she reached toward them, but they darted away. Then she saw a narrow gray shape swimming slowly past her hands. It was longer than the others, and its body swayed gracefully. She tried to grab it, but it slipped easily from her grasp. Frustrated, she bent lower and then gasped as water unexpectedly invaded her nostrils and sloshed up toward her eyes. She fell back in a heap, coughing and sputtering. The antelopes across the pond snorted and leaped away from the alien racket.

Zena retreated, lest the water reach out at her again. She sat and stared at it for a long time. Ripples broke its surface occasionally, but it did not otherwise move, so she ventured close again and dared to thrust one foot, then the other, into the soft mud below the water. Her toes promptly disappeared, but when she pulled them up, they were still there. She waded farther. The air had become blisteringly hot as the sun rose to the top of the sky, and the coolness on her scratched skin was wonderfully soothing.

A trio of tiny yellow birds swam past her, peeping loudly. Zena laughed as they ducked beneath the water, tails pointed high in the air, then emerged with weeds trailing from their pink bills. She scooped beneath the surface to see what they were eating, but the sodden plants she brought up were bitter to her taste. She dug deeper, into the soft silt near the edge of the pond, carefully keeping her face away from the water. Her probing fingers found clumps of snails, a few wriggling tadpoles, and some long, trailing plants with delicious white bulbs.

The tiny silver fish she had seen leaping around the rock were everywhere; they darted away, disappearing beneath the silt each time she moved, so she stood perfectly still. Immediately, the fish began to nibble gently at her ankles, making her jump. The nibbling stopped, but began again as soon as she was still. Her hand flashed through the water, grabbed a tiny fish, and brought it up to her mouth in a single gesture. Smacking her lips appreciatively, she chewed the delicacy. Three or four more times, she repeated this tactic. Then, satisfied, she headed toward her cave.

The eggs were still in the nest; she passed on, leaving them undisturbed. She was well fed already and had no need of more.

Sighing with contentment, she curled up to rest on the ledge. Even when the vulture circled near her, she barely moved. Now that she could duck into a secure hiding place in moments, it no longer frightened her. Only later, when darkness had descended and an animal howled plaintively from the hillside, did her newfound serenity waver. Though the shock of her mother's death, the horror of the tiger's attack, were beginning to fade, the longing to feel, to hear and smell another like herself was strong. But there was no one.

CHAPTER

3

An agonized scream woke Zena. The sound sent shivers up her spine. Before, the tiger's growl had triggered her memory; now the scream itself forced her to remember the time when a member of her troop had been killed by one of the big cats. Shuddering, she listened for more screams, but there was only silence.

For a long time, she lay unmoving, ears and eyes alert. A different sound pulled her into a wary crouch. Barely audible, the scrabbling noise came from the ridge outside. Automatically, she reached for a stone and clutched it in her fist.

A new sound, a thin mewing, joined the first. Zena frowned, confused. This, too, was familiar. It was as if she were hearing herself, when her mother had disappeared beneath the rushing water. Almost a year had passed since that time, but she still remembered.

She hesitated, uncertain how to respond. Then the mewing rose into a cry of fear, and she acted without thought. Pushing herself out, she ran toward the sound. Shivers coursed through her again. The scent that reached her had been imprinted on her brain when she was a suckling infant, had been reinforced when her brother was born. Prompted by an impulse deeper than memory, she gently touched her breast.

Another odor invaded her nostrils, and this time she knew it immediately. It was blood, fresh blood.

Cautious now, she crept toward the smell, but it was quickly

2 5

obscured by the scent of dampness and trampled leaves that rose as she moved. She strained to see, but the sun still hid below the horizon, and everything around her was shadowy and indistinct. She might have missed the still form had the little creature not moaned. The sound drew her forward, and then she saw it. A small body, a miniature of her own, lay motionless on the hard ground, its arms outflung.

She stared, waiting for it to move or make some further sound. Its eyes were closed, and its mouth hung open to reveal toothless gums behind lips just like hers. Like herself, it was hairless except for a dark thatch on its head, but unlike her, it had a small protuberance at its groin. Zena's memory stirred; her baby brother had looked like that. She crept closer, but jumped back in alarm when the little body twitched violently. Then it was still again.

An unfamiliar feeling enveloped Zena as she continued to stare, a feeling that grew stronger when the small male slowly turned, his mouth twitching in pain. Now she could see why he smelled of blood. A long gash had been torn in his back, as if a claw had ripped it. Instinctively, she knelt down and began to lick the wound with long, slow swipes of her tongue. The infant whimpered and turned, raising his arms toward her. She drew back, alarmed. But his hands only flicked gently at her face, then grasped at the matted hair that framed it. She tried to pull away, but the clutching fingers had wound themselves tightly and she could not free herself. To stop the pulling, she picked the baby up and hugged him gently. He gave a deep sigh, and his fingers released her.

Zena stood with him in her arms. His weight and the heat of his body against her chest felt strange, yet somehow normal. Wonderingly, she passed a hand across the small form, so like her own except for the odd little bump between its legs. Tears formed unexpectedly in her eyes. To hold this wounded creature close and comfort him was intensely satisfying. After all the months of being alone, he made her feel complete, as if an aching void inside her had finally been filled. Gently, she pressed her lips against his rounded cheek.

She did not want to leave him again, even for a moment, so she carried him carefully into the cave. There she licked the wound until blood no longer oozed from it. The gash was not so deep, she saw, now that the dirt and blood had been cleaned away. When she had finished, the little one nestled his head at her neck and slept.

Hunger roused her after a few hours. Gently, she slid away from the sleeping baby, trying to get up without rousing him. His eyes fluttered open, and he stared at her with a startled expression. The round, dark eyes were huge in his tiny face. Then he yawned, a wide stretching yawn, and began to whimper. The whimpering quickly accelerated into screams. Zena shifted his weight on her arm, uncertain what she should do. Abruptly, the howls stopped as the little male turned his face toward her chest and began to root around with his mouth, seeking her nipple. He sucked eagerly for a few moments. But when no sustenance came, he uttered a loud and furious screech.

Baffled, Zena set him down. Her action only intensified his screams. Still howling, he tried to walk back to her but his legs would not hold him and he plopped onto his rump. He held up his arms to her, and a look of desperation came over his face. Zena knelt quickly and folded him into her arms, murmuring soothing noises. When his sobs finally ceased, she maneuvered them through the dusty space onto the ledge, to look for food. The baby sneezed, and looked at her in grave surprise.

Bushes with ripening red berries grew a short way up the hill. Zena plucked some and thrust them into the infant's mouth, but he only sputtered and began to whimper again. She chewed slowly on a handful she had picked for herself. Immediately, the little male held up his face, mouth pursed, and stared piercingly into her eyes. Zena stared back, then, prompted by a memory of her mother with her baby brother, she placed her mouth against his and transferred some of the well-chewed berries. He swallowed and held up his face for more. Over and over, they repeated this procedure. Then the small body relaxed against her chest, and the round dark eyes closed again.

Zena's shoulders began to sag under the unaccustomed weight. She carried the baby back to the cave, doubly grateful now for its security, and laid him in a pile of dry grasses she used for sleeping. Then she hurried down to the pond. The little one had eaten most of the berries, and she was still hungry.

The area was deserted except for some small birds that stalked around on skinny legs, peeping frantically whenever she came close. Ignoring them, she pulled up a bunch of the trailing plants to feast on their soft bulbs. She had eaten only a few when a loud screech emanated from the direction of the cave. She jumped up, still clutching the bulbs, and ran back the way she had come.

When she entered the cave, the little male stopped wailing immediately. He crawled toward her, his face expectant, and reached for the bulbs in her hands. He pulled at the long stems, but did not eat. But as soon as she began to chew some herself, he pursed his lips toward her face. She pushed some into his mouth; he swallowed quickly and held up his face for more. She tried feeding him some tubers as well, but they took too long to chew and he became impatient, so she returned to the bulbs.

After a time, she turned away, weary of the procedure. The youngster popped a bulb in his mouth and sucked at it. Grabbing another, he fingered it carefully. Then he began to crawl around the cave. One long stem trailed from his mouth, another from his fingers. Several times, he tried to stand, but each time he plopped back onto his rump. Then he spat out the bulb, crawled into Zena's lap, and slept again.

She watched him, bemused. The little creature had dropped into her life from a place of which she had no knowledge, for reasons she could not fathom. Yet already he seemed a part of her. There was no strangeness to him, only familiarity. Her eyes became dreamy as images of her mother and baby brother appeared. She straightened abruptly, remembering the scream of the night before. It must have been another one, another mother, she had heard.

Frowning, she examined the gash on the baby's back. An image of the great cat came unbidden into her head. She saw again the tearing claws that had scratched the floor of her refuge as she huddled there after her mother's death. A claw had made that gash. The claws and the fearsome teeth had killed the mother. And that meant the great cat was still out there somewhere, feasting on its kill. . . .

Zena wrapped her arms protectively around the little male. He awoke at her sudden touch and emitted a thin screech. Then, feeling himself secure in her arms, he sighed contentedly and closed his eyes. She smiled, amused. He made that noise all the time, when he was unhappy or hungry. She tickled him gently; he screeched again and stared at her crossly. Once again, she tickled; again, he screeched. She left him alone to sleep. But after that, each time she thought of the small creature who had come to her so unexpectedly, she thought of the screech too. In her mind, she called him Screech.

II

For a few weeks, while Screech recovered from his wound, Zena repeated the process of running to the pond while he slept, gathering food for both of them, and returning with her bounty. But one day, he refused to be left behind. He grabbed her legs as she entered the passage that led out of the cave, making small sounds of distress. She kicked him away gently, but he scrambled after her, so she turned and held out her arms. He clambered into them, chortling. His black eyes were lively. Zena rubbed her nose against his; he threw back his head, open-mouthed with delight, then pushed his face against hers again, to repeat the game. She obliged, her own eyes merry. Pleasure welled up in her throat, and she hugged Screech close. His wriggling body was wonderfully comforting against her own.

He struggled away, wanting to play again. She set him down, reluctantly this time. To her surprise, he landed on his feet. For a moment, he rocked back and forth as if he would fall, then he took a few tottering steps. She grinned and clapped her hands together. Screech imitated, his small face split in a beaming smile. Again, he tottered forward, frowning in concentration. When he reached her, he wound his arms around her neck and would not let go. Abandoning the idea of leaving him behind, Zena carried him out of the cave. Together, they ventured into the brilliant sunlight.

The antelopes were feeding quietly. That meant no predators were lurking, so Zena tucked Screech firmly against her hip and made her way down through the thick bushes. Settling him on the grass, she went to drink. He crawled after her at a furious pace, and when she looked around, he was at the edge of the pond, staring into the water. He leaned over and slapped it with one hand. The noise startled him, and he backed quickly away. Zena took a large mouthful of water and put her face close to his. When he opened his mouth expectantly, she squirted the water into it. Screech's eyes opened wide in surprise at the coolness. He forgot to swallow and choked instead. Water dribbled down his chin, his chest, and poured out of his eyes. But he recovered quickly and held up his face for more.

All day they stayed there together. Screech imitated Zena's every move, digging into the earth with grubby hands as she searched for tubers, pulling over and over again at some deep purple berries that had ripened on bushes near the water. Soon his hands and face were stained scarlet with their juice. Zena took him to the edge of the pond to wash him. A big green frog jumped into the water with a loud plop. Screech stared, then struggled from her arms to chase the frog. He tumbled into the pond, landing unharmed on his rump. Startled, he looked up at Zena for reassurance, but the novelty of being in the pond quickly distracted him. He trailed his hands through the cool water, watched them emerge, tangled in weeds. Carefully, one at a time, he plucked the slimy plants from his fingers.

Zena let him play for a while, then she picked him up and headed for the cave. The sun had almost reached the western horizon, and

the heat had gone from the day. These were the hours when predators stalked. She glanced up toward the ledge. Its contours softened
by the setting sun, the area around her shelter looked infinitely
welcoming. Rocks, grasses, and bushes blended together in a soft
palette of pinks and golds, and all the area to the west was steeped
in dusky luminescence.

Screech was already asleep on her shoulder. She lowered him
gently into the nest of grasses. Immediately, he woke and scrambled
back into her arms, whimpering. Zena lay down beside him so they
would not have to be apart. As they had each night since he had
come, they slept with their arms entwined, their breathing light and
steady against each other's cheeks.

The next morning when they left the cave, Screech pointed insis-
tently at the red berries she had fed him that first day. Zena gave
him some from her mouth, then he tried eating them by himself.
They were fully ripe now and not so hard to chew. Slowly, they
made their way up to the top of the ridge, following the bushes.
Zena had not been this way before. Always, she had gone toward
the pond, with its abundant food.

She peered curiously down the other side. Below her lay a deep,
narrow valley, thickly dotted with trees. The ridge wound south
toward the mountains, enclosing the valley on one side, then
dropped sharply into a deep ravine that bordered the other side of
the valley. Beyond the ravine, the land rose gradually toward a
huge green plateau. Many animals, tiny in the distance, grazed in
its lush meadows.

A movement below her caught her eye, and she gasped. A long
tail, tipped with white, had flicked briefly above a clump of grass.
Abruptly, the herd of antelopes feeding nearby became skittish.
Their heads tossed nervously and their hooves beat a fragile tattoo
on the grass. Zena stiffened. It was a sound for which she always
listened, though she was seldom conscious of her impulse.

Mesmerized, she watched as the grasses parted and a leopard
emerged. Tension marked every line of its lean body, and its powerful square jaws were clenched in concentration. Staring fixedly at
the antelopes, it began to slink forward, its belly low to the ground.
Some were already fleeing, but one was slower than the others.
Toward this one, the leopard aimed its hurtling body. Nothing
could stop it now. Every muscle, every sinew had been instantly
intoxicated by the chase, the lightning rush toward its intended
victim, the long, ground-covering strides that followed, the ultimate,
deadly spring. Swerving desperately, the terrified antelope pounded
away. The leopard swooped after it, its tawny body no more than

a blur against the ground. Both disappeared behind the curve of a hill.

Pent-up breath whooshed out of Zena's lungs. Unable to tear herself from the scene, she waited. Soon, the leopard reappeared, dragging the lifeless antelope. Hauling its victim into a tree, it settled down to feed.

Zena stared down at the scar on Screech's back. The scream had come from here, from the ridge. . . . It must have been the leopard, not a tiger, that had made the mark, taken the mother. . . .

Shuddering, she led Screech the other way, to the familiar pond, glad that the leopard did not hunt here. Still, the incident made her nervous, and for many nights her sleep was fraught with dreams, as it had been after her mother's death. Leopards and tigers stalked Screech over and over again, and she could not help, for her legs would not move at her command. The dreams commanded them instead, and they twitched constantly even as paralysis seemed to seize them.

After that, she saw the leopard occasionally, but it never came near the pond. Slowly, her nervousness diminished, though she continued to avoid the area behind the ridge. She found another place with red berries, and when Screech wanted some, she took him there. Soon, he could chew them for himself, for strong teeth had pushed through his gums. His steps became steady as well, and as the months passed, he learned to run so fast Zena could barely keep up with him. He loved to chase her, or run away from her, and stopped only if she called to him in a certain way. She used many types of hoots and calls to tell him what food she had found or animal she had seen, if he should run or hide when danger threatened. Some she remembered from her mother; others, they created as they were needed. Once she had used a certain sound, both she and Screech remembered it and used it again in the same way. Soon, he was as adept at using them as she was. He copied everything she did too. He learned to sniff the air for scents and survey the area before they ventured down to the pond, to listen for the sounds of danger. His hands grew ever more adept at digging for bulbs and tubers, at catching tadpoles and frogs or small fish.

Everywhere, food abounded. Berries covered the bushes, and the trees by the river produced wondrous bunches of fruit and nuts. Grains ripened in the fields, melons and tubers proliferated, and birds laid multiple clutches of eggs. Screech delighted in chasing the disgruntled parents from their nests with loud shouts, while

Zena grabbed an egg or two. The others she left for the watching birds to hatch.

Sometimes Screech tried to catch young animals as well, but Zena always stopped him. There was no need now for flesh to supplement their diet, and it seemed wrong to take a creature they did not mean to eat. Instead, they watched in delight as the tiny antelope or zebra he had found pranced after its mother on wobbly legs. Once, they saw a baby giraffe drop from its mother's rump, then struggle to its feet and follow her, stiff-legged, to the pond. Spreading her legs clumsily, she lowered her head to the water and drank as the calf suckled beneath her belly. Elephants often trumpeted through the valley, the babies clustered under the knees of the adults. Their trunks ripped steadily at trees and bushes to satisfy their insatiable appetites as they plodded along. Zena and Screech did not go too close to the massive creatures, but they watched in fascination as the elephants wallowed in the pond and sprayed themselves with their long trunks. For days after their visits, the pond stayed brown and opaque.

All that was missing from their lives were others like themselves. With Screech nearby, Zena was no longer lonely, but she still felt strangely empty sometimes. Thirteen years had passed now since her birth, and she was three and a half feet tall, as tall as her mother had been. A thatch of dark hair had appeared at her groin, and the flatness of her bony chest had been disrupted by the slow swelling of breasts. She touched them sometimes, and vague sensations stirred inside her, as if she should have or do something she could not imagine. Often the yearning came upon her when she ventured near the top of the ridge. There were scents sometimes, caught briefly when the wind was right, scents from the valley below, that aroused memories of her troop, of her mother and little brother. It was from this place that she had heard the scream of another of her kind. . . .

But she dared not venture down the far side of the ridge. That was leopard territory.

III

One morning, feeling restless and uneasy, Zena loped down to the pond. Huge clouds scudded across the sky, for the season of rain was almost upon them. Screech dashed ahead of her to drink, then he started up the opposite hillside to search for fruit, his favorite food. It was scarce now. For months, creatures large and small had feasted on the succulent harvest, but soon there would be no more until the cycle began anew, after the rains.

Zena did not join him but stayed by the pond, chewing listlessly on some bulbs while she watched a group of ducklings follow their mother into the water. Every year, they emerged from nests around the pond to entertain her with their antics. But this time, her laughter turned to a cry of distress when one duckling disappeared in a roil of muddy water. Moments later, she saw a turtle's head break the surface of the pond. Jaws agape, it snapped at another duckling. But this one escaped into the weeds while its mother hissed angrily at the turtle.

Screech called from the trees, to let her know he had found fruit. Zena answered him and rose to her feet. Another call, a low hooting sound, reached her ears. She stiffened; the call was unfamiliar, and it had come from the rocks behind her refuge, not from the trees. She stared at the ridge, but saw nothing, so she started up the hill to join Screech.

Again, she heard the unfamiliar call. She whirled, and this time she saw movement. A young male, much larger than Screech, emerged from the thick bushes. Alarmed, Zena uttered a shrill cry. Screech rushed toward her, but when he spotted the strange male, he stopped abruptly. The intruder stalked slowly toward Zena, making soft guttural noises in his throat.

Zena stood still. She had no impulse to flee, though she did not know why. Instead, she stood her ground as the young male came close and sniffed her. He tried to mount her, and she snapped at him angrily. He retreated, startled. She ambled back toward the pond, ignoring him. He followed eagerly, though he cringed whenever she turned to look at him. He paid no attention to Screech, and after a few moments, Screech wandered back toward the fruit trees.

Zena led the male to the pond and sat down on its grassy banks. Perching beside her, he stared into her face. When she did not return his gaze, he pulled up some juicy plants and handed them to her. She accepted them, but she still refused to look into his eyes. He sat patiently, watching every movement she made. When she rose, he followed; when she ate or drank, he did the same. All that day, he watched her and followed her, but in the late afternoon he climbed up the ridge again and disappeared. Zena felt an unexpected pang of regret, and her sleep that night was disturbed by the feeling of emptiness that had plagued her so often in recent months. It twisted inside her, almost as if she had not eaten—but she was not hungry.

The next morning, the male was back. This time Zena's treatment of him was less reserved, and after he had come four days in a row, she greeted him with enthusiasm. She enjoyed the attention he gave her, and his presence seemed to assuage at least some of the strange emptiness she felt. Each time he came, he brought a choice piece of food for her to eat, extending it to her with a series of guttural grunts. The grunts sounded like "dak, dak," and soon Zena began to think of him as Dak.

Screech was less enthusiastic about the young male's visits. Whenever Dak appeared, he ran to the fruit trees, or wandered off to sit by himself on the hillside, his face forlorn. He wanted Zena to pay attention to him, not to the strange male. Zena sensed his distress, but for the first time since they had been together, she ignored it. She needed to be with Dak, and Screech would have to wait.

On the fifth day, when she heard Dak call from the ridge, she ran to him and stroked his arm. Then she led him slowly to the pond. They sat there together, almost touching. When Dak handed her some bulbs to eat, Zena looked deeply into his eyes. The expression she saw there brought a strange hotness into her belly. But now it was Dak's turn to look away, almost as if he were embarrassed. Zena persisted, and after a time, he returned her stare. Mewing softly, she came close, so that her body pressed against his. Then she turned and presented her genitals. The hotness built inside her as he sniffed between her legs and mounted her. Moaning with pleasure, she felt him go inside her and thrust vigorously. The hotness grew and grew until it reached a crescendo of excitement. Her body shuddered violently, and she groaned, a low, intense groan of utter satisfaction.

In the weeks that followed, she and Dak mated many times. The act of mating was deeply gratifying to Zena, and she wanted to do it over and over again. Dak was her willing accomplice. Each morning, he approached her eagerly, often carrying a choice bit of fruit for her to eat. They mated, then sat close together for long hours.

Finally accustomed to Dak's presence, Screech often came to join them, clamoring for his share of attention. When he had first seen them mating, he had hooted angrily at Dak, and tried to pull him away. But Zena had snapped at him, and Dak had refused to move. Defeated, Screech had sat by the pond and watched them, a baffled look on his face.

After that, he had ceased to object, and even greeted Dak with affection when he appeared on the hillside each morning. Dak, in turn, was tolerant of the younger male. He played with him, throwing stones into the pond to hear their loud plunk, or running after him in wide, exuberant circles. Sometimes, too, he just sat quietly beside Screech and traced the long, curved scar on the small male's back with gentle fingers, his eyes attentive.

One morning, Dak did not return. Zena was sad, but at the same time, she was strangely content. The emptiness inside her had been filled, and she no longer felt restless or incomplete. When her belly began to swell a few months later, she was not surprised. She had no idea what the distention might portend, but it did not disturb her. Screech, however, was very startled one evening when he placed his hand on her belly and something inside it kicked him. He drew his hand away and stared at her, perplexed. Zena pulled his hand to her belly again and let him stroke her until he became accustomed to the jolts within.

Many months later, strong cramps disrupted Zena's sleep. An impulse deep within her had persuaded her to build a second nest in a far corner of the cave, and she crawled over to it as the cramping continued. She crouched there, moaning softly. Screech came to nestle against her, a worried look on his face. The bond between them was very strong, and whenever she was hurt, he suffered. She touched his face gently.

The contractions became stronger, and she cried out in pain. Screech whimpered and tried to pull her to her feet. Zena waved him away. She had no strength to spare for reassurance now. All her energies were concentrated on her belly, on the feelings inside her. A heavy ache developed in her back, and she felt an immense pressure between her legs. The contractions continued to intensify. One after another, they shuddered through her body, leaving her no time to recover. She barely noticed as Screech stroked her abdomen and mewed softly beside her.

A fierce pushing sensation overwhelmed her, even as the contractions continued. She pressed down hard with her muscles, to make it go away. But the feeling stayed with her; it wrenched and pulled at her, made her torso rise into the air, then arch backward as the need to push, the forceful contractions, surged through her body.

Water suddenly gushed from her, and she felt something hard between her legs. Gathering her strength, Zena leaned over to see what it was. Blood was everywhere; its smell filled the cave. Strangely, it did not alarm her. And when she saw that a form was emerging, she was not alarmed, either. A strong thrill jolted her instead. This was as it should be. She reached down to grab the small body. It resisted for a moment, then came free. She pulled it up to her mouth and licked it energetically. It wailed, and Screech jumped backward. Zena paid no attention to him. All her energies were focused on the little one. She licked it over and over, then held it close to her breast. It rooted for her nipple and sucked eagerly. Screech came close again and watched, his eyes round with surprise.

Light was beginning to penetrate the cave, and Zena could see the infant more clearly. Its face was pink and crumpled, and its tiny skull was covered with black fur. Its hairless body was still covered with a waxy substance that her tongue had not removed. Like her, it had no protuberance at its groin. For a long moment, its eyes opened and it stared at her, unblinking. Zena stared back, entranced. She mewed softly to it and held it close to her breast again. Its tiny hands clutched at her chest, but this time it did not seek her nipple. Instead, it slept, bleating sharply from time to time as a tremor passed through its fragile body.

Suddenly exhausted, Zena lay down on the matted grasses, holding the infant carefully against her chest. But before she could sleep, her belly began to cramp again. She rubbed it hard, trying to make the pains go away. Soon, the afterbirth appeared; following a strong impulse, she ate some of it. Then she cut the cord that had attached the infant to her with her strong teeth. Satisfied, she lay down again and slept far into the morning.

When she awoke, Screech was not there. Alarmed by his absence, she called to him. There was no answer, but soon she heard him lowering himself into the cave. He had bulbs and tubers in his hands, as well as two speckled eggs. His face was covered with yolk and bits of shell. Zena had learned to eat eggs neatly by inserting a fingernail into the top and bottom of the shell and sucking out the contents, but Screech had not yet mastered this technique.

Abruptly aware that she was ravenous, Zena devoured the eggs. They were her favorite food, and satisfied her hunger more than anything else. Screech watched her, his eyes round and serious. Zena held the baby up for him to see. He reached over and touched it gently, then brought his face close to sniff it. The scent was new and complicated. Blood and milk and feces were all intermingled. He sneezed.

Zena put the infant to her breast and suckled it peacefully while she ate some bulbs and tubers. Then she rose to her feet, gesturing to Screech to follow. Gathering a large armful of the soiled grasses, she pushed them up through the entrance to the cave. The smell of birth was strong and would attract attention. Screech helped her; together they carried all the nesting material away from the refuge and scattered it, to dissipate the scent.

Weary but content, Zena stood for a moment gazing at the vista below. Though she had been here for many years, she never ceased to wonder at the beauty and abundance of the place she had so unexpectedly found. Then her eyes were drawn to the plume of smoke that always rose from the mountain with the bowl-shaped top. Today, the plume was thick and very dark.

She frowned anxiously. For weeks, the mountain had been belching smoke and soot, and sometimes it emitted ominous low rumblings. When the wind was right, the air carried a thin layer of grit that covered everything—rocks, grasses, her skin, even the berries she ate. As she watched, a deep russet glow showed momentarily at the base of the plume.

Zena turned away. The belching peak, with its ominous smells and noises, worried her. But for the moment, she was too tired to care. The mountain would have to wait. And for almost a month, it did.

Then, in a momentous explosion of flame and molten rock, it erupted.

CHAPTER
4

The antelopes could not settle to their feeding; their heads snapped up constantly, and they pranced skittishly from place to place as if drawn by an invisible force. Zena watched them uneasily. She did not know the cause of their nervousness, but she felt it too. Some danger greater than a leopard or tiger, or even a storm, was gathering around them. It was like the tingling feeling she had before the rains came, when terrible rumblings came from the sky and flashes of light speared the clouds, but much bigger and more oppressive.

She turned to look at the mountain. For weeks, it had been emitting a strong, acrid smell that coated her nostrils, made her eyes water. The noxious fumes were even stronger today. The light was strange too. A sickly gray-green cast overlaid the normal blue of the sky. She could not see the sun, had not seen it all day. It seemed reluctant to show its face, as if weary of its unaccustomed struggle to break through the constant haze.

Plumes of black smoke spewed from the mountain's bowl-shaped summit. Zena watched as they dispersed into wispy grayness, then coalesced into bulbous clouds edged with sulfurous yellow. They seemed to cover all the world with their ominous pall. Her sense of unease increased. The mountain was the cause of the animals' nervousness; she was suddenly sure of it.

She shuddered, terribly afraid. For the first time in years, she wanted her mother. She did not know what to do, whether to take Screech and the infant away or to remain in the security of the cave until the danger from the mountain had passed. Her mother would have helped her.

She called to Screech and headed for the cave. Night was almost upon them, and there was nowhere else to go. Placing her bundle of long-stemmed plants and tubers on the cave floor, she settled down to feed the infant. She had tried to make Screech understand that he, too, should bring as much food as he could carry back to the cave. It was all she could think of to do against the unnamed threat.

He came almost immediately. He had understood, for his small hands were full of plants and fruits. He nestled close to her, as he always did, but this time his face was uneasy. He seemed to sense her apprehension, and he stroked her arm over and over again. Even the infant seemed to be affected, for she had whimpered off and on all day.

Darkness came, but Zena could not sleep. Low rumblings emerged from the mountain, and sometimes the sound escalated into a sustained roar. Twice, the ground trembled under them as they lay curled up in the cave. After the second tremor, Zena picked up the infant and crawled outside, driven by an impulse stronger than her fear. The air was warm and still, the night silent except for the volcano, as if even the insects were too wary to emit their usual noises. Moonlight bathed the plains, and Zena could see the outlines of grazing animals. They seemed even more restless than before.

One of the heavy black clouds that littered the sky snaked across the moon's face, and the animals disappeared. Now all she could see was the mountain glowing fiercely in the distance. The redness near its top had grown. So had the smoke; no longer a thin plume, it spewed out in voluminous bulges that roiled menacingly into the sky. Behind the smoke came flames, but this time, they did not diminish into a scarlet glow, as they always had before. Instead, the flames leaped into the night, turning all the area above the mountain into a blazing inferno.

Fear slashed through Zena's body. Something terrible was about to happen. She could feel it in the tingling of her skin, the gaping ache in her belly. She must get Screech, get away!

She turned toward the cave, but before she could take a step, the mountain exploded. A massive pillar of smoke and flame shot straight up into the tumultuous clouds, and a deafening roar split the air as thousands upon thousands of tons of molten rock finally escaped the dome of hardened magma that had long held them captive. Moving at hundreds of miles an hour, the scalding rock spewed over the lip of the fractured dome and spilled down the sides of the mountain to the earth below, burying everything in its path in a scorching embrace.

Another explosion rent the air. Fiery balls of rock catapulted into the night sky, then streaked toward the earth in long, burning arcs. Everywhere they landed, fire followed instantly. It sped through the grasses, the bushes, the trees, the animals that sheltered within them, incinerating them in seconds.

Horrified, too shocked to react, Zena stood motionless, watching. Flames covered everything in the valley below her. They lit up the plains, turned the air red. Animals scattered in all directions, trampling each other as they fled the inferno. A band of pigs blundered toward her, swerving at the last moment to charge up the ridge. Not all the animals escaped the fires, and the screams of those who were trapped and burning mingled sickeningly with the crackling of flames, the mountain's roar.

A stronger tremor shook the earth. Zena yelled for Screech, but he was already beside her, his face contorted with fear. Then suddenly he was not there, for the ground had parted beneath them with a huge, grinding crack. Zena fell hard against the ledge, knocking the breath from her lungs. She gasped and tried to call Screech, but no sound emerged. Frantic with fear, she tucked the screaming infant under one arm while she felt for Screech's warm body with the other. But there was nothing.

Relief flooded her when she heard Screech calling from somewhere below. His voice was wild with terror. She scrambled toward him, but another tremor knocked her down. Clutching the infant against her chest, she crawled toward the place where she had heard him. The moon was eclipsed by ponderous clouds, and she could see almost nothing. Then, blessedly, it emerged for a slender moment, and she spotted Screech crouching partway down the slope. She ran to him and pulled him up the hill again, toward the cave. Perhaps they would be safe inside.

They crawled toward the entrance, but nothing was there. Zena stared, so astonished she forgot her fear for a moment. The ledge had fallen on top of it. She pushed Screech ahead of her toward the second entrance, but that too was gone. The whole ridge had collapsed. There was no refuge, no place to go.

The roar of the mountain grew into a sustained shriek. Zena pushed the baby's head against her chest, and covered an ear with her free hand, to try to stop the sound. But an even greater clamor arose as the volcano's savage intrusion on the atmosphere triggered a momentous storm. Thunder split the sky; a wild crack of lightning followed instantly. The bolt hit the bushes at the top of the ridge, engulfing them in flames.

Dazed, unable to think amidst the noise, the horror, Zena could not move. A burning chunk of rock careened through the air and crashed in front of her, jarring her into action. Grabbing Screech's hand, she bolted along the ridge, away from the fires and the belching mountain.

All through the night, they blundered through the murky darkness, falling countless times, until they were battered and bruised all over. Only flashes of lightning gave shape to their surroundings. Then, each rock, each bush and tree stood out harshly against the scarlet sky. But as soon as the incandescent spear had delivered its blow, a curtain of black dust descended once more, making the livid air impenetrable. The urge to stop and rest was strong. But Zena kept them moving, for she sensed a menace behind them even worse than the fires. Twice, she had looked behind her and seen the russet glow of molten rock racing across the plains and up the hills, as if the mountain itself were chasing her.

The ferocity of the storm increased moment by moment. The thunder seemed never to stop, and lightning tore the sky apart in multiple flashes. Wind suddenly blasted at them, driving hot ash at their faces, into their eyes. With the wind came rain. Black and filled with soot, it cascaded upon them in torrents, coating their skin with its residue. Zena stumbled on, clutching the screaming infant with one arm, guarding her eyes with the other.

A tree fell behind her with a deafening thud; she hurried away from the noise, desperate now to find shelter. She could barely see, and branches were crashing all around them. To go on was dangerous.

She reached for Screech, to pull him with her under an overhanging ledge, but Screech was not there. Her fingers touched only air.

She called to him, but got no answer. She called again. He could not be far away; he had been beside her only a moment before. Suddenly terrified, she yelled as loudly as she could into the onslaught of thunder and roaring wind and crackling flames, but still there was no answer.

Frantic, Zena tried to retrace their steps, but in the howling darkness, she could not tell where they had been. She dropped to her knees and crawled, clinging to the infant while she searched the ground with her fingers. Perhaps he had fallen, or was trapped somewhere.

She could not find him. Over and over, she crawled around, trying to search a new place each time. She yelled with all her strength until her voice was hoarse and not even a croak would emerge. Finally, she sank to the ground in exhaustion. Tears poured from her eyes. Screech was gone. He had vanished as her mother had vanished, and now she might never find him.

The infant squealed in her arms, but she ignored the cries. She wanted Screech; even more than the baby, it was Screech she wanted. He was closest to her heart, for he had come to her first, when she was all alone.

Despair overwhelmed Zena. She felt as if something inside her had been killed, mortally wounded in a way she could not understand. She closed her eyes and howled, forgetting the storm, the volcano, the danger of being heard. She howled and howled until all the strength was gone from her. Then she collapsed silently against the ash-laden earth.

II

A total absence of sound woke Zena. The woods were eerily still, as if every creature that had ever lived there had been silenced by the volcano's fury. No wind stirred, no animal moved, no bird called to its mate.

A drop of water made a barely audible plunk as it landed in a puddle, its normal bell-like tone muffled by soggy ash. Zena turned her head toward the sound. It seemed to come from far away, so she ignored it and fell back again toward sleep, but she could not get comfortable. Her whole body ached, and her throat was so raw she could barely swallow.

She rose stiffly to her feet, holding the still-sleeping infant against her chest. For a moment, she could not remember where she was. Then memory returned, and agony bent her double. Screech was gone . . . he was gone. . . . A terrible, drowning heaviness tore at her heart as she thought of him alone and frightened, calling for her.

Abruptly, she straightened and began to search frantically among the stark trees. Perhaps he was still nearby. The night had been so dark, so terrible. Maybe now, with light beginning to creep into the smoky air, she would find him. She tried to remember the way she had come, but nothing looked familiar, and all signs of their passage had been erased by the driving rains. There were no footprints, no scents, so she traversed the whole area, back and forth, calling loudly. But no answer came.

Numb with grief and weariness, she crouched against a blackened stump to rest. Her eyes closed involuntarily, then opened again in surprise as the infant woke and pulled eagerly at her breast. In her searching, she had almost forgotten her tiny daughter.

The baby's suckling reminded her that she was hungry. But the unforgiving landscape did not offer much hope of food. She could see no greenness, no sign of life anywhere around her. Heat and wind had blasted the leaves from the trees; fire had left the earth bereft of plants and bushes. The smell of scorched wood and damp soot was overwhelming.

Zena shuddered. How could she survive in such a place? No warmth came from the sun. No berries grew; there was no pond with bulbs, no fields with tubers to dig. None of these things were here. Perhaps they did not exist anywhere now. She had seen them burning below her as she fled.

She sat up suddenly. Perhaps the pond, at least, was still there. She could go back. Maybe Screech had gone back when he could not find her.

The image of Screech waiting at the pond gave her courage and a purpose. Determinedly, she clambered up a large boulder near the top of the hill that commanded a good view of the area. Twice, she fell back, for the rock was slick with soot. But she kept trying, driven by an overwhelming need to see if the place that had sheltered her for so long might offer refuge once again, if Screech could possibly be there.

The sight that greeted her was devastating. Lava, black and lifeless, stretched as far as she could see in every direction. Nothing moved on all that vast space, except steam rising from the hardening rock. The lava had poured into the long valley below her refuge, obliterating every sign of the abundance that had once flourished there, had spewed up the hills and through the passages between them, had even spread beyond the deep ravine that lay between her and the high plateau she had seen when she had climbed to the top of the ridge with Screech.

Zena's body slumped in utter desolation. She could not go back, and Screech would not be at the pond. There was no pond. Only a small, ash-filled puddle remained in the spot where it had once glittered in the sunlight. There were no grasses, no bushes, no life at all. Even the trees by the river had gone, instantly cremated by the fiery flow.

She could look no longer. Sobs shook her body, and cold fear gripped her heart. Flames still leaped from the volcano, and she could hear it rumbling. The menace could come again, the burning arcs across the sky, the fires, the moving blackness that was worse

than fire, the tremors that made rocks crumble and the ridge collapse. All of it could come again.

She must leave, must look for Screech and then leave as quickly
as she could. But where could she go? She raised her eyes again,
to the high plateau. Only there could she still see the greenness of
trees and grasses, the movements of animals.

Tucking the infant firmly against her hip, she slid down the boulder and began to walk in the direction of the plateau. Hope flared
anew as she trudged across the charred ground. It was near this
place that she had lost Screech. Surely now, in full daylight, she
would find him. She scoured the area with her eyes and called to
him constantly, listening all the while for any unusual sound. But
the woods were startlingly silent, almost devoid of life. Once, a
snake slithered past, leaving a curved gray trail. Later, she almost
ran into a pair of antelopes that had escaped the fires below. They
jumped away from her and disappeared silently behind the blackened trees.

As she neared the ravine, a loud roaring made her frown in
confusion. The sound had not been there last night. Cautiously, she
crept closer, then stood still as understanding dawned. It was water,
rushing water. The storm had turned the gorge into a turbulent,
fast-moving river. The sight filled her with terror. Her memory of
the foaming river was dim, but her brain and her body reacted
instinctively. Leaping away from the dangerous current, she plodded reluctantly up the hill to look for another route to the plateau.
For hours she searched, but always she found herself back at the
ravine. There was no way around it. To get to the plateau she would
have to go through the raging water, but to do that was impossible.

Hopelessness assailed her. Sobbing uncontrollably, she collapsed
in a heap on the unyielding ground. She was trapped here, stuck
in this terrible place without sun or sustenance or any sign of life,
where huge trees menaced her with their dark shapes and there
was no sound, only silence and shadowy darkness and the horrible
stench of smoldering earth and damp ash. And she had not found
Screech, would never find him now; he was gone, burned in the
fires or sucked into the raging water.

The infant's wails roused her. Zena looked down at the small
face, unseeing, and stroked the soft cheek with her fingertips. Gradually her eyes focused, as a picture of lush green grasses, of grazing
animals, of trees and bushes laden with fruit, arose in her mind.
These things existed on the plateau; she had seen them. And the
baby, at least, must live.

She rose wearily and forced her legs back toward the flooded ravine. Somehow, she must get to the plateau. It was their only hope. She walked and walked, looking for a place to cross, but everywhere she saw only foaming rapids, water so swift nothing could step into it without being knocked into the tumult.

Almost bereft of strength now, she stumbled on. A branch tripped her and she fell headlong into the remains of a burned thicket. As she pushed herself up again, her hand met a round object that cracked under her weight. Surprised, she looked down. It was a large egg; four other eggs lay beside it. The promise of food intensified the pangs of hunger that had racked her all morning. Eagerly, she poked a fingernail through one of the shells and sucked. Nothing came out. Too ravenous to wait, she tore at the shell. It splintered off, revealing another, softer egg inside. Zena sniffed it, then thrust it into her mouth. Its solidity puzzled her, but the taste was good. She ate the others and almost immediately felt stronger.

She went on, looking constantly for any sign of Screech as well as a place to cross. Once, a scent caught at her nostrils as she stood looking at a big boulder that still stuck up above the raging water. The smell was familiar; it was not Screech, but it was somehow like that.

The scent wafted away before she could identify it. And then the puzzle was driven from her mind by the sight of a huge tree that had fallen across the ravine. Its massive trunk stretched far into the woods on both sides of the gorge, and branches as thick as the trees she had known by the river thrust up all along its length, creating an almost impenetrable thicket. The trunk and all its limbs were slippery with rain and the constant splash of seething water that churned between boulders in the chasm below.

Zena stared at the tree, terrified by the chance it offered. Tentatively, she touched the trunk. Her hand slid away. She grasped one of the branches above. It, too, was slippery, but the plentiful smaller boughs that sprouted from it kept her hand in place. Slowly, she climbed up and straddled the huge trunk. Holding the infant close, she slid one thigh, then the other, along the wet surface.

A thick, curved limb barred her way. Cautiously, she squeezed around it and straddled the trunk on the other side. A deep breath escaped her. She had managed to get past the obstacle. But there was still earth beneath her. If she kept going, the churning river would be there instead. She peered into the ravine, to judge its depth, and shut her eyes in terror. The water charged between two boulders about ten feet below the tree, then shot through a narrow crevice to create a seething cascade that roiled down a steep fall of rocks. If she fell, she would never get out.

She began to slide off. She could not do this, dared not. It was impossible. . . .

She ceased to think. Without volition, her thighs held on to the trunk and began to squeeze her forward. She followed, hardly knowing what she did. Slowly, with terrible caution, she crept to the next branch that blocked her way, ignoring the twigs that slapped at her face, the rough bark that tore at her legs.

The rapids rushed below her, louder now, but she did not look down. She could not. She looked only at the next branch, at the place she would grab as she swung herself and the infant around the impediment. Now she had to squeeze through a narrow cleft where two large limbs made a sharp angle. Slowly, she pulled herself upright, clutching the baby under one arm and holding tightly to a stout branch with her free hand. She stepped through the gap. Her foot slid out from under her, and she fell heavily. Terrified by the sudden jolt, the infant screamed and wriggled wildly. Zena held on to her with frantic strength. Her knees hit the sleek trunk, and she managed to get her legs around it to clasp it once again.

Her whole body was trembling, and she stopped for a moment to rest. Before her was a long, bare area, with no branches, not even any brush, to hold on to. Only the drenched and glossy trunk lay between her and the roiling water below. Beyond that, the main trunk of the tree rose high in the air, supported by smaller branches that stretched to the ground. Another, narrower trunk seemed more level, but it did not rest as securely on the far bank. Zena stared at them, uncertain which to take, but when she got to the place where the trunks divided, she had no choice. To climb the larger one was impossible. It was too steep, so she ventured onto the smaller one. Forcing her eyes to the opposite bank, she inched forward. She was getting close now. Only a few more feet and she would be there.

Cautiously, she started to pull herself upright to maneuver her way around a limb that rose straight up from the middle of the trunk. She never managed to stand, for at just that moment, the tree shifted. The branches that supported the larger trunk gave way, and it plunged toward the ground. Swaying horribly, the smaller trunk dropped toward the water.

Zena screamed and wrapped her legs convulsively around the plunging trunk. Bushes projected from the top of the opposite bank. She grabbed at them desperately, but she was jerked backward as the trunk fell, and they slithered from her fingers. The movement knocked her off balance, and almost wrenched the infant from her grasp. The baby's body was slippery and stiff with fear, and Zena knew she could not hold onto her much longer. She would drop her soon, into the foaming chasm. . . .

With a momentous effort, she raised her arms over her head as she straddled the sodden trunk, and threw the infant toward the bushes. Then she clung with all her strength to the branch in front of her as the tree swung wildly above the gorge.

The trunk smashed into the edge of the bank, halfway down the steep side of the ravine. Against her will, Zena's eyes were drawn to the seething water, so close now that it splashed unceasingly against her face. With demonic force, it tried to dislodge her; it pulled relentlessly at her feet and careened over her ankles, smashing into them as if reluctant to give way and part around them.

Dizzy with terror, Zena closed her eyes. When she opened them again, she moaned in despair. There was no escape. Beside her, the side of the bank curved sharply inward, hollowed out by the rushing water. It was slick with clay, impossible to climb. The bushes were above her, far beyond her reach. There was no sound from the infant.

CHAPTER
5

Dak stalked silently through the woods. He had left the others crouched under a boulder deep within the ravine. They were safer there. To flee any farther from the blazing mountain tonight was dangerous. They had been walking for hours, ever since the mountain had exploded, but now the storm had become so intense he dared not venture farther. Trees were crashing all around them, and the fire-reddened air was so heavy with smoke and dust they could not see. Besides, Myta was hampered by her two young ones, and Rune, his mother, had slowed with age. His young brother Klep was strong, but his small legs were unaccustomed to walking all through the night.

He would be safer in the ravine as well. He had left it only because of the howling, the terrible, grief-stricken cries that had torn at his chest as if he had uttered them himself. He did not know what creature had made the anguished sounds, or why, but they had seemed to lodge inside him. Even after they had ceased, they had pulled at him relentlessly, had drawn him from the gorge and compelled him to walk through the raging storm to see if he could find their source.

A blazing shard landed close by, igniting a bush. Dak grabbed a stick and beat at the flames until they were gone. He did not want the fire to spread, making it impossible for him to return to the others. Some of the fire stayed in the top of his stick. He looked curiously at the glowing tip. It gave out light, so he kept it with him as he moved on.

The land was rising now under his feet. He was at the far end of the ridge, where it began to slope up steeply and curve south. The area was unfamiliar to him. He and the others lived in the valley to the east, behind the ridge. They seldom climbed up the steep hill, for the leopard hunted there. It had taken his sister, Apar, when she had ventured up one day to look for fruit, and had stayed into the evening hours. Her young one had disappeared as well, though they had seen only Apar's body hanging from the tree.

Long ago, he remembered, he had climbed over the ridge himself, drawn by the scent of others, though he had been careful to avoid the leopard. He smiled as an image of the pond, and the mate he had found there, formed in his mind.

The memory vanished as Dak's attentive ears caught a low sound. It was not the howling; instead, it was a whimper, like the sound young ones uttered when they were hurt, or wanted food. He edged forward cautiously, testing the smoke-laden air with his nostrils. A scent came to him, then disappeared as a gust of wind pulled sodden leaves and ash from the floor of the forest and whipped it at his face, but even in that moment he had known that the smell was familiar.

The whimper was louder now. Dak's forehead wrinkled in consternation. How could a young one be here? He had left all the others in the ravine. None were missing. And the scent was not that of any member of his troop. It was similar, but not the same. He had known it before, though he could not identify it precisely. His eyes clouded as he tried to remember.

Now the sound was right under his feet. It came from beneath a big fallen tree. Dak held his burning stick near the ground and stared into the tangle of branches. His straining eyes focused on a small shape, deep within the brush. The shape twitched. Dak knelt, trying to see more clearly through the driving rain and soot-blackened air. He moved the burning stick closer. The creature flinched. But the stick's glow illuminated the area, and the dark shape took on meaning. It *was* a young one, lying facedown against the damp earth. A branch covered its neck and shoulder, pinning it to the ground. On its back was a long, curved scar.

The hair on Dak's neck rose at the sight. The scar had meaning for him. He knew it immediately, but the meaning would not come clear. He reached into the tangle and touched the small form. A hand thrust toward his face, and the moaning began again. Dak hesitated. To rescue a young one who was not from his troop felt strange, but the nagging sense of familiarity that came with this one tugged at his instinct to protect.

He looked carefully at the fallen tree. Most of its weight was supported by smaller branches. It was one of these that had pinned the youngster to the ground. The others could break at any moment and crush the small form beneath. He tried to raise the branch, but it was held firmly in place by the tree's weight and would not budge. Clenching his teeth with the effort, he crouched below a big limb and pushed upward with all his strength. Unexpectedly, the whole tree lurched toward the ground. He scooped up the small body and leaped away. With a massive crack, the tree settled against the sodden earth.

Dak stared down at the little creature in his arms. Blood covered its face, but its eyes were open and staring. It uttered a new sound, a call unfamiliar to Dak, and raised a hand to his face. Then it sighed deeply and its eyes slowly closed.

Again Dak hesitated. The howling sounds still reverberated within him, and he knew he had not found their source. This one had not made such noises. Perhaps another was pinned beneath the tree, or lay wounded somewhere ahead. He scanned the area carefully, but he could see almost nothing in the blackness.

The wind rose suddenly. It blew thick ashes into his face, whistled harshly in his ears. Then he heard a new noise, one that made him turn sharply toward the ravine. It was the sound of water slapping against boulders. He ran forward and peered into the deep gorge. Already, the water had risen so high it would cover his ankles if he stood there. A picture of the others, crouched under the boulder waiting for him, came into his mind. He hurried back the way he had come, his face wrinkled with anxiety.

The small creature moaned piteously as his hurrying steps jostled it. Dak looked down at the sound, but he did not break his stride. The water was rising fast; he must hurry—but when he reached the place where he had left the others, no one was there. His heart thumped in fear, and he looked frantically around him. Lightning flashed nearby, and the momentary illumination revealed many sets of footprints on the north side of the gorge.

Relief coursed through him. The others had crossed already. Dak stepped cautiously into the ravine. Water swirled around his knees, then for a moment reached his chest. He held the youngster above the torrent as he stumbled to the other side. Soon the flood would be so turbulent no creature could cross. The others had been wise to move on.

He scrambled up the far bank, studying the footprints carefully.

Already rain had obliterated many of the marks, but he was able to tell that the others were still heading north. All the day before, as monstrous clouds had poured from the mountain, his mother, Rune, had gestured in that direction. She knew of places the others had never seen, for she had lived a long time. When the mountain had exploded, she had called excitedly, running north a short way, then coming back to make them follow her. And so they had started off, as fast as they could with the young ones. Dak himself had often seen a high plateau to the north, when he had climbed the ridge to go to the pond. The place had been green, and filled with animals. It was far from the screaming mountain, too. They would be safe there.

The footprints led to a clearing in the forest. Fire had already burned it, so there would be no more flames. A loud chorus greeted his scent, which wafted before him, and the others came toward him excitedly.

Dak's face relaxed. They were all here. They clustered around him, then moved back warily when they spotted the bundle in his arms. Dak gestured that it posed no danger, and they crowded around again. Gently, he held the young one out for their inspection. Rune came close and sniffed, her brow furrowed. She stared at Dak with puzzled eyes and sniffed again. Then she took Screech carefully from Dak's arms and began to lick the blood from his face. Her face was gentle now, and soft cooing sounds of reassurance came from her lips.

Dak looked at her, baffled. This was behavior usually reserved for one of her own young ones, or the young of her daughters. But how could that be? Two of her daughters had died of a sickness that had killed many in the troop; another had left in search of a mate. Of Rune's young, only he and Klep remained in the troop. Before, there had been Apar; Rune had behaved like that with Apar's young one. . . .

Dak gave up the puzzle. Rune's behavior told him that she had accepted the young one he had found, and that was all that mattered.

Rune, too, was puzzled, but she did not doubt her senses. She had known immediately that this was Apar's young one, that he had somehow survived. His scent was unique, and she knew it well. Before his disappearance, she had cared for him many times, had licked him and fed him, carried him in her arms, and the smell of him told her he belonged.

She gathered a pile of leaves that had escaped the fire and laid Screech gently on them. He moaned again at the movement. She studied him, her eyes alert. One of his arms was bent at a strange angle, and it was bruised and swollen. The bruise extended across his shoulder and neck. Rune turned him so the arm did not press against the ground. Blood still welled up from a cut on his head. She licked it until the oozing stopped.

Screech stirred and called out. Myta's little ones, curious about the newcomer, tried to kneel down to look at him, but Rune chased them back. All night, she hovered over him, not allowing the others to come too close. Occasionally, she drank water from a nearby puddle and pressed her lips to his. Most of it dribbled down his neck, but some went down his throat. His face twisted with pain as he swallowed. For hours, the heavy branch had pressed against his neck, bruising everything inside. Rune's eyes were anxious as she watched.

Again, Screech uttered the strange call. Rune bent over him solicitously, but he frowned and looked away. He wanted another face there. He wanted Zena. Her image came into his mind, and he smiled, a tiny, fleeting smile.

Once, he had heard her calling, but he had not been able to tell if the noise was real or part of the dreamlike visions that had come in and out of his mind ever since the tree had knocked him down. He did not know if he had answered, either. Wearily, he shut his eyes again and resumed his waiting. He had waited all through the long hours when he was pinned beneath the tree, and he would wait some more. She would come to him; he was certain of it, for she always had before.

II

Light came softly through the sooty air, many hours later. The redness had gone from the sky, and the rain had stopped. Dak rose from his resting place and stretched. Klep grabbed his hand and pulled him over to the young one on the ground. Ignoring Rune's scolding, he traced the scar on Screech's back with curious fingers. The gesture pulled at Dak's memory. He saw himself at the pond, tracing the scar in the same way. . . .

This was the small male at the pond. But where was the young female with whom he had mated? He frowned. This puzzle was not so easily dismissed. He had cared for that female, and she was missing. Perhaps she too had been wounded, was still lying somewhere. If he searched again, he might find her.

Rune came to him and pointed north, wanting to leave. Dak looked up at the smoking mountain. Fire and the terrible moving blackness could pour from its peak again at any moment, and trap them here. He sighed. There was no time to look for the young female. He was the only adult male left in his troop, and he must help Rune get the others away.

Sadly, he turned away from the mountain and began to walk north. Rune lifted Screech into her arms and followed, but he was too heavy for her and she asked Dak to take him. Klep strode by his brother's side, trying to match his long stride. Myta's two little ones scampered ahead, chasing each other through the woods as if there had been no volcano, no storm to frighten them and make them flee from their home. Myta followed, calling anxiously.

The two young ones had been born together, almost a year after Myta had appeared, thin and frightened, in the valley. Rune had chased her away at first, but Myta had refused to leave. Day after day, she had hung around the places where they slept and gathered food, cringing submissively whenever one of them came close, and after a while they had become accustomed to her presence. Then Myta had signaled her readiness to mate. Dak and another male who had since left had mated with her many times. After that, his mother had accepted her as one of them.

Her acceptance was crucial, for Rune was the undisputed matriarch of the troop. Dak watched her admiringly as she strode beside him, her eyes fastened on the place to the north where she wanted to lead them. Her vast store of experience was invaluable to all of them. She had taught them what foods to eat, where to find shelter, how to protect and feed the young ones; she had led them to new places when food was scarce. During the drought that had killed so many in the troop when Dak was a small child, she had brought them to the valley behind the ridge, where food and water were available to those who knew the territory, as Rune did. Now, she was leading them to safety once again.

Dak looked down in surprise as the thick mat of damp, ash-covered leaves on the floor of the forest abruptly gave way to a squashy substance that almost buried his toes. Looking up again, he realized that they had emerged from the woods. For the first time since they had fled from the volcano, he could see far into the distance. He gasped in astonishment. The whole expanse of land before him had been buried beneath a hard black crust. Above it lay a thick layer of ash, still damp from the rains. The ash-covered lava stretched as far as he could see to the east and west, went all the way to the edge of the deeply eroded escarpment to the north. Above the escarpment stood the plateau. There, at least, he could see some green.

Klep called excitedly. He had found bones, sticking up from the lava. Dak went to see. The bones still had the shape of an antelope. It lay there, as if sleeping, but much of its flesh was gone. He pulled a bit of charred meat from its ribs. The taste was burned and bitter. But in another place, he found flesh not so badly charred, and he called to the others to try it.

Rune pulled off a piece and chewed it thoroughly, then leaned over Screech to put some in his mouth. He choked and cried out in pain. She looked up at Dak, her eyes clouded with worry. The small male's lips were terribly hot.

Myta's little ones swung on the animal's horns, chortling, while the others feasted on its flesh. It was the first food they had found since the day before. When their hunger was satisfied, they moved on across the wide stretch of wet ash, leaving deep footprints behind them. The sun bore down on the prints and baked them dry, leaving an indelible record of their passage.

Suddenly, Klep screamed and jumped frantically up and down. Dak ran to him and began to jump himself, for the ash was hot under his feet. He pulled Klep away from the place, but as the sun climbed relentlessly higher, all the ash began to heat up. By the middle of the day, they had to hop as quickly as possible from one spot to the next, and they could not rest at all. Thirst began to torment them. Dak thought of the wet leaves in the forest behind them, and ran his tongue longingly over his cracked lips.

A big boulder stuck up through the lava just ahead. They collapsed on top of it, drawing their feet gratefully away from the scorching ground, but thirst soon drove them on. Myta especially needed water, for she was suckling two youngsters and they drew the liquid from her body. Rune led them around to the right, pulling Klep behind her. An instinct born of years of experience told her this was the most likely direction in which to find water. The land sloped down on the right side of the plateau, and in such places, swamps sometimes flourished.

Abruptly, Rune began to run, still pulling the startled Klep. She called as loudly as she could without breaking her stride. Dak stopped to listen to the call, then ran after her quickly as pain shot up through the soles of his feet. But his eyes were eager, for Rune had uttered the sound for water.

Then he saw it, a glimpse of muddy liquid, just beyond the top of a small rise. He lumbered forward, his eyes fastened on the sight. So intent was he that he failed to notice the sudden disappearance of ash and lava. At one moment, his feet burned; the next moment, they felt the welcome coolness of grass. He looked down, amazed.

A few long tongues of black reached toward the swamp, but between them was the wonder of green. And beyond that was the miracle of water.

Rune and Klep were already there, kneeling and drinking deeply. Myta staggered behind her two young ones, who ran jubilantly toward the muddy banks. They did not stop to drink, but waded in energetically. Myta screamed, the scream for danger, and they ran out as fast as they had entered. She had spotted an ominous pair of eyes just above the surface. She did not know what the eyes signified, for she had never seen such a creature before, but she was certain it could hurt them.

Dak peered into the water as he knelt to drink. He could see the animal's large body from this perspective, just beneath the water. It was scaly, with a thick tail, and it had a long snout with terrible, gnashing teeth. He pointed toward it for Rune to see. She jumped back, and gestured with her arms that the creature might come close and try to snatch one of them with its cruel jaws.

The two youngsters backed fearfully way from the water, their feet squashing deeply into the wet moss around the pond. But their alarm dissipated rapidly as other novelties distracted them. Tiny colorful frogs, disturbed by their hasty retreat, leaped high into the air. The twins scampered after them. One of them picked up a handful of moss and flung it at his brother. Soon clumps of the soggy stuff were flying in all directions.

The others moved away from the crocodile's place to soothe their blistered feet in the coolness of another of the small ponds that dotted the marsh. Then they lay down on a grassy area above the wetness, grateful to be able to rest. Dak looked around him with satisfaction. Food abounded in this place. The marshes were studded with edible plants, and there would be many kinds of insects and reptiles, as well as small mammals and birds.

Carefully, he lowered Screech to the ground. The small male was frighteningly limp, and he had not uttered a sound for a long time, not even when Dak had run, stumbling in his eagerness, to the water. But his eyes opened for a moment when Dak put him down, and he emitted a weak sound, the same call Dak had heard before.

Rune came to look at him. Dak thought he saw tears in her eyes, and they frightened him further. But she went stolidly toward the water and slurped up a mouthful. The little one needed liquid desperately. The lava's terrible heat had drawn all the moisture from him, and he was feverish as well. Screech did not resist when she placed her lips against his, but he could not seem to swallow. Even when Rune put the water in very slowly, most of it dribbled down his chin.

A clump of wet moss hit Rune's back as she crouched over Screech. She scowled at the twins. Then her face became thoughtful. The moss had felt cool and refreshing. Gesturing to one of the boys to give her the clump in his hand, she placed it gently on Screech's forehead. When she signaled for more, the youngsters set off eagerly and returned with big piles. These she draped around Screech's chest and neck. The coolness seemed to help, for his face became less strained. Satisfied, Rune settled down beside him to wait.

Dak rose and climbed to the top of the escarpment, beyond the marsh. From here he could see all the way to the valley where they had lived. The contrast between the place where he stood and the place he had come from was startling. Here, everything was lush and green, untouched by the volcano. Below, all was black, apparently lifeless. Only the trees in the forest they had left, looming bleakly above the ashes, broke the flat darkness. Then he spotted some antelopes, and a bunch of pigs, taking advantage of the evening coolness to cross the lava. There were not many, but at least some animals had survived. Far away, near the place where they had first stepped onto the lava, he thought he saw another creature, one that walked like himself on two legs. He squinted, trying to distinguish its size and shape. But it was too far to see clearly, and he gave up the effort.

The brilliant horizon caught his attention. The sun had just disappeared, and all the sky around it was fiery red. Its glow lit up the voluminous clouds that still seethed behind the smoking mountain, and turned the lava purple. The vast expanse seemed almost to move before Dak's eyes as the light disappeared against it. He watched for a time, then turned away. Soon it would be fully dark, and he must protect the others. They were safe from the volcano, but other unknown dangers could lurk in this place. He scrambled back to the marsh. Rune had moved them a little higher, away from the water and the crocodiles. Dak picked up a few large stones, to throw at any predator that came near. Klep imitated him. Rune, too, had a stone.

Dak went over to her where she lay beside Screech on a deep pile of grasses. The small male was still and quiet. Once, he cried out and his eyelids fluttered, then he was still again. Dak looked at his mother for reassurance, but the tightness of her lips only increased his uneasiness.

Rune reached out and touched the young one's hand, then his

head. She had kept the mosses damp and cool, but Screech's skin still burned against her palm. She met Dak's worried eyes and shook her head forlornly.

Sighing, he lay down beside her to sleep. But even in sleep, his ears remained alert for unusual sounds. He heard snuffling, as a night creature probed for food, and insects made a wondrous chorus. Once, a bird squawked, and an animal screamed in terror as a predator grabbed it. None of these noises woke Dak, though he was aware of them. He sat up straight, though, when he heard an eerie howling pierce the darkness. The sound stopped, then resumed, from another place farther away.

Dak relaxed and lay down again. It had been a different kind of howling. But after that, he dreamed. As he slept, an image of a young female, the one he had mated with at the pond, came into his mind. She sat in the middle of the steaming lava, her head in her hands, and she howled in anguish. Over and over, the dream raced through his brain, and when he woke in the dawn, he could not tell if he had heard the howling or not.

CHAPTER
6

Zena wrapped both arms around the thick branch in front of her and clung desperately as the trunk slid still lower against the stream bank. It scratched deep gouges in the damp clay; she watched, mesmerized, as displaced globs slithered into the water and were instantly dissolved in swirling foam.

The trunk settled again with a wrenching jerk just above the churning river. Water surged around Zena's knees, splashed relentlessly into her face and eyes, but she dared not wipe it away, lest she lose her grip and fall. She dared not move at all, forward or backward. She was stuck here, at the mercy of the raging water.

She slumped helplessly against the sodden branch. Then a muffled sound reached her, barely audible over the water's clamor. It was the infant; she was almost sure it was.

Resolve returned, and she sat up straight. Somehow, she had to get to the baby.

She dared to let go with one hand and swipe at her eyes, so she could see. On one side of her a waterfall charged through the rocks; on the other side were vine-encrusted brush and branches that hung down from the larger trunk. If she could reach them, she might be able to haul herself up.

Just as she began to move forward, a heavy log careened over the waterfall and charged straight at her knees. Frantic with terror, she stood up and grabbed a thick vine that dangled near her head, to steady herself. Her feet slid away from the drenched trunk and dropped uselessly into the water. It reached as high as her chest now, and only her fingers kept her from being swept away. She held on to the vine with all her strength as the current lashed her, tried to force her into the tumultuous river.

Trembling with the strain, she looked for a place to stand to get a few seconds of relief for her arms. The log that had crashed toward her was down there, bobbing in the restless water. Gingerly, she placed her feet on it. The log held her weight for a moment, then it shot out from under her, propelling her straight up into the thicket. Despite the jolt, she felt immediately more secure. Now the water was below her knees, and she could reach the larger branches above. Slowly, she hauled herself up until her body was free of the current's wrenching pull.

Now she was certain she heard the infant. She was screaming loudly, long insistent wails of frustration. The sound renewed Zena's determination. Doggedly, she dragged herself up through the tangled branches until she was directly below the main trunk. It still rose at a steep angle, but not as steep as before. Wrapping both arms around its wide girth, she pulled herself on top of it. This time, she did not even try to sit, but lay flat on her stomach as she wriggled toward the opposite bank.

She lifted her head, suddenly aware that water was no longer splashing up at her, and steeled herself to look at the torrent below. Her relief was so great that she almost fell. There was no water. There was only ground, solid, ash-covered ground. But she was high above it—too high to jump, and she saw no branches, no convenient tangle of brush through which she could lower herself. All that was visible was a limb below her that angled down toward the ground, above the churning water.

The baby wailed again, a sharp cry of fear. Zena moved without thinking. She slid backward to the limb, rose to her knees and lunged. For a moment, her body hung over the rushing torrent, then she landed with a thump at the edge of the bank. Brushing away the tears that welled up at the welcome feel of earth beneath her feet, she hurried toward the place where she had heard the infant. There had been no more cries.

An unexpected noise made her heart thump with hope. It was a sneeze, the kind of sneeze the infant made when she was carried into the cave through the dusty passage. Zena ran toward the sound, and saw the baby immediately. She was lying in the bushes beside the ravine, kicking her feet and waving her tiny fists, as if trying to extricate herself. An angry red bump showed on her forehead, and there were scratches on her stomach, but otherwise she looked unharmed. She stared up at her mother, whimpering. Zena picked her up and held her close. Tears coursed down her cheeks, and this time she did not try to wipe them away.

The baby sighed contentedly and began to suckle. Zena sat down abruptly, dizzy with the shock of the last few hours. She forced herself up again. Dusk was not far away, and she had to find shelter. Her knees shook with exhaustion as she stumbled on, and her eyes kept closing. Only the infant's movements and noises kept her going. Each time her head nodded and her arms began to sag, the baby wriggled and screamed in fear.

Abruptly, she realized that the trees had thinned, and the ash under her feet felt different. She sank into it with every step, and in some places there was heat below. Frowning, she peered out from behind the last of the trees.

An endless expanse of ash-covered lava stretched as far as she could see in every direction. There was nothing on it, nothing at all—no animals, no trees or bushes or grasses. No movements distracted her eyes; no noises reached her ears.

Despair overwhelmed her suddenly. With it came a terrible feeling of helplessness. She could not think what to do. To reach the plateau, she had to cross the blackness, but to struggle across all that desolate space was impossible. It was too far, too forbidding. But she could not stay here, in this horrible place without light or greenness or shelter.

Cautiously, she took a few steps into the deep ash, to see if she could walk in it. It was hot and burned her feet, so she turned and headed east along the edge of the trees, to look for a cooler place. Then, without warning, hunger and exhaustion claimed her, and she knew she could go no farther. She had to find shelter. The thought reverberated in her mind, and she clung to it tenaciously as she moved slowly toward the woods, looking for anything that might offer safety during the dark hours. Finally, she saw a pile of large rocks in a burned area. She climbed onto them, seeking a crevice she could crawl through, or even a place in which she could huddle unseen.

She was lucky. Near the top of the pile, she was able to squeeze through a crack between two rocks. The space was tiny; she could barely move her elbows, and she could not lie down, but at least no larger animal could get in. Groaning with weariness, she slumped against the hard surface. Her eyes closed, and she slept, forgetting her hunger, her fear, even her anguish at losing Screech. She could rest, finally, and that was all that mattered.

II

An animal padded over Zena's head, its paws almost silent on the gray rocks. She shivered convulsively and huddled lower. The sound triggered a remembered terror so sharp her breathing seemed almost to stop. But the noise disappeared quickly, and she roused herself to feed the infant. Her hungry whimpers would attract attention. Zena placed the tiny female at her breast, but her milk supply had diminished over the past days, and the baby was not satisfied. Sighing, she pulled herself stiffly out of the tight crevice. Neither of them would survive if she did not find food and water soon.

She drank deeply from a shallow puddle left by the rain. The water was smoke colored and tasted of fire, but it quenched her thirst. Food was more difficult to find, but eventually she came across some plants she recognized, ones that she knew had long yellow tubers beneath the ground. To her surprise, they were softer than those she had found near the pond, and she could chew them easily. She dug up a bunch of them with a stone and kept them with her as she headed again toward the lava.

Food and rest had restored her, and the picture of the green plateau was once again clear in her mind. She trudged out across the dark ash without hesitation. No heat came from it now, for the sun was barely over the horizon. For more than an hour, she plodded on, only vaguely aware of the occasional animals that trotted past her on their way to the greenness above. Then an unexpected sight brought her to an abrupt halt. There were marks before her in the ash, marks that she had seen many times before. Her own feet made them in the mud, and Screech's feet. But how had they come here?

Zena looked down at her feet. Carefully, she placed one of them beside a big footprint, then she removed it and stared at the result. Her print looked the same, though it was smaller and not as deep, for the ash was harder than it had been the day before. Other prints were scattered nearby. One set was almost the same size as her own; another was smaller. Zena knelt to look at it, and Screech came into her mind.

She stared into the distance. The unexpected marks excited her, but she was also apprehensive. She sensed that others like herself had made them, but she had been alone for so long, except for Screech, that she could not imagine what *others* might mean. She walked on, watching nervously for any sign of the ones who had made the marks.

The ash began to warm up as the sun rose higher. Zena placed her feet inside the biggest footprints. The ground was cooler there, and she kept on walking inside them until they stopped abruptly beside a large rock. She rested for a moment, then set off again, eager to get off the lava before it became too hot. The green was getting close now; she could see bushes ahead, and she thought she could smell water. The faint scent that lingered around the footprints was getting stronger, too. She had smelled it often as she stood on the ridge looking down into the narrow valley, but never before had it been so powerful, so close. She scanned the landscape ahead of her anxiously and hurried on.

Another scent stopped her in her tracks. Her heart began to thump heavily—but it was too weak to be sure, and Screech could not be here. . . .

Tense with hope, she strode ahead, not even noticing that the coolness of grass had abruptly replaced the hot ash beneath her feet. A slight breeze rippled toward her, bringing with it the smell of water and mud and that other, elusive odor.

Zena began to tremble, and a sob rose in her throat. The scent *was* there; she could smell it clearly now. It was Screech's smell, more familiar to her than any other.

She called to him, a long, anguished call, ignoring the danger that might lie ahead. There was no answer. She moved forward slowly, eyes and ears alert. So intent was she that she almost stumbled into a pool of muddy water. Automatically, she knelt to drink, but midway through a gulp she lifted her head in confusion. The scent was strong here. It was Screech, but not quite the same, as if he had changed somehow.

Bewildered, she called again, the call she had always used to bring him to her. This time she heard a response. The sound was weak, terribly weak, but still she knew it. She sped toward it, forgetting caution, forgetting everything but the need to find him.

An old female rose from the ground at her approach. She growled at Zena and stood protectively over the small body at her feet. Zena paid no attention. It was Screech on the ground; she was certain it was Screech, even before he uttered the call she knew so well. She ran to him, oblivious to the growls. The other female moved aside as Zena knelt beside him and gathered his head into her free arm, cooing to him joyously.

Screech looked at her, and an expression of absolute relief came into his eyes. He felt for her hand and held it to his cheek. She had come for him, just as he had known she would. His eyes closed again, but now the anguish had left his face.

Tears rained down Zena's cheeks, tears of joy and of fear. His face was hot, terribly hot. She pushed the moss away from his forehead, revealing an angry red gash that was badly swollen. And his smell was not right.

Over and over again, she stroked his cheeks, uttering low calls of happiness, and then of distress, at his stillness, his silence.

A sound, an unfamiliar call, made her look up. She had almost forgotten the others, whose tracks she had followed. For the first time, she really saw the female who had stood over Screech. Though stooped and thin, she was strong. There was no hint of submission about her. She had stopped growling and was watching Zena carefully. The eyes of the two females met. Worry clouded them both.

Again, Rune uttered the unfamiliar call. A male appeared behind her. He stared at Zena, and then came closer to sniff at her. She shrank back, protecting Screech and the infant with her body. He retreated quickly and sat down near her, continuing to gaze at her face. She stared back, wide-eyed with astonishment as recognition returned. This was the male who had come to her pond. Tentatively, she reached out to touch his shoulder. Dak smiled, and placed his hand on hers.

Zena sighed, a long, deep sigh, and bent over Screech once again. Heat came from him, and his arm was hurt. It was purple, and bent in the wrong place. She frowned, and cooed to him. His eyes flickered, but he did not respond. His inability to move, to reach out to her with his characteristic eagerness, frightened her terribly. Had she found him only to lose him?

Then practicality reasserted itself, and determination. He was hurt, just as he had been when she first found him. She would treat him the same way, and he would get better. Zena ran to the water and filled her cheeks with it, then ran back and placed her mouth over his. Instinct told her he needed water more than anything else, for the heat inside him was burning the liquid from his body.

With a momentous effort, Screech swallowed a few drops. The movement hurt him badly, but because it was Zena above him, coaxing, and not some other, he would try. His bruised throat was a little less constricted, too, for the terrible tension that had afflicted him as he waited for Zena had finally eased. All through the long nights, the hot days, his muscles had been immovable, kept rigid by the need to listen for her. Now that she had come to him, his whole body had relaxed, and he could try to swallow the liquid he needed so desperately.

Zena went back for more water; again a few drops went down his throat. She chewed one of her tubers, and tried to persuade him to take some from her lips. But he only frowned and turned his head away. Rune came up beside her carrying fresh clumps of moss. As Zena watched, she placed one on Screech's forehead. Then she handed the others to Zena. Feeling their coolness, Zena imitated her, and put them against the feverish small body. She looked up gratefully at Rune.

Another female approached as Zena bent over Screech. Two small ones clung to her. She reached out tentatively to touch Zena. Her hand stopped in the middle of the gesture, and she looked anxiously at Rune, as if requesting permission.

Rune frowned as her eyes moved between Zena and Screech. Screech had a familiar smell, but Zena did not. But Dak had greeted her in a way that implied recognition. She shook her head, confused, and wandered off to sit by herself.

Myta took advantage of Rune's confusion and finished her gesture. She touched Zena, very lightly, and looked curiously at the infant. Then she darted off to join Rune. After a while, both of them got up and went off in search of food. The young ones followed, chattering to each other and tumbling together in the grasses as they went.

Dak disappeared behind a low hill on the far side of the pond. He returned a few minutes later and sat down close to Zena. In his hands were some ripe pieces of fruit. Gravely, he held them out for her to take.

Zena looked carefully at his face, then she reached out and accepted the fruit. It was deep purple, and juicy. She bent over Screech, to see if he might take some. His eyes had opened again, and he was staring up at her. She cooed to him, and showed him the fruit. But he just kept looking at her and did not respond. She lay down beside him to rest. Perhaps later, he would eat more. Joy filled her heart, despite her worry. She was with Screech again.

Her eyes began to close and she blinked furiously, trying to stay awake. She did not want to leave Screech again even in sleep. But exhaustion and the feeling of security that came from having others nearby were too great to deny. Against her will, Zena's eyes closed again, and she slept.

III

When she awoke, the others were grouped around her. Dak lay on his back; a young male Zena had not seen before leaned against him. Rune crouched beside Screech, her eyes watchful. The two little ones were suckling, one at each of Myta's breasts.

Suddenly fearful, Zena turned quickly toward Screech. Seeming to feel her anxiety, he opened his eyes and reached out toward her with his good arm. Lovingly, Zena held his hand against her face. It felt hot to her cheek. She laid the small hand gently by his side and jumped up to get him water and fresh moss, taking the infant with her.

Dak followed and watched carefully as she drank. Now that Zena had returned, he was determined to protect her, and the new infant as well. Crocodiles lurked everywhere in the marshes, ready to grab any creature that came too close. He spotted a pair of eyes and a telltale ripple in the water, and flung a stone at it with all his strength. A scaly tail whipped out of the muck as the crocodile swam away. Zena looked up at him gratefully, and he smiled in satisfaction.

Zena returned to Screech. He took some water, then he stared into her face and opened his mouth, just as he had when he was tiny and wanted food. Overjoyed at this sign of improvement, Zena looked for the tubers she had left near him, so she could chew some for him. They had disappeared. A remnant of one still clung to Myta's mouth. So she approached Dak, and made gestures as if plucking fruit. It was Screech's favorite food. She was certain he would eat some, if she could find more. Dak watched her carefully, then grunted with comprehension and led her to the trees. Together, they gathered a big pile of the succulent fruit and brought it back to the resting place.

Zena chewed the fruit thoroughly, until it was almost liquid. Screech watched her, and opened his mouth obediently when she pressed her lips against his, but he could not seem to swallow more than a mouthful or two. Zena sighed, disappointed. Darkness was almost upon them, and in the dim light his face looked terribly pale.

Later in the night, he began to shiver, and to utter strange sounds, as if he did not know where he was, or that Zena was beside him. He called for her over and over again, but did not seem to hear her reassuring responses. She ran for water, but now he did not even try to swallow, and most of it spilled out of his mouth. The heat had gone from his skin, and he felt cold and clammy. Zena lay close to him to give him warmth, murmuring the sounds he knew so he would understand that she was still there.

He cried out suddenly in fear. Zena took his hand in hers and caressed it. The gesture seemed to penetrate his delirium. He opened his eyes and gazed at her. The moon was almost full, and she could see his face clearly. Now she was certain he knew she was there. She could tell because an expression of merriment, like the expression he had had when he was small and they played games together, came into his face. Zena rubbed her nose gently against his. He responded briefly, as if to assure her that he remembered. Again, he stared deeply into her eyes, and now his expression was utterly peaceful. He sighed in contentment, and his small body relaxed.

Zena held his hand against her cheek as she slept beside him. All through the rest of the night, he did not stir or make a sound. When she awoke in the morning, his hand was cold. She bent over him anxiously and called to him. He did not answer. She called more loudly. Still he did not respond. Daylight had crept across the low meadows, and the gentle light touched his face as he lay there. No color showed in his skin.

Terror seized her heart. Trembling, she laid the infant on the cool grass and pulled Screech into her arms. His body felt stiff against her chest, and the heat had left it. There was no warmth in him at all.

Darkness descended over Zena, despite the glow of the early morning light. She did not see it, did not want to see anything, except Screech's face, eager and warm as it had been before. She did not know what death was, or what it meant, but she knew instinctively that Screech was irretrievably gone. She would not have him anymore. She held him close and howled.

Dak leaped to his feet as her anguished cries broke the early morning quiet. The terrible noise made his scalp prickle, as it had on the night the mountain exploded, and even in his dreams. But he dared not approach Zena to comfort her. The pose of her body warned him to keep away. He looked anxiously at Rune. She, too, seemed to sense an invisible barrier, for she did not move toward Zena. She only shook her head wearily as she returned his gaze. Her eyes were mournful. She was an old female, and had seen sickness and injuries kill many in her troop. She remembered the shivering and delirium, the final stillness that followed.

After he and the others had fed, Dak came to Zena and tried to take Screech from her, so they could head toward the plateau. Rune wanted to go on, for the crocodiles were a constant threat to the young ones, but Zena refused to relinquish Screech. She snapped at Dak, and would not let him close to the infant either. The tiny girl was still lying in the damp grass beside her, whimpering.

Rune gestured to Dak to go with the others. She was not surprised at Zena's behavior, for she knew the death of a young one was hard to accept. Slowly, she advanced toward Zena, holding out her hand. When Zena did not move, she picked up the infant. Then she touched Zena lightly on the shoulder and walked away. Zena rose automatically and followed, holding Screech carefully in her arms.

All that day, she carried Screech with her. He was heavy and stiff, and she stumbled often, but she did not seem to notice. Her howling had stopped, and no tears came from her eyes. She moved as if much of the life had left her when Screech had gone. One foot followed another, and she seldom looked up. Once, Dak tried to take Screech from her, so she could rest. She lurched away from him and lumbered on.

By the middle of the morning, the infant was screaming with hunger. Zena seemed not to hear. Finally, Rune pressed the baby against her and forced her to let the little female suckle for a few moments while the others rested. Zena looked at the tiny girl then, and laid Screech on the ground so she could feed her. But when they resumed their journey, she handed the infant to Rune and picked Screech up again.

They were high now, near the top of the plateau. Grasses waved around them, and animals of many kinds grazed peacefully in the distance. Leafy trees decorated the meadows, and beyond the grasses, a huge lake sparkled in the sunlight. The scene was beautiful, had Zena been aware of it. But she could not see, not yet. All her attention went inward, toward the emptiness of her loss. Because there had been no others, the bond between herself and Screech had been stronger even than the one between mothers and young they had borne themselves. They had loved each other deeply, and Zena was desolate.

Rune led them toward the lake. On its eastern side were tumbled rocks and boulders where they could shelter. Long ago, she had lived here, and although her memory was dim, her feet led them unerringly in the right direction. Zena followed without protest, and when the group settled for the night among the boulders, she laid Screech gently beside her and slept with one arm stretched protectively across his still form.

She woke in the dawn, before any of the others had stirred. She looked down at Screech, and an expression of infinite sadness came into her eyes. Quietly, she picked him up and slipped away. She wandered with him all around the rocky area beyond the lake. She was looking for something, though she did not know what it was. But when she saw a tiny pond shining in the distance, Zena went to it unhesitatingly. She sat beside it for a long time with Screech in her arms. Finally, she rose and placed him in a little crevice between two boulders overlooking the water. Then she turned and went without him to join the others.

CHAPTER

7

Zena sat by the lake, watching intently as the weaverbirds constructed their intricate nests. She used an old nest she had found to hold berries and nuts, but now it was full of holes, and she wanted to make a new one. Plucking a few reeds from the edge of the lake, she tried to put them together as the weaverbirds did. The strands fell apart. She tried again. This time the pieces stayed in place, but Tipp grabbed them out of her hands and threw them into the air, squealing in delight.

Zena hugged her, amused as always by her daughter's lively antics. Tipp was almost as big now as Screech had been when he had died. Many years had passed since then, but Zena still thought of him often. Sadness came with his image, but Tipp could always chase it away with her irrepressible delight in everything around her. She was a curious child, and fearless. Zena had to watch her carefully. She loved to run, and she chased the twins everywhere. Even when she could barely toddle, she had followed them on small, unsteady legs, falling constantly in her eagerness to join. She had tipped over so often that Zena had come to think of her as Tipp.

Tipp screamed suddenly and Zena leaped to her feet. The child had climbed on top of a pile of sand. Always curious, she had dug into it with her small fingers, unaware that it contained a nest of biting ants. They swarmed over her hands and streamed up her legs. She jumped up and down, slapping frantically at the ants. Zena grabbed her and dunked her in the lake. Tipp's eyes opened wide at this unexpected action, and her screams stopped abruptly. The bites forgotten, she chortled with glee as her still-slapping hands made loud splashing noises against the water.

Dak appeared behind Zena, looking worried. Zena made the sound for *stinging ants* and pointed to Tipp. He shrugged, and moved away. Like all of them, he had become accustomed to her escapades.

The twins appeared on the shore, and Tipp called to them to join the game. Shouting eagerly, they charged into the shallows. The noisy play of three young ones was too much for a group of flamingos fishing nearby. They rose into the air and flapped heavily away, their long legs dangling. Zena watched as they settled farther down the shore in a rosy cloud. Behind them, the water heaved and surged as a hippopotamus emerged. It opened its mouth wide, revealing blunt yellow teeth. Another one thrust its head up, then another. Squawking their displeasure at still another disturbance, the flamingos took flight again.

Zena stood quickly and called out the sound for *danger*. The hippos were not close; still, they made her nervous. Their massive bodies could move with alarming speed, and they often charged at anything that annoyed them.

Tipp and the twins scrambled quickly to the shore at her signal. Everyone in the group now understood the sound-words she and Screech had developed. The children especially delighted in learning them, and they made up new ones for every object and situation they encountered.

Tipp yelled a sound she had created for *run*, and began to leap through the tall grasses. The twins scampered after her, calling the word back and forth. Tipp stopped suddenly, and they piled into her, almost knocking her over. Zena started toward them, alarmed. Tipp was staring intently at a small creature that had emerged from a pile of brush. It was about her own size, and it had thick fur and a long muzzle. A larger animal appeared behind it.

Tipp held out her hand, and the little creature sniffed it. The bigger animal turned back to the brush pile and resumed its search for insects. Zena relaxed. She had seen baboons before, but they did not often come so close. Still, they presented no danger unless they felt threatened. She made a detour around the brush pile as she headed toward the resting place above, calling to the young ones.

The children ran after her, a little frightened by the sudden encounter. The young baboon tagged behind them, but turned quickly when its mother uttered a sharp call. Tipp stared after it, disappointed, then ran to join the others.

They had gathered at the resting place, an open space just below the boulders where they sheltered during the night. Rune and Dak and Klep were there, and Myta, with her newborn infant. There was a new male, too. Lop had appeared at the lake almost a year ago. As Myta had once done, he had stayed near the edges of the group for many weeks. He was a shy male who made no attempt to challenge any of the others, and after a while, they had become accustomed to his presence. When Myta had entered her receptive period, she had mated with him as well as with Dak, and after that he had dared to join them in the clearing. Klep had also tried to mate with Myta, but she had pushed him away. He had not been quite old enough then.

Myta was nursing the infant. The little female had been born only the night before. Tipp and the twins stared at it curiously. It bleated at them, and they jumped back in alarm. The others crowded around Myta, wanting to touch the newborn. She held it out for their inspection, but only Rune was allowed to hold it and lick its small body. She let Zena stroke its face and wriggle its tiny fingers, but Dak and Klep had to be content with tickling its curled toes. Lop did not even try to come close. He sat quietly at the edge of the group, as if still unsure of his welcome.

Zena climbed onto one of the big boulders above the resting place. This was her favorite perch. From here, she could see out over the lake, and all around the surrounding countryside. Everywhere, life abounded. The plateau she had finally come to was as fertile as the pond she had left. There was food for all of them in the valleys and meadows around the lake, except during the worst of the dry season. Then Rune led them to places she remembered—first to the marsh, where food was always available, then to a river valley far to the west. Huge trees that fruited late in the season grew there, and the river kept enough water so that tubers near its banks stayed moist, and berries and melons continued to grow. Always, though, the group came back to their place at the lake as soon as the sky began to darken with clouds, signaling the return of the rains.

Dak came to sit beside Zena. He, too, loved to look over the lake, and to listen to the cacophony of sounds that sprang from the African savannah during times of plenty. All around them insects chirped and birds called. A lion's roar punctuated the softer sounds. The lions hunted on the far side of the lake, where many animals grazed. They were well fed for the moment, for they had taken a zebra the night before. The children had found its carcass. They had not gone near, though. They knew that even if the lions had full bellies, they could be dangerous if anything interfered with their kill.

Klep had been more adventurous. He had hidden nearby, then run in quickly to snatch at a bone. Grinning, he had returned to the resting place, proudly waving his trophy. The smaller children had looked at it with awe, but they had not liked the taste when Klep let them chew for a moment on his prize.

Klep had grown much bigger in the last months. He was taller than Dak now, and very strong, though he was always gentle with the small ones. Zena looked at him as he rested in the shadow of a boulder below her, and an almost forgotten sensation stirred inside her. She frowned and turned her gaze to Dak. The sensation grew stronger, and she moved closer so she could rub against him. Intent on watching a long-legged stork stalk fish in the shallows, Dak ignored her. Zena stroked his arms and caressed his face. His attention wavered, and he looked into her eyes. She met his gaze and felt hotness spread between her legs.

Still looking into her eyes, Dak began to stroke her body gently, then with increasing fervor. Zena returned the strokes until the heat inside her was too great to deny. She climbed into his lap so he could go inside her. He thrust repeatedly, and she moaned with pleasure. A series of spasms shook her body; she stiffened, then slumped against Dak. He, too, shuddered and then relaxed. Zena sighed deeply. Her emptiness was at least partly assuaged.

Klep had kept his eyes averted as Zena and Dak mated, but he was still very aware of their actions. He waited until they were resting separately before he approached Zena and began to stroke her. But she had had enough for the moment and wandered away. Soon, though, she called to him to join her in a clump of grass behind the boulders. There she mated with him, patient with his lack of expertise. It was his first mating, and she had to help him find the right position.

During the next few weeks, she mated repeatedly with Dak and Klep, and Lop as well. Instinct told her that to mate with all the males in the troop was crucial. Then there would be no need for them to fight among themselves to be the one to mate, and once he had mated with her, each of the males would help to protect her young one when it was born.

Eager for her company, the three males followed her around and plied her with choice tidbits of food. Sometimes she presented her rump to them; sometimes she lay on her back in the soft grasses, or held herself in their laps, as she had with Dak. Always, the act was deeply satisfying. Mating made her feel complete, and it triggered feelings inside her body that caused her to moan and cry out. Tipp usually came running when she heard the sounds, fearing her mother was hurt. But it was pleasure, not pain, that prompted Zena's cries.

Gradually, Zena's need to mate diminished, and she forgot about it. Once again, her belly began to swell. This time it was Tipp who patted it and was surprised when something within her mother pushed strongly against her hand. But it was Rune who helped Zena through the birth.

The contractions began early one afternoon. Zena went to an enclosed area among the boulders where she had built a nest of grasses. Sensing her need to be alone, the others stayed away, except for Rune. Zena was glad of her company. All afternoon, all through the night and into the following morning, the spasms rocked her body, each more painful than the last, but still there was no sign of the infant. By the middle of the day, she was exhausted and frightened. This was not like Tipp's birth, which had happened so quickly and easily.

Rune's wrinkled face furrowed with worry as she watched. She had seen many births, and she knew something was wrong. When the next contraction came, she crouched down to peer between Zena's legs. A tiny rump showed there. Rune pulled at it. Zena screamed in pain and tried to push her away. But Rune would not let go. She pulled harder when Zena's muscles tightened again. Blood poured from a jagged tear in Zena's skin, but still the infant would not come. Shaking her head worriedly, Rune sat back on her heels to wait.

As evening approached, Zena became still, and her groans subsided. Rune sensed she would not last much longer. Desperate now, she tried again. Rubbing her hands with dirt so they would not slip away, she pushed her fingers down on each side of the tiny rump and pulled with all her strength. Once, twice she pulled, and then, so abruptly that she fell over backward, the infant emerged, already squalling. Rune smiled in satisfaction as she handed the little creature to Zena.

Zena took it in her arms, momentarily forgetting her pain, her utter exhaustion. The infant was red and wrinkled, and had the protuberance at its groin. She licked it vigorously for a moment, then fell back against the grasses. The licking had used the last remnants of her strength, and she was not sure she could move again. Her body felt as if it had been pulled apart, and strong cramps still wracked her belly. By the time the afterbirth appeared, she felt incapable even of lifting her head.

Rune seemed to understand. Signaling to Zena to lie still, she cut the cord with a sharp rock, then she disappeared. In a few moments she was back, clutching some soft bulbs and a pile of spongy mosses she had dipped in the lake. They were full of water, and Zena sucked at them eagerly, but she was too exhausted to eat.

Darkness came, and she slept. Rune stayed close to guard her. Once, when a large hawk settled nearby, she called for Dak. He chased the bird away, and left again.

The tiny boy began to whimper, and Rune placed it gently at Zena's breast. It suckled vigorously; when it had finished, Zena slept again. All through the night, the infant was quiet, but just as dawn broke, it started to wail lustily. Zena knew she must force herself to move. To stay in the birthing place was dangerous. The smells, the sounds, could attract predators.

She struggled painfully to her knees, then to her feet. Tipp heard her movements, and peeked out from behind a rock. Her small face was perplexed. She could not understand her mother's long absence, nor did she know why Zena carried a squirming bundle that made noises like the ones Myta's baby had made after it was born.

Zena held the newborn out for her to see. Tipp's eyes lit up as she understood. She reached eagerly for the infant, but her mother pulled it back again. Tipp turned away dejectedly. But when Zena called to her, and gestured that she should help to pick up the stained grasses, her face lightened. Eager to help, she grabbed a big pile and followed Zena and Rune to a place farther from the resting area. They threw the grasses into some thick brush. After she had made one trip, Zena let the others complete the task. She felt terribly weak, and her legs shook under her when she tried to move.

She staggered back to the resting place, holding Tipp's small shoulder for support. The others crowded around her, wanting to touch the newborn. Rune snapped sharply at them, and they backed away. Grateful for her protection, Zena lay down to rest. Later, she tried to get up again, so she could go to the lake and wash the stains from her legs. But as soon as she stood, the world went dark and she slumped to the ground.

She did not move again for many days, but only lay there as if dead. Blood dribbled incessantly from a place deep inside her and stained the dusty ground. At night, she shivered; by day, the hot sun tormented her feverish body. The others watched, their faces bleak with worry. Zena had found a special place in their hearts, and they did not want to lose her. They tried to protect her from the burning sun with leafy branches, and slept close beside her at night, to lend her their warmth. Tipp searched the area for choice bits of food, to tempt her mother, but Zena lacked the strength to eat. Each time she refused, Tipp's eyes grew sadder, her face more forlorn. Zena drank, though, and Rune kept her constantly supplied with wet mosses. She made Zena drink a liquid from the leaves of special plants that helped sickness, too, grinding them carefully with her own worn teeth and mixing them with fresh, clear water.

Dak watched over them all, his heart leaden with fear. Always, he had felt Zena's pain as if it were his own. Long ago, her howling had lodged inside him; now her terrible weakness seemed to fill him as well. It dragged at his limbs, made it hard for him to gather the food he knew they needed.

The days crept by, and his fear increased. The bleeding had finally stopped, but Zena had barely moved, and she had not eaten at all. Then, one morning, Tipp came running with a big egg, the first they had seen in months. Eggs, she knew, were her mother's favorite food. She poked her fingernail into one end, then the other, as Zena had taught her, and dribbled the contents into her mother's mouth. Zena's eyes opened, and she sucked eagerly. Tipp smiled, the first smile that had crossed her face since the birth of her tiny brother. She hurried off to find another egg.

That night, sweat poured from Zena's body, despite the cool air. Every time Dak touched her, her skin was wet, and in the morning, her forehead felt cool to his touch. Frightened, he called to his mother.

Rune placed a hand on Zena's forehead, then on her belly, and nodded gravely. Her shoulders slumped, and tears poured from her eyes. Dak stared at his mother, his face frantic with worry. He could not tell if her actions meant Zena was better or worse. He thought she must be worse, because of Rune's tears, but when he came to see for himself, he knew the answer. He covered his face with his hands and wept, for Zena had looked up at him and smiled.

II

The rains that year were hard and long. Monstrous black clouds slithered across the sky, and they did not disappear after a few hours, as they usually did. Instead, they loomed over the bleak landscape for days at a time, dumping torrents of rain that seemed never to stop. The thick, heavy drops battered the lake and flattened the withered grasses against the darkening ground. Miniature rivers descended from the boulders where Zena and the others huddled miserably, tracing ever-widening paths as they tore through the cracked earth toward the lake.

Zena shivered as the rain pounded at her shoulders and pulled the infant closer, trying to keep it dry. But there was no escape from the wetness. She had no cave to shelter in here, only the scattered boulders, which were useless against the driving rains.

She rose, made restless by the constant discomfort and by her hunger. She had been ravenous ever since she had begun to recover from the birth, but in the interim between the end of the dry season and the fulfillment of the rains, food was hard to find. Soon all manner of bounty would decorate the hillsides, but until the plants matured and the new berries ripened, they struggled to find enough.

Tipp followed her mother. Since her brother's birth, she had been reluctant to let Zena out of her sight. Zena stretched out her hand and Tipp grasped it eagerly. Together, they headed for the grove of trees on the hillside. Nuts could still be found on some of their limbs—if they could be reached.

Zena paused beneath the big trees. Here, the rain hardly touched her. She peered up into the leafy canopy. She could see nuts, but they were too high to reach. Reluctantly, she passed out from the trees' shelter and felt the rain pound once again at her unprotected back and shoulders. She hunched low to avoid it, and almost tripped over a tangle of limbs on the ground. A tree at the edge of the grove had been felled by lightning the night before, and its branches were scattered over a wide area.

Tipp let go of Zena's hand and ran to explore the fallen tree. Squealing with glee, she returned with a bird's nest. Four small eggs still lay within it, their shells cracked but the contents intact. She and Zena each ate two of them, then they scoured the branches for nuts. There were plenty, so Zena called to the others to come and join the feast.

They came running, chattering excitedly at the unexpected bonanza, and began to stuff themselves and their baskets with nuts. Zena had finally succeeded in making herself a container like the weaverbirds' nests she so admired. It had worked so well that she had made a basket for each of the others.

The twins, however, did not bother with the fallen tree. They wanted an excuse to climb. Myta watched worriedly as they shimmied up a tree and shook its branches to loosen nuts high above their heads, but the nuts clung stubbornly and would not fall. Klep grabbed a long, slender stick and climbed after them. He hit hard at the high branches. There were swollen pods up there, as well as nuts. Dak found a stick and tackled another tree; the twins found sticks as well. Soon nuts and pods were falling to the ground in indiscriminate showers.

When they had eaten their fill, Zena and Tipp returned to the boulders. Zena brought a branch filled with nuts for Rune to eat. Dampness made the old female's joints stiff and painful, and she could not walk very far. All of them helped by bringing food back to the resting place, so she could share whatever they found.

Zena held the leafy branch over her head to protect her from the driving rain. Tipp watched with wide, interested eyes. She scampered back toward the fallen tree and returned, holding a branch proudly over her head, just as her mother was doing. Unwilling to be outdone, the watching twins ran off to find branches. Grinning at their accomplishment, they positioned a bundle of leafy twigs above their heads while they dragged two stout limbs behind them.

Now Dak joined the game. He went to the fallen tree and came back with an unusually thick-leafed branch. He propped it up in a crevice between two boulders so that it sheltered part of the area where they sat. Lop put some smaller branches on top, to provide more cover from the rain, but it was Zena who suddenly saw the potential in their arrangements. Signaling to Dak and Klep to help her, she placed the twins' stout tree limbs across the tops of the boulders that enclosed their sleeping area. Dak's leafy branch went above them. The others gathered still more twigs and branches to pile on top. Before long, they had a roof.

Tipp and the twins crawled under it, squealing with delight. The others followed. There was room for all, if they squeezed together. That they were happy to do, for the cool air made them shiver. Zena smiled with satisfaction. Now, at last, she could keep the infant warm and dry, and Rune could escape from the rain.

She settled back and began to work on a new basket. The others brought out digging sticks and stones to sharpen. There was little else to do until the rain stopped. For weeks, they huddled together, chipping and scraping and weaving. Zena began to wonder if they would ever again feel the warmth of the sun. But one morning, it finally burst through the clouds, and she crawled out to toast herself in its welcome glow. Rune followed, but she was not content to rest in the clearing; she wanted to go down to the lake where she could watch the storks and flamingos, and all the animals that gathered to drink.

Zena frowned anxiously as Rune rose painfully to her feet and started down the muddy path, still slippery from the rain. She called to Tipp to go with her.

Tipp's usually cheerful face was somber as she adjusted her pace to match that of the old female, but once they reached the lake, she regained her high spirits and ran off to look for frogs and turtles. She loved to creep up on them and hear them leap into the water with a resounding *plop*.

Rune settled herself near the water, where she could reach bulbs and mosses. Zena watched her for a time, then closed her eyes and basked luxuriously in the sunlight. She did not see the ripples, the rounded back, as a hippopotamus surfaced near Rune. Rune did not see it either, but she looked up abruptly when a second hippo, a huge, lumbering male, charged out of the reeds near her to challenge the one in the water. It was the rutting season, and they were irritable and full of aggression.

The hippos thrust their massive heads at each other, mouths open to reveal sharp, tearing incisors. Their bodies lurched through the water, and big waves rolled toward Rune's feet. Locked in combat, the massive creatures came closer and closer, until they were almost on top of her. Screaming, she tried desperately to crawl away, but she was too late. By the time Zena had sat up to see what the racket was about, Rune's frail body had disappeared beneath the lumbering monsters.

Zena ran down to the lake, calling frantically to Tipp. When she got there, the hippos had retreated to the water, but they were still fighting, tearing at each other's thick hides and bellowing loudly. Rune lay in a crumpled heap near the place where she had sat so peacefully.

She and Tipp looked down at the old female's lifeless body. Tipp began to sob. Tears rose in Zena's throat, too, but they did not come out. It seemed as if her sadness was too great for tears. Rune had cared for her and protected her, had taught her from her great store of living knowledge. Now she was gone.

Dak came up behind Zena. Grimacing with emotion, he knelt beside his mother and pulled her into his arms. He held her for a long time, his head bent with grief; then he carried her to a safe place among some tumbled boulders at the edge of the lake. Gently, he lowered her broken body into a protected crevice. All that night, he watched over her, hardly aware of the others as they came to see what had happened. Sadly, Zena gestured to the hippos, and made the sound for *dangerous animals*. They understood. Each of them came up to Rune and touched her gently, then went away.

Her death left a massive gap in their lives. Even though she had been old and frail, Rune had been their leader, the one who had accumulated the wisdom and judgment to see them through almost any disaster. She had led their travels, monitored their behavior, helped them when they were sick or fearful or uncertain. Often, they went to the place where she lay and sat there with her, to pay their respects and remember some of the things she had taught them.

A few days later, rain began to fall again. The lake grew wider and deeper as the torrent continued, and before long, the lapping water reached the rocks that held Rune's body. The lake enfolded her in its grasp, and when Dak next went to look at her, she had vanished.

Her final disappearance made everyone uneasy. Squabbles broke out in the group, as if without Rune's alternately sharp and patient guidance, they did not know how to behave. Klep punched one of the twins when he took a piece of fruit; his brother came to the rescue, and Dak tried to restrain all of them. Tipp jumped up and down, excited by the unaccustomed disturbance. Zena, however, was irritated, and she snapped at them sharply, just as Rune had once done. Immediately, they were quiet. After that, they looked to her for leadership. She was the one who was most like Rune, and they trusted that she, too, would lead them well.

When the dry season came again, Zena took them first to the marshes, as Rune had. But just as the rains had been unusually hard and long, so the heat and dryness that followed were more intense than ever before. Even the swamps were drying up. Food was hard to find, and the once-lush ponds had turned to thick mud that sucked at their legs. One of the twins started to wade toward the clearer water in the middle. Zena pulled him back quickly, remembering the experience with her mother long ago.

The next day, she led them on again, across a wide plain. The vast expanse was littered with termite mounds, some as tall as Klep, to sustain them as they traveled, and they found three unprotected ostrich eggs to eat as well. Water was harder to find. They had brought wet mosses from the swamp, but all moisture was soon sucked from them by the terrible heat.

They settled that night in a dry stream bed. Zena dug into it with her stick until a small puddle of water appeared. The others copied her, so that each got at least a dribble to sustain them. But in the morning, Dak found a good place, where a larger puddle formed. Zena bent down to drink as deeply as she could before they left, and gestured to the others to do the same. She wished they had kept the mosses, so they could saturate them again, but they had long ago been discarded.

Her eyes lit on the three ostrich eggs. Loath to relinquish the new objects, Tipp and the twins had kept them even when they were empty. Zena picked one up and regarded it speculatively. The thick shell was intact except for a hole at the top, where they had sucked out the contents. She lowered it into the puddle and watched with satisfaction as water slowly oozed in. Dak and Lop filled the other eggs, and once again they set off for the sanctuary of the river.

The river did provide sanctuary for a time, but then, just as it had when Zena was young, drought began to stalk the land. The rains never came that year or the next, nor did they come for three more years after that. Ponderous gray clouds filled the sky, but no moisture came from them. Only deafening claps of thunder emerged, and lightning. The jagged streaks lit up the sky as they plunged toward the dry earth, sparking fires that burned feverishly across the parched plains.

The river ran sluggishly, then became still. Its once-abundant water coalesced into hot brown puddles that shrank visibly every day, leaving white-edged rings on the drying mud. The grasses withered and burned as fires raged across them, but no new shoots appeared against the blackened earth as they usually did. Berries failed to grow on the bushes or fruits on the trees; insects ceased to buzz and chirp. The birds and animals that fed on them vanished, and after that the larger animals began to disappear. Only predators thrived, for a time, and then even they began to grow desperate.

Zena watched and remembered. The terror and loneliness of her early years returned as she saw the land dry out, the plants and animals disappear. But it was water that worried her most. Every day, she eyed the shrinking puddles and wondered how they were going to survive if the rains failed for still another year.

Early one morning, Klep came up to Zena and touched her shoulder. The twins were behind him. There was a terrible sadness in his eyes that she did not at first understand. He pointed into the distance and said the word for go. He hugged each of the others, repeating the word. The twins did the same, lingering longest with their mother, Myta. Then the three males turned and began to follow the river downstream.

Tipp lunged after them, as if to follow. They waved her back, and she returned to stand by her mother. Sobs wracked her body. Every day since her birth ten years before, the twins had been her constant companions. Now they were leaving, and she might never see them again. All vestiges of the happiness she had felt when the two young males had hugged her drained from her face.

Zena placed a comforting arm around her shoulders. Dak came

close, and Myta. As always, Lop stood a short distance away. Together, they watched until the three males were out of sight.

Zena stared at the place where they had disappeared, and her
eyes burned with tears she refused to shed. The others depended
on her to be strong. Klep and the twins were right; they would
have more to eat alone, and the group would fare better without
them. The twins were almost as big as Klep now, and all of them
needed a lot of food. Still, she did not want them to go.

It was the beginning, she knew. First one would go, then another,
and finally all of them would have to separate. Soon, there would
be no choice.

She turned and saw Dak watching her. She went to him and held
tightly to his hand. To think of leaving Dak was more than she
could bear. He was her special companion, the one who was always
there to help and comfort her. They held each other for a long
moment, then Zena pulled reluctantly away. The sun was high already, and they must begin the arduous search for food.

In the days that followed, Zena and the others stayed close together, suddenly more fearful than before. Without Klep and the
twins, they felt strange, as if they were missing some integral part
of themselves. Klep especially had made them feel safer, for he was
the largest and most fearless of all. But even worse than the fear
was the sorrow. Tipp could not stop crying, and Myta's face was a
mask of grief. Zena saw tears in Dak's eyes as well. Klep was his
brother, the one he had cared for and taught. Now he was gone.

She watched their faces despairingly. The bonds the group had
developed were different than anything she had known before.
They cared deeply for each other, and suffered when they were
apart. But she could think of no other solution.

Dreams began to torment her at night, as they had when she was
young and all alone. She saw the vulture that had terrified her so
long ago, watched it plunge from the sky, its savage beak ready to
tear into her flesh. Before it reached her, it became the tiger, the
huge, ferocious tiger. She was running, and it was behind her, ready
to spring. She heard herself scream—

Zena sat abruptly. Something was screaming. The dream was still
in her mind, and she could not tell if the screams had come from
her throat, or from some other.

Dak lifted his head and stared at her, his eyes wide with fear.
He picked up a big stone and sprang to his feet. Zena jumped up
beside him. The screams came again, long, deep yells that resounded in the quiet night.

More noises came, strange, wild noises. Never in her life had

Zena heard such a fearful racket. Her small son and Myta's daughter woke and added their terrified screams to the clamor. Tipp huddled beside them, shivering with fear. Zena grabbed her stone and stood over the children defensively. She had no idea what sort of animals might make such an uproar, but whatever they were, they were coming closer.

CHAPTER

8

The sounds were almost upon them. Zena and Dak stared at each other in bewilderment. It was shouts they were hearing, not screams. Shouts, and something that sounded like laughter. What kind of creature would shout and laugh?

Dak suddenly leaped over the wall of thorn branches they had placed around the shelter to protect them, and ran into the clearing. Horrified, Zena lunged after him to pull him back. But he was peering into the darkness and shouting as if demented, and he paid no attention to her frantic tugs.

"Home!" he was saying, over and over again. An answering cry came from the woods beyond the clearing. Dak sprinted in that direction and disappeared among the trees.

Zena stood still, and a spasm of joy constricted her chest. It could not be. . . .

Tipp came running out of the shelter and grabbed her mother's arm. A gamut of emotions crossed her face. Confusion showed first, then astonishment, then a sudden spurt of hope. After that came a burst of pure happiness. Her mouth creased in the widest smile Zena had ever seen.

"Two!" she called out excitedly, for that was how she had always referred to the twins. Laughing and crying at the same time, she ran after Dak.

Zena saw them then. Four shadowy figures had appeared at the edge of the woods, their bodies almost invisible against the backdrop of trees. They were laughing and talking and crying, jumping up and down and hugging each other.

Tears poured down Zena's face. She had not wept when Klep and the twins had left, for she had wanted to be strong. But now she made no attempt to control the flood of emotions that surged through her. They had returned. Klep and the twins had come back, and her troop was whole again.

Klep strode over and hugged her warmly. He waved jubilantly to Lop and grabbed his arm, shaking it over and over again. The twins leaped wildly around Tipp, pulling at her hair in their teasing fashion, making sure she knew how glad they were to see her. Their eyes sobered when they saw their mother. She pulled them into her arms, her face twisting as she wept with joy. They stroked her gently until she recovered, all the while trying to comfort their little sister, who was still crying in confusion.

Klep called to the twins, his deep voice booming into the darkness, and the three of them ran back into the trees. Tipp's eyes widened in consternation. Were they leaving again?

A moment later they reappeared, carrying something heavy. Zena stared, astonished, as they dropped their burden at the edge of the clearing. It was the carcass of a pig, and almost all the meat was still on it. Pigs were fast and dangerous, and they had sharp, tearing tusks. Never before had they managed to capture one, at least not a big one like this.

With a few words and many dramatic gestures, Klep and the twins described their adventure. They had spotted the pig trapped in mud, nearly dead, but they were afraid to pull it out lest they be trapped themselves. They prodded it with sticks, and its frantic movements brought it a little closer to the edge of the muddy pit. Finally, it came close enough so that they were able to pile branches on the mud, to stand on, and wrestle it out. Then they had looked at each other, remembering those they had left behind, knowing they were hungry. The pig would feed all of them for days. And so they had come home again, lugging their prize. They had shouted and laughed and made up loud combinations of sound-words all the way, to frighten off any creature that might try to attack them, or snatch the pig.

As soon as there was light enough to see, they butchered the pig with their sharpest stones and stuffed themselves joyously on the tender flesh. It tasted magnificent, but the smell of blood was strong. Vultures were soon circling overhead, and Zena could hear the whine of hyenas nearby. In the daylight, they would not come close, but as soon as darkness fell, they would attack, unless a lion or tiger got there first. They would have to be careful.

Lightning zagged across the sky toward the end of the day. Once again, clouds were beginning to form, but it was still too early to hope for rain. A patch of brush in the distance began to burn. Zena called to her son, Hoot, named because of the hooting sounds he liked to make, and Myta's daughter, who was his constant companion, and wandered toward it. Sometimes fires flushed out birds, and their eggs were left behind. Eggs would be good for the children. Hoot was as tall as Screech had been when he had died, but he was much thinner. He was always hungry. In five years of life, he had known nothing but drought.

She picked up a stick from the edge of the brush pile and poked it into some bushes the flames had not yet reached, but no birds emerged. Few were left now; fewer still made nests. She and the children searched the whole area, but found no eggs. Disappointed, she started back toward the clearing.

A hyena passed by, cringing low. Zena called sharply to the children and waved the stick to scare it off. It turned and fled. She stopped, surprised. Never before had she been able to frighten away a hyena so easily.

A glow at the end of the stick caught her attention. It was burning there, she realized, and when she had waved it, the fire had brightened into flames. Perhaps that was what had frightened the hyena. She ran back for Dak and led him to the pile of smoldering brush, leaving the children with Myta. Motioning to him to do the same, she found another stick with fire at one end. Together, they approached a grassy area where the hyenas often hid and waved the sticks. Low whimpers of fear emerged, and then the sound of many feet loping away.

Zena and Dak stared at each other, intuitively aware that they had discovered something very important, something that would change their lives. They called to the others to get more burning sticks, as many as they could find. When darkness came, they placed the sticks around the pig and piled dry grasses and brush on top, to make the fire bigger. Then they concealed themselves in the shelter and watched to see what would happen.

A young lion came first. It slunk around the edges of the clearing, eyeing the fire cautiously. Twice, it darted forward, as if to grab the pig. But each time, it retreated, and finally it disappeared. The hyenas came next. They crawled stealthily toward the pig, then turned away, whimpering with fear. Even the vultures would not approach.

The others looked at Zena and Dak incredulously. The burning sticks worked! They crept warily out of the shelter and approached the fire. Its fierce heat seared their skin, and the crackling blaze spat sparks at their faces. They drew back and watched from a distance until it burned less fiercely, then they came gradually closer. The leaping flames mesmerized them, held them motionless with their strange beauty. For a long time, they sat as if hypnotized, staring into the scarlet flames, soaking up their warmth and power.

Slowly, the fire died down and became embers. Released from its spell, they shook themselves and went to find more dry brush and grasses. These were like food to the flames, they knew, and would keep them alive. All night long, they took turns watching the fire and feeding it so it would not disappear. When Zena awoke in the morning, its pungent smell still filled the air, and she sighed with relief. Already, fire seemed an essential part of their lives, and she did not want to lose it.

The pig kept them fed for many days. Then it began to rot in the hot sun, and the smell became overwhelming. There was not much left anyway, and they let the vultures have it. After that, there was no more food, and Zena knew they would have to leave. Klep and the twins had seen antelope and zebra still feeding in the vast grasslands to the north, so she led the group in that direction. They brought burning sticks with them, to make fires at night, and tended them carefully so they would not go out.

The sky was thick with vultures as they approached the grasslands. Their soaring bodies almost blocked out the sun, and their hoarse croaks filled the air. Zena stared up at them, shivering despite the heat. Vultures no longer frightened her, but never before had she seen so many in one place. The constant swirl of heavy wings, the ceaseless clamor, made her skin prickle, gave her a strange feeling of wrongness. There was a smell too—the smell of death.

She looked down to see what had attracted the vultures. At first, she did not see the carcasses, for they were almost hidden by the mass of ungainly birds. Then she made out the shapes of muzzles, of curving horns and splayed hoofs, and she cringed. Bodies were everywhere; they littered the baking ground, filled the air with their stench, as if this fourth year without rain had abruptly pushed the weakest animals past the breaking point, and they had all died at once.

In the distance, she saw lions fighting over a dead zebra. Off to the left, a tiger dragged an antelope into the trees. Hyenas snapped and whined behind it. Wild dogs with big, upright ears trotted through the carnage, their bellies distended with gorging. Over it all, the vultures soared, then dropped to tear at the stinking flesh.

A bitter taste of nausea rose in Zena's throat. She swallowed it back determinedly. They needed food desperately, and at least some of the carcasses would be fresh. If they waved their burning sticks, they might be able to frighten the other animals away and grab some chunks of meat.

Myta and Lop stayed behind, in a dry stream bed shaded by trees, to guard Tipp and the two younger children. The others followed as Zena picked her way through the long grass until she came to a carcass that seemed fresh. Vultures covered its head, and a group of hyenas snapped at its haunches. Yelling loudly, she brandished her burning stick. The males added their deep voices and swung their sticks fearlessly. Yelping in fear, the hyenas slunk a short distance away and sat watching them. The vultures were harder to frighten, but eventually they lumbered into the air and flew just above the carcass, croaking angrily.

The group worked quickly. They slashed big chunks from the carcass with their sharp stones, twisted and yanked at bones so they could take a whole leg. Then they turned and ran. The hyenas were already beginning to creep back, snarling with renewed courage, and the vultures had landed again. Their stringy necks flashed in the sunlight as they jabbed furiously at the invaders.

The next day, and for many days thereafter, they raided the carcasses. It was dangerous work, but they did not mind. For the first time in years, their bellies were full, their spirits content. Each morning, they feasted on the juicy flesh of a zebra or an antelope; each night, they slept contentedly, knowing the fire would keep them warm and safe. It drew the chill from their bodies, kept the impenetrable darkness at bay. Beyond it, lions roared and hyenas snarled, but none dared to come close.

Most satisfying of all were the evenings, when they plied the glowing embers they had tended so carefully with fresh brush, and waited for the fire to settle into a steady blaze that enclosed them in its magic. They felt intimately connected to each other during these hours, as if the fire had somehow made them one. Sometimes they exchanged words, tried to recount the day's adventures, or tell each other about a new source of food, or an unusual animal or bird they had seen. Sometimes, too, they tried to find words for the thoughts in their minds. But just as often, they fell silent and stared into the crackling flames, seeming to understand each other's thoughts without words. It was at these times especially that Zena knew they must stay together. To be apart was wrong.

Slowly, the carcasses were reduced to piles of gleaming bones, and hunger began to plague them once again. Zena sent the others out in groups of two or three to look for food, so they could cover as much territory as possible. At the end of the day, they returned to the clearing to share anything they had found, and to sleep near the safety of the fire. Foraging in small groups was dangerous, but she could think of no other way to survive, unless the troop dispersed entirely. That she refused to consider.

Lions and tigers had become a terrible problem. Their numbers had increased dramatically in the early years of the drought, when weakened and dying prey had been plentiful. Now even the carcasses were gone, and the big predators were starving. Hunger made them bold. Whenever one of the troop failed to return before darkness, the others were frantic with worry. Once, Dak did not come back to the shelter until the following day, and Zena suffered agonies of fear.

But it was Lop, not Dak, who finally became the victim. One evening, he went with Myta to dig for water. Myta laid the infant she had recently borne beside her as she worked. She did not see the tiger that slid noiselessly out of the bushes and crept toward the baby—but Lop saw it. Waving his stick and yelling fiercely, he ran to stand over the tiny boy. Usually timid, Lop became violent when anything threatened his troopmates, especially the young.

The tiger roared but did not run. Lop moved closer and hit it over and over again with his stick. Maddened by the blows, the tiger turned on him instead of the baby. Raising its heavy paw, it killed him with a massive strike to the head. Zena and the others ran to help, but they were too late. By the time they got there, the only noise was Myta's screaming, as she watched the tiger close its cruel teeth around Lop and drag him away.

His death left a gaping hole in their lives, despite his quiet ways. Always, he had been there to help, to pull back a child that had wandered too far, to sharpen sticks for all of them—for his were the best—to gladly give the others the food he had found. They felt suddenly vulnerable too. The tiger had attacked despite the fire that burned a short distance away. They pressed close against each other in the shelter that night, afraid to sleep lest another tiger come.

They should leave, Zena realized, get away from the grasslands where the big predators hunted before any more were killed. But she could not think where to go. No area had escaped the ravages of the drought, and at least in this place they could still dig in the stream bed for water.

Another danger, one she had not expected, finally persuaded her to leave. She had stayed in the clearing with her infant daughter, born this time without difficulties, while the others searched for food in the fields nearby. Only Tipp was with her.

A twig snapped behind her. She whirled, fearing a predator. But no lion or tiger appeared. Instead, a big male, a stranger, stepped out of the bushes and eyed her pugnaciously.

The baby whimpered in her arms, disturbed from its sleep. The male's eyes shifted. With a quick movement, he grabbed the infant's leg. It screamed in pain. Zena twisted away and managed to free it from his grasp. Pushing it into Tipp's arms, she mouthed the word for *run*.

Tipp hesitated. She did not want to leave her mother alone with the violent stranger.

"Run!" Zena screamed the word this time. When Tipp still did not move, she added another sound.

"Others," she said forcefully. Tipp turned and ran.

Zena faced the male. He was huge, larger even than Klep, but scrawny with hunger. Instinctively, she knew she could not trust him. There was no softness in his eyes, only challenge.

The male turned away from her and started to run after Tipp and the infant. Zena plunged after him and grabbed his arm, to make him stop, but he was too strong for her, and she was dragged along as he ran. Pulling herself forward, she leaped in front of him. The male tripped and fell on top of her. He stared at her, surprised. Taking advantage of his confusion, and his position, Zena turned her genitals toward him. As he leaned down to sniff her, she picked up a large rock and brought it down on his back with all the strength she possessed.

The male howled and rolled away. Zena landed another blow on his shoulder. He grimaced and raised his clenched fist. But before he could hit her, angry shouts distracted him. Dak and Klep, with the twins and Tipp behind them, came charging across the dry grasses, yelling as they came. The big male leaped to his feet and crashed away through the bushes. But the next day, he came again, and the next as well. Every day he returned, always at a different time. He was watching them, Zena realized, waiting to snatch an infant while it was unguarded.

She shuddered. The big male frightened her even more than lions and tigers. He was like themselves, except there was no caring in him. He was desperate for food, and even the flesh of infants of his own kind would do. She kept all of them together, ready always to repel the next attack.

One day, the big male did not come, and Zena knew they must

escape while they could. Gathering the others around her, she whispered the word for *go*. They nodded, understanding, and followed her silently from the clearing. Determinedly, she turned in the direction of the river. They would probably find water there, too, if they dug deep enough. Besides, there was nowhere else to go.

The number of predators declined as they traveled away from the grasslands, and there was no further sign of the big male. Some of their fear dissipated, but their hunger and thirst did not. Once, the twins found a termite nest that still held insects, and Dak found some stringy tubers, so dry they could hardly be chewed. After that, three days passed with nothing but an occasional sip of water from the shell of an ostrich egg they had brought. Zena watched Tipp and the younger children rub their hands over their hunger-swollen bellies, as if to massage the emptiness away, and her heart ached with sorrow that they should suffer. She gave them the last dribble of water, to comfort them, and wondered if they would ever find more.

They staggered on, bellies distended, throats raw with dryness. Another day passed with agonizing slowness; the night was spent dreaming of food and water that never came. Only the thought of the river kept them going, made it possible to put one foot in front of the other. Always before, the river had provided sanctuary, and they clung to the thought that it would do so again. But when they finally reached their goal, the hope that had sustained them drained away. There was no food, and no water at all. No matter how deep and hard they dug, not a single drop emerged.

II

The small group sank to the ground in despair, too exhausted, too filled with hopelessness even to raise their heads. Then, as if on a prearranged signal, the others looked up at Zena, and some of the anxiety left their faces. Staring morosely at the ground, she did not notice at first. But then her skin began to prickle as the force of their gaze pierced her absorption.

She raised her eyes and saw their expectant faces, saw their hunger, their thirst, the fear lodged deep in their hearts. Anger possessed her suddenly. She stared up at the sky, at the black-edged clouds that refused to drop their burden of rain, and she shook her fists at them harshly. The rains should come now. For weeks, clouds had been converging. They were swollen with moisture, and they should send it here, to the earth, where it was needed. They would die; all of them would die, unless the rains came. These were her troopmates, the ones she loved, and it was not right that they should die.

Over and over, Zena pounded her fists against the dry earth, then shook them violently at the sky. She screamed the word for *rain*, hurling it at the stubborn clouds until her voice was hoarse. But there was no response.

The anger dissipated as suddenly as it had come. In its place came a terrible feeling of helplessness. She felt as she had long ago, when her mother had been killed, and the huge tiger had prowled overhead. Without her mother to guide her, she had not known what to do. She did not know what to do now, either.

Lowering her eyes so the others would not see her uncertainty and fear, she handed the infant to Tipp and went to sit by herself in a small glen near the clearing. It was a peaceful place. She had often rested here when times were better, enjoying the sounds and scents. Now birds no longer sang, and no aromatic smells arose from the brittle grasses.

Questions raced through her mind. Should she leave the river again, take the others with her, hoping they would come across a place where food and water still existed? Should she tell them to go off by themselves? The thought of separating was too terrible to consider. She did not think she could make the sounds, the gestures that would drive them apart.

Zena shook her head hard in refusal, and the gesture dispelled some of her helplessness. Slowly, determination returned. The group belonged together, and she would keep it together. Long ago, her mother had led her through the horror of a drought, and she had survived. Now it was her turn to find a way to keep the ones she loved alive.

Zena sat and pondered. Slowly, her restlessness diminished, and a quietness she had never felt before rose inside her. Images drifted into her mind, of her mother, of the grandmother she barely remembered, of Rune. Over and over, their faces floated past her. It seemed to Zena that they were here with her, comforting her with their presence. Strangely, though, they were not separate. They were all in one, as if they had somehow merged into one mother, a mother who was much bigger, much wiser and stronger than any of them alone. But even that was not enough to describe the mother they had become. She seemed to hold within her all the females who had ever struggled to help those who depended on them, as Zena was doing now. They understood; they could guide her, as her mother and Rune had once guided her.

For a long time Zena sat without moving, feeling the presence of these mothers who were one. Sleep did not come to her, but dreams did. She closed her eyes, to see the dream better. There were stones in her dream, a circle of stones. She frowned, surprised. But then she forgot to wonder at them and just watched the dream unfold in her mind. She saw herself picking up a stone and placing it carefully on the ground. It was round, weathered, as if the storms of thousands of years had taken away its sharpness and made it gentle. She put another stone beside it, then another, until there was a circle, a big circle, that would enclose many besides herself. Now she was standing inside the circle. . . .

The dream faded. Zena looked around her. There were stones like that nearby, at the edge of the woods. They were big and round, but not too heavy to lift. She picked one up and placed it firmly against the earth in the middle of the glen. It was cool to the touch, and her fingers lingered against its smooth surface. As if still in her dream, she went to get another, and another, and placed them in a wide circle.

Dak came to look for her, worried by her long absence. He stared incredulously. But the look on Zena's face kept him silent. She was there, but not there, as if some other were looking from her eyes. Frowning, he watched her pick up a stone and place it carefully, then go back for another. Her actions lost their strangeness, and he began to help. The others came behind him. Like Dak, they looked at Zena in amazement, but then the atmosphere in the small glen infected them as it had infected Dak. They began to gather up the big stones, using only the ones that were smooth and rounded, as if they, too, were part of the dream. Soon, the circle was complete.

The trancelike look on Zena's face deepened. Slowly, as if she were being led, she walked to the center of the circle of stones and held up her arms to the sky. She said the word for *mother*, the word that all the young ones used to name the one who cared for them and kept them safe, the word they uttered when they were frightened or hurt or needed help. They used this word, too, to describe the feelings of comfort and peace, the certainty of food and shelter and warmth that came from their mothers' presence. It was a powerful word, one that contained both joy and fear.

Zena said the word aloud, over and over again. Her tone rose with every repetition, then softened until she spoke almost in a whisper. She raised her face to the sky, then turned it toward the earth, while she stamped her feet in a rhythmic pattern. Now she was calling another word, the word for *rain*. Again and again, she shouted the word, stamping her feet hard against the dry earth.

Mesmerized by her movements, the others began to shout the

word and stamp their feet. One at a time, they joined her in the circle and turned their faces toward the clouds, then the earth, as they called and shouted and stamped. Thunder cracked over them, and they stamped harder, called louder, to match the deafening sound. Lightning followed, and with it came the smell of ozone. The pungent scent excited them still further.

Dak leaped from the circle and grabbed a stick. He brandished it in the air, scraped it noisily against the ground. Klep imitated him, the twins as well. Leaping wildly, they shouted the word for *rain* as they beat their sticks against the earth, then pointed them toward the sky.

The females stayed in the circle, belonging there. But now they were stamping in patterns, moving slowly, then quickly, in a rhythmic movement. Both words came from their throats; first the word for *rain*, then the word for *mother*, in rhythm with their movements. The feet of the males outside the circle pounded in rhythm with them, and their voices repeated the words. The glen, the woods, the earth itself, resounded with the incessant stamping, the powerful words.

The atmosphere was heavy with the odor of an impending storm. They smelled it, felt it in their bodies, and they pulled at it, willing it to come down and drench them in its welcome downpour. Over and over, their heads lifted to the sky, to the pregnant, moisture-filled clouds, then returned to the dry earth, as if they were showing the way.

The tempo increased. Their pounding became frenzied, and their voices cracked with the strain of shouting the words faster and faster, over and over again. They knew the rain was coming now; it could not resist.

When the first drops hit, they stood perfectly still and bowed their heads in gratitude. Tears cascaded down their cheeks, tears that could not be stopped any more than the rains could be stopped. More drops came to fall delicately on the backs of their dusty necks, then more, and then, suddenly, the heavens opened. Their heads snapped up again to welcome the blessed wetness. The rain streamed across their thirsty skin and into their parched throats; they felt it heal their cracked lips and cleanse their grimy bodies, and they raised their arms in a gesture of pure ecstasy.

Joy filled them, a joy that came from the return of the rains, but from something deeper, too. It was as if another presence moved among them, a presence far greater than any creature they had ever known. It flooded their hearts with its magnificence, as the rain was flooding the river.

Zena slumped suddenly to the ground, and they came back to themselves. Dak ran to her, frightened. She lay motionless for a long moment. Then she shook her head hard, as if to clear it, and sat up. She stared at Dak, at the others. Smiling, she held out her hands to the rain. The others stared back, relieved. She was seeing with her own eyes, acting like herself again. They did not speak but only sat beside her for a long time, cherishing the rain that pounded their parched bodies, smelling the wondrous scents that came with wetness. When darkness came, they rose slowly and went to the shelter.

The next morning, water rushed through the river's banks. Insects and shrimp, even tiny fish, emerged from the mud where they had lain dormant until the rains came. Tadpoles squirmed in the puddles; thin green shoots appeared like magic in the clearing. Zena ate and drank, then she walked slowly to the glen and sat down in the circle of stones. The peace she had felt the day before was still with her. There was a wondrous gratitude in her as well, for the rains, for the mothers who were one who had helped her. She wanted to thank them, not just this day, but every day of her life.

The glen sparkled as sunlight caught the drops of water that still clung to each stem of grass, each twig and stone. Zena watched them slowly evaporate and disappear. Tomorrow, the drops would be there again, of that she was certain. She was certain, too, that rain would fall later in the day and each day thereafter, until the rainy season had ended. The rains would come every year as well. The knowledge was as much a part of her as her legs or her arms or belly. She knew the rains would come, for each year without fail she would return to the circle of stones to speak the words again, to move in the special way the dream had shown her. Never would she forget this magic, the magic that had come from the mothers who were one.

III

Zena kept her promise. Each time she returned to the river, she went first to the circle of stones to thank the mothers who were one for their help all through the year. And when the rainy season approached and clouds began to loom against the darkening sky, she gathered the others around her to re-enact the ritual that brought the rains. Every year, for all the years that remained of her life, they came. Whenever she spread her arms to the sky and chanted the sacred words, the clouds loosened their hold and dropped their precious burden. Whether the ceremony was responsible, none could know. But Zena took no chances.

The group expanded during these years. Klep disappeared one day, and they were afraid he had been hurt, or killed. But he soon returned, holding a round young female by the hand. Another female appeared soon after Myta had died, and a new male joined them, one as gentle and cooperative as Lop had been. A male who tried to attack them, as the hungry one had before, was driven away. Zena would not allow such a male in her troop. There were many births too. Tipp mated with the twins, and had twin boys herself, and both the new females gave birth soon after. And after that, Myta's daughter and Zena's son, Hoot, were almost ready to mate as well.

Zena watched over them happily. She had never forgotten the solitude of her early life, and her growing troop was a constant source of joy and satisfaction. She listened to their ever-increasing chatter, settled disputes, helped them to make decisions, snapped at them occasionally, and loved them all.

The years sped by, and Zena became old and frail. She spent most of her time now sitting peacefully on her boulder above the lake, or in the circle of stones, remembering. Sometimes Screech's face appeared in her mind, and she saw his eyes grow round with delight, or wrinkle in merriment as they played together. Often, she thought of Dak. He had died during their last trip to the river, and she missed him badly. Always, he had known her thoughts, felt her pain and joy as if they were his own. She thought of Rune as well, with her wise, appraising eyes, her sharp voice and comforting ways, and of all the mothers who had come to her when she needed them so desperately.

One day, as she sat in dreamy silence in the circle of stones, she slipped a little lower against the warm earth. When Tipp came in the evening to look for her, she was no longer breathing. Tipp smiled at her gently, but she did not weep. Her heart was too full for tears. She sat beside her mother for a time, then she went to get the others. Hoot came first, holding his own son by the hand, and after him came Zena's youngest daughter, clutching a newborn infant against her chest. The others came behind them, to touch Zena once again, to see her face, so they could keep it in their hearts.

They were saddened by her death, for she had been mother to them for almost twenty years, and they had loved her dearly. But in another way, they were glad, for it seemed to them that Zena belonged in this special place. Now she could stay here always, safe within the circle of stones she had created And every time they came here, she would be waiting, ready to offer help and guidance. They covered her with leafy branches and slowly turned away. The rains had come again, and it was time to leave for the lake.

Tipp took her mother's place. Like her mother, she was brave and resourceful, worthy of respect. She gathered the others around her and led them along the familiar paths from river to swamp, then to the lake, and back to the river when the dry season came again. Each time they returned, they went first to the circle of stones to remember Zena, the one who had called the rains from the sky and kept them alive when all of them had thought they would die. And just as they had expected, she was always there to greet them. Sometimes her voice came to them in the wind; sometimes they thought they heard her speak through the stars or the moon, or through the creatures of the woods.

Soon, though, it was not just Zena for whom they listened. Her voice became the voice of the mothers who were one, and her presence merged into the presence they felt when they performed the ritual to bring the rain. They called this presence "Mother," as Zena had. She was all the mothers who had ever given birth and nurtured those around them; She was the powerful force that brought storms and rain, the force that created new life and took the old or the injured back again. The Mother lived in the earth, in the sky, in the rivers and lakes, in every creature that walked or crawled or flew. But Her special home was the circle of stones, where Zena's compassion for the ones she loved had caused Her to be born.

PART II

From the Rift Valley to the
shores of the Red Sea—between
five hundred and
two hundred thousand years ago

CHAPTER
9

The herbs had dulled Mina's pain. Cere could see the change in her sister's face. For hours, her jaw had alternately clenched and widened, as if she was about to scream but lacked the strength and had to swallow her agony instead. Sweat had dripped unceasingly from her forehead. Over and over, Cere had wiped it from her with the soft bundle of fragrant leaves. Now the sweat had ceased to come and Mina's jaw had relaxed.

Cere looked up at her mother. As always, Kalar's face was serene, as befitted her position. She was the tribe's wise one, the woman who advised them and helped them to make important decisions. Kalar was closest to the Great Mother, and without the Mother, the tribe could not survive. They were all Her children, for She was Life-Giver, who caused infants to grow in their mothers' bellies.

The Mother spoke to them through Kalar, so it was to Kalar the tribe now looked for reassurance, when so many of the young women were dying. Pictures of those already dead arose in Cere's mind. Mina's face slid beside them. She shuddered and thrust the picture away. It was a bad omen. Surely the Mother did not want to take Mina back so soon. Only three days ago, Cere herself had given birth, and she had not died. That was a good sign. Her infant, though, had lived less than an hour. It had been born too soon, without the strength to breathe, so the Mother had taken it back until it was stronger. Sadness filled Cere as she thought of its tiny, puckered face, the cruel stretching of its lips as it sucked for air. It had never sucked milk, though her breasts were ready. They swayed with unfamiliar heaviness as she bent over Mina, and she could feel milk trying to push through her nipples even though there was no baby to feed.

Mina seemed to be sleeping now. Her lips were soft in repose, and the lines that had marred her brow had disappeared. Like Kalar, Mina was one of the long-headed ones. Some in the tribe had low, sloping foreheads, but Mina's brow was high and wide, her head unusually large.

Mina's eyes opened suddenly, and she stared straight ahead, as if she saw something surprising.

Cere looked up, puzzled. There was nothing to see here, in the birthing place, except the trees that surrounded the small glen. They had chosen it as the birthing place because of the blessed circle of stones that lay within it. No one knew how the smooth, rounded rocks had come here, but they did know they were sacred, and a good place for new life to emerge. Cere herself had felt their power, and so had Mina. When they had first entered the circle as children, strange prickles had slid up their spines. They had scampered away to find Kalar, to ask why that should be.

"The Mother's spirit resides there," she had answered, and after that, the children had regarded the stones with awe.

Mina's eyes closed again. Cere spoke the word of caring to her and stroked her cheek, but Mina did not seem to hear.

Cere raised her face to the sky, wishing the moon would come out and bathe Mina in its soft light. It had been full and bright when Cere herself had given birth, but all through this night it had hidden behind thick, black-edged clouds. Labor was easier when the moon was full, Kalar said, for then it had power and could help to pull at the life within.

She looked down again. Mina's eyelids fluttered briefly, and a small sigh escaped her lips. Cere could see a line of darkness around her mouth, where blood had stained it when she bit her lips in pain. Gently, she wiped the stains away with the fragrant leaves.

It was good the pain had left her. But surely her labor was taking too long. Mina had entered the birthing place soon after sunrise, and now the night was almost gone. At first, she had crouched, to ease the pressure, or walked a little, but for many hours, she had been lying down. Perhaps she was gathering her strength, so she would be able to push hard when the time came.

Cere looked at the other women, to gather a clue from their faces. But there was only patience, and weariness. All night long, they had watched over Mina, tending the fires that lit up the small glen, fetching water and leaves for compresses, rushes to soften the bed, anticipating the moment when she would give that final push. But it had not come. Instead, hours ago, when Mina had begun to writhe in agony, Kalar had called for her special herbs, the ones to dull the pain. She did not often do that, but she had given the herbs to Mina many times, pushing the concoction into her mouth, and stroking her throat until she swallowed.

Cere frowned, worried. Dawn was sliding into the air, and still nothing had happened. Her own labor had lasted only a few hours, and she had not needed the herbs. So many of the births had been like that. When labor was short, the baby died, too small to live. When it was long, the mother died. The tribe had looked to Kalar for answers. She had tried to reassure them, but the words to say what was in her thoughts were few. They had words for animals and objects, for their activities, for people and the relationships between them, even for the caring in their hearts. But knowledge of other things came in pictures in their minds, and it was hard to show these pictures to one another. Still, Kalar had tried.

"The Great Mother changes us," she had told them. "Then pain comes. But good comes too. We must wait."

The response had meant little to Cere at the time, and it did not help her now. All she wanted was for Mina to be all right. Mina was the one who had comforted her each time she fell, who had shown her how to use her digging stick, how to pound nuts and tubers. They had gone everywhere together, leaping through the fields in imitation of the graceful gazelle, or splashing happily in the lake when the air was hot. Together, they had stared down at the faces they saw in the water and wondered at the sameness to their own faces, then at the strange distortions that came when the water moved. Cere wanted badly, still, to ask Mina about these things. Mina would know how to answer. She had the promise of wisdom already upon her, like Kalar when she was young. Cere knew this from listening to the other women.

She smiled down at her sister, remembering, and touched her cheek to reassure her, as she had so many times this night. Her hand leaped back involuntarily, for Mina's skin was cool, as cool as the rocks when no sun had come for many days. A cry rose in Cere's throat, but she could not utter it. Fear choked her, made her heart jump fiercely. There was no color in Mina's face, only grayness. The tiny infant's face had looked like that, at the end. Was Mina gone too?

She was aware of sudden movement. Kalar had called sharply to one of the women, who had run off in the direction of the clearing. Her footsteps thudded on the well-worn path; Cere heard a shuffling noise and another sharp command. Her cutting stone—that was what Kalar had called for. Why should she want that right now?

Kalar was kneeling by Mina, gently kneading her swollen belly. Her eyes were closed in concentration, and she did not see Cere, nor did she respond when Cere called out to her in fear. She seemed to be aware of nothing but the messages that came from her fingers as they probed carefully all across the distended mass where the unborn child still rested.

The woman returned and handed Kalar the cutting stone. It was her best stone, the one Lett had struck from his special flint and sharpened many times, so that it would cut easily through the tough hides of the carcasses they sometimes found. Still kneeling by Mina, Kalar held it to her lips, then raised it into the air in blessing. She touched Mina's face, and spoke to her quietly. Cere could hear the caring in her voice.

"Love is in my heart, in my hands, as I do this, Mina. Go now to the Mother, for She takes you back to Her heart."

Placing the stone reverently on Mina's chest, Kalar rose to her feet and stood, straight and tall. Arms outstretched, she spoke in a full, strong voice that all could hear.

"Great Mother, Giver of Life, take Mina, my eldest daughter, to Your heart. I, Kalar, will keep the little one, as Your picture told me. Great Mother, give me strength to do as You have asked."

For a long moment, she stood absolutely still, her face raised to the sky. Slowly, the brilliant red ball of the sun slid over the horizon and touched her eyelids with pink. It was the signal for which she had waited.

Once again, she knelt and placed her palms against the stretched skin of her daughter's stomach. Her long fingers probed and pushed as she tried to feel what lay within so she would know how to accomplish the task the Mother had given her. The weight of her actions compressed her lips and furrowed her brow, but her hands did not falter. Taking a deep, calming breath, she grasped her cutting stone. Slowly, with great deliberation, she cut a long, shallow slit across Mina's belly. Blood welled up; one of the women knelt and sopped it up with fresh leaves. Again, Kalar cut, deeper this time. Then she shoved her hands into the wound and felt for the life within. Around and around her hands went, feeling, exploring, hoping.

Cere's stomach heaved and bile rose in her throat. She thrust the sensations away. She must be strong, for her mother's sake, for Mina's sake.

Kalar's hands leaped, as if she had been kicked. She withdrew them and made another careful slit, opposite to the first. Her eyes wrinkled as she struggled to see into the dark wound. Abruptly, she thrust both hands back into Mina's belly and pulled. Blood spurted up around her; Mina's blood, her daughter's blood. It showed darkly up to her elbows, stained her knees and chest as she leaned over to pull harder. Then the infant came, so suddenly she almost fell backward. It squirmed in her hands, bloodied, nearly unrecognizable. A thin wail rose from its tiny chest, but the cry seemed to strangle in its throat. Quickly, Kalar placed her lips over the infant's mouth and sucked hard. Hearing no further sounds, she held it upside down and slapped gently at its back. She sucked again, more strongly. Another wail emerged, then another.

Kalar called for fresh leaves to wipe the squalling infant. Exhaustion marked her face, but there was exaltation in it, too. She had done the thing that had come to her in a picture, a picture that had come from the Life-Giver. Never before had an infant been plucked alive from the belly of its dead mother. Now it had been done, and it could be done again. She could not save the tiny babies, the ones born too early, but she could save some of the others, the ones too big to be born. Even if the Mother took the women who tried to bear them, she, Kalar, might keep the precious life within. Until this time of change was over, they did not need to lose them all. And perhaps, as her vision had told her, good would finally come from their ordeal.

Sunlight bathed the birthing place now. Kalar could see the infant clearly. It was a girl child, and like its mother, it had a long, high forehead. Its head was very big; never before had she seen a head so large in a newborn infant. Perhaps, she thought, that was because it had lingered such a long time in the womb. What might such a thing portend?

Kalar frowned. She must ask the Mother, seek Her wisdom. But now there were practical tasks, tasks associated with life, to attend to. She signaled to Pote, the most experienced of the women, to help her cut and tie the cord. The baby was quiet as they concentrated on making a knot close to its round belly, but this time Kalar was not alarmed. Its breathing was regular, its skin darkly pink and healthy, unlike the poor little male child Cere had borne, with its translucent skin and frail body. Kalar turned and approached her other daughter. It was good, after all, in this way.

Tears sprang unbidden into Cere's eyes as Kalar placed the infant in her arms. Her mother honored her to trust her with this special child. She glanced up at Kalar, to express her knowledge of the honor, but her throat was too full for speaking words. Kalar grasped her message anyway, and inclined her head to let Cere know she understood.

The infant began to wail lustily again. Cere held it close, to comfort it. Her own had never cried like that. It had never made a noise at all, except to gasp for breath it could not draw. This one was much bigger, and it wriggled energetically. She touched its round cheek gently, marveling at the perfection of its features. Its head jerked immediately in the direction of her hand, and its tiny lips pursed. Amused, Cere turned its face toward her nipple. The infant stretched its body taut and began to suckle eagerly. Its fingers scrabbled at her chest.

A strong, sharp thrill shot through Cere as the sucking at her breast intensified. She had never felt such a sensation before. It was like fire, except much softer. It settled, glowing, in a place just below her belly. She stared at the baby, entranced by its tiny form, by the feelings it evoked in her. She hardly noticed the other women as they gathered around her to peer at the tiny one. Each of them touched it gently and murmured a blessing.

Then, one at a time, they went to Mina's body. Chanting the word of caring, each woman placed fragrant leaves over her, until the terrible wound was covered, and kissed her forehead. Cere rose, to take her turn. She held the infant over Mina, so her spirit could see that the baby lived.

"See your small one, Mina." She pointed to herself, then to her heart, then to the infant. "I will care for it now; it is in my heart, more precious even than my own."

Emotion overcame her as she kissed Mina's forehead, and she began to sob. Kalar raised her gently, signaling to two of the women. With comforting hands, they steered Cere away from the birthing place toward the shelter in the clearing. There they prepared fresh bedding of rushes, and settled her on it. They brought cool water from the stream that flowed into the river, fruit and nuts for her to eat. Cere accepted them eagerly. All through the long night, she had taken neither food nor water. But even as she stretched out a hand for more, sleep claimed her, and she did not move again until the infant stirred in her arms.

When she awoke, Kalar was standing beside her. She reached for the baby and juggled it expertly in her arms. Once again, her face was serene, as if the night had never happened. The infant turned its head toward her breast and made sucking noises with its tiny pink lips. When no food came, it screamed in protest. For a long moment, Kalar stared into its rapidly purpling face, then she handed it to Cere. Triggered by the baby's cry, milk was already leaking from her breasts. As soon as the infant touched a wet nipple, its squalling stopped. Cere and Kalar laughed at the suddenness of the silence.

Kalar turned away, her laughter suppressed by the questions that had arisen as she stared at the baby. They had been with her for so long. Would she never understand? This infant was well grown, sucking strongly before it had been in the outer world for even a few hours. It was big enough to live, but too big to be born. After such a long time in the womb, its head, especially, was too large to fit through the narrow passage between its mother's legs. Cere's infant, and many others who had emerged at the normal time, were not developed enough to live. But they could be born, the others could not. What was the answer? For a moment, her brow furrowed. Then her habitual serenity returned. When the time was right, the Mother would provide an answer.

II

That is how Zena was born. The story was told over and over again, as the group sat around the fire in the long evenings. It was such an astonishing event, that Kalar had plucked a living infant from its dead mother's belly. Just as remarkable was Zena herself. Even as a small child, she was determined to make sense of everything she saw and heard and felt. She examined the world around her—animals and birds, plants and flowers, even tiny insects or seeds—with endless curiosity. Sometimes the others laughed at her for looking so serious and asking so many questions. Cere, though, never laughed. She listened carefully even when she was incapable of understanding what Zena meant or of answering her, and she watched over the child with great care.

Kalar, too, watched Zena carefully as she grew, seeking clues to the problem that confronted her. It was obvious that the child had abilities the others did not possess. Zena could make words easily, for her thoughts as well as for objects, could accomplish things with her hands and form ideas that never occurred to any other. Was it, perhaps, her unusually large head, that had made it impossible for

Mina to bear her, that also made Zena so intelligent? If that was the case, Kalar could think of no solution. It was good to be intelligent, bad to be unable to be born, and she could not imagine how even the Mother could resolve such a cruel dilemma.

Sighing, she went off to help still another woman struggling in childbirth. Again, the woman died; again, Kalar wielded her sharp stone and pulled the infant out. It, too, had an unusually big head, she noticed, not as big as Zena's, but still bigger and with a much higher brow than babies in the past.

In the ensuing years, Kalar repeated her procedure many times, sometimes for the women of her own tribe or another tribe that lived nearby, sometimes for women in more distant tribes who sent for her in desperation when babies were unable to emerge. Some of the infants lived, but many were born dead when she was too late with the cutting. But always the mothers died. Kalar gave them her herbs, over and over again, to ease their suffering. And she waited, wondering if her tribe would survive the decimation. Six women had died already; now only five were left.

Surely, she thought, the Mother would send her another message soon, so she could help her tribe. But all that came to her was a picture of a female with enormous buttocks and large, pendulous breasts.

She looked down at her sturdy, wide-hipped body. Then she thought of Mina, with her boyish frame. Most of the women who had died had looked like Mina, with hips no wider than those of the men. But she, Kalar, had given birth to Mina, whose head had been big and high-browed, to other young ones as well, and she had lived. Perhaps, after all, the Mother was showing her a solution.

Kalar knelt and scraped at the earth with her digging stick. After much effort, a sketch of the imagined female emerged. The figure had almost no head, for its features were not important, but it had wide, encompassing hips, and huge breasts that hung luxuriantly across its swollen belly.

A woman like this could give birth with ease, Kalar thought with satisfaction, and feed the infant well.

She went to find Lett. Handing him a chunk of wood, she showed him her picture and indicated with gestures and a few words that he should carve the figure from the wood.

Lett stared at her, astonished. He made cutting and scraping stones of many sizes; he sharpened digging sticks for all of them, for his were the best. But never before had he made a carving in wood.

He shook his head doubtfully, but he went off to try. All day, he sat by Kalar's drawing and stared at it while he chipped at the piece of wood, trying to make it conform to the picture on the ground. The wood broke, and he threw it down in disgust. But now, Kalar could see, he did not want to give up. He was the most skilled of all of them with cutting stones, and he did not want the others to see him fail. He went off to find more wood, stronger this time, and set to work again.

Two days later, he approached Kalar with his handiwork, and she was pleased. The figure was clumsy, but it resembled the picture the Mother had given her. The hips were wonderfully wide and encompassing, the belly extended, the breasts full and drooping. She smiled gratefully at Lett, and showed the figure to the others in the tribe. Some of them leaped away from it in fear. Kalar said the word *Mother*, to reassure them. They did not touch it, but they looked at it curiously when they passed it at the birthing place. Kalar placed it there, certain that the Mother intended it to help those who would come next.

The figure did seem to help, for in the years that followed, the women's birth problems slowly began to ease. The first sign came early one morning, when a live female infant was born to Nyta at the usual time, after ten cycles of the moon. Twice before, Nyta's infants born after ten moons had died. Like Cere's, they had been too small to breathe. But this time, the infant lived despite its apparent frailty. It was much smaller than Zena had been, for more than thirteen moons had passed before she had tried to emerge. Unlike Zena, Nyta's infant could not support itself at all, but just flopped helplessly. Still, it had a lusty scream and seemed quite healthy.

Feeling the baby's skull with her sensitive fingers, Kalar discovered a soft place near the top, where the bones did not meet. Consternation creased her forehead. Never before had she seen an infant with a soft skull! It would probably die. How could a child with a hole in its head manage to live?

Disappointed, Kalar returned the baby to its mother. She showed her the soft place, and gestured that she should be careful not to let the baby drop. But she did not think her warning would do much good. Even if the infant grew stronger in its body, it would never be able to play normally. One blow to the head would kill it, if it even lived that long.

In the years that followed, three more infants were born that resembled Nyta's. Like hers, they arrived after only ten or eleven moon cycles, and they had the strange soft places in their skulls.

Two of them lived, but still Kalar shook her head in despair. It seemed impossible that they could survive for long. But to her surprise, they seemed to thrive, as did Nyta's infant. Even more surprising, the holes in their heads gradually closed. All three children were slow to develop; even after a year, they were unsteady on their feet. Zena had walked after only seven moons. But in spite of their slowness, it seemed to Kalar that they possessed some of the abilities Zena displayed. They spoke words very early and watched everything that happened around them with bright, inquiring eyes. Like Zena, they had heads that were disproportionately large for their bodies.

They could never have been born had they stayed longer in the womb, Kalar realized. Perhaps that was the Mother's solution, to cause infants to emerge as soon as they were strong enough to live, but before the big, high-domed heads that promised such intelligence were too large to fit through the passage to the outer world. If that was true, good might come from their ordeal, as She had promised.

Kalar was gratified to see, too, that as the years passed many of the women really did begin to look more like the figure Lett had carved. The Mother's sign, so incomprehensible at first, had been a good one. Almost every woman who survived a birth was wide hipped, and as they grew, their daughters' hips became even more rounded. Kalar had lived through almost three generations, and she was certain she could see the difference. She could not be absolutely sure that the picture the Mother had given her, and Lett's carving, had helped to make the changes, but she took no chances. She instructed Lett to make many of his figures, and each time the Mother caused an infant to form in a woman's belly, she gave her one to keep in the sleeping place.

Soon the women became accustomed to the figures, and were reassured by them. They felt closer to the Mother when they had one in their hands. In the years when they had watched so many die in childbirth, all the members of the tribe, men as well as women, had become closer to the Mother. They came often to the blessed circle of stones to ask the Mother to let the women who labored there live. The first figure Lett had made still rested within the circle, and they stood before it or held it in their hands as they spoke. And as the years passed, She continued to hear their pleas. Women still struggled in childbirth, but they no longer died in such terrible numbers, and more infants lived, even when they were born very early.

There were other changes. Some Kalar could see; others were

invisible, or part of a process that would continue long after she had returned to the Mother. The widening of the women's bones beneath their newly rounded hips was hidden from her eyes, though she suspected it must be there. She would have been surprised to know, though, that beneath the big skulls she observed, brain tissue would become ever more convoluted, turning over and over on itself so it could grow without taking up more space. That skulls continued to become thinner and less rigid, she did perceive. Zena's skull had been huge and thick, as hard as a rock. Now, almost all the infants that lived had thinner skulls, with the worrisome holes that closed up later. Kalar had realized, finally, after assisting at so many births, that the gaps allowed the skull to be compressed as the infant struggled to emerge.

Truly, she thought, the Mother had wondrous solutions. Kalar thanked Her constantly, especially when she attended a birth and saw labor progressing as it should. The pain of watching women struggle uselessly all through the long nights had become almost too much to bear. But at the same time, she was aware that the welcome changes were causing unexpected problems. In the past, infants had always been able to hold on to their mothers, but now they could not even hold their heads up or keep their backs straight. Kalar was sure they would one day be very intelligent, but in the meantime they were completely helpless. Their mothers had to use both arms to keep them safe, and that made food gathering difficult. If a mother wanted to pick berries or dig tubers, or drink water, she had to put the infant down. Then it screamed and she was forced to pick it up again lest it attract predators.

The difficulties did not disappear as the babies grew. They became stronger, but they also got heavier and heavier, and they had to be carried for almost two years. Nyta and the other women with little ones came back exhausted each night, without food for the group, for they could carry little besides their babies.

Life was harder for the women now, Kalar mused. But almost before the thought came to her, she chastised herself for her complaint. After all, the problem was not so severe. Their women were no longer dying, and that was most important. The Mother would send a solution to this newest difficulty, just as She had for the last one, and all the others through the years. And just as they had before, the tribe would manage until the Mother spoke. Those without infants—the men and the older children—could bring back most of the food. Already, the men were helping more, and that, surely, was good.

Still, she listened carefully in case the Mother should send another message. Each day when she awoke, each night before sleep, she lay quietly in the shelter and held her mind ready. Often, she clasped one of the figures in her hand as she waited. These moments were precious to her, whether or not a message came. She loved to lie there anyway, hearing the slow, steady breathing of the others as they slept, watching the moon or the morning sun filter through the branches above her, just as the pictures the Mother sent filtered into her thoughts.

Tonight, no pictures emerged. But she was content, for all was well with her tribe. Cere lay beside her, one arm curled protectively around Zena. Kalar was pleased, for Mina's spirit and for Cere, who loved Zena as her own.

The name suited the child, she reflected, glad now that she had chosen it. Zena meant *remarkable woman, one who would lead*, and Kalar was certain that would one day be true. It was an old word, and no one could remember its origin, but her grandmother had told her she thought it came from a long-ago ancestor who had served the Mother well.

One of the infants squealed, the sound loud and abrupt in the still air. Its mother held it close to her breast, and stillness fell again. Abruptly, as if on a prearranged signal, the cicadas and frogs began their nightly chorus. The whirring calls rose and fell and rose again, lulling Kalar into sleep. Other sounds broke their rhythm as the darkness deepened; a lion roared from the hillside, and hyenas began to bark. The herd of wildebeest across the river shuffled uneasily.

Kalar yawned. They were safe in the shelter. Constructed of thick rows of branches from the thorn trees that grew nearby, it was almost impenetrable. The walls rose as high as their shoulders, and a low fire in the hearth guarded the entrance. No animal would try to get in, for the thorns were sharp, the smell of people strong.

It was a good shelter, and she did not want to leave it, but the time had almost come. Always, she led the tribe south to the lake just before the rainy season. Nuts and fruits were already ripening on the big trees that grew there, fish and frogs would soon leap through the water, birds would lay their eggs in the rushes. But when the dry season came again, they would return to the river, to the thick shelter and the circle of stones she loved the best.

Kalar's eyes closed, and at just that moment, a picture came into her mind. She saw an animal, small and like a rat, except that it had a pouch on its belly where its young sought refuge. Why should the Mother send her this creature, one that she had seen only once before?

She shook her head, unable to think what the picture could mean. She would describe the animal to Zena tomorrow. Already, the child knew more than any other. Perhaps she would have an answer.

CHAPTER

10

The acrid smell of smoke stung Zena's nostrils. She sat up abruptly. The others were still sleeping. In the dim light, they were little more than indistinguishable bundles huddled against the earthen floor of the shelter.

She stared toward the hill where lightning had struck the night before. Fires at this time of the year were not unusual. As the rainy season approached, clouds gathered each afternoon and covered the sky in thick gray layers. But for many weeks, no rain fell from them. All they generated were ominous rumbles, and heat lightning that struck savagely at the baking earth and bone-dry grasses. Usually the fires that resulted died out during the night, when the wind dropped. But this time, the fire was still burning fiercely.

Zena reached out and touched Cere, to awaken her. Cere sat immediately, alert as always to Zena's slightest movement. Their eyes met briefly, then Cere turned to scan the group. The sun had just broken free of the horizon and she noticed what Zena had been unable to see. Kalar was missing, and Lett. She pointed to their empty places, mouthing their names quietly.

Just at that moment, shouts pierced the stultifying air. Leaping to her feet, Zena ran toward the sounds. Bran, Kalar's son, and Agar, another adult male, followed.

Lett and Kalar emerged from the crest of a hill to the north of the clearing. The fire burned behind them, outlining them in scarlet. They were dragging something, struggling with its weight. When

112

Zena reached them, she saw that it was an antelope. How had they managed to capture such a prize? The tribe hardly ever found more than bones or scraps left by predators, but this was a whole animal. She grabbed a leg and pulled, eager to get the antelope back to the clearing before a lion or tiger came to claim it.

Thick smoke swirled suddenly around their faces, covering them with a thin layer of soot. Kalar turned to study the shifting blaze. Zena watched her anxiously. At eight years, she was old enough to understand the wise woman's dilemma. Soon Kalar would lead the tribe south to the lake. But if the wind changed or the fire continued to spread, it could cut across their path.

Fires were strange, Zena thought. They were welcomed in many ways, yet feared in others. A smoldering stick found in the woods after lightning had struck lit the hearth fires that kept the tribe warm, and frightened predators away at night. Whenever their fire went out, they hoped for lightning, so they could find another burning stick. Fires brought abundance, too. Tender new shoots poked through the revitalized earth where they had burned, and the next year berries proliferated on the bushes. But when they burned out of control, fires were menacing. She had seen animals fleeing in panic before them, and one of their group had been killed when he was not quick enough to escape a change in the wind. He had not burned, but had died when fire had encircled his hiding place among the rocks. Perhaps that was what had happened to the antelope.

Zena shuddered. What if the fire came here, and trapped all of them? The winds were unpredictable this time of year. It would be better to leave soon, not take any chances.

Kalar's words confirmed her thoughts. "We must get ready," she told the others. "It is time to leave. Tonight, we feast, and thank the Mother; when the light comes, we go."

No further instructions were necessary. Each member of the tribe knew what he or she had to do, and they set about their tasks without hesitation. They must fill the baskets they had made of reeds and vines with food—melons and tubers, and any nuts and firm fruit they could find. There were gourds—or ostrich eggs, if any were left—to be filled with water. And this year, they had the antelope to consider. It would have to be butchered and cut into small pieces, so they could take at least some of the meat that was not consumed tonight.

Zena was glad they would not leave until morning. She loved the times when they gathered around the hearth fire to feast on an unusual treat like the antelope. First, of course, they thanked the

Mother for Her special gift. Then the story of the animal's capture was told over and over again as they savored its succulent flesh. Often, Zena ended up telling the tale, for she had more words than the others. Once those who had found the animal had made the event clear with gestures and actions and a few words, she elaborated, and taught the new words as she spoke. The young ones picked them up quickly, as did Kalar. The others were slower.

Lett had already begun to make some new flints so they could cut up the antelope. Patiently, he grasped a stone in one hand and chopped at it with another. Sparks shot out, and small chips flew in every direction. Sima, Nyta's four-year-old daughter, picked up one of the sharp chips and screamed as it cut her hand. Nyta came running, but Lett paid no attention; he did not look up from his work until he had forged three sharp cutting stones. He handed one to Cere, another to Bran, so they could help him cut the meat. Slitting the antelope's belly from tail to chin, he stripped the pelt from the carcass and tossed it aside. Later, he would take it to the river and scrape it clean.

The children stood around him, chattering excitedly. As soon as Cere and Bran began to cut the meat, their small hands flashed out to grab chunks. Zena grabbed some, too, then she picked up the discarded pelt to help Lett by carrying it to the river. She held it against her cheek for a moment. It felt soft and supple, even though it smelled of smoke.

Suddenly the picture Kalar had described to her a few days before, the one that had come from the Mother, appeared in her mind. She saw the small animal, with its soft brown fur, its little one peeking from the pocket on its belly, just as if it were there in front of her.

Zena held the pelt against her body, frowning deeply. As she stood there, Nyta came to the river to wash some chunks of antelope flesh that had fallen into the hot ashes. She laid the infant she had recently borne beside her. Suddenly deprived of the warmth of her body, it began to wail. Nyta grimaced and picked it up again, to suckle it for a moment. But as soon as she put it down, the wailing resumed.

Zena looked at Nyta, then at the infant, then at the pelt. Back and forth her eyes went, considering. A dreamy look came over her face as she pictured the small animal once again. Abruptly, determination replaced her abstraction. She spread the pelt on the ground, then she ran over to Lett to ask him for a scraping stone.

He gestured toward his place in the sleeping area, where he kept a supply. Zena took one and set eagerly to work. Sima came to help. Her skinny arms moved back and forth with surprising strength, and soon all the flesh was gone. Zena dunked the skin in the river, rubbing it vigorously against the rough sand, then stretched it out to dry in the hot sun.

The pelt dried quickly. Sima watched curiously as Zena cut a long strip, wider in the middle, from one edge of the hide. She tied the ends together in firm knots, then she placed the strip over her shoulder and across her belly. It was too long; the sling came down to her knees. Patiently, she undid the knot and shortened it. Then she asked Nyta to stand and arranged the pelt around her shoulder and chest.

Nyta was puzzled, but she submitted good-naturedly to the procedure. She began to object when Zena took the infant from her and placed it inside the loop of pelt at her chest. Then her eyes lit up in wonderment as she suddenly understood. The baby was slung tightly across her chest where it could easily reach her nipple. But both of her hands were free! She could pluck berries from bushes, dig for tubers, reach for fruit high in trees, wash food—all without putting the infant down. She could not believe what Zena had accomplished, and she danced around and around in a circle, hooting with glee.

Her hoots brought the others running. Eyes wide with amazement, they gathered around Nyta to examine the device. Zena paid little attention to the chorus of appreciation. The sling was not very secure, and the knot was clumsy. She had been in too much of a hurry. The next strip was wider in the middle, more tapered at the ends, so it tied better. Cere and Tempa, a young female who had joined the tribe a few years ago, vied for a chance to try it, but Zena could make only one more of the devices from the pelt, so they took turns.

A small piece of usable hide was left. Zena cut it carefully like the others, except smaller, and tied it around Sima's shoulder. The child stood up straight and tall, carrying her small sling proudly. It was she who found Kalar, to show her. Kalar's eyes went straight to Zena's face when she saw it. She shook her head, bemused. So *that* was what the Mother had been trying to tell her. But it had taken Zena's special intelligence to make it happen. Surely, she thought, the Mother's ways and Zena's gifts were a wondrous combination.

Her face grew serious as she realized what a difference Zena's device would make in their lives. Now, early birth would no longer be such a problem. Mothers could keep their babies close against their hearts, even suckle them, while they gathered food, or drank. They would be able to carry food too.

The thought of food-carrying brought mischief into her eyes, and she grinned. Zena had found a way to carry infants; perhaps she could find a way to carry flesh. They would feast on the antelope tonight, but much would still be left. They dared not linger another day to eat more, lest the fires trap them. Still, it seemed a shame to waste the Mother's bounty.

"Carry antelope?" she questioned, pointing to the carcass, and then to the sling Zena had made. Her eyes were merry, for she did not really expect Zena to take the question seriously. Meat rotted too fast, anyway, and only attracted predators.

But Zena took her very seriously indeed. She considered the problem, her head tilted to one side, her lips compressed. Bran and Agar started to laugh at her thoughtful expression. Zena stamped her foot in frustration. The two men always laughed when she tried something new.

Cere came to her rescue and scowled crossly at Bran and Agar. "Get fruit," she told them sharply, knowing they were the best at climbing to the high branches where fruit still lingered. They ambled away, still grinning. Then she came close to Zena and patted her on the shoulder.

Zena smiled gratefully, but she was still distracted by Kalar's question. She had noticed before that when the flesh of animals fell into the ashes and stayed there for a long time, it became smaller and lost all moisture. Once, she had taken such a piece with her when they traveled, and chewed on it slowly as they walked. It had been tough, but the taste was good, and it had suppressed her hunger. It had not become rotten, either, for many days.

Lett had pulled most of the flesh from the antelope's body and was cutting it into chunks. Later, they would put them on sticks and roast them in the fire. Zena asked for a slab and cut it into long, thin strips. She pushed them into the hot ashes with a stick, then she went to a place where the vines were especially thick and supple. Cutting off long pieces, she constructed a loosely woven basket. She wove one piece over another, as they always did, but she made the basket very big, and she left two long strands that could be tied over her shoulder.

In the morning, before they left, she pulled out the pieces of dried meat and washed them carefully in the river. Frowning seriously, she handed one to each of the others to put into their baskets. The remainder she placed in the bigger basket she had made and slung it over her shoulder.

Kalar shook her head in astonishment. She was not sure they would be able to chew such stringy pieces of meat, but the child really had tried to answer her question!

Bran and Agar, however, looked at Zena suspiciously. They did not understand at all. Why did she want them to carry such a shrunken piece of flesh? They poked her, wanting an answer.

Zena refused to explain. Instead, she stuck out her tongue at them and stalked away.

Nyta and Tempa giggled at the males' discomfiture. Soon the whole group was laughing, not at the men, but at Sima and Lupe, Pote's small son. Pote had died soon after her son's birth, but Nyta and Tempa had suckled Lupe and he had lived. The two children were swinging the long pieces of dried flesh wildly through the air, throwing them up and catching them again before they landed on the ground. Then Lupe stuck one in the corner of his mouth and began to strut around, twirling it with his teeth. Dorn, Tempa's son, who had been born the same year as Lupe, imitated him. Even Zena began to laugh, her good feelings restored.

Abruptly, the merriment stopped. Kalar was ahead, leading them along their usual route. They saw her stop and hold up her hand. The fire had died down during the night, but it had not gone out. Now, as Kalar had feared, it was burning slowly into the wide plain they habitually traversed to reach a swamp, where there was almost always water to refresh them after the dry, hot crossing. They might be able to get across before the fire reached them—but if the wind strengthened, they could be trapped.

Kalar made up her mind. They could not risk it. Instead, she would lead them south along the river. The first part of the track she knew well, for a group like themselves lived a day's journey away. The two tribes interacted often, to mate, or when Kalar helped their women in childbirth. Beyond that point, the way was unfamiliar and more dangerous. Predators could lurk in the thick brush, and both elephants and rhinoceros were attracted to the thorny bushes and tall trees that grew in wide swaths near the river. Elephants could usually be avoided since they made so much noise, but rhinos could lurk unseen in the bushes and charge at anything that came too close.

Another problem worried Kalar even more than the bad-tempered rhinos. Along the river were scattered groups of small-headed creatures they called Big Ones. Her grandmother had told her that they were like people long ago, but the Big Ones had never changed, as others had. Like themselves, Big Ones walked on two legs, but in other ways they were very different. They did not speak at all, but only grunted. The females were no larger than themselves, but the males were huge, with thick, strong bodies and massive jaws. Kalar had always avoided them, unwilling to provoke a challenge by intruding on their territory. As far as she knew, the Big Ones had never caused any harm, but never before had she attempted to walk through the areas where they lived. Now, she had no choice.

II

Zena was delighted with the change of plan. She loved exploring new places, and she had no fear of Big Ones. The area around the shelter, or even the variety of places where the tribe searched for food, had never satisfied her boundless curiosity, and she often wandered far from their usual haunts. Only Cere had joined her in these adventurous forays. She had followed patiently, interfering only to keep Zena from hurting herself, for she knew it was impossible to stop her from looking behind every bush, into every hole in the ground or nest in a tree, from exploring every hill and valley. Still, she never let the child get out of sight. Zena was more important to her than any other, even the young one she had recently borne. The Mother Herself had trusted her to care for Zena and keep her safe.

One day, Zena had come across a group of Big Ones who lived a few hours north along the river. After that, she had visited them often. She had few playmates, since so many infants had died in those years, but there were many her age among the Big Ones. She liked the strange youngsters. They never answered when she spoke to them, but that did not deter her from showing them everything she noticed—a butterfly, a baby gazelle leaping after its mother on spindly legs, the shape of an animal in the clouds. They followed her pointing finger or excited gestures with their eyes, and listened intently as she gave words to her discoveries. But they never responded in the same way.

Cere shuddered, remembering. The Big Ones had never seemed aggressive, but they had still frightened her. She was glad Zena was older and no longer yearned so strongly for the companionship of other young ones. Now she spent more of her time helping the adults and experimenting with objects she found around her. Some were not very useful, like the stringy meat, but others surely were. Cere adjusted the sling, marveling once more at the freedom of her hands.

The tribe started off again, heading south this time. Zena strode beside Kalar, glad to have this chance to learn from the wise woman. Whenever she saw a plant she could not identify or some behavior in an animal that was unfamiliar, she asked about it. Kalar had observed animals for years, and could usually answer. As well as warning of predators, animals often told her that storms were coming, or where food or water could be found. But plants were Kalar's specialty. She knew all the flowers and shrubs and herbs in the areas where they traveled. Her mother had taught her their uses; she had added her own knowledge, acquired through years of patient observation, and that of the wise woman from the nearby tribe. Kalar was as eager to teach as Zena was to learn, and she watched carefully for specimens as they walked, so she could identify them and explain how to use them.

"See the shape," she said, holding out a leafy twig she had plucked from a nearby bush. "It goes many ways, like the fingers on your hand. It goes many ways inside you, too, to help sickness."

Zena nodded. Once, she had seen baboons eating this plant, as if they, too, knew the faintly aromatic twigs would help.

"This one is soft," Kalar continued, bending to pull up a succulent plant. "It goes on the skin and draws out the pain." She crushed it into a ball and placed it on Zena's arm, where vines had scratched her. The small cuts soon stopped throbbing.

Another she held up for all to see. "This kills," she said sternly to the children. "Do not eat it." Kalar knew that from her mother, whose young one had died after eating this plant.

The children stared, their eyes wide with alarm. Zena held the plant, with its deep purple flower and narrow leaves, and stored its appearance in her memory, as she had stored the others.

A loud trumpeting made her jump. Kalar led them quickly away from the sound. The track they were following had been made by elephants. The herd ambled along, pushing down trees and uprooting bushes with their strong trunks, and gradually a cleared path emerged from the brush. The track made walking easier, but if the elephants were using it, the tribe moved out of their way. The massive creatures would not harm them unless they felt threatened, but sometimes the males were aggressive, especially when the time of mating came.

They went on, walking through the brush beside the track, and watching carefully. There were no more loud calls, only a low rumbling noise that seemed to come from a single animal, a lone female elephant who stood in the middle of the track. Her feet were planted protectively over a tiny calf. Zena watched as she prodded the calf over and over with her trunk. The small one did not move. She looked questioningly at Kalar.

"It has died," Kalar said, her eyes filled with pity. "Its mother mourns, as we mourn when young ones die."

Zena took a last look as Kalar urged them away from the place. The elephant raised its head and stared at her, but Zena thought it had not really seen her, for its eyes were clouded with grief. Her own eyes filled with sympathetic tears, and for a long time, she was quiet.

A brown chameleon darted across the ground in front of her, distracting her from thoughts of the elephant. It scuttled onto a leafy branch and then stood perfectly still, its body stretched out along a green stem. Slowly, as Zena watched, it turned green itself. She called to the children, to show them. They watched, open-mouthed, as its color continued to change.

"It hides that way," she told them. They looked at their own bodies, as if expecting them to change too. Zena laughed. "Only ones like this change," she explained. Then she had an idea, and ran back to get some purple berries they had passed. Standing Sima in front of her, she drew a long line of purple, squeezed from the berries, across Sima's small belly. The two boys shoved at her, wanting a line too. Zena obliged by making a big circle on each, as well as a line. They ran off happily, sticking their decorated stomachs out as far as they would go.

Soon after, they decided to stop for the night near a deep depression in the earth, where elephants had rolled during the rainy season. There would be water if they dug deeply, for the elephants' heavy bodies had compressed the earth so that it held water even when there had been no rain for months.

Agar had brought a burning stick, and had managed to keep it going. Sometimes the glow at the tip burned out as they traveled, and then they were without the protection of fire, but for this night, at least, they would be safe. They gathered sticks and brush and settled themselves around the fire, glad to rest.

A call from the bushes brought Bran and Agar to their feet, clutching the big stones they always kept near them. The others grabbed their own stones and drew together, protecting the young ones with their bodies. But when she heard the call again, Kalar relaxed. These were people from the tribe near the river, whom they had often visited. They would be welcome.

The bushes parted to reveal an old woman. Her face was wrinkled, her teeth so worn they barely showed above her gums. She moved with dignity as she approached Kalar and touched her gently on the shoulder.

"Greetings," she said, lowering herself slowly to the ground. She was the wise one for her tribe, and Kalar was glad to see her. This was the one who had added so much to her knowledge of plants. She knew them all, especially those that cleansed wounds and helped to make pain go away.

Three others came through the bushes. In their hands were some big fish. Parts of the river near their gathering place had dried up, leaving fish stranded and easy to catch.

"You eat," one of the men told Kalar, handing her the fish. "We have many." Kalar inclined her head gravely, to thank him.

Bran found sticks that did not burn easily and speared the fish so they could be held over the fire. Soon their tantalizing aroma filled the air. When they were cooked, he signaled to Zena to find some big leaves, so he could place the fish on them to be passed around. Kalar took the first bite, for she knew the fish was in thanks for her help when the women labored, and then passed it to the old female.

"You eat, too," she told her, knowing the soft flesh would be easy for her to chew.

After that, all of them dug their fingers eagerly into the fish. When only bones were left, they snuggled companionably around the fire, talking and relaxing. Then Nyta rose, calling to one of the young men from the other tribe. Tempa signaled to the other one, and they went off behind some bushes to mate. The young woman who had accompanied the group took Bran with her, and Agar followed, to wait for his turn. After each couple had rested, they would trade partners, so that everyone who wished to had a chance to mate with everyone else.

Kalar watched them go, smiling. To have this opportunity to mate with men and women from another tribe was good. Mating was a gift from the Mother, one She wanted them to use often. It also gave much pleasure, especially to the women. Often, the tingling sensations and the warm glow lasted for many hours. Men tired more quickly, and she did not think their pleasure was as great. But mating calmed them, and that was important. It was the Mother's way of reducing the fighting that occasionally broke out between males, even those like Bran and Lett who were usually peaceful. Mating pulled a fluid from them, a fluid that made them aggressive if it stayed too long within them. Kalar had often observed this, and she was grateful to the Mother for providing a solution.

Once, she, too, had eagerly sought out men from other tribes for mating, but now only Lett seemed to spark desire. A ripple of remembered delight coursed through her body, and she rubbed Lett's leg and touched her lips to his, considering whether or not to leave the warm fire and seek the privacy of the bushes. Lett looked into her eyes, understanding her perfectly. Without speaking, they decided they were too lazy and content to move. They settled back against a fire-warmed rock, touching often, rubbing their faces together in a gentle rhythm. There would be other times, and they could wait.

The children followed the mating couples, eager to peer at them through the bushes. Sima and the two little boys watched with great interest, but Zena had seen this many times before and quickly became bored. Mating seemed a silly activity to her, and she could not understand why the adults spent so much time doing it. Even Kalar did it, especially with Lett. She had often watched them. Zena had asked her about it, and Cere, too, but neither had provided a satisfactory answer.

"It gives great pleasure to those who do it," they had told her, but she had not believed them. The groans they uttered, and the grimaces on their faces, made her think that mating must be a very uncomfortable process. She was certain she would never do it.

She wandered away from the fire. Darkness would come soon, and she wanted to explore while the light remained. Handing her infant to Kalar, Cere followed. Zena liked to be independent, and she was old enough now to stay out of danger, but Cere still worried when she went off by herself. She stayed a short distance behind, so Zena would not see her.

The sun was approaching the western horizon, and Zena stood to watch the colors. Always, they astonished her with their beauty. She had asked Kalar why the colors came, but this answer had not satisfied her, either.

"The Mother makes the colors," Kalar had said. But Zena thought the sun itself made the colors when it was squeezed behind the earth, just as berries let out color when they were squeezed. Still, she was not sure. The sun reappeared each morning, full and round, while the berries stayed flat.

Antelopes of many kinds grazed in the distance. Some were tall, higher than the zebra that grazed among them. Others were small, graceful creatures with pointed horns. All of them suddenly leaped straight into the air, as if to see better over the tall grasses, then ran out of sight. Probably a lion was chasing them, Zena thought, glad to be far away.

She froze. A rustling sound had come from the grasses beside her.

Nothing sprang, and Zena relaxed enough to turn her head to look. The rustling came again, so faint she would not have heard it had she not been listening hard. She raised her arm, her fist clenched around the rock she always took with her, and bent down to look more closely.

At first, she could see nothing, so well did the small creature blend with its surroundings. Then a gasp of surprise escaped her; she quelled it quickly lest she startle the tiny gazelle that lay huddled almost under her feet. She would have stepped on it had she not heard the rustling.

Why had it not run? And where was its mother? Although gazelles had little fear of creatures like themselves who did not prey on them, they usually ran if *any* animal came too close. There must be something wrong with this one, to lie so still even when she knelt directly beside it. But it was not dead. Breath went in and out of its body, and that stopped when death came. Could it be hurt?

The calf's eyes were closed, and its muzzle lay along its front feet. As Zena leaned closer, the fringed lids slowly opened, and the baby gazelle turned its head to stare at her. She stared back, entranced. The limpid brown eyes seemed to her to contain everything she had ever seen in the savannah—the beauty as well as the fear, the enormity of the sky and grasses, the incredible intricacy of the many living forms. Zena could not find words to express the immensity of her thoughts, but still she saw it all in the tiny creature's eyes.

Her arm dropped, and she placed the stone silently on the ground. Slowly, with infinite caution, she reached out to touch the calf. It moved slightly, but did not try to rise. Her hand came closer. A long shudder of anxiety rippled through the fawn-colored body when her fingers made contact, but still it did not run. Zena rubbed it gently, then more vigorously, as if her hand were its mother's tongue. Over and over, she stroked the soft fur, from neck to rump, with smooth, strong gestures.

Another noise made her look up in alarm. But it was only Cere, coming to see what Zena had found. Fear showed in the calf's eyes as Cere approached, and it struggled to rise to its feet. But its legs would not hold it, and it fell back against the ground, bleating piteously.

"Quiet," Zena whispered. "It is hurt, I think."

Slowly, almost imperceptibly, she moved her hand down the calf's rump until she was touching a leg. Again, a shudder ran down its body, but it stayed still. Returning her hand to its back, she stroked it slowly, over and over. The calf relaxed and breathed more calmly. Zena tried again, stroking first one leg, then another. It did not move. But when she tried to touch the third leg, the calf stiffened and butted her fingers with its head. Zena stopped, and returned her hand to its back.

Cere watched, unmoving. She had noticed before that animals did not seem to fear Zena. They did not run, and sometimes, like this one, they allowed her to touch them. She sighed, sorry for the small creature. Before the night was over, it would be dead. A lion would come, or the hyenas.

She rose to leave, but Zena stopped her with an imperative gesture. "We must heal it," she said.

Cere stared at her. How could they make an animal's leg work again? That was impossible. But Zena would not be deterred. She was certain she could fix the calf, with Kalar's help. Surely, there were herbs for this, too.

She drew the small creature into her arms, murmuring low bleating sounds all the while. At first it struggled to escape, but when she rubbed her face gently along its flank, in the same way her hands had moved, it lay still again. Cradling it in her arms, she walked slowly toward the fire.

The others were already sleeping. There were many now, for the visitors had stayed so they would not have to walk in the darkness. Zena was glad they were asleep. The flames and the smell of many bodies made the little gazelle tremble and squirm, but at least there were no voices to frighten it further.

She lay down beside it, a little away from the others, and soothed it with her hands, with low, cooing noises. It settled beside her. Slowly, as she watched, its deeply fringed lids drooped over its eyes. As long as it felt her hands on its back, it was still. But as soon as she stopped stroking, its eyes opened again, and it tried to rise.

Zena stroked and stroked, trying to stay awake, but the warmth and her full belly conspired against her, and her eyes finally closed. Twice, she awoke when the calf moved against her, and she stroked it until sleep claimed her once again. But when she awoke in the morning, just as light began to filter through the trees, the tiny creature was gone.

CHAPTER

11

Apprehension turned Zena's stomach into a hard knot. Pictures flashed through her mind: she saw the calf dead, killed by a hungry animal that had managed to creep up in the night without waking her, or by one of the visitors, for food. But the others were still sleeping, and she saw no footprints of animals. She sprang to her feet and began to search through the sleeping bodies, all around the area of the fire, and beyond, in the bushes. Perhaps the calf had managed to struggle to its feet and had hobbled away, frightened by the smell of many people.

Kalar sat up and rubbed her eyes. She watched curiously as Zena leaned down to look under a bush.

"What do you look for?" she asked sleepily.

"My gazelle," Zena replied, her voice tremulous.

Kalar sighed, and almost laughed. The child had such strange ideas. But the laugh died in her throat when Zena raised her face. She was truly distressed, Kalar saw.

Cere awoke, hearing the voices. She jumped up and began to help Zena.

"Zena found it in the grasses," she explained, seeing Kalar's perplexed face. "A young one."

Kalar frowned. "But it must go back to its mother," she said firmly. "Only the mother can feed a young one."

"Its mother cannot help it," Zena said, peering into a clump of small trees. "Its leg is hurt. We must heal it."

Sympathy sprang into Kalar's eyes, but her voice was still firm. "That is for the Mother to do," she said. "The gazelle is the Mother's creature, for Her to care for."

A stubborn expression came into Zena's face. "I must care for this one," she stated, and resumed her search.

Kalar and Cere looked at each other with raised eyebrows. When Zena had made up her mind, there was little anyone could do to change it. They, too, began to look for the little gazelle.

The others woke, disturbed by the noises. Zena had disappeared to search near the place where she had found the calf, so Cere tried to explain. Bran and Agar grinned at yet another of Zena's strange behaviors. But when Zena returned, her downcast face aroused even their sympathy.

"I will help," Agar said.

Zena's eyes lit up in relief. Agar knew more of animals even than Kalar. Bran was big and gentle, but Agar was a small, quick-tempered male who often aroused the wise woman's wrath because he struck out or yelled at one of the others. Then she stared at him until he retreated to cool his anger. He went to the animals at these times, and watched them for long hours. He knew how they behaved, what they ate, and where they hid.

Agar asked her to describe the calf and where she had found it. Nodding, he went immediately to a small area of brown grass she had not noticed.

"It could be here," he told Zena, "where it can hide. It looks for grass of this color."

He was right. The gazelle was lying just as she had found it, its small muzzle stretched on its feet. It was almost invisible against the brown stalks. Zena looked up at Agar in immense gratitude. Never again would she provoke him, as she and the other children sometimes did, to watch him lose his temper.

The calf's eyes opened a little when Zena bent over it, but it barely resisted when she picked it up.

"It needs food," Agar said. "It is weak."

"What does it eat?" Zena had often watched gazelles feeding, but she was not certain which of the many grasses they liked best.

"It eats from its mother," he replied. Seeing the dismay on her face, he added, "But it is old enough to eat grasses, too, and leaves. We can try."

He strode quickly toward the plains where Zena had found the calf and began to pull up the smallest, most tender shoots he could find. There were not many, for the grass became high and tough at the end of the dry season. He held the pieces flat on his hand and placed it under the small animal's nose.

It roused, and nibbled a little. Agar put the rest of the grass in Zena's hand and went to a nearby tree. Miraculously, even before the rains came, this particular tree always managed to produce new growth. The small leaves were pale green and tender. When the little gazelle smelled them, its nose twitched, and it raised its head eagerly and ate.

"Good," Agar said. "Perhaps it will live."

Zena watched, astonished, as the calf gained strength before her eyes. She called to Sima and the two boys. They had been watching from a distance, warned by Cere not to go too close lest they frighten the small animal.

"Find more," she instructed, showing them the grass and the tender leaves. Thrilled with the task, they scurried off and soon returned with a big bundle. Zena let them offer some to the calf, and they giggled as its rough tongue scraped their palms.

"Water?" she asked Agar.

He shook his head. "It needs little," he replied. Still, she offered it water and it drank a small amount.

When it stopped eating, she laid the gazelle gently on the ground to examine its leg. The calf turned its head toward her, bleating, and tried to get back into her arms. It seemed to feel safe there, and nowhere else.

Kalar came to watch. "It needs herbs to pull out the hurt," Zena told her. The slender leg, hardly thicker than her finger, was discolored and had a deep cut. Nodding, Kalar went to find some of the leaves she had shown Zena the day before. Together, they prepared a poultice. They began to wrap the leg in the crushed leaves, but the old wise woman from the other tribe stopped them.

"Wait," she said. She shuffled away and returned with two slender sticks, very straight, and some supple vines.

"It is broken," she said, indicating the leg. "This holds it straight. I have done this before, on a young one."

Gently, she straightened the leg and bound the sticks to it with vines. The calf flinched when she touched the leg, but she spoke to it soothingly, and stroked it as Zena had done. It submitted to her ministrations, seeming to sense the old female's calm and long experience.

"Place the poultice over this," she told Zena. "It must have the sticks for many moons, until the leg heals."

Under her watchful eyes, Zena placed the poultices around the sticks and bound them.

"Good," the old wise one said, and rose painfully to her feet. "We go now." She touched Zena softly on the shoulder, and took Kalar's hand.

"Go with the Mother," she said, looking straight into Kalar's eyes. Kalar returned the long, deep look. The two women understood each other now without words, for they had joined so many times in the long wait for death to come, or life if the Mother willed it, that their minds worked as one. The old one was bidding her good-bye, Kalar knew, for she might not live until the next meeting.

"May the Mother take you gently," Kalar replied.

The wise woman nodded, and turned away, signaling to the others of her tribe to follow. Zena watched her go, impressed by her courage and dignity.

"She is very wise, I think," she remarked to Kalar. "More wise than any I know but you."

Kalar smiled gravely in agreement. "We have learned much from the old one," she replied. "She is of the Mother."

When the time came to resume their journey, Zena set the calf on its feet, hoping it would be able to walk now that its leg was supported. It hobbled a short way, then lay down, bleating. She sighed, and picked it up again. Somehow, she would have to carry it.

Her eyes lit on the big basket she had made. She laid the gazelle in it, on top of the dried meat, for she did not want to leave that behind, and raised the basket to her shoulders. The calf sniffed delicately at the strips and wrinkled its nose, then settled itself against her warm belly.

The group set off, heading south along the river. Zena felt her body bend under the unaccustomed weight of the calf. She straightened quickly, determined not to ask for help. But when Agar took it from her later in the day, she did not object. Her shoulders were raw from the straps, and her back was terribly sore. The way was harder now too. They had left the wide track made by elephants, and had entered terrain unlike any she had seen before. Tall trees festooned with vines and ghostly clumps of moss closed in thickly all around them, hiding the sky, and the spongy undergrowth was warm and damp beneath their feet. The air was hot and thick with moisture.

Zena shuddered. She felt uncomfortable in this place. Everything around her was shadowy, indistinct. The thick canopy reverberated with bird song and other noises, but she could see neither birds nor any other animal in the dark mass of leaves. She clutched Cere's hand for reassurance, but soon the foliage became so dense they had to creep through it single file, and she had to let go again.

They came to a small clearing among the vegetation, and decided to rest. A shallow pool of dank brown water tempted the children. They ran to it and bent down to drink.

"No!" It was Lett shouting. Once before, he had been in a place like this, and he knew the pools could be dangerous. There was something in them that hurt the belly, so that those who drank became hot, and all moisture fled from their bodies.

The children leaped back. Lupe had already swallowed some, but he spat out what was in his mouth. The others drank sparingly from the gourds they had brought, and looked around them nervously. There could be other harmful things in this strange, damp forest, but they did not know what to fear, for none but Lett had been in such a place before. Kalar especially felt anxious, almost as if she were being watched. She stared into the impenetrable green that surrounded the clearing, but she could see nothing.

Zena took the calf out of the basket, so it could stretch, and went to look for some broad leaves to place on her shoulders, where the strap rubbed. The little gazelle followed her, hobbling on its three good legs.

"Three-Legs," she decided suddenly. "It is called Three-Legs."

She reached for a large, thick leaf, and examined it curiously. It was larger than any she had seen before, and downy white hairs clung to its underside. It might be good to heal skin, she thought, since skin, too, had hairs. She reached for another one, to show to Kalar, and jumped in astonishment. Behind the leaf was a face, the face of a Big One. Its eyes met hers for a moment, then they turned. Zena followed its gaze and called out sharply. It was staring straight at Three-Legs.

Kalar and the others ran over to Zena. The Big One emerged from the leafy brush, and as he moved, many others also emerged. The females were no bigger than themselves, but the males were massive creatures. Dark hair covered most of their bodies, and their jaws were huge, though their heads were relatively small. They shuffled rather than walked, but still they moved with surprising agility.

They had been all around the clearing, Kalar realized, watching them. Her skin began to crawl in apprehension.

But the big male who had emerged first made no move that signified aggression. Instead, he continued to stare at the little gazelle. He and his tribe had not seen meat for many moons. The herds had gone south, following the rains, and other animals were hard to catch in the dense foliage. This small animal would make a tasty meal. His mouth began to water, and he went toward it, to catch it before it leaped away. Guessing his intention, Zena ran to the calf and pulled it into her arms.

The big male stopped, surprised, and gestured to her to put it down. Zena shook her head. He made motions, as if eating it. She shuddered and held Three-Legs closer. He frowned, and looked at the others in his group, as if asking them what he should do next. They regarded each other closely, and seemed to decide something without words, for the whole group moved closer to Zena, surrounding her as they reached for the calf.

Lett and Bran and Agar broke through the group, raising their clenched fists to signify that they would defend Zena. Puzzled, the Big Ones backed away. Again, the big male made gestures, as if eating. To keep an animal and not eat it was incomprehensible to him, and neither he nor the others could understand why these strange ones were defending it.

He became impatient, and began to pound his chest angrily. His urge for meat was strong, and these others were preventing him from satisfying it. The other males copied him; soon the small clearing resounded with their drumming. The females did not pound, but they screeched over and over in high-pitched voices. The noise became deafening. Kalar's skin prickled as she felt the danger escalate. She signaled to her tribemates to retreat, but the Big Ones would not let them go. They surrounded them, gesturing repeatedly toward the frightened calf.

"We must let them have it," Kalar whispered. "It is the only way. There are many of them, too many."

Zena held on stubbornly. She looked around the circle of threatening faces. One of the females was frowning in confusion, and Zena recognized her suddenly. It was one of the Big Ones with whom she had played, when she was younger.

"You come from the place by the big rocks," she said, referring to a large pile of rocks near the place where the Big Ones she had visited lived.

The female looked startled. The words had no meaning for her, but the sound of Zena's voice jogged her memory. She made a guttural sound of recognition, and stretched a hand toward Zena. Her companions looked at her searchingly. She uttered a series of grunts, combined with quick gestures, that seemed to signify children playing. The others looked back at Zena, and some of the hostility left their faces. But then the calf bleated and began to struggle in Zena's arms. It was terrified of these large, noisy creatures, and Zena was holding it so tightly it could hardly breathe. The Big Ones lurched toward it, their interest revived.

"Wait!" Zena's voice stopped them, though they did not understand. Still clutching the struggling calf, she ran over to her basket and pulled out some pieces of dried meat, which had begun to smell in the intense heat. The Big Ones sniffed appreciatively as she dangled the strips near their faces. The male took one and placed it between his huge teeth. The others reached for strips and began to chew. Their eyes lit up at the strong meaty taste, and they nodded to each other in agreement. This was not an animal, but it was satisfying anyway.

Zena looked straight into the big male's eyes and pointed to Three-Legs. "No eat," she said clearly, shaking her head firmly as she made eating gestures. Then she pointed to the strips in the basket, nodding vigorously.

"Eat these," she told them. "You take." She pointed into the foliage, the way they had come.

The big male seemed to understand. He took the basket and signaled to the others to follow him. They disappeared quickly into the dense cover, making almost no noise. The female who had recognized Zena touched her gently on the shoulder, and looked into her eyes before she followed. Then she, too, vanished.

Kalar went to a fallen log and sat abruptly. Even her calm had been shattered by the unexpected encounter, and she was not certain her legs would hold her any longer. Lett came and put an arm around her. The others followed, still blinking at the suddenness of the Big Ones' departure. They had seemed literally to melt into the forest. But it was Cere who was most affected. Zena, the one she loved more than any other, had been threatened, and she had been powerless to defuse the threat. She went to Zena and held her close, sobbing with relief. Zena hugged her back, trying to hold on to Three-Legs at the same time. The little animal bleated and stuck its head comically out between their bodies.

The children started to laugh unrestrainedly at the sight, releasing their tension in merriment. The adults joined in, and soon all of them were holding their stomachs, trying to contain laughter that threatened to explode into hysteria after their frightening experience.

The merriment faded quickly when a big shadow passed across the clearing, darkening it still further.

"The clouds come," Kalar said. "We must go."

She turned to Lett, seeking his help. His sense of direction was superb, even better than her own, and she relied on his judgment when she was unsure.

"We go to the grasses again," she told him, "away from this place, before the dark comes."

He nodded, agreeing, and pointed west. "We go that way first," he replied. "I do not know how far to the grasses."

They pushed their way into the thick foliage. Zena ran after them, desperate now to get away from the towering trees and clinging vines, the suffocating air, the dimness. Soon, they would not be able to see at all, and then the Big Ones might come back.

Shivering with fear, she pulled Three-Legs close against her chest. She had seen the big male's last, covetous glance. If he came again, she would not be able to save the baby gazelle, for there were no more strips of meat. She hurried on, unaware of the eyes that still peered at her from behind the lush green cover. But Kalar felt them, as she had felt them before. The Big Ones were following, so quietly she had not once been able to hear their footsteps.

II

For hours, they struggled through the dense greenness, unable to find a clear place where they could hold themselves erect. Since the basket was gone, they took turns carrying Three-Legs. Bran and Agar, who did most of the carrying, often looked pointedly at Zena, as if to express their disdain at her foolishness. Still, they handled the calf gently. Like the others, they had quickly become attached to the little creature.

Soon, however, they stopped glaring and looked at Zena with new respect. For the first time, they grasped the importance of the slings she had made. With Three-Legs in their arms, they were unable to slap at the bugs that had begun to torment them, or even to push vines aside to pass. Soon they were bitten and scratched all over, and short-tempered with exhaustion.

Bran thrust the calf at Agar, unable to hold on to it any longer. Shaking his arms with relief, he looked back at the others to see how they were faring. It was Tempa's turn for the sling, and Cere was struggling to creep under the vines while she held on to her infant. Newly aware of the difficulty of carrying a helpless creature for many hours, he reached for the infant so she could rest her arms. She shook her head, panting, and pointed to Lupe. The child was doubled over with cramps from the water he had drunk. Dorn was trying to help him walk, his small face puckered with worry for his companion. Bran picked Lupe up and slung him over his shoulder. At least the child was old enough to hold on, so that one of his hands remained free.

Finally, they came across a vague track that seemed to lead in the right direction, for the way before them lightened even as the sun began to ease behind the horizon. They struggled down it, too weary even to notice that the trees were thinning, that vines had ceased to grab at their shoulders. And then, suddenly, they saw grass. They stumbled into it and sank to the ground.

Zena looked at the sky as if she had never seen it before. Its huge arc rose all around her, and the western horizon was gaudy with orange and rose. She stared at it gratefully, but then her eyes began to close. She snuggled down next to Three-Legs, too tired even to eat. The other children slumped down beside her. Limp with fatigue, they fell asleep immediately.

Kalar looked at them dubiously. The group should move farther from the trees, but she was not sure she would be able to rouse the young ones again. She decided to let them sleep, but she did not relax her guard. She and Lett watched long into the night, then the others took turns guarding the group. All night long, she was aware of the Big Ones lurking behind the green cover, but no sound or movement betrayed their presence.

As soon as there was enough light to see, she roused the children and pushed them forward, toward some tumbled rocks she had sighted in the distance. If they could get that far, they would be safe, for she was certain the Big Ones would not venture far from their shadowy home in the forest. Gradually, as the distance from the forest increased, she realized that she no longer had the sensation of being watched, and she relaxed for the first time since they had set off the day before.

The rocky escarpment she had sighted proved even more hospitable than she had hoped. Wide trees covered with pod-bearing vines grew on the slope, and a shallow pond nestled behind the rocks. It was empty but still damp, and when they dug into it, they found both water and masses of clams. They feasted on them, smacking their lips at the fishy taste and the welcome juice that surrounded the pink flesh.

All they lacked now was fire. The burning stick they had brought with them had gone out as they had traveled through the wet forest. But even that problem was solved later, when lightning started a small fire. Sprinkles of rain, forerunners of the real rains, quickly extinguished it, but they managed to get fire into some sticks before the flames disappeared. They gathered more sticks, to keep the fire going, and settled down to stay for a few days while the children recovered their strength.

Kalar was especially worried about Lupe. He was weak and shivery, and he could not keep food down. She placed damp wads of leaves on his forehead to take the heat from his skin, and sent Zena off to find the herbs she had showed her earlier, for sickness in the belly.

"The bushes grow among the pebbles, in dry places," she told Zena, indicating an arid hillside just beyond the rocks.

Zena set off happily, proud of the responsibility. Three-Legs followed. The calf would not let her out of its sight, and if she did not pick it up, it hobbled after her. Already, it was learning to walk on its three good legs, though it still tired easily. Zena had fashioned a kind of leash, to keep it close. There were vultures soaring overhead, and she had seen an eagle earlier. The huge, crowned birds could lift newborn gazelles off the ground and into the sky with little effort. She did not know if they could carry Three-Legs, but she took no chances.

A thickset animal with light fur on its back ambled by her, snarling ferociously. She backed away, giving it plenty of room. It was an animal they called honey-digger, for it dug up the nests of bees and of ants that also made honey. Despite its small size, it would attack anything that got in its way.

Three-Legs gamboled clumsily toward the honey-digger, wanting to play, and was rewarded by a savage swipe of the animal's heavy paw. Zena pulled the calf sharply backward just before the claws hit. The small gazelle snorted with dismay and began to tremble. Zena picked up her pet and followed the ferocious creature from a careful distance. Perhaps it would lead them to honey. All of them craved the sweet stuff, especially during the dry season, when fruit was hard to find.

The honey-digger lumbered on, then stopped, as if looking for something. Zena noticed a small bird, just ahead of it. The bird flew a short distance, perched on a branch until the animal saw it, then flew again. The honey-digger followed. Intrigued, Zena followed as well. Abruptly, the bird ceased to fly and stared intently toward the ground. The honey-digger stopped in front of it and began to dig energetically. Soon bees were flying everywhere. Zena ran a safe distance away, but the animal ignored the furious insects. It just kept digging, and as it dug, it ate, shoving its face into the gaping hole to consume any bees that remained in the nest, the honey, the young ones inside—everything but the waxy coating around the beehive. This it left for the bird that had guided it. The bird pecked daintily, satisfied with its prize.

Remembering her task, Zena began to scour the rocky hillside for the leafy twigs Kalar needed. When she had a big bundle of them, she hurried back to the others, eager to tell them about the bird and the honey-digger. Agar and Cere followed her back to the place, hoping for some of the delectable treat, but nothing was left. Disappointed, they turned back. Then Agar spotted a hole filled with scurrying honey ants. The voracious digger had unearthed it as well, and the ants were trying to repair the damage it had made. On their abdomens were globules of honey, twice the size of the ants themselves.

Zena's stomach rumbled in anticipation. Grasping the ants carefully so they would not pinch her, she bit off the tasty bundles of sweet stuff until her craving was satisfied. Then she and the two adults scooped some of the scurrying insects into a basket and hurried back to the resting place. The others greeted them joyfully. Honey was a very special treat, especially for the children. Even Lupe ate some, to wash down the bitter brew Kalar was forcing down his throat. The other children ran back for more, and soon became expert at grabbing the wriggling ants and nipping off the delicious honey without being pinched. It seemed to restore their energy, and they began to romp and play with their usual abandon.

They rested for one more day and then went on. Lupe was now recovering quickly, and Kalar wanted to get to the lake before the rains came to batter them as they walked. Once at the lake, they could build a sturdy shelter to protect them, or repair their old one, if it was still there. But when they reached the familiar spot, two days later, they found their old shelter occupied by others. Bran and Agar, irritated at seeing strangers in the place they considered their own, started toward the intruders, to force them to leave. Kalar called them back.

"We will build another," she said. Reluctantly, they turned back.

"That is our place," Agar objected.

"All places are the Mother's," Kalar replied. "The land is Hers, not ours."

Agar looked sullen, but he did not argue. He was tired and sweaty after the long journey, and wanted more than anything else to jump in the lake and clean himself. All of them preferred to bathe every day, but that was hard to manage when they traveled. He ran to join the others, who were already cavorting in the fresh, cool water. When the grime of the past week had been removed, they rubbed themselves with clumps of sweet-smelling leaves and lay drowsily in the sun to dry. After that, they began the arduous job of constructing a shelter. Grasses had to be gathered for thatch to protect them from the rain. There were thorn bushes to cut with their sharp stones, then rocks had to be found to support them, and long, slender branches for the roof.

Kalar took Zena with her to search for a suitable site. It had to give them a good view of the lake and be placed against the rocks on the other side, to protect them from winds as well as predators that might creep up unseen from behind. In front, they would have the fire, if they could keep it going during the rains to come. That was always a problem. If the fire was lit inside the shelter, they could hardly breathe, but if they left it outside, it was soon extinguished by the torrential afternoon rains. Night after night, Kalar had opened herself for a picture from the Mother that might help them with the problem, but so far, no message had come.

Perhaps Zena will solve that one, too, Kalar thought wryly as she wandered around the lake.

She came to a place where large boulders littered a gentle hillside. One boulder, especially, provided a wonderful view of the lake and all the land around it. Zena had already climbed up on the boulder; she stood there, arms outstretched, as if embracing everything before her. Kalar watched, intrigued. Zena looked so serious, as she often did. But she looked dazed, too, as if she were seeing something far away.

The small gazelle clambered stiffly up beside Zena and nuzzled her hand. For once, Zena paid scant attention. She felt as if her mind were somewhere else, almost as if another were seeing through her eyes. A picture began to form, of the lake, but it was not the lake as she saw it today. The reeds were thicker, and there were many birds. . . .

Three-Legs nuzzled her hand again, harder, and the picture disappeared. Zena laughed and pulled the insistent calf close against her. She would have to watch her pet carefully, now that there was another tribe living nearby. Like the Big Ones, they might not understand that Three-Legs was not food.

Kalar pronounced the site with the boulders perfect for their needs. There was a large level area where they could gather around the fire, and plenty of space for the shelter. They lugged their materials to the place and began to build. A day later, just as the rains began, they attached the last bundle of thatch, bound with vines so it would not blow away, and snuggled happily inside. This shelter was much better than the old one, they decided, glad now that they had built it.

Cere sat Zena in front of her and began to comb her tangled hair with a bunch of twigs she had bound together with a vine. The hair was thick and unruly, and the comb broke. Sighing, Cere set it aside. Tomorrow, she decided, she would hold Zena's hair under water, to clean it, so the combing would be easier.

Freed from Cere's pulling, Zena began to work on a project that had formed in her mind as they had traveled. They needed one more sling, and there was little chance that they would come across another antelope. She had decided to try making another big basket of vines, like the one they had used to carry Three-Legs. It would have to be sturdier, though, to carry an infant safely. She set to work with some vines she had brought with her into the shelter, trying to weave them back and forth more closely than she had before. Cere saw what she was doing, and came to help. Her long, slender fingers were nimble and quick, and Zena soon turned the project over to her. When the basket was finished, they padded it with soft grasses, and put Cere's infant, a girl-child called Filar, inside. She stuck her thumb in her mouth and slept.

After that, all of them tried making big baskets that were carried across their shoulders, as well as the small ones they normally carried in one hand. The larger ones were wonderfully useful. They could hold twigs and sticks for the fire, large melons and tubers, or piles of clean grasses to line the shelter where they slept. Cere's were always the best. None of them could weave as neatly and securely as she, and whenever one of them wanted a new basket, they asked her to make it in return for food or the performance of various tasks. Cere loved basket making and was always delighted to oblige.

The females living in their old shelter were fascinated by the slings. They had watched curiously as Kalar and the others built the new shelter, and had even imitated some of their techniques, piling on clumps of twigs and grasses where the old roof leaked. But it was the slings they really coveted. Every day, they came a little closer to the place where Cere worked, holding their infants tightly against their chests as they stared at her handiwork.

The children of both groups were not so restrained. They spent a few moments examining each other, then began to play noisily together, splashing through the shallows and hiding from each other behind rocks and trees. Only Zena stayed away. She was growing fast, and play was less appealing now than watching the birds and animals, or helping the adults, or working on one of the projects that often sprang full-blown into her mind, as if they had been there all along, only she had not seen them before.

The children's spontaneity seemed to give the women of the other tribe courage. The one who appeared to lead them pointed at the sling Zena was using, then at herself, as if asking to try it. Zena took the sling off and placed it around her shoulders. The strange female's eyes lit up in delight as she displayed herself proudly to her companions. They all began to point and gesture excitedly, wanting more of the slings.

Zena and Cere looked at each other in dismay. There were many of these women, too many to make slings for all of them. Zena held up a hand for silence, and gestured for the women to follow her. She led them to the place where the vines they used for baskets grew, and had each of them collect a bunch of long strands. Then she sat them down beside Cere to watch closely while she worked. Cere moved her fingers slowly, so they could imitate. Frowning in concentration, they began to copy her. At first, their efforts were clumsy, but they quickly became more adept at weaving the vines securely together and tying them in neat, strong knots.

Zena helped them for a time, then went off to sit by herself on the big boulder above the resting place. She kept Three-Legs close beside her, worried that the men of the other tribe might harm her pet. The women and children seemed to accept the little gazelle as a strange kind of young one; they laughed at its antics and fondled it gently. But she was not sure about the men. Males were different, she thought, more apt to kill quickly. That was true even among children. Yesterday, Kalar had become intensely angry with Lupe and Dorn. The two boys had killed all the baby birds in a nest, though they had no need for food.

"These are the Mother's creatures," she had told them, not raising her voice but speaking with such severity that they had trembled before her. "Never should you kill more than you need, lest there be none for the next year. You should thank the Mother for Her abundance, not use it for play!"

She had taken the bloody stones from the boys' hands and looked at them with despair in her eyes, as if feeling the pain they had inflicted on the birds.

Then she had turned and screamed at them, frightening them so badly they had not spoken for the rest of the day.

"Go, and do not come back to my presence until you have spoken words of sorrow to the Mother for what you have done."

The two boys had run off, shamefaced. Lett had followed them to make sure they did as Kalar had asked.

Zena stared at the landscape before her and thought of these things. She never had the desire to kill, except for food as she needed it, and then she always blessed the food, as Cere and Kalar had taught her. All creatures came from the Mother, and if they gave their lives for Zena or any of the others, they should be thanked, and remembered to the Mother, so She would receive them back into Her heart.

Zena sighed heavily, aware that the senseless killing had hurt her too. She could not understand it. Kalar had told her there was a force in males, some much more than others, that had to be controlled, lest it be used to harm others or hurt the Mother's creatures. Always, she had said, the men needed a wise one to help them control this force.

The thought confused Zena. The men she had known were so kind. Agar had helped her with Three-Legs, and Bran was always good to her, even if he teased. She thought it strange, too, that the Mother should make men this way. Next time she talked to Kalar, she would have to ask why this should be so.

She sat on, aware of a sadness in her that had a deeper source than the puzzling behavior of males. It came instead from something deep inside herself, from the questions always in her mind, questions that had no answers, about men, about mating, about why some had words and some did not, why the Mother gave young ones only to females, why animals behaved as they did. She wanted to know especially why the Mother allowed bad things to happen, like the killing of the birds or the harming of other animals for no reason. That seemed wrong to Zena and she wanted to fix it, as she wanted to fix all things.

None of the others seemed to be bothered by these questions, she reflected, except for Kalar. But when she had questions, the Mother gave her answers, in pictures. Why did the Mother not answer her, Zena, when she wanted to know something? Kalar had told her she must be patient, and wait many hours, many days or moons even, to receive the pictures. That seemed a long time to Zena. She wanted to know the answers right away.

She remembered that a picture had almost come into her mind when she had stood on this boulder, before they had built the shelter, but it had been swept away, when Three-Legs had nuzzled her. Zena decided she would try to get it back.

She stood, arms raised, as she had stood before, and closed her eyes. Three-Legs nuzzled her again. She frowned sternly at the little gazelle and put her hand on its back so it would be content and not bother her. Then she closed her eyes again and waited.

Slowly, a picture began to form in her mind, though she did not think it was like the one she had almost seen before. This one felt different, and it was not here, by the lake. Instead, Zena realized that she was standing in the clearing by the river, near the shelter there. The air smelled smoky, and there were noises, loud, terrifying noises that made her want to clap her hands over her ears, to protect them. The sounds came from animals, she thought.

She saw Kalar, standing near the river. The wise woman's face was contorted with fear. She was screaming, calling out a message. Zena heard her voice, but she could not make out the words. There was too much noise; it was worse now, a thunderous racket that got louder and louder. . . .

And then Kalar was running, running as if her life depended on it.

Zena screamed. She did not like this picture, did not want to see it. Sobbing, she thrust it from her mind. She pushed it away so hard that when Cere came running to ask what was wrong, Zena could not tell her what she had seen. The river, the noise, and the confusion were gone. All that remained was Kalar's terrified face.

Zena rubbed her eyes hard, to make the face go away too. Ignoring Cere's questions, she jumped from the boulder and ran off to play with the children. For all the time that remained at the lake, she played with frantic abandon, as if willing herself to be a child again, a child like them, who did not get pictures from the Mother.

CHAPTER

12

Zena and the children from both tribes sat under a clump of trees, shading themselves from the hot sun.

"We do words," she told the children. "Pictures too."

They looked at her expectantly. Zena had created games for them, games of naming things and making scratches in the earth that looked liked the named object, then trying to count the pictures. The children loved the games, and so did Zena. They distracted her, kept her thoughts busy so they could not return to her frightening vision on the boulder.

"Fish!" Zena called out.

Sima and Lupe immediately began to scratch a fishlike picture on the ground. Dorn managed a good imitation. The children from the other tribe copied them enthusiastically, but their scratches did not look much like a fish. Zena did not press them. They were eager to learn even if they were slower than Sima and the boys, who had been playing word games with her since infancy.

"Bird!" Zena instructed. This one was harder, but they scratched away industriously.

"Many," Zena said, pointing to all the scratchings. She held up her fingers. Sima pulled down one of Zena's fingers for each drawing, saying a word they had devised for each. When she got to the end of the fingers, she frowned, unable to think what to do next.

Zena laughed and rumpled her hair, too hot and thirsty to start on another hand. Instead, she led the children to the lake to drink and cool off; then she wandered over to join Kalar and Cere. They, too, were sitting under big shade trees, surrounded by eager students. Cere was helping the adults from the other tribe to make baskets, and Kalar was speaking to them of the Mother, as she had many times before. They had grasped the idea immediately, almost with relief, as if the Mother had long resided in their hearts and minds, and Kalar's words had confirmed their belief. It seemed obvious to them that a force greater than themselves must exist, since the sun rose each day, the moon each night, and storms came, and life renewed itself continuously. That the force was Mother was obvious, too. Each of them had a mother, so the earth itself and everything in it must have a mother as well.

The Mother was like their wise one, they realized, only much more wise. The Mother was the Great Wise One, the one to whom they could now turn whenever they had problems they could not solve. She was Life-Giver, too, who caused new life to form in the bellies of females, and in the earth after the rains.

Lett appeared, holding a bunch of the big-breasted, wide-hipped statues. At Kalar's request, he had made some for the women from the other tribe. She wanted them to have a tangible symbol of the Mother, to help them remember.

Kalar thanked him and stood. "May the Mother be with you always," she said, as she gestured to their wise one to come forward and accept the figures. She, in turn, handed one to each woman whose belly was round with child.

The children scrambled up from the lake to watch the ceremony, their eyes wide with awe. Zena beckoned to the smallest one, a boy from the other tribe who had just learned to walk. He toddled over and plunked himself into her lap.

She would miss them, she reflected, rubbing her hands over his smooth, sun-warmed skin. But in another way she was glad the time had come to leave the lake and head back once again toward the river. Travel always excited her, and they could not stay much longer. The rains this year had been sparse, and with two tribes in residence, food was already hard to find.

The next day she waved good-bye to the children, calling out a word that meant *next time*. The children repeated the word, but their faces were sad. They cared deeply for Zena, and for the games that challenged their imaginations. They loved to puzzle over everything they saw, to think of new words and ideas. Now they would have to do it by themselves.

The adults stood in a cluster around the children. Each member of the tribe held a basket, and each woman proudly wore the sling she had made. One of the women held up her basket in one hand, the figure Lett had made for her in the other, and spoke the message Kalar had taught them. The others imitated her gesture and repeated her words.

"Go with the Mother," they said, and their voices were a chorus of blessing in the still air.

Kalar turned once and waved. "May the Mother live always in your hearts," she answered. Then she moved on without looking back. When the time came to lead her tribe, she wanted only to look forward.

She led them first to a marshy area where food and water were almost always abundant, then they slowly worked their way north and east in the direction of the river. They were in no hurry this time, for food was still available along much of the route. Often, they spent many weeks at one site. They built a shelter and stayed there until food became hard to find, then they moved on. Zena loved these prolonged stays, for they gave her a chance to teach children in nearby tribes. She gathered them around her, to show them her games, while Cere taught the adults how to make baskets and Kalar spoke of the Mother. Both children and adults listened avidly, their faces intent. It was almost as if they had been waiting, Zena thought, as plants wait for rain, for someone to teach them the new ideas and skills. When she tried to express this thought to Kalar, the wise woman nodded agreement.

"It is in this way the Mother has changed us," she said gravely. "All now have the desire to learn."

"You must teach others as we have taught you," Kalar told the eager listeners, and they did. Each tribe passed on all they had learned to others they met in their travels. These tribes taught other tribes; each generation taught the next, and so it went, year after year, generation after generation, until almost all the tribes in the area had become familiar with Zena's inventions, with the concept of the Mother.

When they finally reached the river, Zena felt a pang of sadness despite her pleasure at being once again in her favorite place. There were no new children here to teach, and she would miss watching their faces light up when they first discovered new words and ideas, found answers to their questions. In another way, though, teaching frustrated her. She could answer questions for others, but no one could answer hers.

She watched a group of antelopes grazing in the distance. Some of them were jumping on the backs of other ones from behind.

"What are they doing?" Sima touched Zena's hand to get her attention.

"They mate," Zena answered, "like the adults."

Sima nodded, content with the explanation. But Zena was not content. She wanted to know if mating gave antelopes pleasure, as Kalar and Cere told her it gave adults pleasure. She did not think so. The female antelopes usually tried to run away when the males approached them. If the act gave them pleasure, why did they run? And if it gave no pleasure, why did they bother to do it at all?

Lions, she had observed, were different. A group of them often lazed around the lake. She had watched the females nudge the males, over and over again, trying to get them to mate. The males often seemed reluctant, but the females insisted.

"It is the Mother's way," Kalar had told her when she had asked. "All animals mate, and all are different." But that answer, too, failed to satisfy Zena. She wanted to know why it was the Mother's way, and why animals were different.

The question took on renewed urgency some months after they had returned to the river. Three-Legs was a full-grown female now, her leg long ago healed, and she was becoming more and more interested in other gazelles. Zena was sure mating had something to do with her interest. Twice already, she had run toward a herd and had let a male sniff at her. Each time, she had run back to Zena. But now she was approaching the herd for the third time, and she was much less skittish than before. Zena watched with a heavy heart as the big male approached her once again. This time, Three-Legs let him mate with her; then she disappeared into the herd.

Zena turned and ran into the trees, trying hard to suppress the sobs in her throat. If Three-Legs wanted to be with her own kind, she could not keep her. Kalar had told her that over and over, and Zena knew she was right. Three-Legs was not Zena's; she was a gazelle, and gazelles belonged with each other.

A solid lump of misery settled in Zena's belly. She felt as if part of herself had been suddenly wrenched away, that she would never be quite whole again, without Three-Legs.

Bowing her head so none of the others could see her contorted face, Zena trudged slowly toward the small glen where she had been born. She felt more peaceful here than in any other place. Even her questions seemed to lose their urgency when she sat in the circle of stones, as if there were no need to search for answers, to struggle to understand.

Closing her eyes, she forced herself to pay attention to the sounds of birds calling to each other, of water splashing through the stream. Another sound made her sit up straight. Something was munching right beside her. Puzzled, she opened her eyes. Three-Legs was standing near her, browsing contentedly on some low bushes. She had come back!

The tears Zena had been trying to control poured from her eyes as she ran over and hugged the little gazelle. Three-Legs nuzzled her affectionately and went back to her browsing, as if nothing had happened. When Zena rose to leave, Three-Legs followed close behind her, and she did not stray toward the herd again.

Toward the end of the day, heavy clouds gathered, and a jagged streak of lightning struck the hillside where the gazelles were grazing. Fire spurted high into the air as the dry grasses were instantly consumed. The rainy season was approaching once again, and because the rains had been so sparse the year before, the fires were unusually ferocious.

The gazelles began to run, their backs creating delicate arcs in the air as they leaped away from the danger. In minutes, the whole herd had disappeared. Zena was relieved. Now she would not have to worry about losing Three-Legs, for a while at least.

Early the next morning, she wandered up behind the clearing toward the fires, to look for burning sticks. Their fire had gone out during the night, and sticks were always plentiful in places where the flames had passed already. This time, she left Three-Legs behind with Sima and Lupe, fearing the gazelle would burn her feet or her delicate nose as she sought green fodder beneath the layers of soot and blackened grass.

Zena clambered up a steep slope to reach the level, burned area beyond. A short, overhanging cliff blocked her way; she pulled herself up the rocks on one side of it. A movement just beneath her caught her eye, and she froze. A lion, or more likely a leopard, could live in the dark space beneath the overhang, but she had never seen one anywhere near this place. There was no smell of a den, either. Probably it was just a small animal of some kind.

Hugging her body against the ground, she peered cautiously over the cliff. Nothing moved now, but she could make out a dark bundle lying on the rocky ground. Perhaps it was an antelope, like the one they had found last time there were fires. That would be a wonderful discovery. She would be able to make some more slings, and the meat would keep them fed for days.

Zena went closer. The creature on the ground stirred and made a moaning noise. She jumped in surprise. The sound was not that of an animal; it was the sound of another like herself. She ran over, fearing that a member of the tribe had been hurt. But it was a stranger, a young male a little larger than herself.

She bent over him. His eyelids fluttered open, revealing eyes of a pale, nut-brown color. Yellow flecks were sprinkled on the pupils, as if bits of sunlight had caught there. Zena stared at them, entranced. She had never seen eyes like that before.

The young male uttered a stream of words she could not understand. Most of the tribes they encountered had words very much like theirs, but this one seemed to have entirely different ones. She watched closely as he spoke, as if her eyes might grasp what her ears were unable to comprehend.

The torrent of words dried up abruptly as he realized she did not understand. Fear came into his eyes then, and a terrible sorrow. He tried to lurch to his feet, but he fell back again, overcome by dizziness.

"I help you," Zena said. She pointed to herself, and then to him. The boy did not answer, but watched her warily as she leaned close to examine him. A big bump on the back of his head explained his dizziness. There were scorched places on his hands and feet, as if he had run through fire and fallen into it as well, and one wrist was swollen and discolored.

"Wait!" Zena commanded, as she rose to her feet. She would have to get help; she could never manage to carry him by herself.

The fear in his yellow-flecked eyes increased as they heard steps on the hillside. Zena called out, hoping it was one of the others, and heard Bran answer. He came quickly, alerted by the anxiety in Zena's voice. The boy tried desperately to get to his feet when Bran bent over him, but the concern in the older man's face was so obvious that he relaxed again. Together, Zena and Bran helped him to stand and walk slowly into the clearing.

The others came running, calling excitedly to each other. Kalar said nothing, but gestured to Zena and Bran to bring the stranger to her. She examined him closely.

"His wrist may be broken," Zena told her, "and his head is hurt. He fell, I think. I found him under the cliff."

Kalar nodded. "Get the herbs for burns, and for swelling," she instructed Zena.

The young male watched curiously as they bound his swollen wrist between two straight sticks, as the old wise one had taught them. Kalar did not think it was broken, but the splints would keep the wrist from bending. After that, they prepared some poultices. One went on the boy's head, others on his feet and hands; still another was bound around his wrist. Sima and the two boys began to giggle. The stranger looked funny with all those bandages. And his eyes were so odd!

He looked up at them and grinned, but the expression did not last. Pain quickly clouded his face again. Zena did not think the pain came from his wounds. It seemed instead to come from his thoughts.

Cere appeared in front of him with a melon and some pieces of meat from a small pig Bran and Agar had caught the night before. He nodded to her, thanking her with his gesture, and began to eat voraciously. He was famished, Zena realized. The questions she could not ask battered at her. Where had he come from, and what had happened to him? Why was he alone? He was taller than she was, but she did not think he was much older, and that was too young to be alone.

She tried to think how she could ask what had happened to the others in his tribe, but finally she gave up and simply looked at him questioningly as she gestured toward the hillside and the fire above it.

The pain in his face increased. He passed his hand across his eyes wearily, and his whole body seemed to slump. Words tumbled from him, but Zena understood nothing. She shook her head in frustration. He stopped speaking and began to show her with his body what had happened. He pointed to himself, then made figures in the air with his hand for others. Pulling himself to his feet, he ran a few steps in one direction, pushing the others the opposite way. He gestured wildly toward the fire, and his hands surged in the air, representing the flames and the heat. Fear enveloped his face, then a terrible sadness. He pointed to Zena, then to Cere, and tears began to run down his cheeks. Finally, he fell to the ground, gesturing with one arm, to show he had fallen.

Zena watched, transfixed by his performance. Had the others of his tribe died? Or had he been separated from them in the fire? And why had he pointed to her, and then to Cere?

She would never know unless she learned his words, or taught him theirs. She decided to start immediately.

"Zena," she told him, pointing to herself.

He regarded her seriously and then pointed to himself, saying a word that sounded like their word for *fish*.

Zena tried to say it, too. The boy laughed, and repeated the word. "Lotan," he seemed to be saying. Zena tried again, and this time he nodded.

So his name was Lotan. That was a start. She pointed to Sima and said their word for *child*. Then she gestured strongly with both hands, as if trying to draw a word from him.

The young male's eyes lit up with comprehension. He uttered a word, pointing to the child.

Zena committed it to memory and tried another. Soon, she understood his words for most of the objects and people in the immediate vicinity, as well as a word for Lotan's wounds. She was especially interested in Lotan's expression when she asked for the word for *mother*. The sadness came over his face when he uttered his word, and stayed there. He pointed to Bran, and then made gestures, as if fighting.

"Male wound mother?" Zena's words were halting, but Lotan understood. He nodded vigorously, and rose to his feet again, pointing to the place from which he had come.

"Help mother?" Zena pointed to herself and Bran and Kalar, then at Lotan, hoping he would get the meaning of *help*. Again, his eyes lit up.

"Help mother," he repeated, nodding furiously.

Kalar spoke for the first time. "You must sleep first," she said firmly.

Zena translated this message as well as she could, and Lotan nodded reluctantly. He would not be able to walk very far until his burns improved, anyway.

All that afternoon and into the evening, Zena sat by the fire, which they had managed to relight, and learned words from Lotan. Kalar watched her, frowning a little. The child was so intense, so determined to learn everything she wanted to know immediately. She did not stop to eat, to rest, even to pat Three-Legs.

It was time to start teaching Zena seriously, she realized, not just of plants and their uses, but of the Mother, of what it meant to be a wise one. Almost ten years had passed now since Zena's birth, and she was old enough. Already, she knew so much, more than any of the others, about the world around them. She could imagine, and invent, find answers to puzzles. But that was not enough. She needed to understand and accept the Mother's ways, Her infinite patience and strength.

Zena was of the Mother, destined to serve Her and speak for Her, of that Kalar was certain. But she knew, too, that Zena would find the task of learning the Mother's ways more difficult than some. She was impetuous and often stubborn, too ready to find her own solutions without help from any other. Zena needed to learn to open herself to the Mother's wisdom, combine it with her own abilities. Otherwise, her intelligence could lead her astray. Especially, she had to learn to accept. The Mother's ways were mysterious, harsh as well as kind. No one could understand them fully. Even Zena could not. No; she must learn to accept. It was the only way.

Tomorrow, Kalar decided. Tomorrow, as they prepared to go to the lake once again, she would begin the initiation.

II

The tribe gathered around the hearth fire toward the end of the day, as was their custom. Lotan hovered uncertainly at the edges of the group. Seeing his unhappy face, Zena pulled him down beside her with a reassuring grin.

"Lotan is his name," she told the others. "He showed me some of what happened. He went one way, and his tribe another. A male hurt his mother, I think, and he worries about her. I will know better when I learn more of his words.

"He is very sad, I think," she added, regarding Lotan's pensive expression.

The others nodded sympathetically. Kalar was about to reply when a commotion brought everyone to their feet. The wildebeests across the river had begun to bellow and stamp restlessly against the dry earth. All day, Zena and the others had watched clouds of dust billow into the air as thousands of the shaggy animals traveled slowly south. They passed this way each year at the same time, seeming to smell even the possibility of rain. The tribe had not paid much attention to their passage, except to realize that if the wildebeests were moving, the rains would surely come soon.

Kalar went down to the river to see what was happening. Lett followed. They stared at each other, frowning. No words were needed to express what was in both their minds. They had watched the wildebeests for many years, and knew that the huge herds were closer than they had ever been before. They also knew the wildebeests had to cross the river to get to the grassy plains to the south. Usually, they crossed beyond the river's deep bend, about half a day's journey away. It seemed impossible that they might cross here; they had never done such a thing before.

Still, their nearness made Kalar uneasy. It was hard to tell exactly which way the animals were heading, or even to see individual bodies among the churning mass. The dust was too thick, and the light was beginning to fade as well. But it did look as if the agitated beasts were coming this way.

She yelled to the others to go into the shelter. Unless the big

beasts stampeded, they should be safe there. She turned for a last
look at the plain across the river, and her eyes widened in dismay.
There was fire behind the wildebeests, fire that was moving fast.
Only a moment before, the horizon had been clear. Now it glowed
orange, then scarlet, as the fire caught a grove of trees and hurled
flames into the sky. Fires were burning to the south of the wildebeests, too, blocking their normal route. That was why they seemed
to be heading for the river. There was no other way to go.

A thick spear of lightning sheared across the sky and hit the
ground in the middle of the throng of animals. Another came, and
then another. Deafening claps of thunder accompanied the brilliant
flashes. They were so loud that Kalar's eardrums felt pierced. They
boomed and reverberated across the plains.

Bellows of fear sprang from the throats of hundreds of the burly
creatures across the river. Then, abruptly, they began to run. A few
animals thrust themselves forward, jostling and shoving for position; the others followed. Within seconds, all of them were galloping
in a thick, fast-moving line of thrashing hoofs and heavy bodies
and impenetrable dust. And now there was no doubt about their
direction. They were running straight toward the river and the
clearing that lay beyond it.

Lett screamed into the clamor. "Go to the trees," he shouted.
"Into the trees, fast!" But his voice was lost in the thunderous
pounding of hoofs.

Kalar whirled and sprinted for the shelter. The massive body of
animals, so large it covered almost the entire plain, was stampeding.
The ground shook beneath her feet, and the noise was overwhelming. She did not think the others could possibly have heard Lett's
warning. But even if they had, there would barely be time to get
to the trees. Wildebeests ran like the wind when they were frightened. And they would trample everything, everyone, in their path.
Nothing stopped them, not water, not a thick barrier of thorns.
Only the big trees on either side of the clearing might deter them.
They would be funneled between the trees, through the clearing,
through the shelter. . . .

She ran faster. The first animals would be upon them in moments.
The river would not even slow them down; it was shallow at this
time of the year, and not very wide.

"The trees," she screamed, as she saw Nyta hesitating in the
middle of the clearing, uncertain where to go. Nyta sprinted for
the woods with her infant, pulling Sima behind. But the child was
paralyzed with fright, and dropped to the ground. Kalar saw Zena
grab her hand and drag her toward a big tree. She shoved her into

the arms of the strange male and scrambled up the tree. He pushed the child up into Zena's arms and climbed up himself.

Good, Kalar thought, *Zena is safe*, but she kept going, for she had not seen Cere, or any of the others. The dust was so thick it was hard to see anything, or even breathe.

She looked up again, toward the shelter. There was movement in it, she was sure of it. The others must still be huddled there, believing they were safe. She must warn them, get them out.

The wildebeests had started to cross. She could hear the splashes, the roars and bellows and screams as smaller animals were trampled by bigger ones. They had gone into a frenzy of panic; they knew nothing except that they were running. They would run and run even if they killed each other, even if they killed themselves. Kalar could feel their panic in her bones.

Lett passed her, breathing hard. Had he, too, seen movement in the shelter? Kalar tried to catch him, to send him into the trees, while there was still time, but the breath had gone from her body, and she could not make her legs go any faster. She staggered and almost fell.

Suddenly she saw another figure, sprinting toward her from the edge of the woods. It was Cere, searching the clearing before her with frantic eyes.

"No," Kalar screamed. "No! Go back! Zena is safe!" But Cere did not hear. She ran on, her face transfigured with fear.

A roiling cloud of dust enveloped Kalar. The wildebeests were right behind her; she could feel the thuds in the earth, hear the hot breath of the panting animals. It was too late. . . . She knew it was too late.

In the instant before the huge beasts reached her, she looked up and saw Lett near the edge of the clearing. A child was tucked under each of his arms.

He had gone to rescue the others before he ran himself. Kalar knew that wordlessly, and so he would die, and the little ones with him, for the wildebeests were almost upon him too. Their horns were lowered, and their eyes gleamed red with panic. She saw Lett throw one of the children toward the trees, and then he disappeared beneath the thrashing hoofs.

Kalar closed her eyes. Lett; they had killed Lett. He had been her mate so many times, and she had loved him. . . . Always it was Lett she could count on to give advice, to soothe her. More than any other, he had understood how hard it could be to speak for the Mother, to know Her ways—

She felt the first hoof crash into her back. Kalar bent low to the dusty earth, seeking its embrace, and called out to the Mother. She did not know if she said words, but her message was clear in her mind.

It is to Zena I entrust my place. It is Zena who will hear Your messages. Zena will hear if You give her time. . . . Spare her, Great Mother, so she can grow to be the one who speaks for You.

Then the hoofs passed across her body and broke it, and she ceased to know at all.

High in the tree, Zena felt an uncontrollable tremor pass through her body. She shook her head, bewildered, then she began to cry in huge, wrenching sobs. She did not know why she wept so suddenly, except that she was frightened, but she could not make herself stop. She wept and wept, as the wildebeests crashed below her, and neither Sima nor Lotan could comfort her.

Finally, the wracking sobs diminished. Zena leaned her head against a branch in exhaustion. She lacked the strength to cry any longer, but the agony that had unleashed her tears remained stubbornly lodged in her belly. There was a terrible feeling inside her, as if she had done something wrong, but she did not know what it was.

And then she remembered, so suddenly that her whole body stiffened in horror, and she almost lost her grip on the tree. This was the picture she had seen. It was the Mother's picture.

She gasped, struggling to breathe. The Mother had tried to warn her, but she had not listened. Kalar—she had seen Kalar running, but then she had pushed the vision away, and now there was no way to know what had happened, if she could have helped. Why, why had she not listened to the Mother?

Zena pounded her fists against the tree, desperate with fear and guilt. Were they all dead? Was that why she had such a terrible sick feeling in her belly?

She did not know, could not tell. She could see nothing but the furry backs of animals, writhing and seething below her. Billowing clouds of thick dust, colorless in the fading light, obscured everything else—the clearing, the trees, even the sky. She could not hear either. All other sounds were lost beneath the overwhelming rush of pounding hoofs, the brutal bellowing, the dreadful screams as fallen animals were trampled, the thick sound of gasping breath as the wildebeests ran and ran and ran.

For hours they passed. Wave after wave of them surged across the river, through the clearing. Some, blinded by dust, charged into the woods. Trees shook and branches fell. They swerved in a body, to find their way out again, leaving a trail of devastation behind them. Others crashed drunkenly into the shelter. The high wall of thorns stopped the first animals that hit it; they fell to their knees, their bones shattered and their skin lacerated. Their fellows kept on going, using the fallen animals as a bridge to go up and over the formidable barrier. Screams filled the air, closer now, and Zena could not tell if they came from the wildebeests or from her tribe-mates. She pulled Sima's head close against her chest to drown out the terrible noises.

Darkness descended, and the sounds began to diminish. Slowly, the pounding of hoofs, the bellows, became more distant, and the dust settled. Then there was only silence.

Lotan touched Zena's shoulder gently, and pointed to the ground. But now she could not bear to go down. She did not fear the wilde-beests; they had spent their passion. She feared what she would find. The branch that supported her seemed infinitely comforting in contrast to the horrors that might await her below. She clung to it doggedly, and would not move.

All night, she stayed there, desperate with uncertainty and fear. At intervals, she called out to the others. Once, she thought she heard an answer, but she could not be sure.

When the light came again, she forced herself to move. Slowly, reluctantly, she lowered herself from the tree and ventured into the clearing. Lotan and Sima followed. The child was weeping quietly.

Zena tripped over a body and knelt to look, but she rose again quickly. Once, it had been Lett. She had loved him dearly. In his quiet way, he had helped them almost as much as Kalar. By his side lay a shapeless bundle. It was one of the children, she thought, but it was hard to tell. Its head had been trampled. Another small form was sprawled near the trees. Zena did not stop to examine it.

A warm nose nuzzled her hand. Zena jumped and whirled around. It was Three-Legs! She must have run away, terrified by the commotion. She hugged the little gazelle briefly, and then went on. She was glad Three-Legs had not been trampled, but it was the others she wanted most.

She came to the remains of the shelter. It was nothing more than a bundle of flattened sticks, covered with the bodies of wildebeests. A few still struggled. Arms and legs stuck up through the carnage— arms and legs that did not belong to the wildebeests. None of them moved. Zena looked at them almost dispassionately, and wan-dered away.

A wildebeest calf rose on wobbly knees, bleating piteously, and stumbled off toward the burned hillside. Zena paid no attention. She walked slowly into the clearing as if she were not there at all.

None of this seemed possible. Last night, they had sat together, talking, and now there was nothing.

Cere, she thought suddenly. *Surely Cere had escaped.* She must have heard Kalar's warning, must have known she should go to the trees. She had been standing near Nyta, and Nyta had run for the trees. Bran had been there, too; she was sure he had.

As if reflecting her thoughts, a cry suddenly came from the edge of the woods on the far side of the clearing. It was Bran calling, and Lupe was behind him. Bran had recently become Lupe's hero, and he followed him everywhere. He must have followed him last night too; his devotion had saved his life.

Zena ran to them, rejoicing. If *they* were alive, Cere and Nyta must have escaped too. She looked eagerly into the woods behind them, but no one else emerged. The hope that had been in her heart sank heavily, and she broke away from Bran's warm hug.

Lotan called sharply from the trees. She ran to him, hope flaring again. He pointed to the ground. Nyta lay there, the infant in her arms. No sound came from the baby, usually so lusty and demanding, but Nyta's eyes were open. Tears squeezed from them when she saw Zena's face. She tried to get up, but dizziness swamped her, and she fell back, moaning.

Zena knelt beside her anxiously and started to examine the wound on her head. Nyta pulled her hands away and gestured toward the infant. Zena took it from her, and knew immediately that the baby was dead. Its tiny body was cold, already stiff.

"He has gone back to the Mother," she told Nyta gently, as she placed the infant beside her.

Nyta turned her face away, and made no further effort to rise. But then Sima saw her mother. She burst into loud and happy weeping, and flung herself against Nyta. Zena left them there together and went toward the clearing again. She had to find Cere, Cere and Kalar. Theirs were the faces she most wanted to see.

A vulture flapped noisily over her head, as if to land beside her. Zena waved her arms and shouted. It rose again and perched clumsily in a tree. Its eyes were fixed on the ground near her feet. Against her will, for she was terrified she would find something she did not want to see, Zena looked down.

It was Cere. Zena knew her immediately, though she could identify her only by her hands, the long-fingered, nimble hands that had made such perfect baskets. The rest of her had been trampled beyond recognition. Why? Why had she not run for the trees?

Zena pushed her fists hard against her eyes to stop the tears, to stop herself from looking at anything else. She did not want to see, did not want to know. She wanted only to be left alone, to be taken from this place of horror, to run away, not to look for more of the ones she loved, especially not for Kalar.

Kalar was dead. She knew that. Kalar had to be dead, because she would have tried to save the others before going to the trees. Kalar was near here too. Zena could sense her presence, even in death. But she did not want to see.

She looked up at the sky. It was brilliantly blue, cloudless, as if nothing had happened. But the vultures knew. They soared in lazy circles, awaiting her departure. Zena kept her eyes fastened on them so she would not have to look down as she wandered on.

But when she came to the place where Kalar had died, Zena looked down anyway, compelled by a sense that the wise woman's face might tell her something, might give a reason why these terrible things had happened. And she was right. Kalar's face was buried in the earth, and when Zena turned it over, it was almost intact. Her eyes were closed, and her face wore an expression of reverence, as if the last thing she had done was speak to the Mother.

Anger suffused Zena, unexpected, boiling anger. It overwhelmed her, filled every part of her. Nothing was left inside her but anger. She jumped up and stormed around the clearing, picking up everything she could find, bits of tools and baskets, smashed now beyond recognition, pieces of wood from the fire, from the shelter, and flinging them wildly into the air. When she had thrown every object within reach, she pounded the earth with a rock, and screamed at the sky.

"No," she screamed. "You cannot have her. You cannot have any of them. You are Mother, the Mother we trusted, and this is what You have done. No! No, no, no!"

She screamed until her voice was hoarse, then flung herself against the ground and wept. Her body shook with anguished sobs. But just as abruptly as they had started, the sobs stopped, and she sat up, a stubborn expression on her face.

"No," she muttered again angrily, between her teeth. "This cannot be. You are Life-Giver. Kalar loved You. We all loved You. No. You cannot do this. It must be changed."

She waited, fists clenched, as if she expected that at any moment, the clearing would be as it had always been before: Kalar would appear, and so would Cere, and Lett would be there, and all the others. The sound of their voices would come, and the babies would wail again.

Zena whirled. A baby *was* crying. She heard it clearly, just for a moment. But she couldn't have heard it. They were all dead; she would have heard an infant before now if any were still alive.

She ran in the direction of the sound. It had come from the shelter, from somewhere beneath the horrible battered bodies, the broken limbs and mangled flesh, the blood and bone and bits of wildebeests and people that littered the trampled ground in unimaginable mixtures. She began to paw through the refuse, but bile rose in her throat, and she had to stop. No further sound had come, anyway, and she thought she had only imagined the cry, as in a dream. But Lotan and Bran were there, too, searching frantically beneath the bloody piles.

It was Lupe who found the infant. Less horrified by the litter than the others, for he was too young to understand fully, he dug without inhibition beneath a battered carcass. He felt something move and pulled it out. Zena ran to him and grabbed the tiny female.

Filar! It was Filar, Cere's infant. Sobs constricted Zena's throat as the infant nestled at her neck. She swallowed them determinedly. Perhaps the Mother had helped a little, by giving her Cere's child, but She had still killed Cere herself, and Kalar, too, and most of the others.

Miraculously, Filar seemed unhurt. But she was terribly hungry, and once she felt herself free of the body that had saved her life even as it pinned her to the ground and made breathing difficult, screaming nearly impossible, she took a deep breath and yelled. The sound roused even Nyta, who came hobbling out of the woods. She had twisted her ankle when the wildebeests had knocked her from the tree, as well as hitting her head.

She looked gravely at the screaming infant. It was not hers, but she would gladly feed it. Her breasts were painful with unused milk, anyway. The little one could take it.

Zena went back to the place where Lupe had found Filar. She felt compelled to know who had saved the baby with her body. But when she looked more carefully, it was hard to tell. She thought it might have been Tempa, or maybe Agar. Perhaps Cere had handed the infant to one of them and then tried to come back to retrieve it.

She would never know now, but Zena knew she would always wonder. The knowledge that she had been more important to Cere than any other lay heavily within her. Always there would linger in her heart the terrible thought that Cere had been looking for her, not the infant, that she had not seen her reach the trees, and had come to find her beloved Zena. Instead, she had found a cruel, unnecessary death.

Zena's anger hardened, obliterating all other feelings, even her guilt because she had refused to listen when the Mother had tried to warn her. Her tears dried with her anger; after that day, she did not weep, or even mourn. There was no room inside her for anything but rage at the Mother for allowing those who loved Her to die such horrible deaths. The anger churned deep and strong within her as she and the other survivors traveled far from the verdant clearing by the river that had sheltered them so many times. Overnight, their peaceful refuge had become a place of terror and death, of mangled bodies and the smell of rot.

She would never return, Zena vowed, never think of this place again, of the horrors that had happened here, or even of the loved ones she had lost. Especially, she would not think again of the Mother. The Mother had betrayed her, had betrayed all of them, and that she would never forgive.

III

The vultures descended, the hyenas and wild dogs came, and a lioness that passed by fed herself and her cubs. Other predators joined her, drawn by the scent. For once, they did not have to fight for a chance to gorge on the carcasses. There was plenty for all. When they had finished, smaller animals gnawed the bones, and hordes of insects cleaned them. And after that came heat and dryness, and fires, and finally the rains. Brief, savage storms sent the river seething over its banks, depositing silt and debris that further erased the signs of destruction. Soon, all that was left to mark the place where Kalar and her tribe had lived was the blessed circle of stones in the secluded glen beyond the clearing, where Zena had been plucked from the belly of her mother.

CHAPTER
13

Two months earlier, Lotan had sat quietly beside his mother, Ralak, and watched her face harden with worry as the hours passed. The men had left before the sun had come over the horizon, to look for the carcass of a zebra one of the women had spotted the day before. Now night had almost fallen, and still they had not returned.

Ralak rose to gather more of the pungent twigs she had put on the fire so the men would smell it from afar. She handed the infant to Lotan, to free her hands for the task. He accepted the baby gladly. Her funny smell and the cooing sounds she made amused him. He tried to elicit a few noises by jiggling her gently, but she was sleeping soundly and did not respond. He contented himself with watching her eyelids flutter and her tiny mouth purse up as if she were sucking.

She had been born only a few moons ago. Lotan remembered the night well. His mother had struggled all through the day, all through the dark hours, to bring the infant forth. When it still had not come at daybreak, Toro, the other adult female, and her almost grown daughter, Metep, had looked at each other with despair in their eyes and quietly muttered a word. Lotan's heart had gone rigid with fear. He was certain they had said the word for *death*.

But Ralak was strong, and refused to give up. She was the tribe's wise one, and she knew the others needed her. Digging her fingers into the earth, she called upon the force that lived deep in its bowels, the force from which all life emerged, and asked for strength to bear the pain, but even more, she called on her own reserves of stamina. Steeling herself to endure still more of the brutal contractions, she gave up her body to the labor. Each time her muscles tensed, she pushed with all her might, ignoring the terrible ripping of skin within her. Finally, when the sun had almost reached the top of the sky, she felt the baby's head between her legs. She called to Toro.

"Pull!" she commanded. Toro placed her hands on each side of the slippery skull and pulled as hard as she could. Her hands slid off. She rubbed them against the earth and tried again. This time the infant came out. It wailed immediately.

"Good," Ralak thought. "It wails, so it will live." Then she closed her eyes and lapsed into a time of semiconsciousness. The place where she lingered hung somewhere between sleeping and waking, between living and dying. The present had no meaning for her; she was aware of nothing except a tingling pull at her breasts when Toro placed the baby there to suckle. But her inner world was filled with sounds and sensations, and memories.

Long ago, Ralak had lived in a damp, forested area. She went to this place again in her mind. Tall trees closed in around her, filtering out the sun, so that her world grew dim and shadowy. She smelled ferns, and mosses, the moist earthiness of decaying litter on the forest floor. She saw the tribe into which she had been born, watched it disintegrate until only she and her brother were left. One at a time, the others had died of a sickness that robbed them of strength until they could no longer eat or even stand.

Her mother had been the last to go. Ralak saw her face again, heard her speak of the earthforce that gave life and took it away again in endless, random cycles—only her mother was not speaking, for there were few words to describe such things. Ralak listened in another way, hearing her mother as if their minds were one. In that manner, she came to understand that just as the earthforce caused new grasses to grow, bushes and trees to bear fruit, gave life to animals of every kind, so, too, it caused death and destruction, when mountains exploded and the ground cracked into pieces. At other times, the earthforce grew restless and escaped to the skies. It flew upward like a great bird into the tumultuous clouds, then charged toward the ground again in brilliant spears of lightning that burned everything in their path as it sought re-entry to its home.

Ralak's eyes rolled and twitched behind her closed lids as the memories coursed through her brain. No other part of her moved at all. Her stillness, and the blood that came from her, terrified Lotan. The faces of the others frightened him too. They seemed astonished that Ralak still breathed, that milk still flowed from her breasts, even when she lay there as if dead. But she *was* alive, and Lotan decided he must keep her that way. Over and over, he tipped cool water into her mouth, using a small gourd so he could dribble it in slowly. The first time, Ralak choked, but after that, she seemed to sense his presence and was able to swallow.

On the fourth day, her eyes opened. She looked as if she were far away, in some other place. But when Lotan put some berries he was holding into her mouth, she chewed them slowly. The next day, she raised herself on her elbow and called to Toro.

"Infant," she said weakly. "See infant." Toro brought the little one to her. Ralak's cracked lips, still caked with the blood that had accumulated when she bit herself in pain, widened into a smile. She reached out and took the baby for a moment, then sank back in exhaustion. Lotan bent over her, afraid she would not move again. She pressed his hand briefly, in reassurance. Heartened by the gesture, he soaked soft grasses in the stream, and gently wiped the blood from her face.

When the light came again, Ralak crawled toward the stream and immersed herself in a shallow pool to cleanse her body. The action seemed to revive her. She directed the others to remove all signs of the birth, so predators would not be attracted. Then she lay still again for many days, but now, Lotan saw, her stillness had energy in it. She was herself again even if she barely moved. She told all of them what to do, called for the infant, ate and drank with enthusiasm. Fear drained from his body for the first time since the birth.

Now, three moons had passed, and Ralak seemed to have recovered completely. Until tonight, when the two men had failed to return, her features had been free of strain.

The baby stirred and began to root against Lotan's thin chest, seeking food. He rose and went to his mother.

"She is hungry," he told Ralak, handing her the infant. "I find sticks now. I watch."

Ralak nodded and went to sit by the fire while she nursed the baby. She peered nervously into the woods. Though Lotan did not know it, another problem worried her almost as much as the missing men. For many days now, a strange male had been lurking in the area. Ralak did not like the look of him. Instead of approaching, to see if he might join the group, he had peered at them from the trees with hard, angry eyes. Whenever one of the men had gone closer to challenge him, he had disappeared.

She hugged the infant protectively. Once, long ago, a male had attacked her tribe while the men were half a day's journey away.

He had killed her tiny brother and another infant before the men had returned to help her mother and the other women drive him away. Males like that had too much of the harsh earthforce in them, her mother had told her, and could not control their violence. Ralak did not fully understand how this could be, or why they should kill infants, but she was terribly afraid the stranger was one of them. She must find the men quickly, lest he attack while they were gone.

At daybreak, they set out to look for them. Lotan trudged beside his mother, scanning the area with his eyes, listening, raising his head to sniff the air, as she had taught him. For a long time, no signals came to him. Then he spotted the vultures, heard their noisy fighting. His heart thudded in his chest, lest it be one of the men they were stabbing with their fearful beaks, but it was only the zebra. The lion that had killed it had finished, the hyenas had gone, and only the vultures were left. There was no sign of the men.

Lotan went on, following a vague track through the brush. Something had passed this way recently, something that was tall enough to part the tops of the grasses as well as pressing them against the ground. Perhaps the men had been here.

A strange scent came to his nostrils. It was like the smell of some badly rotted eggs he had once found, when an ostrich had deserted its clutch, but much deeper and stronger. The smell became more and more pungent as he approached a small pond. The water in it had a sulfurous yellow cast.

The grass beneath his feet felt suddenly hot and dry, and it crunched strangely. Startled, Lotan backed away, almost bumping into his mother, who had come quietly up behind him. Together, they stared toward the pond. Dozens of carcasses, stripped of all flesh, littered the area. They were covered with pale yellow dust. A thick substance, orange in the sunlight, oozed up at the edges of the water.

Lotan frowned, aware of another strangeness about this place. There was no sound, no movement at all. No insects buzzed around the dead bodies, no vultures fought over them. The whole area seemed dead.

He jumped violently as a harsh croak broke the silence. A large bird he had not noticed before was lying half submerged in the shallows. It opened its beak and shrieked again, a cry of pure desperation. For a moment, it thrashed weakly, as if trying to escape some invisible force that held it down. The sound faded into a gurgle, and the bird lay still.

Lotan took a step toward it, to see better, but his mother pulled him back. "It burns," she said. "This water burns." There was a terrible sadness in her voice, as well as a warning, and he turned quickly to look at her. She was staring at an object not far from the dying bird. Lotan gasped in horror. It was one of the men, his arms stretched out in front of him. He was almost invisible, for his body was camouflaged by the sickly yellow powder. Beyond his out-stretched arms, Lotan could just discern the outline of another famil-iar shape.

Sickened, he turned away. He did not understand how water could burn, but he knew he would never forget this ghastly place, the silence, the reek of death with no purpose. Death to satisfy hunger, he understood. Death without benefit baffled him.

Ralak stood still, unable to move under the weight of her grief. She had recognized the scent, though she had smelled it only once before. There were places, sometimes, where the yellowish stuff in the water grew so strong that it burned, as if the earthforce had lingered there too long. As soon as she had smelled it, she had known her brother was dead. Even before that, she had known. All during the long night, she had been haunted by a feeling that some-thing terrible had happened to him. Her brother had been her com-panion since birth, and each of them had always been able to feel the other's pain. Now he was gone.

She reached out a hand, as if to touch him once again. Only he had understood her, knew the words she knew; only he had grasped her meaning when she spoke of the earthforce. The others, the ones she and her brother had joined when all in their tribe had died, were different. They had no knowledge of the earthforce, did not seem capable of understanding.

Except for Lotan. He understood a little, though he was still young. At least she still had Lotan.

Ralak turned toward him, her face crumpled with grief. He put his arms around her, to comfort her. His gesture released the tears she was trying not to shed, and for a moment she sobbed without restraint. Then, determinedly, she pushed her sadness away. She could not afford to grieve. With only women and children in the group, they were terribly vulnerable. Predators were one problem. The deep voices and large frames of men were often enough to frighten a lion or tiger away. But it was the strange male who frightened her most. Now that the men were gone, he would not hesitate to attack. She must be constantly on her guard, never stop listening, never miss a scent or a movement.

Ralak straightened her shoulders and gathered the others around her. They would have to keep moving all the time, so the big male could not find them.

She led them east, away from the gathering place. Lotan looked at her questioningly. He could not understand why they were going away from the place where they had slept so often.

"Why?" he asked her.

"Danger," she replied. "There is danger now, with no men. A bad male might come and hurt the infants."

Her answer puzzled Lotan. The men he had known had always been kind. But he trusted his mother's judgment, and he could tell that she was frightened. She scanned the landscape constantly, and tested the air for scents. She kept a stout stick in one hand, putting it down only when she gathered food. Lotan found a stick for himself, and practiced swinging it as he trotted beside her protectively. He was the only male left now, and although he was small for his eleven years, he would do his best against any danger that threatened her.

A week passed without incident. Ralak kept them moving; they gathered food as they traveled, and slept in a different place each night. Lotan began to relax his guard. Then, late one afternoon, he spotted a lone male staring at them from a ridge. He shouted a warning and ran to stand beside his mother. Toro followed, dragging Metep with her. She clutched her new infant tightly against her chest, instinctively aware that it could be in danger.

The male ambled toward them. He was huge, almost twice as big as Ralak, for she was a diminutive female. She watched him carefully. It was the same male she had seen before, and already she was certain she was right. He was one of the violent ones. Though he moved slowly, there was no hesitation in his step, and he stared straight at her with challenging eyes. A normal male would lower his eyes, approach with caution. She saw no hint of kindness in his face.

She handed the infant to Lotan and moved in front of both of them. Growling low in her throat, she faced the intruder. He paid no attention. Still staring at Ralak, as if he recognized her leadership, he lunged unexpectedly toward Toro's infant. Toro screamed and ran. The big male followed. Turning her back, Toro bent protectively over the baby. Metep pummeled the big male with her fists as he approached her mother.

Lotan gave the infant back to his mother and swung his stick hard at the male's massive back. Startled, the intruder turned to face him. Lotan held the stick high, ready to swing it again. But the male only shook his head in confusion and pushed the stick away, then turned back toward Toro. Lotan hit him again. This time, the male whirled and struck him a vicious blow to the chest. Lotan staggered backward, fighting for breath.

Toro took advantage of the momentary distraction and ran for the trees. The male stared after her, then turned suddenly and charged toward Ralak. Crouching low, she presented her genitals, to distract him from the infant. He sniffed her, puzzled by her action, and tried to force her to the ground. Ralak hit him with her stick, but she had only one free arm, and the blows had little force. Lotan struggled to his feet and went to help. Toro and Metep came back and grabbed sticks as well. Together, they pummeled the male, screaming and shouting as they rained blows against his back and shoulders.

Howling, he retreated to the hillside. But he did not go away. He stayed nearby all night, and he followed them as they traveled the next day. Though he did not come close, Lotan knew he was still in the area. He had a distinctive smell, stronger than that of other males he had known, that could not be missed.

Suddenly, just as the sun was lowering, the male charged toward them again. This time he moved with sure purpose. Before Toro could take a step, he was upon her. He snatched her infant and ran into the woods. The whole group followed, screaming wildly. Toro grabbed his arm, but she could not make him stop. He swung the infant by an arm and smashed its head against a tree, killing it instantly. Sobbing, Toro retrieved it and cradled it against her chest.

Anger suffused Lotan. He hit the male so hard that his stick broke, then began to pummel him with his fists. The male roared in anger and raised his arm high to strike.

Ralak pulled frantically at Lotan. The male would kill him, too, if he did not stop. She could not lose Lotan.

The male's fist came down, and Lotan crumpled at her feet. Ralak bent over him. Terror filled her, but it was instantly replaced by rage, a rage so fierce and consuming there was no room for fear. Slowly, she raised her eyes to confront the huge creature above her. He backed away, unaccustomed to such fury.

"Bad! Bad male!" she screamed at him. "I, Ralak, have no caring for one like you!"

Ralak repeated the words over and over, alternately shouting and hissing them through her teeth. But they did not satisfy her. She hated this cruel male; she wanted to curse him, to tell him all of them cursed him. Never before had she needed to express the opposite of caring, and she had no words for the hatred that surged inside her.

She wanted to tell him something else too. Again, there were no words, but the meaning was clear in her mind: if he had killed Lotan, she would make him pay. She did not know how she would manage it, but she knew she would find a way.

II

When Lotan opened his eyes, the light had begun to fade. He tried to sit, but the pain in his head forced him to lie down again. Ralak's heart leaped with joy to see him moving, but she hurried over and whispered that he should be quiet, lest the big male attack. Lotan was glad to comply. He felt dizzy and sick, incapable of standing. But in the morning, he felt well enough to get up and try to walk. He was still weak, but the pain in his head had diminished.

The male stared angrily at Lotan as he hobbled around the clearing, but he made no attempt to harm him further. He was wary of the tiny female who showed no fear and shouted words that seemed to penetrate his flesh as sharply as the blows of sticks. Ralak had not been satisfied with her words, but their effect had still been strong.

Ralak was relieved that there were no more attacks, but she was still furious. She would not look at the intruder or acknowledge his presence in any way. Ignoring him completely, she signaled the others to follow her to a small field with fruiting bushes. When they had finished eating, she went on again as if he were not there, and she continued to treat him this way for many days.

The big male plodded behind her, nursing his anger. He did not understand why the others had attacked him so ferociously. He had only tried to kill the infants so their mothers would mate with him, and then he could join the group. They needed a male to protect them. That did not seem wrong to him, but still the females had struck him over and over again. Bruises from the pounding they had inflicted showed purple against his dark skin, and a large welt throbbed where Lotan had hit him. But even more painful than his bruises was Ralak's refusal to pay any attention to him. She reminded him of his mother, whom he had loved, but she acted like the female who had driven him from his tribe when his mother had died. He hated that female. She had been jealous of his mother and had tried to drive her away, too, and as soon as his mother had died, she had turned on him instead. Day after day, she had tormented him relentlessly until he had left, long before he was full-grown. He had been alone ever since.

His frustration grew as the weeks passed and Ralak continued to ignore him. He could not vent his feelings on her; he wanted her to like him, not scream at him or ignore him. Nor did he want to harm the other females, for they were potential mates, so all his wrath was directed at Lotan. It was because of Lotan that Ralak had screamed scathing words at him, and then refused to acknowledge his presence at all. It was Lotan's fault that she still glared at him with loathing instead of accepting him. He wanted to grab the younger male and shake him until he could never move again, but he did not dare. Instead, he tried to intimidate Lotan by watching him constantly and following him everywhere. Lotan felt the hard, vengeful eyes on his back as he dug for tubers, and smelled the strong, rank odor close beside him as he slept. Not for a moment could he relax his guard, and his constant state of watchfulness was exhausting.

Ralak decided to try to sneak away with Lotan. Toro and Metep would be all right with the male. Metep was as tall as her mother now, and would soon be ready to mate. Once he had mated with them, the male would protect them and any infants they bore.

Whispering to Lotan to follow, she crept farther and farther from the others as they gathered food, then ran as fast as she could into the trees. The big male saw what was happening and rushed after them furiously. He grabbed Ralak's arm and pulled so hard she screamed in agony. Lotan ran to defend her, his face contorted with fury. Ralak stopped him with a quick command, certain that the male would kill Lotan if he hit him again. Reluctantly, Lotan obeyed.

In the weeks that followed, Ralak changed her tactics. Instead of letting her anger show, she tried to become friendly with the intruder. She and Lotan would have to escape; of that she was certain, but they would be more likely to succeed if the male thought they had accepted his presence.

"I Ralak," she told him one evening, pointing to herself. He grunted and did not respond. He seemed to have few words, fewer even than Toro and Metep. Perhaps solitary males like him had no need for words.

She pointed to the others, and named them. The male followed her pointing finger, seeming now to understand.

"Kropor," he said clearly. It was not a name Ralak had heard before. She wondered where he had come from.

"Mother?" Ralak said the word in a questioning tone, hoping to elicit more information. Most males were more attached to their mothers than any other, and preferred to stay with their mother's tribe as long as they could.

She pointed to herself, then to the infant, in case his words were different.

Kropor frowned and looked away, and for the first time she saw softness in his face. She was certain he had understood her word, and that he had cared for his mother.

The softness vanished as Kropor watched Lotan place an arm around Ralak's shoulders. Ralak was no longer ignoring him, but it was still Lotan she cared for most. Kropor wanted her to care for him more than any other, as his mother had. Except Ralak was not mother, but potential mate, and while Lotan remained with the group, Ralak would always care most for him.

Kropor thumped a fist against the ground. He was not accustomed to these complicated feelings, and his confusion made him angrier than ever.

"Gone," he barked in answer to Ralak's question, and closed his lips firmly, to discourage further discussion.

Ralak soon realized that her attempts at friendliness were not defusing Kropor's anger toward Lotan, as she had hoped. Instead, as she became less abusive, the big male tried to keep her with him all the time, and he became even more blatant in his attempts to get rid of Lotan. Once or twice, Ralak saw his eyes linger on her infant, too, as if he were gathering the courage to attack it. Baffled by this unexpected response, she began to shout at him again. She kept Lotan close beside her, and refused to let Kropor come near her or the infant.

These efforts failed even more miserably. Bewildered and hurt by her renewed hostility, Kropor became more aggressive than ever. Ralak knew they must leave soon, and watched anxiously for an opportunity.

Her chance came late that day, when she crested a low hill and saw fire in the valley below. At the end of the dry season, the earthforce was always restless. It swirled among the bulky clouds and charged over and over again toward the earth in long, crackling spears of lightning, triggering brush fires in the dry grasses. The fire below her was still small, but it was very smoky, so that much of the valley was hidden by a thick gray haze. Under its cover, she and Lotan could escape.

Kropor seemed to read her mind, and would not let her out of his sight. When she moved a few paces away to suckle the infant, he grabbed her arm again. She screamed in pain, but he would not let go. He shook her savagely, finally venting his frustration with this female who had become friendly and then inexplicably refused to tolerate his presence. Why was she cruel to him again? He cared for her, wanted her to care for him. He felt a security in her presence that he had not known since his mother had died. He did not want her to leave him, make him be alone again. He wanted to keep her.

Lotan could stand no more. For weeks he had endured Kropor's constant staring, his increasing possessiveness toward Ralak. All his accumulated tension exploded when he saw the big male grab her arm and heard her scream. He charged at Kropor, waving the digging stick he held in his hand wildly. He did not hear Ralak's cry of warning, or see the rock the male grabbed from the ground. He saw only the truculent face, the hard eyes, and he struck at them with all the force he could muster. The pointed end of the digging stick went into one of Kropor's eyes. The big male clutched it, screaming in agony.

"Run!" The words penetrated Lotan's blind fury, but he did not respond. He could not run without his mother.

"Run," she screamed again. "I follow!"

Kropor raised an arm to throw the rock. Toro grabbed his hand, destroying his aim, and the rock fell harmlessly by Lotan's foot.

The huge male growled deep in his throat, enraged by her interference. He hit out at her, but she ducked away.

Lotan hesitated, paralyzed by indecision. Ralak ran toward him. "Run!" she screamed again. The terror in her voice galvanized Lotan. He turned and fled. Kropor pounded behind him. Blood from the wounded eye covered his face and neck, and his mouth was open in a terrifying snarl.

Lotan ran faster. There were patches of fire in front of him now. He ran between them, dancing from one clump of grass to another to avoid the flames. He heard Kropor scream as fire scorched his feet. The pounding footsteps slowed, then stopped, but Lotan could not tell whether the big male had given up the chase or if the sound of his movements was hidden by the wind, the noisy hiss of burning grass and wood. He kept on running, first in one direction, then another, as new fires spurted up around him. Only when he was certain Kropor was no longer behind him did he stop and begin to pick his way back through the burned grasses to look for his mother. She had said she would follow. He scanned the area, blinking furiously in an effort to clear his eyes. He could see only an arm's length in front of him, and the smoke made objects seem to appear and disappear as he stared. He started toward the hillside where he had left his mother, but then he realized he did not know where the hillside was. He had run in so many directions he could not remember.

Calling frantically, he tried to retrace his steps. But fire had destroyed any sign of his passage, and the crackling of flames, much louder now, obscured his voice and all other sounds. If his mother answered, he did not hear; if she was nearby, searching for him, he could not see.

Tears ran down Lotan's cheeks, from the heat and fumes, from the terrible anguish that gripped him. His search was useless. He would never be able to find Ralak in all this smoky blackness—if she was even here. She might not have been able to follow him, as she had promised. Maybe Kropor had dragged her back, was still holding her arm as she screamed in pain.

Lotan was sure of it suddenly, as sure as if he had been there, and the realization gave him strength. He *had* to find his mother, had to find his way back, so he could rescue her.

The wind rose as he stood still, trying to get his bearings. All around him, flames suddenly shot high into the air, then flattened as they attacked the dry grasses. Smoke blew in thick, murky clouds against the ground, spewing cinders into his eyes, obscuring his vision completely. Flames licked at his legs, and blistering heat seared his body. The fire was coming at him from all directions now.

Terrified, Lotan covered his face with his hands and ran. He ran anywhere, toward any small oasis where the fire was not yet burning. He no longer knew where he had come from, where he was going. There was no way to know as the fire chased him, sent him careening in every direction.

The flames rose still higher; they singed the downy hairs from his body and scorched his blistered feet. He blundered on, reeling with fatigue, dizzy from the pungent fumes. Twice he fell and almost stayed where he landed, too exhausted to move. Each time, the burning forced him to leap up and stagger on. But the third time he fell, the ground was not so hot. Dazedly, he looked down and realized that the fire had passed this place already. Smoke rose thickly from the ground, but the flames were gone. Perhaps he could rest here for a moment.

A large animal moved suddenly in front of him, and he jumped to his feet. He could not see what it was, but he thought he heard a menacing growl above the noise of the wind. Panicked, Lotan charged forward. He felt rocks under his feet, hard and sharp against his scorched soles. And then, abruptly, there was nothing beneath him, nothing at all.

III

On the hillside above the fire, Ralak winced sharply, as if she had been hit. But there was no one near her. Even Kropor had retreated, alarmed by her overpowering grief.

She had tried to follow Lotan, had tried to leap from one clump of grass to another as he was doing, but the infant had screamed and wriggled with fear, making movement impossible. With her wounded shoulder, the pain of trying to hold on to the baby had quickly become intolerable. Smoke and cinders and heat had blinded her, and she could see nothing.

And then, out of the fiery gloom, Kropor had appeared and dragged her back to the hillside.

Furious at Lotan, at his own burning feet, at the agony of his bloody eye, he had pulled remorselessly at her injured arm, so she would have to follow. Even when she had fallen, overwhelmed by the pain, he had not let go. Only when they had reached the others had he released her. Then he had been frightened, for she had uttered a howl of absolute anguish and folded to the ground. Her body had started to shake so hard he had feared she would break, and she had screamed at him with such vengeance that he had gone away, afraid for himself as well as for her, that she would never be friendly again.

Ashamed now of his cruelty, Kropor returned and offered Ralak a piece of fruit, to try to make amends. He had not meant to hurt her so badly. He had just wanted to keep her with him, keep her from following Lotan.

Huddled over the infant, weeping in great, wrenching gasps, Ralak neither saw nor heard him. There was room only for Lotan in her thoughts, her heart. His slender body had disappeared behind a thick curtain of smoke, and she did not know if he was dead or alive, if he was wounded, waiting for her to come to him. He had vanished, as her brother had vanished, and she might never see him again.

The infant nuzzled against her, and Ralak held it closer so it could suckle. The familiar sensation calmed her. Slowly, her sobs diminished. Maybe Lotan was still alive, still wandering out there somewhere, looking for her; maybe she would be able to find him when the light came again and the fire had died down.

A torrent of anguish threatened to overwhelm her again, but Ralak pushed it away. She had seen something, in her mind. It was a picture of Lotan, lying on the ground.

She frowned deeply, trying to hold on to the image. Long ago, with her mother, she had often been able to see this way. But so much time had passed, with no other who could help her, that she had almost forgotten. Even her brother had been unable to help, for he did not see the pictures.

Ralak closed her eyes, so she could see better. The picture came into focus for a moment and then vanished, as Lotan had vanished. She clenched her fists in frustration. Then fatigue overtook her and she relaxed. Listening absentmindedly to the baby's sucking noises, she let her mind go loose.

The image came again. She watched it carefully. She saw Lotan lying motionless against the ground. There was no fire around him, only smoke. He did not move or call out, but she did not think he was dead. It was as if a connection existed between herself and Lotan that would have broken had he been dead. But he was hurt, hurt and frightened.

The image disappeared again, but it had given Ralak courage. She would find him. As soon as the light came again, she would look for him. And this time, Kropor would not stop her.

Early in the morning, long before the sun had come over the horizon, she crept away from the others. Her wide feet were soundless against the dry grasses, her lithe body almost invisible against the still dark air. Kropor did not stir. Only Toro awoke. She sat up and stared at Ralak's shadowy figure. Her mouth opened, but then she pressed her hand firmly against her lips and did not move or make a sound until the small form had disappeared.

Ralak glanced back at her gratefully. Toro had few words, but still she had understood. She hurried on, stepping with infinite caution, holding the infant close against her breast so it would not cry. She did not go to the burned place, but to the trees above, where Kropor could not see her. All morning she waited there, while he searched and called for her in mounting frustration. Then, when he and Metep and Toro had disappeared, she crept soundlessly down the hill to look for Lotan.

For hours Ralak searched, as the sun beat heavily down on her back, but she could find no trace of him. The pungent smell of smoke obscured his scent; there were no revealing footsteps, no trail of blood. Surely if the fire or Kropor had killed him, she would have found some sign. The recognition gave her hope even as she struggled with despair. Then, suddenly, hope kindled into excitement as she caught a whiff of Lotan's scent. It came from a rocky area beneath a short, steep cliff, below the place where the fires had burned.

He had been there; she was certain of it. His scent was strong, for the fires had not come this far. There was a hint of another scent, too, the scent of others like herself.

Puzzled, Ralak sat back on her heels to think. A violent clap of thunder interrupted her absorption. Lightning followed, as the afternoon displays that were a prelude to the rains began. Abruptly, she became aware of a commotion in the distance. Dust was rising thickly to the east, and she heard the sound of thousands of hoofs, as if a huge group of animals had suddenly started to run.

It was the wildebeests, she realized, on their annual migration. But why were they moving so fast? She heard another noise, faint above the din of pounding hoofs. She thought it was a scream—a scream of fear.

Ralak leaped to her feet, galvanized by the sounds, and ran up the hillside, to see better. There were fires, far away, across the slim ribbon of river she could see from her vantage point—only the river was no longer there, for it had been obscured by the bodies of wildebeests. They were surging across it in an enormous clump, as if they were one, and they were moving in this direction.

Was it Lotan who had screamed? Ralak did not know, could not tell. She wanted to run down to look for him, but she dared not go closer. The animals had stampeded, and they would trample anything in their path. They would trample Lotan, if he was there. They would trample her, too, and the infant.

Tucking the baby securely under her good arm, Ralak ran for the trees where she had sheltered earlier. She could not climb them with her wounded arm, so she ran deep into the woods and lay close against the earth, trying to pull its force into her, to give her strength. All through the long night she huddled there, listening to the wildebeests thunder past, pushing away the grief that threatened to tear her heart into pieces. Lotan was still alive; she was certain of it. She had seen the place where he had been, smelled his scent against the rocks. He could not die now. The fire had not killed him, Kropor had not killed him. The wildebeests would not kill him, either.

Ralak closed her eyes firmly, squeezing back the hot tears that burned behind them, and told herself these things over and over again, willing herself to believe. Lotan would not die. In the morning, she would search again. And this time, she would find him.

CHAPTER
14

Bran's fist lashed out and caught Lotan squarely on the chin. The boy stumbled backward and almost fell. A mixture of astonishment and anger showed on his face. The blow had not been hard, but it had caught him completely by surprise. Bran had always seemed so amiable.

Bran looked even more surprised. Lotan had inadvertently jostled him, but he had not expected to hit the younger male in return. He was appalled and embarrassed by his action. He glanced apologetically at Zena, but she only shook her head in dismay and wandered off to sit by herself.

Ever since they had left the clearing, incidents like this had occurred with increasing frequency. Grief lay heavily in their hearts, making them short-tempered. But their discord had a deeper source. Without Kalar's quiet guidance, they seemed unable to control themselves. They fought over petty incidents and selfishly grabbed food for themselves instead of sharing. Worse, in losing Kalar, they felt they had lost the Mother as well. Kalar had been Her representative, and with no one to speak for Her, they seemed to forget how to cooperate or express the concern for each other that still lurked deep within them.

The others turned instinctively to Zena for leadership, sensing, as Kalar had, that she was destined to speak for the Mother. But Zena stubbornly resisted. To take Kalar's place would mean giving up her anger, and that she would not do. Anger protected her. It gave her strength to move through the days and kept her grief at bay. Most important, anger made it possible for her to keep her heart closed against the Mother. The Mother had killed Kalar and Cere and the others, and Zena had no intention of forgiving Her. Each day when she woke, each evening before sleep, she prodded her anger, so she would not forget. It spread within her, coloring all her thoughts and actions.

Bran went to sit away from the others, with his back to them. Lupe started to follow, but changed his mind, confused by Bran's uncharacteristic behavior. Sima began to cry quietly. Lupe put his arm around her, and they huddled together, apart from the others. This, too, had become a frequent occurrence. Bran and Zena sat alone, brooding, leaving the two young ones to comfort each other as best they could. Nyta paid no attention to any of them. Ever since she had fallen from the tree, she had existed in a kind of trance, as if she did not remember what had happened to them. She fed Cere's infant and sometimes helped Sima, but she seldom spoke or responded to the others.

Lotan sighed heavily, remembering the time before the stampede, when everyone in the tribe had cared for each other. He had never known such friendliness and warmth. Now there was only indifference, the numbness of overpowering grief.

The misery in Zena's face made him want to comfort her, but he did not dare. She refused comfort from any of them. Only Three-Legs could get close to her, and often she seemed barely aware of the little gazelle's gentle nuzzling. She hardly spoke either. Before, she had been so eager to talk to him, to learn his words. Her curiosity had vanished, and she wanted only to be left alone.

He understood. He, too, had lost the one who was most important to him. His mother was always in his thoughts, and he looked constantly for any sign of her or the others.

He went to Zena and pointed south. "That way?" he asked.

She shrugged and shook her head wearily. She could not answer him. Probably they should go south, to the lake, as they always had in the past. But once again, fires had cut across their normal route, and without Kalar and Lett to guide them, they felt helpless. Nothing seemed to matter to any of them, except the need to feed themselves and stay alive.

Finding food was harder now. All the implements that had made it easier—the digging sticks, the sharp stones, the carrying devices— had been destroyed in the stampede. Bran had tried to make some stones like Lett's, but they did not work very well. And every time Zena started to make a basket or sling, she thought of Cere and the tears she refused to shed pricked behind her eyes with such force she could not see to work.

Only two items had been salvaged. Nyta still used the sling Zena had made for her, and just before they had left the clearing, she had gone to the circle of stones, for Zena would not, and had picked up the first wide-hipped figure Lett had made. She kept it with her always. Zena saw her holding it as she suckled Cere's infant, and the familiar anger rose forcefully within her, giving her energy.

"We must find shelter," she said. The others rose quickly and followed her, glad of any activity that distracted them.

Each afternoon now, they shivered miserably under a tree or rock, or whatever meager protection they could find from the heavy downpours. All of them knew they should build a more permanent shelter, but they lacked the motivation.

Zena spotted a pile of rocks below them. If they gathered some branches, and a burning stick if they could find one, they would have some shelter at least, and be safe from animals.

Lotan stiffened suddenly as they approached the rocks. A scent had come to him, a scent so heavy and unmistakable he could not be wrong. He grabbed Zena's arm.

"Male," he said urgently. "Bad male!"

She stared into his face. Fear dominated his features, but she saw hope there too.

Bran came closer, alerted by the tension in their bodies. "We go back," he said, when Zena had explained Lotan's words.

Lotan shook his head. "Find mother," he insisted.

"We hide to look," Bran said.

Zena nodded and they started back up the hillside to find a place where they could observe unseen, but they were too late. The big male had spotted them. He stood on a rock, squinting in an effort to see clearly. Even at this distance, Zena could see that one of his eyes was puffy and discolored. He wiped at it constantly, trying to clear his vision.

"Eye?" She looked questioningly at Lotan.

He pointed to the digging stick he carried, and gestured as if to poke it into his eye, then pointed to Kropor. Zena grimaced. This male must be very angry at Lotan, if he had hurt his eye so badly.

The big male uttered a low call, and two females appeared behind him.

"Mother?" Zena watched Lotan's face as she asked the question. He shook his head, disappointment heavy in his eyes.

Lotan moved closer, one step at a time, trying to see past Kropor and the others. Perhaps his mother was behind them; perhaps she was wounded, and could not walk.

"Mother! Ralak!" He called her name loudly.

Zena saw the big male's head turn sharply at the sound of Lotan's voice. The bigger of the two women came up to him and put a hand on his arm, as if to restrain him.

"Toro," Lotan called. "Toro, where is Ralak?"

"No. Go away. Not here." Toro waved him away frantically. Lotan paid no attention. He continued to come closer, calling his mother's name over and over again.

Kropor roared with sudden fury. He could barely see from his wounded eye, and until Lotan had come close, he had not known who he was. Now he did, and all his rage returned.

He leaped from the rock and charged at Lotan. Bran grabbed a stick and ran to defend the young male. Zena picked up a rock and followed. Nyta began to scream, wrenched for the first time from her dreamy complacency. Toro and Metep screamed, too, and Cere's infant began to wail loudly.

Kropor roared again and raised his fist to hit Lotan. Bran was just about to strike the fist with his stick when a piercing yell broke through the pandemonium, paralyzing all of them with its suddenness.

A tiny woman with an infant under one arm came hurtling toward them. She was shrieking words at Kropor with such force that he flinched as if she had hit him. Zena understood the words, for Lotan had used them too.

"Bad male!" she screamed. "Bad male!"

Kropor's arm went down and he stared at her in wide-mouthed astonishment. She had come back! He had thought he would never see her again, and she had come back!

"Ralak!" he said, and to Zena's amazement, a huge smile creased his face. He beamed at the small, shrieking female as if she were the most wonderful sight he had ever seen.

Ralak was even more surprised than Zena. She had expected Kropor to strike her, not welcome her. Despairing of ever finding Lotan again, and knowing she could not survive on her own, she had been following Kropor, trying to summon the courage to join the group. And then she had heard Lotan calling her name, and had run to defend him, and Kropor had beamed at her.

It was all very perplexing. Ralak nodded authoritatively, to hide her confusion, and uttered a torrent of words Zena could not understand. It was clear, however, that they were directed at the big male, who had raised his fist as if to resume his attack on Lotan. But

when Ralak's words lashed him, his body slumped. He looked at
her pleadingly and held out a hand in a gesture of submission. She
did not take it, for her anger was still too strong, but she did come
closer to look at his eye.

She gave a sharp command, and Toro and Metep ran off. Totally
bewildered, Zena turned to Lotan. But he had no time for her. He
ran to the tiny woman and hugged her as tears poured from his
eyes. Her face alight with joy, she tried to hug him back but winced
instead. Lotan drew away, concerned.

"Arm hurt?" Zena asked Lotan. She did not need to ask if this
was his mother. The expression of relief and caring in his face told
her that. But she had also noticed that Ralak held her infant under
one arm, while the other hung limply by her side.

Lotan nodded, and anger flashed in his eyes as he glanced at
Kropor, making the yellow flecks glow like sparks.

Ralak intercepted the glance and spoke firmly. "No fights. I will
not have fighting."

She looked sternly at Kropor, then at Lotan, then back again. She
still had no idea why Kropor was behaving in such a submissive
fashion, but she was determined to take full advantage of her apparent power over him.

Bran came to stand beside Ralak, to reinforce her authority. He
did not understand her words either, but he knew Kropor had to
be controlled and was willing to help. Even bigger than Kropor, he
was a formidable adversary, and Kropor's eyes dropped quickly.

"Now we fix the eye. Sit," Ralak commanded Kropor when she
thought he was sufficiently cowed. She pushed his shoulder to
make sure he understood.

Toro and Metep had returned with a bunch of plants and some
water in a gourd. Toro took the infant as they handed both to Ralak.
Zena came close to watch as Ralak carefully stripped the leaves and
immersed them in water. Her hands itched to help, and she looked
questioningly at the older woman.

Ralak nodded, understanding. Together, they finished stripping
the leaves and soaking them. Ralak squeezed gently and placed the
poultice on Kropor's eye. Then she sat back on her heels and regarded Zena with a look so intense and direct it seemed to penetrate
all the way to Zena's heart.

Zena returned the look without embarrassment, without restraint.
Ralak's eyes seemed already to have laid bare her heart, so there
was no point in evasion. Instead, she simply absorbed the feelings
that came to her from this extraordinary woman. There was little
comfort in her candid gaze, but still there was solace, a kind of

understanding, as if she had known Ralak for a long time already. Somehow, she seemed infinitely familiar. . . .

A strange tremor, like the one that had jolted her when she clung to the tree, coursed through Zena's body. She shook her head hard, as if to clear it.

Ralak reached out and patted her arm. "We will speak of many things," she said enigmatically. Then she rose quickly to her feet. The first drops of the afternoon rains were falling, and it was time to seek shelter.

She trotted toward the pile of rocks Zena had spotted earlier. Zena clambered up on them and pointed to a place where there was room for all of them to sit, and branches could be placed overhead. Ralak nodded vigorously and issued instructions to Kropor and the two females.

"We help them build a shelter," Zena said to Bran and the others. They ran to break off leafy branches and gather piles of twigs and mosses, as Toro and Metep were doing. Kropor stood uneasily by himself, but when they began to make the roof, he shouldered the heavy branches and helped to shove them into place. Before long, they had constructed a solid shelter that hardly leaked at all. They piled in together as the downpour increased, and looked at each other self-consciously.

Kropor especially was uncomfortable in such close proximity to many strangers, and glared at them fiercely. Ralak saw him glaring and hurled another barrage of words in his direction. He looked up at her, his eyes forlorn, and subsided in a corner. Ralak had come to fill a place in his heart he had not known existed. The agony he had felt when she had disappeared had frightened him, and he did not want to experience it again. He wanted only to please her, and if that meant he must tolerate strangers, he would manage it. He would tolerate Lotan, too, if only Ralak would stay nearby. He could not bear the thought of losing her again.

Toro and Metep moved over to sit beside him. They were used to Kropor, and his surliness did not bother them. But Zena and the others were not accustomed to males of his type and watched him suspiciously. Agar had sometimes lashed out at others, but he had never harmed a female, as Kropor had harmed Ralak. They slid as far away from him as they could get, while Bran kept his eyes on the big male's face, challenging him. Then Three-Legs poked her wet head into the shelter, looking comically eager to join them. The children's laughter dissipated the tension. Toro and Metep exclaimed with amazement and delight as Zena drew the little gazelle in to sit beside her.

Zena looked around her in astonishment. Only a short time ago, she and the others had been alone, feeling miserable and angry; now they were sitting peacefully in a new shelter with a strange group of people—and it was Ralak who had brought about this remarkable transformation. She looked again at the tiny woman, marveling at her composure. She was like Kalar in that way, except Kalar had been quiet and slow, always serene. Ralak was quick and energetic, full of animation.

Zena realized with a start that thinking of Kalar had not brought the familiar twinge of unbearable anguish into her heart. Somehow, in Ralak's presence, the agony was more tolerable.

A spasm of pain crossed Ralak's face as her shoulder was jostled in the confined space. Zena frowned in consternation. She had been so busy watching Ralak that she had forgotten she was wounded.

She crawled over and began to examine the shoulder with gentle fingers. She did not feel any broken bones, but the upper part of Ralak's arm was bruised and swollen. It seemed to hurt most when she moved her shoulder. Zena decided that she would bind the arm to Ralak's body, so it would stay still.

As soon as the rain subsided, she took Sima with her and went to look for leaves for a poultice, to draw out the swelling, and vines to bind the arm. Thrilled to help Zena, after all the weeks of being ignored, Sima quickly pulled down more vines than Zena could possibly use. Zena thanked her and bound Ralak's arm to her side, after she had placed the soft leaves all around the shoulder. Then she looked resignedly at the remaining pile of vines. With one arm strapped down, Ralak would not be able to carry the infant very well. She would have to have a sling.

Keeping her head low so the others could not see her face contort with the effort not to weep, she set about making a sturdy sling. For hours, she worked, squeezing her eyes tightly over and over again to force the tears back. A few of them dribbled through anyway, and she gritted her teeth in anger. She hated them, hated everything that had caused them. Especially, she hated the Mother, for hurting them so badly.

Rage came flooding back as she continued to battle her tears. But now it was stronger than ever because she was furious at herself as well as the Mother. She had allowed herself to be distracted by the unexpected events, had allowed herself to feel almost happy again, instead of nourishing the anger that would pay the Mother back. She pulled at her anger, forced it to fill her, used it to keep her heart hard against the Mother and to dampen the terrible grief that threatened to overwhelm her as she concentrated on the task Cere had loved so well.

Bran saw Zena's struggle; he also saw that the others were staring. Once, he might have teased her; now he wanted only to help. He pulled out some sticks he had collected and began to sharpen them with a stone. Soon everyone's eyes were on him instead of Zena, and all the others wanted to sharpen sticks too. He sent Lupe out to find more. Like Sima, Lupe was thrilled to be included again, and returned with a big armful. Despite his bad eye, Kropor especially proved to be good at scraping, and soon produced a number of well-sharpened sticks. The activity seemed to calm him. Concentration replaced the hostility in his face, and he forgot to glare.

Ralak, too, was aware of the battle Zena was waging, but she did not try to help. It was good that the child struggled. The anger and grief Ralak had seen when she stared into Zena's eyes had to emerge. Until they did, Zena would be paralyzed, unable to make use of the gift that lurked deep within her. Only a few had the ability to see and hear and feel with their minds as well as their senses. Though she did not know it yet, Zena was one of these.

Tears of gratitude came into Ralak's eyes. Since the death of her mother, there had been no one who could grasp what was in her mind, no one to whom she could pass on her knowledge. But Zena would understand; even without words, the knowledge would go into her. Ralak knew this because already she had seen Zena's thoughts, felt them as if they were her own, as she had once known her mother's thoughts.

The rain stopped and the others went outside to look for food. Intent on finishing the sling, Zena did not move. Ralak watched her carefully, keeping her eyes soft so she would not disturb her. But when Zena leaned over to give her the sling, Ralak placed a hand under her chin and raised Zena's face so she could look into her eyes. She saw the held-back tears, the pain, the stubborn anger. Shaking her head slowly, she drew the girl against her and uttered a flow of soothing words.

Something broke in Zena; she felt it break, as if a hard barrier had dissolved. The tears she had refused to shed ever since the stampede streamed down her cheeks onto Ralak's warm skin. With them went the anger, the terrible, paralyzing anger. Ralak felt it emerge and fill the shelter, and she willed it away. Anger, like fighting, had no place here. She would not have it. Digging her fingers into the earth, she called on the earthforce for strength. It had helped her before and it would help her now, as she pulled the anger from Zena's heart and sent it reeling into the clouds, so it would never be able to enter her again.

Zena gasped and shuddered, her body tormented by the bitter flood that spewed from it. After the anger was gone, the grief that had been locked behind poured out in great, gulping sobs of anguish. All of it drained out of her, leaving her exhausted and empty. But when her sobbing had diminished, the faces of the ones she had lost came into her mind, and the caring in her heart for each of them filled the emptiness. All the space her anger and grief had occupied was inundated with the strength of her love for them. She knew now that even though they were gone, they were with her still. She did not understand how that could be, but to feel their presence within her was enough.

As suddenly as it had begun, Zena's weeping stopped. She uttered a final wrenching sob, then she laid her head in Ralak's lap and slept. All through the night, she did not move. When she finally raised her head, brilliant beams of light were dancing through the cracks in the roof. They landed on her arms, her head, her belly. She lay still, feeling them course through her body. It seemed to her that they were giving her back the warmth and energy, the curiosity, that had once been hers. She smiled, and welcomed the new day.

II

Zena and Ralak and Lotan sat with their heads close together, speaking of the Mother and the earthforce. Many seasons of rain and dryness had passed since they had come together, and they understood each other well. Each tribe had learned the other's words; the words had merged and multiplied in the process, as they put meanings together and found new ones.

Sima and Lupe crouched nearby, making pictures of words as they listened, and mouthing them so they would remember. Bran and Kropor were sharpening stones and digging sticks. Kropor excelled at this task, and the others had become dependent on his special expertise. Their praise made him less wary, and he was seldom violent anymore. He was still easily irritated, but he was also fiercely devoted to Ralak and did not want to displease her. When anger overcame him, he disappeared for a time, and when he returned, he behaved.

Toro and Metep sat nearby making slings. Toro had a new infant now, and Metep was pregnant, so they needed them. Nyta helped, patiently showing them how to weave strands together and make firm knots. The presence of others seemed to have revived Nyta. She still did not remember what had happened to them, but she was cheerful and active now, no longer in a trance. All of them had improved in the time they had been together. Though they thought often of the ones they had lost, grief no longer robbed them of energy and motivation.

Zena had grown quickly in the years since the stampede. At thirteen, she was taller than Ralak, and her hips and breasts had filled out. She moved with grace and authority, and sometimes Lotan looked at her longingly as unfamiliar sensations stirred in his loins. Her curiosity had come back, but so had her stubborn independence. She wanted to figure out everything for herself, without waiting to listen to others. Especially, she did not want to listen for the Mother, or feel Her presence. Though her anger had gone, she still did not trust any force beyond herself, lest it betray her.

Ralak despaired sometimes that Zena would ever fully open her heart again. It would be necessary, soon, to challenge her, she thought, as she herself had once been challenged. That was why she had brought them to this place.

She had told Zena many times of the earthforce, and had heard from her of the Mother, of Kalar, who had represented her. That the earthforce should also be Mother had seemed instantly obvious to Ralak, as if a connection between her mind and heart had suddenly slipped into place. She had always understood the power of the earthforce, but she had felt, too, that there was something closer, warmer. She had found it in the Mother.

Still, both could be harsh as well as gentle, and it was this that Zena would not accept. She knew with her mind that the earthforce and the Mother could kill as well as offering the promise of life, but she did not know it in her heart. To make the heart accept was hardest of all.

Ralak held up the wide-hipped statue Lett had made. "The earthforce is in this one," she said. "I feel it. You feel it now." She handed it to Zena and waited.

Zena took the small figure reluctantly. A shudder ran through her. It seemed to come from the statue, and she put it down again quickly.

"I feel it," she agreed. "But there is fear in it too."

"The fear is in you, not in the figure," Ralak retorted. Then she softened.

"The earthforce and the Mother are the same," she told Zena patiently. "And both can hurt. From them come the mountains that explode, the lightning, even the dryness that kills. But from them, too, come rain, and life. They are both—death as well as life, pain as well as joy."

"Why must that be? Why is the Mother cruel?" Zena's lips twisted with remembered grief, and she pounded the ground for emphasis.

"There is no answer. Only that the Mother is as She is, and the earthforce is all that happens."

Ralak sighed as she answered. She was not sure herself; she knew only that it was necessary to accept. Especially, it was necessary for Zena to accept, and little time was left to teach her. The pain low in Ralak's belly, the blood that dribbled from a place deep inside her told her this. Hardly noticeable at first, the symptoms had worsened fast. Each day, she seemed to be weaker.

Lotan spoke for the first time. "We are not so important, I think," he mused. He pointed to Three-Legs. "We are like her, only one of many. That some should feed the lion while others live is good. The lion must eat too."

Zena nodded. That made sense to her. Lotan often made sense. She looked at him appraisingly. He, too, had gown, though he was not big like Bran. He was small and wiry and strong, and sometimes when he glanced at her she felt a strange tingling.

"I still do not think the Mother should have killed so many, and for no reason," she said stubbornly, to cover her confusion.

Sima volunteered a thought. "But now we have others," she commented, "and that is good."

Zena smiled at her. "You are right, Sima. The Mother has given us Ralak and the others instead."

She thought seriously for a moment, trying hard to set her doubts aside. She had learned from Ralak; knew her as she had never known another, as if their minds were one. Was that, perhaps, the Mother's way, to give her Ralak instead of Kalar, to teach her? Though she often tried to avoid the thought, Zena knew she was destined to speak for the Mother. She knew it, but pushed the knowledge away, lest she be hurt again.

She pushed another thought away as well, a thought that was deeper than knowledge, for it came from her body and her heart, as if they were connected to Ralak's heart and body. Ralak was dying. The life force was slowly draining from her. Ralak had never spoken of it, but Zena knew.

She jumped to her feet. "Let us look for food now," she said. "Soon the light will be gone."

Lotan followed as she ran toward the hill where fruit had ripened on the trees. Together, they gathered a big pile to take back to the others, then they sat down to eat some themselves. This was the time of day Zena loved best, when brilliant hues of pink and orange and crimson lit up the sky, and the birds clustered in the trees, jostling and screeching at each other as they settled for the night. It was the time when animals came to drink in the pond below them, and predators stalked the unwary.

She shivered and moved closer to Lotan. He put an arm around her, and when he touched her, a ripple of pleasure coursed through her body.

Lotan stiffened, and pointed wordlessly. She followed his finger, but still she had to stare for a long moment before she saw the tawny lioness crouched in the long grasses. A herd of zebras had come to drink, and her golden eyes were fixed on them with utter concentration. The herd had not yet detected her, and were drinking peacefully. Then, suddenly, one of them caught her scent and leaped away. The others followed, thrusting themselves forward in lunging strides, to put distance between themselves and the lioness. But now she had eyes only for one of them, one who had ventured deeper into the water than the others. Some zebras were closer to her, but she ignored them and charged toward the one she had chosen.

The frantic animal lurched through the water in a desperate effort to reach the safety of the herd. But it was too late. The lioness sprang on its back and grasped its neck with her powerful jaws. Another lioness, hidden until now, attacked from the front and closed her teeth on its muzzle. The zebra screamed and went down. Its legs thrashed wildly as it tried to regain its feet, then it shuddered and lay still. But it was not dead yet: its head came up sharply, and the lioness at its muzzle lost her hold. She sank her teeth into its throat instead, and held on until the dying zebra ceased its feeble struggle.

The two lionesses settled down to feed. They had taken only a few gulping bites when a thick-maned male shouldered them aside, growling and snapping. They retreated, then crept slowly toward the carcass again. One of them reached it and began to feed, but the male knocked her away. She waited again, then returned. The second lioness followed, and this time the male could not drive them away. They fed voraciously. A group of cubs arrived, and imitated their mothers, but they were not allowed to feed until the others were almost finished.

Zena's breath escaped with an audible hiss. She had seen lions kill before, but never had she been so close. This time, she had seen the zebra's frantic eyes, heard its final scream, watched as the life drained from its body. It seemed to her that she had seen something else, too, something even more powerful than the tableau that had played itself out below her. She was not sure what this thing was, except that it had to do with the earthforce, with the way it moved from one to another. The life had gone from the zebra, but it had gone into the lions. The zebra's death was the lions' life.

"The lions must eat too," she mused aloud. Then she sat up straight.

"But why does the female kill and the male eat?" she asked indignantly. "The lioness should eat if she kills, and the cubs too. Why do they wait?"

"All creatures are different," Lotan responded. He grinned. "I like this," he teased her. "She gets the food and he eats."

Zena poked him playfully. "I do not," she retorted. "I am glad I am not a lioness."

She lay back to enjoy the last blazing moments of the sunset. Lotan lay close beside her. His body was smooth and warm. A slight breeze blew across them, and Zena shivered as her skin cooled. She turned to draw more of Lotan's warmth; but he had turned, too, and when their bodies met in the new position, a sudden, piercing thrill passed between them. Zena felt it course through her body, and she knew Lotan had felt it, too, for his eyes widened in surprise, and he drew away.

They stared at each other. At first, their look was restrained, but gradually their eyes softened so that they were seeing not each other but the feelings between them, feelings that surged beyond any possibility of retraction. Without volition, Zena's hand moved to caress Lotan's thigh. He moaned with pleasure. The sound excited her, made her feel powerful, and she stroked harder, all over his body. His hand returned the caresses. Her skin seemed to burn where he touched her, but it was a glowing burn of pleasure, not of hurt. She pulled closer until her belly and breasts seemed almost to melt into his warm skin. Now the glow had spread deep inside her, low between her legs.

Lotan's hand moved down to caress her just outside the place where the glow was strongest, most demanding, and she cried out with delight. She felt her legs open, and was surprised. But then the sensations became so strong, so far-beyond her power to control, that she ceased to think at all and just moved where passion took her. Groaning, she entwined her legs with his to get closer still. But it was not enough; she wanted more, wanted to feel him inside her.

Again, her hand moved without volition as she guided him into her. He went deep, and deeper still, then retreated and came back.

Zena clutched him, holding him in there, where she could feel something growing, swelling, as if it wanted to explode, like ripe fruit suddenly shedding its skin. And then it shattered. A place of pleasure she had never known before grew and grew, then cracked into pieces, so that the sensations radiated all over her body, into her arms and legs, her fingers and toes. Pleasure was everywhere, hot, overwhelming.

Lotan lurched against her, then his body wrenched backward, and he screamed, a soft, urgent scream of passion. Zena thought she could feel in him what she had felt in herself, and she held him close until his shuddering subsided. Unexpectedly, the intense tingling filled her again, and she felt another swelling begin to grow, then explode. Twice again, her body filled and shattered, and she gasped as the sensations coursed through her.

Lotan was still now, helpless against her. Zena did not move or speak. She could not. Somewhere deep inside her mind, she remembered Kalar's words, and Cere's.

"Mating gives much pleasure," they had told her. They had been right.

After a while, Zena realized that darkness was almost upon them. She shook Lotan.

"We must leave. The sun has gone," she whispered.

Lotan sat up and yawned. Then he seemed suddenly to remember what had happened, and he looked at Zena with startled eyes. In the dim light, the yellow flecks were almost invisible. "I have never mated before," he said.

"I have not either," Zena told him. "I did not think I would mate, ever. I did not know it gave such pleasure."

She grabbed his hand and they ran down the hill toward the clearing. Their group had built a good shelter, one that would last, with a large flat clearing where they could make baskets and sharpen sticks, and gather around the hearth fire at the end of the day. The fire was glowing now, welcoming them.

Ralak looked up as they entered the circle of firelight. There was rapture on their faces; she saw it immediately, and knew its origin. There was no mistaking that special look. She was glad. Mating was of the Mother, for it involved feeling, not thinking. It would help Zena when the challenge came.

She sighed. It had been many years since she herself had mated. Since the time when she had struggled so hard to give birth, something had felt wrong inside her. Once, she had tried to mate with Kropor, but it had hurt her, and she had sent him to Toro and

Metep. It was not such a loss, she thought. She was not strong enough for mating anyway.

She rose painfully to her feet, to go to the shelter. The ache in her belly was always there, deep and insistent, and the blood flowed harder. Her strength was waning fast.

Kropor saw her struggle and came to help her. He never strayed far from her side, except when he disappeared in a temper, and he seemed always to know when she needed help. She smiled up at him gratefully. He was a valued companion now. She still had to shout words at him sometimes, for he was often irritable with the others; but he no longer seemed to mind her occasional anger. In fact, he appeared to enjoy it, and often grinned widely as her words pummeled him.

She had finally come to understand why he had changed. Zena had explained it to her, while she listened in amazement.

"He cares for you more than any other," Zena had told her. "When you left to look for Lotan, he felt a terrible sadness. He blamed Lotan, so he tried to hurt him. He said these things one day, but I knew already."

Zena had discovered other things about Kropor too. Ralak was not sure how she had managed to elicit the story, for Kropor did not use many words, but somehow Zena had learned that he had been forced from his tribe when his mother had died, long before he was grown. He had been alone until he had found Ralak.

That, Zena pronounced, was why he cared most for Ralak. At first, he had thought she was like the bad female who had forced him to leave, and had hurt her. Then he had realized she was like his mother instead. He had loved his mother too.

It would be good, Ralak thought wryly, if Zena would put as much energy into listening to the Mother as she did listening to others. She loved to ask questions, and had pulled most of Ralak's story out of her, too, though Ralak had not intended to tell of her struggles. Zena knew of the deaths of her tribe and her brother; she knew how Ralak had clung to the earth in labor, how she had suffered when Lotan was gone. But Ralak had not told her of the challenge. That she must know without words.

Zena came to give her the fruit she and Lotan had collected. Ralak took a few bites, and then lay back wearily.

Zena took her hand and spoke softly. "If it pains you, I will give you the herbs."

It was the first time she had referred to Ralak's illness. Her words signaled acceptance, and Ralak was grateful. If Zena could accept the Mother's way in this matter, she could accept it in others. She would be ready soon.

Ralak's eyes closed, and the strain left her face. "Perhaps later," she said. "I sleep now."

Zena continued to hold Ralak's hand. It was dry, the skin like thin bark stripped from a tree, and she could feel the bones clearly against their fragile covering.

Darkness fell, and still Zena did not move. She felt connected to Ralak through her papery hand, as if she could feel Ralak's feelings, see and hear through her eyes and ears as well as her own. Together, they saw the fire flicker as Lotan placed more sticks on it, smelled the fragrance of the leaves he threw in the flames. They heard the noises around the clearing, of insects chirping and small monkeys chattering to each other as they prepared to sleep. They were different noises than Zena had known before, for Ralak had led them to a place where she had lived long ago. Even though all her tribe had died in this place, she had come back. Zena did not know why.

Tall trees grew close around the clearing, filtering the moonlight, and the moss that hung thickly from their branches cast strange shadows. Frogs called in a cascading chorus that mimicked the water cascading through the many small streams. The smells were strong and moist. It was not like the place where they had met the Big Ones long ago, Zena reflected, for that had been dark and musty, as if the sun had never penetrated. Here, there were fragrant flowers and dappled sunlight, and greenness. Even the mountains were green. They rose from the valley floor, taking the vegetation with them into the swirling clouds.

Zena sighed, and lay down beside Ralak, still holding her hand. She did not sleep, but she dreamed as if she were asleep. She saw herself walking toward a tall mountain that rose steeply from a misty valley. She recognized the mountain, for it was not far away. She had often stared up at its conical peak spearing through the clouds that hugged its upper slopes. But in her dream, there was no peak, for where the top should be were only more clouds, heavy and white. They circled slowly, thinning as they moved, then dissipated suddenly. For an instant before they regrouped, Zena saw the summit, golden in the sunlight. It seemed to beckon her.

She saw herself begin to climb the mountain. Moss and ferns grew thickly beneath her, and the earth was damp. Even in her dreamlike state, she felt the dampness clearly, smelled the dank odors that rose into the air as her feet pressed against the lush growth.

She wanted a track, she realized, so she could find her way through the mist and the clinging undergrowth to the top of the mountain. She was supposed to go there. Something waited for her there.

Sleep overtook Zena and the mountain faded. She slept soundly, unaware of the others as they slid quietly into the shelter. But just as dawn crept across the land, sending fingers of pale light into the shelter, she heard Ralak stir beside her and utter a sharp cry.

Alarm woke Zena quickly. She leaned over Ralak, trying to see her face clearly in the dimness, but then she realized she did not need to see. She knew already. Ralak was slipping away; she was going somewhere, and Zena could not stop her.

Tears poured down her face and fell onto Ralak's thin cheeks. The wetness seemed to rouse Ralak, for she opened her eyes wide and stared straight at Zena.

"Go!" she said hoarsely. "Go while I can help. You must go now. They will guide you."

For a moment, Zena was confused. Where should she go, and why? Then she remembered. The mountain; she must go to the mountain. The dreamlike vision came back to her as if she were still within it.

She placed her lips against Ralak's cool cheek, to let her know she had understood. Then she rose silently and slipped from the shelter.

CHAPTER
15

Mist hung heavily in the air. Wisps of it clung to the shelter, wrapped themselves sinuously around the lower branches of the trees. Zena felt the soft strands tickle her arms, caress her forehead. Despite their fragility, they seemed solid in the dim light, as if she would have to push them aside to walk.

No noises, no movements interrupted the early morning stillness. The birds were still sleeping; the tiny monkeys had not yet left their leafy nests. Even the insects had fallen silent in the brief interim between night and day. Zena looked up, searching for the sliver of rosy orange that preceded the sun, but only the moon was there; it hung above the mountain's shrouded peak, remote and cool and beautiful.

She shivered. The moon had always made her uneasy. It was the sun she loved, with its warmth and brilliance. She remembered Cere's words. On the night that her mother, Mina, had struggled to bear her, the moon had hidden behind dark clouds and refused to emerge. But the sun had come. Just as Kalar finished speaking to the Mother, it had slid over the horizon and touched her eyelids with rose, so that she would know her actions were blessed. The sun had given her light to see as she pulled Zena from the dark womb that had enclosed her for so long, had warmed Zena in her first moments.

A filmy cloud slid across the moon's watching face. Tendrils from the clouds reached down, far down, all the way to the earth and touched her arm. Zena felt them like fingers, drawing her toward the mountain. Something waited for her there; she could feel it, almost smell it. She must hurry.

Darkness enclosed her as she entered the woods. She could see the dim outlines of trunks, a ghostly network of branches against the pale sky, but the solid reality of trees dissolved into moving shadows when she looked too hard. She left them with relief and entered a narrow strip of marsh that bordered the mountain. Her feet squashed soddenly into dank vegetation, and a myriad of scents rose to her nostrils. She breathed them in, aware of each separate smell and then the mass of scents. They seemed to enter her through her eyes and ears as well as her nostrils, just as she thought she could smell the color of the brackish water as well as see it. All her senses were intermingled, fully alive.

She came to a shallow pool and bent to drink. Her face stared back at her, startled, then split into many fragments as she splashed cool water against her skin. The ruffled surface settled again, reflecting the tall reeds that surrounded her. A vague track led her through them to higher ground. The foliage was dense now, and dripping with moisture. She pushed her way into it until the wall of green became impenetrable. There was no sign that any creature had ever ventured this way before. Zena stopped, uncertain.

A flash of brilliant blue caught her eye as a bird flew past and settled on a rock beyond her. Its feathers were the color of the sky in all its moods, from palest blue to sparkling turquoise to the ominous purple that preceded a storm. Long, golden streamers issued from its tail.

Zena stared, entranced. Never before had she seen a bird like this one. She climbed toward it, to see better. The bird rose into the air with a flurry of wings and flew to another rock, farther on. Zena followed. The bird waited, but as soon as she approached, it flew on again.

It was leading her, she realized, as a bird had once led the honeydigger while she watched.

She followed unquestioningly, immersed in her quest. Up and up she went, straining her eyes to see in the dim predawn light. Everything around her spoke of mystery, of challenge. It flowed into her heart and pushed her forward, even when the way grew so steep she could barely stand without falling. Only once did she stop to rest. The bird waited patiently on a branch that hung directly above her head, so that she had to crane her neck backward to see it.

She looked down from her precipitous perch. All the earth

seemed to be below her now. Trees, plains, marshes, rocky hill-sides, rivers and lakes spread away in an array so vast her eyes could scarcely encompass its dimensions. And as she watched, the orange orb of the sun popped suddenly over the horizon and covered it all in sparkling layers of brilliance. Every leaf and flower and twig in all that panorama held a drop of water, and every drop welcomed the sun's light and reflected it back in glittering splendor.

Zena's eyes filled with tears at the spectacle; her tears caught the light, so that even within her there was radiance. She pulled it into her, marveling. The golden glow filled her completely, erasing her hunger, her fatigue, even the sadness that caught at her when her thoughts went for a moment to Ralak. It was all the same, she realized. The radiance was in the trees and grasses, the earth itself, as it was in her, in everything that lived. She breathed it in, felt it enter her body in waves of gold that she could see and hear and taste and smell.

The bird's feathers flashed past her face; then it vanished into the mist. Zena scrambled after it. Now all her attention was focused on her movements, for the way was so steep and slippery she had to crawl. Water was everywhere, rushing down in streams and rivulets between the mossy rocks, the clumps of ferns and flowers. Multicolored and delicate, the flowers nodded on their tall stems like fragments of a scattered rainbow. Swaths of red and blue and purple and yellow dotted the hillside, and behind them all was the velvety green.

The gurgle of rushing water became a thunderous racket as Zena scrambled higher. Rounding a bulky promontory, she discovered its cause. A massive waterfall cascaded from a cliff hundreds of feet above her head, plunging straight down in heavy, immutable torrents. A frenzy of white foam surged wildly below her feet. Sheer cliffs surrounded her on both sides.

No one could go up this way, she realized. She would have to find another route.

The bird waggled near her, catching her attention. To her horror, it flew straight into the waterfall and disappeared behind it. For the first time, she was afraid. Must she follow?

The bird reappeared and repeated its maneuver. Reluctantly, Zena approached the falls, but when she came close, she saw that there was a small opening, just to the left of the major cascade. She squeezed through it and found herself in a protected place behind the crashing water. Even the thunderous noise was muted here, so that she could hear soft drips as moisture fell in glittering beads from the rocks above. There was no other movement, no sign of life, only the muffled splashes.

She looked for the bird. It was perched on a ledge, watching her. She recognized it by its shape alone, for light barely penetrated the cavernous space, and the bird had lost its brilliance. It flew into a small tunnel. Zena crawled after it and emerged into another chamber. For a moment, she could see nothing, then her eyes adjusted and she saw that a wide pool spread across the entire space. The water was black, unmoving. Beyond that, all was darkness.

The bird flew across the pool and landed on a half-submerged rock. Zena frowned. The bird could fly, but she would have to go through the water. It loomed before her, opaque, forbidding, and utterly still. Everything in the cave was still, except her fear as she faced the murky water. Her fear resonated in the silence, bounced into the dank air, and then returned to lodge deep in her belly.

Abruptly, the stillness was broken as hundreds of bats took flight. They poured from their hidden perches above Zena's head, flapping in strong, audible swaths as they swirled through the dark cavern. Zena felt the current from their wings touch her face, her hair, but not one of the flying animals touched her with its body. The scream that had risen in her throat subsided, and miraculously, her fear went with it.

She waded into the inky water. Water slapped at her chest but rose no farther, only cleansed her, pulled all the itching from her skin, the grime from her feet and legs. She relaxed into the pool's womblike softness, allowed it to enclose her, comfort her in its dark embrace. Its water was blessed; she was sure of it. She placed a hand on the glimmering surface in thanks as she slid from its gentle grasp.

Echoes of the rustle of bats' wings, of water lapping against rock as the pool settled again into stillness, bounced hollowly around her as she followed the bird up steep rocks that rose like steps in the back of the cavern. Then, suddenly, there was light ahead. Zena emerged into it and stared, surprised. She was more than halfway up the falls, but all around her were steep, water-drenched rocks, too treacherous to cross. Below her was a sheer drop into nothingness. She began to shake. A thick vine hung near her head. She grabbed it, to steady herself. Before her, the bird perched on another vine and waggled its tail. Zena took a deep breath and clutched the vine with both hands as she inched forward. Just as the vine slipped from her fingers, she grabbed another, and another, until she stood panting on a narrow ledge. She dared not look down; she looked up instead.

A level swath of green beckoned. She crawled to it, almost weeping in relief to be away from the slippery rocks, and sank down to rest. For a long time, she lay quietly, listening to birds calling to each other in high, musical voices, feeling strength flow into her from the earth. Purple berries grew on low bushes near her; she ate them, and they seemed to relieve both her hunger and her fatigue. She rose to continue her climb. The brilliant bird stayed always visible before her.

Abruptly, between one step and the next, she emerged from the clinging vegetation into sand-colored rock, heavily streaked with orange. Exquisite flowers, with delicate waxy faces like tiny gourds, grew in clumps between the rocks. Zena knelt to examine them, entranced by their beauty. A sweet smell permeated her nostrils; she drew it in and felt it swirl through her body. Looking up again, she saw that everything above her was open to the sky. Even the summit was visible. It rose above her, golden in the sunlight, as she had seen it in her vision.

Slowly, she climbed the last distance and lowered herself onto a flat boulder where the bird had perched. She sensed she had come to the end of her journey, and she was right, for when she looked again for the bird, it had disappeared.

For a moment, the valley spread below her once more; then the clouds closed in until she could see only the small area around her boulder. All else was wreathed in mist. Zena waited, aware of an intense stillness within her. There was no need to move, to search further. What she sought would come to her.

Time passed, and she did not know it. There were only the scents, the sounds, the stillness in her body. Presently, she became aware of a rustling noise as something slithered toward her across the sandy soil. She sensed rather than saw what it was, and although her heart leaped into her throat when the huge snake stopped before her, she was not surprised. It was thick, as thick as her arms together, and wide stripes of coral and tan decorated its long body. The serpent never took its eyes from her face as it coiled itself by her feet and raised its flat, triangular head. Its forked tongue darted in and out of its mouth, and its small black eyes stared at her unblinkingly. It began to weave its head back and forth before her.

Zena did not move. The breath went in and out of her body so slowly she could barely feel it. Only her eyes responded, widening almost imperceptibly in fear that was not really fear, so tinged was it with fascination. She knew that if she moved the snake would strike, but she knew, too, that it did not matter, that nothing mattered except to watch the snake and follow its movements.

She stared into the snake's eyes, and as she stared, they became pools, and then they were one great pool of blackness that held everything she had ever known or heard, everything that was. She saw Kalar's eyes there, and Ralak's, and the eyes of many others, wise ones. All their knowledge, their awareness and wisdom lay submerged in the fathomless depths of the serpent's gaze. Zena drew it in, through her eyes, her ears, her skin and nostrils, and felt it settle in her heart.

The snake's venom was there, too, its power; she did not forget. If she broke the connection, it would be merciless. It would strike and she would die.

She swayed with it instead, slowly, in perfect rhythm, drowning in its eyes. Down and down she flowed into the depths of all that had happened before, all that would come to be. And slowly she knew what it meant to accept; to accept was all. There was no other way, only to absorb and to know all that came to her from the deep pool of wisdom in the snake's eyes. And when she knew that this was so, with her heart and body as well as her mind, she emerged from the depths of the all-encompassing blackness. Now all was radiance, as she had seen it earlier, except this radiance was so great it could not be absorbed. It washed over and through her and out upon the earth. Voices came through it, Kalar's voice and Ralak's, the voices of all those who would come after to live and die by the Mother's ways. They spoke to Zena, only there were no words. Their messages came from the knowledge of their bodies, knowledge distilled from the earth and sky. Zena felt the power that came from their wisdom, as if a cord as thick as the serpent connected her to a place deep within the earth, then stretched high into the sky to touch the sun and the moon. They were her body and she was theirs, inseparable. To break the cord would be to risk not just her death but the death of the earth as well, for all life was the same. One life merged into another; each returned to the earth so that new life could begin again. And all of it was the earthforce and the Mother.

The wisdom coursed through Zena, wisdom that came to her body and heart when her mind forgot its struggle to comprehend. She felt it fill a secret place inside her, a place that had waited, haunted in its emptiness, while she had raged against the Mother. There was nothing in her now but her body's knowledge of earthquakes and storms, of droughts and floods that had come and would always come, of the passage of the cool, impervious moon through its phases, of the rains that would drench the earth or stubbornly refuse to fall. Above them all was the sun, the glorious sun, pouring its warmth onto the earth. It pulled the plants, the trees and flowers upward with its energy, then sucked all moisture from the land with its brutal heat. Like the rains, it gave life and took it away. Always it was so.

Still now, quiescent, she felt another truth emerge. The Mother was the earthforce, as Ralak had said, but She was more. The earthforce was all that had ever happened, all that would come as the moon grew round, then shrank to a sliver, as the sun rose and disappeared, as the rains came and the earth cracked apart with drought. The Mother was all these things and more. She was the very best of all that came to their minds and hearts: the caring that bound them to each other, the hope they carried with them when an infant was born, the joy they felt when the rains came, even the pleasure of an unexpected piece of ripe fruit, or a brilliant bird or flower. The Mother was their sorrow when illness came, their pain when She took the ones they loved back to Her heart in death. Even as they grieved, She gave them something precious, in the caring they felt for the one who suffered, in their awareness of Her all-encompassing heart, the heart that absorbed them once more when they ceased to breathe. The Mother was wisdom and knowledge and love.

Zena opened herself to the Mother. No thoughts, no feelings intruded as she sat motionless, knowing only the Mother. Time passed that was not time, for each instant was as brief as the darting of the snake's tongue, even as it stretched to encompass all the time that had ever passed.

Slowly, so slowly she did not know it had happened, Zena crumpled to the earth and slept.

II

When she opened her eyes, the snake was gone. For a moment, Zena wondered if it had been there at all, or if she had only dreamed its presence. But then she looked down at the earth by her feet and saw its skin. It had shed its skin as she had shed the skin of her childish anger.

She reached down to touch the transparent tissue, as if to touch herself as a child for the last time. Then she jumped to her feet, compelled by a sudden sense of urgency that drove all other thoughts away. Ralak had been with her on the mountain; Zena had felt her thoughts, known her presence. But now the wise woman's strength was almost gone. Zena could feel it fading. The earthforce, the Mother, were waiting to reclaim her.

Heedless of the steep descent, Zena began to run. She slithered and tumbled down the mountain, barely noticing the steep, slippery cliffs, the wild scramble beside the waterfall or the struggle to part the heavy vegetation that followed. All her energy was focused on reaching Ralak. Only when she found herself beyond the marsh and entering the woods did a brief awareness of her route return, and she wondered how she had managed to find her way without the bird to guide her.

Terror drove the thought from her mind as she raced through the trees and into the clearing. She did not see the others staring; she saw only the shelter, then Ralak's face. She was still, too still. Her eyes were closed, her skin waxen. Zena knelt beside her, fear thudding in her heart. She had never been able to speak to Kalar again, but she wanted to hear Ralak's voice, just one more time.

"Please," she breathed to the Mother, "please let her live a moment longer."

As if she had heard, Ralak slowly opened her eyes. Zena took her hand, so thin now it was no more than a bare bit of skin with bones beneath, like the fragile skeleton of a baby bird that had never eaten. But though it came as no more than a whisper, there was still power in Ralak's voice.

"You have been to the mountain," she said, staring into Zena's face. "Good." She smiled, and some of the old spark came into her eyes.

"Now you are of the Mother, truly Hers. But still you must find food and water, as the others do. The Mother trips those who become proud."

The typically pungent words brought a smile to Zena's anxious face. She would not forget them. The smile faded quickly as humility poured into her. Ralak was dying, and now she must be the wise one. She must learn to be like Ralak, like Kalar and all the other wise ones who had come before and would come after. It was an awesome challenge.

Ralak spoke again, but now the power had left her voice, and Zena knew she was almost gone.

"Be of the Mother," she whispered in blessing. "Your strength will come from the earthforce, your wisdom and courage from the Mother. Only listen, and they will guide you."

Ralak stared once more into Zena's eyes, then she sighed, a long, deep sigh, and gave up the effort to stay alive. During all the long hours Zena had spent on the mountain, she had clutched at the earth, willing its strength into her frail body so she could take just one more breath. Now she could let go. The earthforce was waiting to reclaim her, and she slid willingly into its grasp.

Zena felt her go, as if a connection between the earth and Ralak's hand and her own fingers had been broken. Even as she neared death, Ralak had transmitted the power of the earthforce through her hand. Now the flow was reversed, as her life drained back into the earth that had sustained her so many times. Zena let the lifeless fingers slip to the ground.

An agonized howl broke into the silence. Zena jumped up, startled. She had almost forgotten the others. The howl had come from Kropor. He ran to Ralak and bent over her, but leaped up again immediately. No breath moved between the lips of the tiny female he adored, and her eyes stared at him sightlessly. He howled again, over and over, long, anguished howls that resounded through the clearing, caused all the birds to take flight, the animals to run into their burrows.

The howling seemed suddenly not to satisfy him. He looked wildly around until he spotted a large branch that had fallen from a nearby tree. Grabbing it with both hands, he began to run around the clearing, sweeping the limb noisily behind him in huge arcs. Everything in its path, digging sticks, baskets, food, even the children, were swept away. When there were no more objects anywhere in the clearing, Kropor stood still and raised the big branch over his head, then brought it to the ground with all his strength. Again, he raised the limb, again it plunged to the ground with a fearful whack.

The children huddled near the shelter, terrified by the noisy display. Kropor approached them, seeming not even to see them, and raised the stick again. They ran, all but Clio, Ralak's young one. Her prolonged and arduous birth had left indelible marks on her as well as her mother. Caught too long between womb and outer world, she had received sustenance from neither. No watery nourishment had come through the cord that attached her to her mother's body, and she had been unable to reach the life-giving air that would replace it. And so a part of her had died.

At first, the damage had not been apparent, for Clio grew like any other child. But when the time came for her to speak, her tongue seemed unable to frame words, her brain unable to comprehend them. She did not understand fear, either. As precocious physically as she was limited mentally, she had quickly learned to run without inhibition in any direction that pleased her, toward any creature, any cliff or body of water, however dangerous.

The child stood now and regarded Kropor without fear, unaware that his behavior posed a threat. He raised his stick high, as if to bring it down on her head. Zena thought he did not see Clio at all, and she jumped forward to pull her out of the way. But Toro got there first and grabbed the child just before the stick crashed. Clio clung to her, finally frightened by the abrupt gesture. Toro was her mother even more than Ralak had been. Once Clio had started to run, Ralak had been too weak and ill to care for her, and Toro had taken over. It was always Toro Clio wanted when she was hurt.

Kropor dropped the stick suddenly. He ran around the edges of the clearing, picking up everything the branch had swept away, and threw each object to the ground with angry force. A cutting stone bounced near Bran's foot, and he charged at Kropor, to stop him. Kropor paid no attention.

Zena called his name loudly, trying to penetrate his agony. But Kropor only stared at her unseeingly. She came closer, to touch him, but backed away quickly when he raised his arm as if to strike her. Bran and Lotan appeared by her side. Kropor roared at them, but there was no aggression in his tone, only helplessness. He began to shuffle despondently in ever-widening circles, moving away from the others. Bran and Lotan let him go.

Just as he entered the trees, Kropor raised his head and stared at the group huddled on the opposite edge of the clearing, as if he were seeing them for the first time since he had begun to howl. His eyes widened in an expression of horror. Another wrenching howl escaped him, then he turned and ran, crashing through the underbrush like a demented animal.

Toro looked after him, her face reflecting an agony of indecision. Kropor was her mate; she had been with him now for many moons. With Ralak gone, her loyalty was to him, not the others. Holding Clio tightly with her free hand, she followed his retreating form. Metep trudged after her mother, one hand resting protectively on her swollen belly.

Zena looked after them sadly. There was nothing she could do. Toro had always cared for Kropor, despite his devotion to Ralak, and Metep needed to be with her mother. Zena was certain Kropor would not harm them now. He had spent his rage, and only grief was left. Perhaps Toro could help with that.

Clio was another matter. Zena wanted badly to call the child back, but she knew it was no use. Clio would not leave Toro. And in the end, only the Mother knew the answer to Clio; only the Mother could keep her safe, for she was uncontrollable, like the earthforce at its most extreme. Zena saw it in her wild, fearless eyes that flashed like lightning when storms came, in the exuberance of her body as she ran to greet the thunder. Clio loved storms. She danced then, frenzied, graceful dances that lasted until she sank exhausted to the earth, and had to be carried back to the shelter. Only at these times, and when she slept, could she be restrained for more than a moment.

Ralak had understood. "I pulled too hard on the earthforce when Clio was born," she had said once. "Now she belongs to it, and not to us." There had been no sorrow in her tone, only acceptance.

Zena struggled to accept, as Ralak had accepted, as she knew Kalar would have accepted. To be truly wise, she must trust.

Determinedly, she turned back to Ralak. Lotan was kneeling beside her, crooning her name in sorrow. He had loved his mother more than any other, and to be without her seemed impossible. Zena left him there and went to the stream, where bushes redolent with snowy blossoms grew in thick clumps. She broke off a bundle of fragrant branches and carried them back to the shelter. Gently, she placed the soft clusters on Ralak's body, covering all but her face. The pale blossoms gave off a tangy scent that seemed right for one such as Ralak. They would protect her and sustain her with their fragrance.

When she had finished, she gathered the others around her. From this moment on, each death, each birth, each animal that gave its life to feed them, each season of life-giving rain, each gathering of the earth's bounty, must be remembered and blessed. That was the Mother's way, and she would honor it. She stood at Ralak's head, and her voice rang out as if she had spoken thus all her life.

"Great Mother, Earthforce, Giver of All Life, take Ralak back to Your heart. Always, she has been one with You, one with the earthforce that gave her strength, one with the Mother whose love she came to know. Now she is Yours once more. We commend her to You."

Zena looked down at Ralak. "Go with the Mother, Ralak," she told her quietly. "The love in our hearts goes with you."

Struggling to control the tears that had welled up when she looked into Ralak's still face, Zena continued. There was more she must say, words she should have said long ago but had been unable to utter. Now her voice was low, filled with sadness.

"Great Mother, hear me now. It is of Kalar I speak, and Cere and

Lett, and all the others who died so brutally. Still, I do not know why this should be so, but I know You have taken them back to Your heart, and that is enough. I speak to You now of them, and through You, I speak to them.

"The love in our hearts goes with all of you," she told the ones who had died. "Always, you live within us. I feel your wisdom, Kalar, and I feel Cere's love, and the loyalty of Lett, the knowledge of the Mother's creatures that came from Agar, Tempa's willingness always to help . . ."

Zena named them, one at a time, names she had not spoken for so long her mouth had almost forgotten how to frame the sounds, as she remembered each face and personality. When she had finished, she commended them to the Mother.

"Keep them safe in Your heart," she concluded. "Like Ralak, they live within us, but they are Yours now."

Zena's voice faded and she sat down abruptly, exhausted by her efforts. Bran watched her, astonished at the change her trip to the mountain had wrought. Zena, the serious child he had once teased, had become a wise one. He had seen the new strength in her stature when she had risen, had heard the unmistakable power in her voice when she had spoken to the Mother. She reminded him of Kalar, with her sturdy body, her wide hips and big head.

He yawned and went to put wood on the fire. Darkness would fall soon, and it was his job to keep them safe.

Zena lay near the fire as silence descended on the clearing. She felt cleansed of a burden she had carried too long, and ready to listen for the Mother's message. It was always at these times, when day turned into night, or night became day, that the Mother had spoken to Kalar, for these were the times of silence. She must learn to listen in the same way.

Zena opened her mind and waited, but weariness undermined her resolve, and she slept until a frantic voice aroused her. She sat, suddenly awake. It was Toro shouting, and her voice was full of fear.

Zena ran to the edge of the clearing, calling loudly as she ran. Bran and Lotan sprinted beside her.

Toro burst from the trees. "You must come," she said. "Clio has gone. She was sleeping beside me, but now she has gone. It was the moon—"

She broke off, sobbing, but Zena knew what she meant. Like storms, the moon attracted Clio powerfully. It seemed to pull at her, as it had pulled at Zena earlier. Sometimes, when the moon was full, Clio ran toward it as if she thought she would fly, as the birds flew, and reach it.

"Bring sticks with fire," Zena instructed. "Nyta can stay to guard the others. Bran can come with me, and Lotan."

"Keep Three-Legs," she added. "Do not let her follow." They each grabbed a burning stick and hurried after Toro. The trees were dark, despite the full moon, but presently they came out into a small, clear space, where some light came through.

"We were sleeping here," Toro explained. "We could not find Kropor. He moved too fast."

Metep was huddled fearfully in the darkest corner of the clearing. She did not rise, but clutched her belly, groaning, as a strong contraction racked her.

Toro's eyes widened, and she bent anxiously over her daughter. "The infant comes," she said to Zena. "We must go back to the shelter."

Zena nodded. The night would be busy between Metep and Clio. The Mother had certainly not waited long to provide her with challenges!

"Take Metep back while she can walk," she instructed. "We will look for Clio and follow."

Metep struggled to her feet and set off, leaning heavily on her mother. Zena looked at Bran and Lotan, seeking their advice. The search seemed almost impossible. Clio could have run in any direction. They could call her name, but she might not answer, might not come even if she saw them. A child of the woods, she had no fear of being alone among the dark trees. She did not understand the dangers.

"We must try," Bran said, answering her unspoken question. Lotan nodded vigorously. Clio was his little sister, the one he had held close when she was tiny. She was all he had left of his mother.

"We each go a different way, and return here to meet, then try again," he suggested.

Clutching their torches, they trudged separately through the dark forest, calling loudly as they walked. There was no answer; they met and tried again, but still there was no sign of Clio.

"We wait here with a fire until the light comes, and then look again," Bran said. "You return to Metep."

Zena nodded reluctantly. Bran was right. They would never find Clio in the darkness. The moon had vanished behind thick clouds, and now the night was utterly black. Still, she did not want to give up. Without the moon to follow, Clio would surely be afraid. She might have fallen, could be lying somewhere, hurt and crying. A predator might find her, or the hyenas.

Zena thrust her fear away. Fear would not help Clio; only calmness and trust would do that. Closing her eyes, she tried to will feelings of peace and security to Clio, tried to visualize her accepting the certainty of the Mother's protection. Clio had no words, but Zena was certain she could feel thoughts in her own way. She had the earthforce strongly within her as well, and it would guard her. Comforting herself with these thoughts, Zena trudged wearily back to the shelter.

III

Deep in the woods, in a hole between the roots of a tree, Clio frowned. The moon had disappeared, and without it, she did not know where to go. She had followed it, and then it had hidden, so she had crawled beneath the tree to rest.

Something rustled in the underbrush, as if a large animal were moving. Clio froze. Her breath barely moved in her chest, and even her scent seemed to disappear. It was not fear that kept her motionless, but instinct, the instinct of an animal with no other form of protection. The rustling stopped. Clio's eyes closed, but even in sleep, her body was utterly still.

Toward morning, a shadow passed over her. Sleeping soundly now, Clio did not see it. She did not hear, either, for the creature that stared down at her made no sound as its feet trod the damp earth. Perhaps, though, she felt the strength of its intent gaze, or smelled it, for she suddenly opened her eyes. A scream rose in her throat, but she did not utter it. Instead, she held out her hand.

CHAPTER
16

Sima burst into the clearing, her body tense with fear. "Lion!" she gasped. "I saw its tracks, near the place where we lost Clio."

Every morning since Clio's disappearance, Sima had scoured the nearby woods looking for her. She was nine now, and took a keen interest in all the young ones, but Clio had aroused a special protectiveness, since she could not speak like the others, and seemed to understand so little.

Lotan dropped the statue he had been carving and jumped to his feet. He, too, spent most of his time looking for Clio, and refused to believe she could not be found. How could she disappear without a trace? But if a lion was in the area, that was possible. It could have sprung on her and dragged her away, and they would never know.

"Show me," he said urgently to Sima, grasping her hand. Together, they set off into the trees. Bran grabbed a stout stick and followed, with Lupe behind him, as always.

Zena watched them go, anxiety stilling her fingers in the middle of a stroke as she sharpened her stick. Over and over, she had waited for a message from the Mother that might help them to find Clio. But nothing had come.

That was not true, she realized, sitting back on her heels to reflect. Each time she thought of Clio, a strange feeling of peace washed over her, erasing the anxiety that had accumulated as the days passed without any sign of her.

Perhaps the peaceful feeling itself is a message, she thought hopefully. It seemed impossible that the child could still be all right, after so many days and nights wandering by herself. But if the Mother was protecting her, perhaps she was safe.

Still, the appearance of a lion was worrying. Normally, lions stayed in the plains, where the zebras and antelopes they preyed on were plentiful. Only hunger would have brought it so deeply into the woods, and Zena could not imagine how even the Mother could protect a helpless child against a hungry lion. Worse, if one lion was in the area, there must be others. At this time of the year, each lioness was trying to feed herself, her growing cubs, and one or two males for whom she hunted.

Sima and Lotan returned, interrupting her thoughts. They were flushed and breathless, and worried. Lotan nodded soberly as Zena raised a questioning face.

"Lion," he said. "Many, I think." His lips tightened, and he went off to sit by himself, with his head in his hands.

Zena looked compassionately at his slumped figure. All of them had been upset by Clio's disappearance, but for Lotan her loss had been devastating. She was always in his thoughts. Only when Zena mated with him did he seem to forget. Then, both of them lost themselves completely in the sensations. For Zena, the pleasure was more than physical. Mating gave her a feeling of closeness to the Mother that reminded her of the intense unity she had felt on the mountain. Strangely, as she immersed herself in purely sensual feelings, she seemed to spring free of the body that created them and enter the realm of her heart.

Lotan felt some of this unity as well, but it quickly disappeared. As soon as they had rolled apart, his face grew strained and weary once again, as thoughts of Clio returned.

Zena shook her head in dismay. If lions were hunting near the shelter, they would have to leave even if they had not found Clio. The danger of an attack was too great, especially without fire. All their burning sticks had gone out in a drenching rain, and they had been unable to find more. The thought of leaving distressed her because of Clio, but in another way it was a relief. Ever since her trip to the mountain, she had felt a terrible restlessness, a restlessness that grew each day until she thought she would burst with it. She was supposed to lead the tribe to a new home; she knew it absolutely, from the dreams.

They came every night, and they were always the same. She saw herself walking in a lush valley enclosed by high plateaus. Smoking mountains loomed behind the hills. Far ahead was a body of water that stretched all the way to the horizon. As she came close to it, her feet sank into soft, grainy earth that sparkled white in the sunlight, unlike any earth she had seen before. Always, the sun rose on her right as she traveled, and set on her left. Always, too, she felt a strong sense of urgency. She must go to this place soon, and she must take the others with her. Sometimes she thought she saw Clio with them as well, although that seemed impossible, and a big, stooped male that looked like Kropor.

The big male's face never came clear, so she could not tell. Now it dissolved into Bran's face. He was standing in front of her, waiting for her eyes to focus on him.

"They hunt near here," he told her soberly. "There are many. Two cubs at least, more than half grown, and one or two males, and the lioness. We must keep the young ones close, and never go alone to look for food."

She nodded, appreciating his knowledge. Bran could understand tracks better than any. All of them were becoming increasingly dependent on him, as the oldest male. Always, his advice was helpful, his support unstinting.

"We must leave soon," she murmured, so quietly that only Bran heard. She hated to say the words aloud, for they meant Clio would never be found. Still, she must not shrink from uttering them. The whole tribe was her responsibility, more than any single member. Sometimes, it was necessary to be ruthless. And it was possible that the child was all right. Otherwise, why would the Mother give her that feeling of peace?

She went to Lotan and put an arm around his shoulders. "Perhaps Clio is all right," she told him. "The Mother sends peace to my mind when I think of her."

Her words did not comfort Lotan as she had intended.

"Perhaps that is because She has taken Clio back to Her heart already," he replied bitterly. "Perhaps that is why you feel peace, why we cannot find her. The lion may have taken her, or some other animal."

Zena grimaced. She should have thought of that explanation. Lotan was right. Probably Clio was dead.

Lotan picked up the statue he had been carving and scraped at it furiously, but after a time his movements slowed and he became absorbed in the task. He loved carving, and had become very skillful at making wide-hipped figures, like the ones Lett had once made. Zena had realized how important the statues were when Metep had given birth. She had struggled all through the terrible night when they had lost Clio, and by morning, Toro had been desperate with anxiety.

"She is too small," Toro had wailed. "The baby cannot come, and she will die!"

Seeing her distress, Nyta had brought out the figure she had rescued from the circle of stones. Reverently, she had placed it in Zena's hands. Following a strong impulse, Zena had drawn it slowly along Metep's straining body from navel to crotch, over and over again, as if pulling the infant forth. The gesture seemed to help, for the baby had been born soon after.

Now Metep, and Toro, even Sima, wanted a figure. Toro especially had been impressed by the statue's magic. She had stared at Zena with awestruck eyes as Zena had drawn the figure along Metep's body, and had wondered at her power. Ralak's talk of the earthforce and Zena's explanations of the Mother had never made much sense to Toro. But she did understand this. The small figure contained powerful magic, and the magic came through Zena. Toro began to listen carefully to all that Zena said, and the clumsy but recognizable statue Lotan made for her became her most prized possession.

Zena patted her own belly. She needed a figure for herself. An infant was growing in her body, still so tiny it could barely be felt. The Mother had blessed her in this way, too.

When the day ended, she called a council, so that all could participate in making the decision.

"I have not spoken before because of Clio," she told the others, "but now I believe it is time to tell you what the Mother shows me." She described the vision she had seen so many times, told of the beautiful valley and high plateaus, the vast water that seemed to have no end, and the strange white earth. She did not mention Clio and Kropor, lest she raise false hopes, but spoke instead of the peace that came to her when she thought of Clio.

"Perhaps the Mother protects her, and she is all right; perhaps She has taken Clio back to Her heart, as Lotan thinks. I cannot tell," she finished.

Subdued murmurs greeted her statements, but for a long time no one spoke. Bran broke the silence.

"We must leave," he said quietly. "Zena has seen the Mother's way in her visions. We must follow.

"I, too, believe the Mother has taken Clio back to Her heart," he added, glancing at Lotan. "The child belongs to Her now, and we need not worry anymore."

Toro looked mournful. "It is hard to leave without Clio, but I would also like to see Kropor again," she said sadly. "He was part of this tribe too."

The others nodded, understanding that she had cared very much for Kropor. They missed him too. Kropor had been difficult sometimes, but still his absence left a hole in their lives.

"He could return one day," Zena comforted Toro, "when his grief is less."

Toro shook her head. "We will leave, and he will not find us," she said sadly. "And I think he likes best to be alone, with Ralak gone."

Loud roars, harsh against the background of gentle night sounds, interrupted her words. The lions were calling to each other. Perhaps they had made a kill. The children shivered and moved closer to the adults. Three-Legs cuddled against Zena, her liquid brown eyes full of alarm. Even the frogs and insects ceased their chirping, as if to listen.

"We must leave. I agree with Bran." It was Nyta's voice, firm despite the fear the lions' roars had aroused.

"The Mother has given me a new infant, and I do not want it born here, where the lions might take it," she added, looking down at her swollen belly.

Lotan nodded reluctantly. "One more time I will search for Clio, when the light comes. Then we leave."

There was no sign of Clio in the morning. There had never been any sign of her. Once, Bran had found some footprints that led to a tree, but then they stopped abruptly. *It was as if Clio really had followed the moon straight into the sky*, Zena thought, *leaving no tracks behind her.*

They set off eagerly despite their sorrow. The lions had snuffled around the clearing during the night, frightening all of them, and they were glad to get away. They moved fast, for the route was cool and pleasant, through deep forest that stretched north for many miles before giving way to open savannah.

By nightfall, they had reached the edge of the woods. Zena decided to stay in the trees. A storm was brewing, and she did not want to spend the night unprotected on the open plains. All afternoon, heavy black clouds had spilled from an invisible place beyond the horizon and stretched across the sky, thickening as they moved. As darkness descended, they solidified into an impenetrable mass that blotted out the stars. The wind rose and began to shriek through the closely packed trees, so that they rubbed together and made ominous, creaking noises.

Rain slashed suddenly at their faces. Quickly, they gathered branches to make a shelter, but as soon as they had the branches in place, a howling gust of wind tore them down and scattered them around the forest floor. Lotan pointed to a deep depression in the earth, where a huge tree had been uprooted.

"In there," he shouted above the still-rising wind. "Pull the branches over our heads."

Metep and Toro ran to the hole and crouched against the ground, trying to shelter the infants with their bodies. The little ones would not be able to tolerate exposure to a storm as violent as this one for long. The rain was torrential, the wind merciless, and it was very cold. Even Three-Legs was shivering, despite her fur.

Zena grabbed a branch and pulled it after her as she slid into the hole. The others imitated her, but it was no use. The wind tore them away, and finally they gave up the struggle and simply huddled together for warmth. The huge root ball of the fallen tree protected them from the wind, and after a while, the heat of their closely packed bodies provided some relief.

Another tree crashed to the ground behind them. Its heavy trunk slashed through the air and came to rest on the earth-encrusted roots that sheltered them. Miraculously, no one was hurt. The leafy crown of the tree hung over them, scratching their arms and faces, but it also protected them from the driving rain. Zena was grateful but uneasy. The tree could settle again at any moment, and crush them with its weight, but there was nothing she could do. It was too cold, too dangerous, to try to move. She would have to trust in the Mother's protection.

Gradually, the wind dropped and the rain became a light drizzle, but the night was utterly black, and the temperature continued to drop. They huddled still closer and set themselves to survive the night. Zena tried to imagine the sun beating down, pulling the cold from them with its fiery heat. Then she visualized the warmth of fire, imagined her hands and feet tingling in its glow. After a while, her body did seem to grow warm with the imagined heat. She took the young ones into her arms and held them tightly, one at a time, until she felt the warmth enter their bodies, too. But as soon as she let them go, they started to shiver again. Filar, Cere's little one, who had so magically survived the stampede, was shaking so hard her teeth clacked together.

A low growl and the sound of padded feet brought Zena upright with fear. Something was out there, prowling.

"Leopard." Bran's voice made her jump. He stood and began to yell loudly, waving his arms. The others woke and added their voices, and the babies screamed. The clamor was deafening, and Zena saw the leopard's shadowy form bound away, but toward dawn, she heard it again, pacing restlessly near the hole where they lay miserably shivering, stiff with cold and fear.

"We need fire," she said to Bran, her voice low and desperate. "If we had fire, it would not dare to come so close." But she knew there was little chance of finding it. The storms that brought lightning came only during the season of rain, and that was still many moons away. Until then, there would be no burning sticks.

Zena crouched deeper in the hole, trying to stop the constant shaking of her body so she could concentrate on opening herself to the Mother, as she always did when they needed help. Her eyes closed despite her resolve, for she had not slept all night, but even in sleep, her mind continued to wrestle with the problem, and she dreamed. She saw Lett, long ago, sharpening his stones in the clearing by the river. Sparks flew from the stones as he worked. Zena stared at the sparks, watched them scatter and go out, and then she saw them merge into one big spark, a spark that began to burn fiercely.

Filar's straining body interrupted her dream. The child was trying to clamber out of the hole, but she was only four and her legs were too short. Zena pushed her up and followed her slowly into the cold morning air, still preoccupied with her dream.

"Stones," she said to Bran. "We must strike them together, very hard."

Bran looked at her dubiously. Had the terrible night affected her senses? But when he saw her striking one stone against another with utter concentration, he, too, found some and imitated her movements, trusting that she knew what she was doing. Lotan watched, and found stones for himself. They struck them against one another over and over, but nothing happened.

"We need different stones," Zena decided, realizing that she had never seen sparks come from the stones they usually used, but only from the ones Lett had used. She searched a nearby pile of rocks, straining to remember the look and feel of Lett's stones. One of them had orange in it, she thought, but the other was hard and dark. She grabbed a rock streaked with rust-colored stains.

"The other must be smooth," she told them. "Dark and smooth, and very hard."

Lotan came running with a rock that looked promising. Zena handed him the stone she had found, and Lotan struck them sharply against each other. His forearms were strong from carving, and he could use more force even than Bran.

A spark appeared, and his eyes lit up with comprehension. If he could make a spark, perhaps they could make fire! He struck harder. Another spark came.

The others gathered around to watch, sensing the excitement. All of them, even the smallest children, understood how important fire was to their lives.

"Dry leaves, or grasses," Zena called out suddenly. "And twigs too."

They scattered to find anything dry, a difficult task after the storm. But finally they had enough, and they gathered to watch again, unconsciously holding their breath in anticipation.

Lotan shook the tension out of his arms, then started again. Harder and harder, he slashed one stone against the other. A spark shot forth, then another. Zena was ready, and held some dry grass close. It caught suddenly, and almost burned her hands. She dropped it. With a quick movement, Bran poked some sticks into the tiny blaze. It burned sluggishly for a moment and then went out.

A groan of disappointment filled the air, but now everyone was determined to succeed. Lotan's hands slashed again; again, the sparks flew. This time, an even bigger bundle of grass lay beneath them. A spark caught in the grass and began to burn, then it slowly fizzled out. Zena blew on the tiny flicker, very gently. The fire flared up. Silently, their bodies tense with patience, the others plied it with more dry grasses and twigs. The flames burned, then threatened to go out once more. Bran blew this time, harder, as if he were the wind that made fire spread. Again, it flared. Lotan poked a larger stick into the flames. Zena blew from one side, Bran from the other, while the others kept on adding twigs and branches.

The fire was burning more steadily now; they watched, mesmerized, afraid even to breathe hard lest it go out again. Then, suddenly, the flickering glow burst into leaping flames. They shot into the air, crackling and spitting, then flattened to burn strongly.

A long, collective sigh escaped the group. Astonishment marked their faces, then incredulity, and after that came relief, and finally, gratitude.

"We have fire!" Lotan's voice cracked as the enormity of their discovery became clear.

"And we can make it whenever we want it," Sima added, her eyes round with wonder.

"We must thank the Mother." Zena rose to her feet, and her voice rang with emotion as she spoke.

"Great Mother, we thank you for this gift. Of all that You have given us, the gift of fire, fire that we can create as we need it, is the greatest. It keeps the numbing cold from our bodies, protects us from the animals that prowl in the darkness. It cheers us, brings us close to You in body and in heart as we sit together, watching the mystery of its flames."

Remembering that fire could be dangerous as well as helpful, she added more words. "Always, we will use Your gift well, Great Mother, so that it may never do harm to the earth that is Your home as well as ours."

The voices of the others rose in unison, to confirm Zena's words. To be able to make fire was a wondrous gift, a gift beyond anything they had ever anticipated. Spontaneously, they joined hands and began to circle the fire they had created, as they spoke to the Mother of their gratitude. Around and around they went, until weariness made their feet stumble. They slid to the ground, still close to each other, and stared into the sparkling flames. Abruptly, their animation returned, and they began to chatter excitedly.

"We will not be cold again!" Sima hugged Filar in delight.

"Not be cold again," Filar repeated over and over, pleased with the sound of the words.

"Meat tastes better after it has been in the fire," Lupe volunteered. "Tubers too."

"We will be safe now, even when we travel." Bran's voice was full of satisfaction. More than any, he felt responsible for keeping the others safe. Now his task would be much easier.

"The infants will be warm," Metep said, looking down protectively at her tiny son. Toro nodded happily.

"No lion will dare take this one," Nyta said, pointing to her swollen belly.

Lotan rubbed his forearms. "That is hard work! But I will get better at making the sparks."

"We must all learn," Zena said. "Those who are strong enough, at least. Then, if one is lost, we can make a fire to tell the others where to look."

Her words brought Clio into their thoughts, and the joy left their faces. Zena wished she had not spoken. A picture of Clio lying helpless on the ground, her features crumpled in pain and fear, flashed into her mind, and she could not make it go away. Always before, Clio's face had been peaceful. Perhaps she really was hurt now, and needed their help.

Zena rose, her composure shattered by the distressing image, and climbed to the top of a small rise to survey the landscape. Waving grasses stretched ahead in all directions. Termite mounds stuck up at intervals, their skinny peaks almost as tall as the wide-crowned trees that gave shape and meaning to the otherwise endless expanse. Puffy clouds skittered against a sky so blue and bright she had to lower her gaze and see them instead as moving shadows that turned the soft yellow of the grasses into somber brown.

Bran came to join her. He did not speak but only stood beside her, comforting her with his presence. Zena leaned against him, grateful for his support. Bran was brother to her, in a way, for he was Kalar's son. She had never felt the desire to mate with him, nor he with her. They cared for each other in a different way, but their caring was deep and strong.

Slowly, calmness replaced the turmoil in Zena's heart, and the picture of Clio faded. But soon after she fell asleep, Clio's face returned. In her dreams, Zena saw the child smile, one of the rare smiles that obscured for a moment the impenetrable blackness of her eyes, eyes that never expressed anything but wildness. But then Clio began to cry, an action as rare for her as smiling. She cried and cried, and would not stop.

Zena sat bolt upright, listening. She was sure she could hear the crying, still. Lotan rose to his knees beside her. His face was strained, incredulous.

"Clio!" he said. They stared at each other, not daring to believe.

II

The young lion thrust his nose toward the outstretched hand, then jumped back, sneezing. The scent that came from the hand was strange, unlike anything he had smelled before. His mother had brought him zebras and antelopes and many smaller animals to eat, but never anything that resembled this. He did not trust it. He sank to the ground and watched the creature, his yellow eyes unblinking.

His ears pricked up as his mother's roar sounded from the field that bordered the woods. He rolled lazily against the ground before he rose and loped slowly toward the sound.

Clio drew in her hand, disappointed. She had liked the lion. Its movements had fascinated her. Imitating its low crouch, as if momentarily a lion herself, she crawled to the place where it had sat. The scent that permeated the place pleased her, and she rolled in it as the lion had rolled.

The lion returned. His mother's roar had not signified food, as he had hoped, and he was beginning to realize that he must learn to hunt for himself. Perhaps the small creature huddled against the tree would still be there.

Clio was delighted at his return. She reached out to touch the lion's soft fur. Startled, the lion backed away. Hunting involved chasing, but this small animal did not run. Instead, it lay on the ground and batted at him like one of his littermates. It smelled like them too. The lion batted back, wanting to play. This time, Clio was startled. The padded paw was soft, but very powerful. She was not sure she wanted to feel it again, and she was certain she did not want the lion to come any closer. She lay perfectly still, as she had the night before, seeming not even to breathe.

Tentatively, the lion batted again. The heavy paw struck a glancing blow on Clio's shoulder, but she did not move. Twice again, the lion struck at her, but still there was no response. Bored by the game, he yawned and ambled away. Clio did not stir until he was out of sight. Then she opened her mouth wide, as the lion had done. The rows of sharp teeth and the long red tongue had impressed her. She poked a finger into her mouth, to feel her own teeth, and stuck out her tongue, trying to see it. But it was too short and her efforts were unsuccessful.

A sparkle of water in a nearby stream distracted her, and the lion disappeared from her mind. She wriggled over to it, liking the feel of soft, damp ground on her belly, and crawled into the shallows to drink. The water was cold against her skin, and she jumped up abruptly. Her feet splashed as she jumped; delighted with the sound, she began to run noisily downstream. For almost an hour, she skipped and cavorted through the water.

A mossy glen attracted her attention, and she left the stream to investigate its smooth green carpet. A few nuts were scattered on the velvety surface, reminding her that she was hungry. She popped them into her mouth, but they were too hard to chew, and she spat them out again. She whimpered and looked around her expectantly. Always before, someone had come to help her with nuts. But no one was there. She snuggled into the soft moss and curled herself into a tight ball to wait.

Something rustled in the bushes in front of her. Clio's eyes opened but she did not move. A large bird came into view and settled itself atop its nest, ruffling its feathers carefully to cover all the eggs. Then it sat perfectly still, its brown-streaked body invisible against the bushes.

Clio frowned. The bird had disappeared even as she watched. Perplexed, she jumped up to investigate. At her approach, the bird shot from the nest with a loud whirring noise, leaving a clutch of speckled eggs. Clio put one of them in her mouth and clamped her teeth down hard. Yolk shot out and dribbled down her chin. She slurped it up again and swallowed, pushing the bits of shell aside with her tongue, then spitting them out. She ate another egg, then lay down to sleep. Content in the protected, shady greenness, she lay quietly all afternoon and through the night, moving only to eat another egg and to drink. When the light came again, she rose and wandered off.

Now her movements were random, without purpose. Something was missing that she needed to have, though she was not sure what it was. But when she saw a pair of legs striding through a field in front of her, she knew immediately that they were what she wanted. They were not exactly the right legs, so she followed them a distance instead of running up to them. A child of the woods, Clio moved as quietly as the smallest animal, and the creature above the legs did not suspect her presence.

She followed the legs all day, stopping when they stopped, running when she had to, for the legs were twice as long as her own. Just as the light began to fade, the legs came to a full stop and folded against a tree. Now Clio could see the whole creature. His big, hairy body and bristly face were familiar. The matted hair made him seem like an animal, and Clio liked that. Once, though, he had frightened her. She hid behind another tree and stared at him.

The creature's face disappeared between his hands. He brought his knees up to his chest to support his shaggy head, and his shoulders drooped forward. Clio tilted her head to one side, puzzled. He had never looked like that before. A feeling of sadness emanated from him, and it came into her, erasing her fear. She moved toward him, her hand outstretched, as it had been for the lion. It was a gesture she used often, for it permitted her to touch others, but prevented them from coming too close. Clio hated to be held or fondled or carried, and her extended arm created a barrier that few violated. But her need to make contact on her own terms was strong. She wanted to feel and smell and stare at everything she saw. Especially, she wanted to touch.

Clio's feet made no noise, and the big male did not look up at her approach. Gently, she placed her fingers on the back of his hand, a touch so light and fleeting he did not notice for a moment. Then he raised his head sharply, and his jaw dropped in astonishment.

This was the strange little one, Ralak's child. What was she doing here? Were the others here too? Kropor looked around him incredulously. They could not be here. He would have heard them. He did not want them here either. He wanted to be alone.

He stared at Clio, his eyes hard with indignation. If she was here, the others must have followed him. He sprang to his feet and began to search the area, calling loudly. No one answered, and he saw no tracks or other signs to indicate that the rest of the tribe was nearby. Was it possible she was alone?

He looked back at the tree. Clio was sitting against the trunk, nibbling at some berries he had dropped.

"Where are the others?" he asked her. She did not respond. He named them, one at a time, hoping she would grasp his meaning. When he spoke Toro's name, she frowned, and a fleeting look of anxiety crossed her face. Then she began to crawl around the base of the tree, searching for more berries.

"Food?" Kropor's voice was gruff. If she really was alone this far from the shelter, she must be very hungry.

Clio knew this word, and she held out her hand as if expecting him to put food in it. But he had no food, only the berries she had already eaten.

"Wait," he told her. "I find food." He lumbered off toward the stream, where he had found the berries. Before he entered the bushes, he looked back to make sure Clio was waiting. She had vanished.

Impatiently, he returned to the tree. How had she managed to disappear so quickly? If the child could not stay in one place, he could not get food for her! He scoured the field, becoming ever more irritated. He had never paid much attention to the little ones. They were noisy and demanding, and he had stayed well away from them. But now this one, the one who understood almost nothing, had found him, and he could not simply abandon her. She was too small to be alone, and he had seen lion tracks earlier.

A soft sound made him whirl in alarm. Clio stood behind him, staring at him with her impenetrable eyes. Had she been behind him all the time? Angry now, he stamped his foot at her. Clio looked at the foot, then at her own small feet, and imitated his movement. She raised one foot and stamped it down, then the other, and then began to leap up and down with both feet at once.

Despite his anger, Kropor laughed. She looked so funny and determined. Clio looked up, startled at the noise.

"Come," he told her, beckoning, and this time, he did not let her out of his sight as she pattered lightly behind him toward the stream. There they feasted on the bright yellow berries. Kropor found a few snails, too, and pounded them open with a rock for Clio. She stuffed them into her mouth and chewed with relish.

Abruptly, her eyelids began to droop. She yawned widely and nestled down among the bushes. Kropor looked at her curiously. She was asleep already, he realized. She had simply curled up on the ground like a little animal and gone to sleep.

Reluctantly, he knelt and picked her up. He did not want her with him, but he could not leave her here unprotected. He would have to keep her at least until the morning. Perhaps then the others would turn up and take her back with them.

Clio sagged heavily in his arms. Awake, she could not be carried, for she wriggled so determinedly that she had to be put down. Asleep, her defenses disappeared, and she seemed to welcome the closeness she could not tolerate by day.

Kropor carried her toward a cluster of boulders he had noticed in the field, and piled grasses between two rocks to make a soft place where they could sleep. Hunching his shoulders against the evening chill, he sat on one of the boulders to watch while the light remained. Thoughts of Ralak crowded his head. The child reminded him of Ralak. Perhaps it was her diminutive stature, or the blackness of her eyes. But Ralak's eyes had been lively, full of expression. Clio's were inscrutable.

Kropor sighed resignedly and slid down beside her. At least for tonight, he would watch out for her. Clio snuggled against him trustingly, her body soft and warm against his hard chest. He covered her small form with one of his large, hairy arms, and fell asleep with her breath on his face.

When he awoke, she was staring at him. He sat up, startled. For a moment, he had thought it was Ralak's face, for he had been dreaming of her. But it was only Clio. Angered anew at her presence, and because she was not Ralak after all, he rose abruptly and began to walk, watching constantly for any sign of the others. Clio followed, unperturbed by his brusque behavior. All that day, he paid scant attention to her, though he did help her find food. In the evening, she fell asleep as abruptly as she had the night before. Again, Kropor hoisted her into his arms. She felt more familiar this time, and he carried her for some distance, toward some fruiting trees he had seen. They would provide food in the morning. She snuggled close when he lay down beside her, sighing contentedly in her sleep.

They continued in this way for many days. Each morning, Kropor awoke to find Clio looking down at him, and each time, he thought he saw Ralak. To think Ralak was beside him and then be disappointed brought intense pain, and he became angry with Clio for causing him such agony. She stayed a distance away from him until his anger dissipated, but she never cried or complained. Instead, she seemed content simply to follow him. If she needed his help with food, she ran up to him and tapped his leg, then she let a short distance come between them again. But she never let him out of her sight, and each night, she snuggled in his arms as if she belonged there.

One morning, Kropor woke first. Clio lay beside him, her round face peaceful in sleep. Thick, dark lashes curved gently against her cheeks, and one of her small hands rested against his belly. He picked it up and looked at it. Clio's eyes opened, and she smiled up at him, a rare, enchanting smile that lit up her face and gave expression to her eyes. Then the long lashes fell again, and she turned away.

Kropor stared down at the sleeping child. This time, he did not see Ralak. Instead, he heard her. "Keep her safe for me," Ralak was saying. "Keep her safe."

Tears sprang into Kropor's eyes. He wiped them away angrily. But then his anger vanished, replaced by a feeling of bewildered joy. Ralak had spoken to him; he had heard her, felt her presence. Somehow, she was still there.

Another thought intruded. Perhaps that was why Clio had come. Perhaps Ralak had sent her, so he could keep some small part of her at least. Could such a thing be? Kropor did not know, did not care. He had heard Ralak again, had felt her near him, and that was enough. His beloved Ralak had not left him completely.

The dam of anguish that had grown in Kropor's heart ever since Ralak's death suddenly broke. He began to sob, loud, agonizing sobs that resounded in the still air and distorted his face into a terrifying grimace.

The sobs woke Clio. She sat up and stared, worried by his uncharacteristic behavior. Her small hand touched his face tentatively, then she put her arms around his neck and rubbed her soft cheek against his rough one. Never before had she made such a gesture. And when Kropor drew her close and hugged her, she still did not resist. His agony had reached some unknown place deep inside her, and the need to comfort him had overcome her terror of being held.

Kropor let her go again quickly, sensing that her tolerance for closeness was almost gone. But he continued to hold her hand, and she did not pull it away. Together, they set off in search of the fruit.

Days passed, and there was no sign of the others. Kropor ceased to look for them, no longer wanted to find them, lest they take Clio and leave him alone again. Clio had pulled the agony from his heart, and he did not want to lose her. She seemed as attached to him as he was to her, and seldom strayed far from his side. She often held his hand as they walked, and sometimes she even let him carry her for short distances when she was tired or they needed to go faster.

Another week went by in perfect contentment; then, without warning, Kropor's newfound happiness dissolved. Late one day, the sky darkened so suddenly he thought at first that night had come. But when he saw the massive black clouds that seemed to have sprung up from nowhere, felt grit lash his face as violent winds swirled in all directions, he realized a storm was upon them. He hoisted Clio into his arms and began to run toward a rocky hill, where he had spotted a dark hole that could signify a cave. They could shelter there until the storm had passed.

Clio resisted strongly. She beat at his arms with her fists and kicked against his belly, uttering sharp cries of distress. Kropor set her down, alarmed by the wildness that had come into her eyes. All day long, she had skipped peacefully beside him, but now there was a look of savage excitement on her face, as if she had suddenly been transformed into another creature. She did not seem to know him, or even see him, or anything else around them. Her frenzied gaze was focused on something far beyond, something no one else could see.

"Clio!" He called her name sharply, hoping to penetrate her wild oblivion. She did not respond, but began to run toward the cliffs ahead. Frightened, he picked her up again and tucked her under one arm, ignoring her screams and the frantic pummeling of her small fists and heels. He sprinted into the cave and gently set her down. As soon as her feet touched the ground, she slid from his restraining hands and charged out onto the rocks. He leaped after her, his heart thumping with fear.

Rain slashed abruptly into his face, blinding him. Kropor swiped frantically at his eyes, unable to see where Clio had gone. In that instant, she had vanished, as she had vanished when he had first found her. Sobbing now with terror, he ran into the driving storm, straining to locate her shadowy form against the dark cliffs. The light was almost gone, and if he did not find her soon, he might never find her.

His heart twisted so painfully he doubled over. He could not lose her, could not lose Clio as he had lost Ralak.

Rocks clattered behind him. He whirled. She was there, on the top of the highest boulder, dancing, leaping, seeing nothing in front of her, behind her. He could tell she did not see, for her eyes were focused inward, on the demon that possessed her. She did not see the precipices on all sides, did not know the rocks were slippery with rain—

Kropor lunged, but he moved too late. He saw her fall, saw her small body hurtle downward, as if she were flying. She landed on the rocks below and did not move again.

CHAPTER
17

Kropor staggered through the woods, Clio in his arms. He paid no attention to her frantic cries or the fists that flailed unceasingly at his arms. There was room for only one thought in his mind: he had to get back to the shelter, so Zena could fix Clio. All the love he had felt for Ralak had transferred itself to her tiny daughter, and the thought of losing her, too, could not be borne.

After she had fallen, he had carried Clio to the cave. Her stillness had terrified him, and at first he had thought she was dead. Then he had seen that her chest still rose and fell at regular intervals, and he had realized she was alive. Still, he had not trusted the rhythmic movements, had watched them compulsively lest they cease when he looked away. Exhaustion had finally forced him to lie down beside her, but he had slept with his face against her lips, as he had slept that first night, so he could feel her breath on his cheek and know it had not left her.

As soon as there was light enough to see, he had headed for the shelter at a run. It was then that Clio had suddenly opened her eyes and begun to cry. He had been overjoyed to hear sounds coming from her, but she had been crying ever since, and her screams tore at his heart.

He looked down at her contorted face. He had never heard her cry before, and he knew the pain must be terrible. It clouded her eyes, twisted her lips into a pathetic grimace, especially when he moved fast. To see Clio in pain was monstrous. To know that he worsened the pain by running was unendurable. But he *had* to run, had to find help quickly, lest she die. And so he simply ceased to hear and ran on, his breath ragged in his throat.

Darkness had already fallen when he reached the trees near the shelter. He called out, but there was no answer. Perhaps he was still too far away for them to hear. He came closer and called again, but even before his voice died away, he knew no one was there. No sounds or scents emanated from the clearing; there was no babble of voices, no smell of sleeping bodies.

Kropor's shoulders slumped in despair. The others had left, and now he might never find them. Then Clio would die, as Ralak had died.

Tears came to his eyes, but he was too drained to shed them. He sank down onto the earthen floor of the shelter and laid Clio tenderly beside him. Grasping one of her tiny hands in his big palm, he willed her to stay alive. There was nothing else for him to do until the light came again, when he could see to look for tracks, try to follow the others.

Twice during the night, the sound of lions snuffling around the clearing propelled him upright in terror. The second time, a young lion poked its head into the shelter and sniffed the air inquisitively. In the bright moonlight, Kropor watched a deep crease of perplexity appear in the thick fur between its shining yellow eyes. Then it turned and loped away.

His heart thumped with fear. It must have been the lions that had forced the others to leave. Never had he known one to come so close. He pulled Clio into his arms, afraid to close his eyes again lest the young lion grow bolder still and snatch her while he slept.

The sun still hid below the horizon when he ventured out to look for tracks. Even in the dim light, lion prints showed all around the clearing. Kropor shuddered and stared fearfully into the trees. Then his straining eyes spotted footprints left by the others, heading north out of the clearing. Even when the prints disappeared in the woods, he had no trouble following the trail. There were broken twigs and trampled grasses, and more footprints where the earth was soft.

Momentarily cheered, he began to run through the shadowy woods. The jostling movements woke Clio; again, he closed his ears to her agonized cries. He had to find Zena and the others before they had gone so far he would never be able to find them.

Another thought broke through his preoccupation. Ralak had asked him to keep Clio safe, and he had failed. Over and over, the thought repeated itself, an agonizing refrain that kept time to his hurrying feet. He ran faster, to escape it. He ran until the sun was high, and then he knew he had to stop for a moment to rest. Clio was struggling desperately, and he did not think he could hold on to her any longer.

He lowered her carefully to the ground, fearing that the movement would hurt her even more. But her wails stopped immediately. She pushed against the damp earth, trying to rise to her feet. One of her legs folded under her. She stared at Kropor helplessly, howling in pain and frustration. She wanted to follow as she had always followed, and she could not. He pulled her into his arms, murmuring soothing noises, but his efforts to comfort her were unavailing.

He lumbered on. Finally, Clio stopped crying, worn out with the effort, and lay limp and quiet in his arms. Kropor was relieved. The light had almost gone, and he was tired, so tired he had to make a conscious effort to put one foot in front of the other. He knew he should stop, but the scent of the others was getting stronger, and he could not bear to give up yet.

A big fallen tree blocked his way. Kropor struggled across it, and suddenly the scent of the others was all around him, distinct and unmistakable. They had been here—all of them had been here—not too long ago. He studied the ground, straining to see in the darkness. Their footprints were everywhere, deeply embedded in the still-damp earth. There were other prints, too, the prints of a leopard. He shivered. If a leopard prowled the area, he must move on quickly.

Excitement and fear revived his flagging strength, and as soon as he emerged from the woods, he broke into a run. The sudden movement woke Clio, and she began to cry again. Her screams pierced the quiet night. Over and over, she screamed, then settled into a steady, monotonous crying.

A different scent came unexpectedly to Kropor's sensitive nostrils. It was fire! He smelled fire! They must be ahead somewhere. He staggered toward the smell, not stopping even when he twisted his ankle sharply. He had run now for two days, without food, and he dared not stop lest he fall and be unable to get up again.

The smell of fire grew stronger. Then he saw it, glowing in a nearby clump of trees. A figure sprang up against the fire. Another figure appeared, then another. Kropor ran toward them, too exhausted even to call out, but through his daze, he heard them calling, heard them shouting Clio's name.

The fire was close now, right in front of him. Kropor stood still and held out the bundle in his arms. He was conscious of Clio's weight disappearing as hands reached out to take her from him. Then he swayed and fell to the ground.

Confusion surrounded him. He heard voices, felt someone press a gourd to his lips. The soothing water ran down his throat and across his face. Another sound broke through his stupor. It was Clio's voice. She was calling for him with the odd little croak she had developed, to let him know she needed him. He struggled up and went to her.

She reached for his hand and clutched it, refusing to let go. Kropor held it gladly. Someone moved beside him, and he saw that it was Zena, examining Clio. His terrified eyes searched her face, seeking reassurance.

"She is all right," Zena assured him. "Her leg is broken, and she has knocked her head hard. But she will live."

A great sigh escaped Kropor's lips. Clio would not die. She would not disappear, as Ralak had, and leave him alone, with no one to care for. Zena had said she would live, and so she would. Perhaps he had kept her safe, after all. Still holding Clio's hand, he lay down beside her to rest, his big, stooped body curved protectively around the tiny child.

Zena stared down at them, trying to understand. Somehow, Ralak's strange little one had penetrated Kropor's grief, as he had penetrated her isolation. She had never seen Clio reach out to hold a hand before, or call to anyone, and never before had she seen Kropor's eyes brimming with tenderness, except for Ralak. How had they become so attached to each other?

Lotan's hand touched her shoulder. "You were right," he confessed, his voice thick with emotion. "The Mother was watching Clio, and that is why you felt peace. She sent Clio to Kropor, so he could keep her safe."

Zena nodded, thinking that the Mother's ways were surely wondrous. But then, unexpectedly, Ralak's face appeared in her mind, eclipsing thoughts of the Mother. Zena saw her as clearly as if Ralak were standing before her. She was smiling, and her eyes glittered with mischief. Her mouth opened in speech, and although her words made no sound, Zena heard them distinctly.

"Kropor needed another one to love," she said. "And Clio needed help. So, here they are!"

Ralak's face disappeared. Zena began to laugh, and Lotan looked at her, frowning. How could she laugh at such a time?

Zena glanced at him apologetically. "The Mother's ways can be remarkable," she told him, "especially when Ralak helps Her."

Lotan did not look convinced, but his joy at seeing Clio again quickly drove all other thoughts from his mind. He stared down at the sleeping child. Zena had given her herbs to drink, to quiet her and lessen the pain. She was scratched and bloody, and she smelled like an animal. Lotan wrinkled his nose. Clio hated being washed, but he would have to wash her anyway, as soon as the light came again. The smell was very strong.

They lingered in the area for two more days, while Zena treated Clio's leg and Kropor recovered his strength. No one wanted to travel anyway. They were too excited by the miracle of Clio's and Kropor's return. Sima kept hugging Clio over and over, despite her objections, and Toro gazed at Kropor with longing in her eyes. Once, they went off together to mate, but Kropor did not linger long, and soon returned to Clio's side. Still, Toro looked happier than she had since the big male's disappearance.

By the third day, they were ready to set out again. Kropor hoisted Clio into his arms. She tolerated her position for a few hours, then she began to struggle, trying to get down. Her leg did not hurt now and she wanted to walk. Kropor tried to calm her, but she only wriggled harder, screaming furiously. Unable to hold on to her any longer, he put her down, looking baffled.

Zena stared at Clio in exasperation. She had become increasingly restless as their journey was delayed, and she was anxious to move on. Must they stay in one place until Clio's leg healed? Surely, there must be a way to carry her that would not bother her so much.

She scanned the area, seeking inspiration. Her eyes lit on Three-Legs. Clio adored her, as she adored all animals. Perhaps she would sit on the gazelle's back. Three-Legs was strong now, and big enough to hold a child as tiny as Clio. But would the gazelle tolerate her presence?

She led Three-Legs over to Clio and let the child rub her hands against the soft fur, as she loved to do. Then she put a leash around the gazelle's neck and handed it to Sima.

"Hold her still," she instructed. Sima nodded confidently. Three-Legs followed her now, as she had once followed Zena, and Sima could always calm her down.

Moving slowly, Zena picked Clio up and placed her on the small gazelle's back, so that one leg hung down each side. Three-Legs jumped skittishly, but Sima rubbed her nose and uttered soothing noises, and she quickly stilled.

Clio's body went rigid. Her eyes opened wide in astonishment and her face puckered as if she were going to scream. But it was not a scream that emerged. Instead, Clio laughed, a small, croaking sound that they knew was a laugh because her normally expressionless eyes lit up with glee. She was part of an animal now. She could touch it any time she wanted, and it would not run away.

The others shook their heads in amazement. Kropor, however, looked worried, and went to stand next to Clio so he could catch her if she fell. But Clio had no intention of relinquishing her new position, and held on firmly. She rode Three-Legs as if she belonged there, and her whole body radiated delight.

The small procession set off once more. Zena and Bran strode in front, leading the way. Behind them came Sima, holding Three-Legs, with Clio on top and Kropor close beside. Nyta and Toro and Metep clustered around them, carrying the little ones, and Lotan and Lupe guarded from the rear.

Every day, they proceeded in this fashion. They started at dawn, while the air was cool and refreshing, and walked until the sun was high. During the hottest part of the day, they sought shade under one of the wide-crowned trees that dotted the plains, then they walked again until dusk, gathering food as they went. At night, they sheltered in a clump of trees or near a pile of boulders, with fire to protect them. They brought burning sticks with them as they traveled, but the knowledge that they could create a new fire if all the sticks burned out was immensely reassuring. Everywhere they went, they looked for the special stones that gave off sparks, and saved them in their baskets.

Only twice did they stop for more than a night or a few hours of rest. The first delay came when Three-Legs spotted a herd of gazelles like herself. All during their time in the woods, she had seen no other gazelles, and Zena thought she had forgotten about them. She was wrong. Once Three-Legs had spotted the herd, she was uncontrollable. Wrestling the leash from Sima's hands, she dashed forward, unseating Clio. Fortunately, Kropor was close and caught Clio before she hit the ground, already screaming with indignation. This was her special perch, and she did not want it to go away.

But Three-Legs could not be stopped. She disappeared among the gazelles, still trailing the leash behind her. Later, Zena saw her mating, and wondered at the strength of this impulse. It was mating, more than a desire for the company of her own kind, that had once again drawn Three-Legs to the herd.

They waited all the following day and the next, hoping the gazelle would return as she had before. And just as they were preparing to sleep the second day, she trotted back to them as if nothing had happened. Zena tethered her, so she would not leave again, but the mating seemed to have satisfied her, and she made no further effort to rejoin the herd.

The second enforced stop came when Nyta's infant was born. The birth was easy and Nyta did not suffer, but Zena knew immediately that something was terribly wrong with the infant. The tiny boy's head was misshapen, and his limbs were not fully formed. Worse, he seemed to be in pain. His wizened face was puckered in agony, and he was gasping for breath.

Sorrowfully, she handed him to Nyta. Tears streamed down the older woman's face as she looked at her newborn son, but she recovered quickly and handed him back to Zena.

"He suffers," she whispered, still weak from the birth. "We must send him back to the Mother. He cannot live, but we must not let him suffer."

Zena nodded. Holding the infant tenderly in the crook of one arm, she placed her hand over his mouth and nose until he stopped breathing, as she had seen Kalar do long ago, when an infant like this had been born. To let an infant suffer was unforgivable. That was not the Mother's way.

"Great Mother, Giver of Life," she said, quietly, "take this little one back to Your heart. Though he has no name, we cared for him, and our caring goes with him. Nyta loved him most of all, for she carried him under her heart for many moons. Now he is with You again, and will suffer no more. For that, we are grateful."

The others gathered around as she placed the dead infant among a clump of rocks and covered him with branches. To lose a child was sad, but to keep one that suffered and would not live anyway was wrong. It was the job of a wise one to help an infant like this return to the Mother as quickly as possible, and they were glad Zena was with them to do it.

When Nyta felt strong enough, they resumed their journey, traveling slowly but steadily, always with the rising sun on their right, the setting sun on their left, as Zena had seen them in her vision.

One day, as she lifted Clio onto her perch, Zena was surprised to see that Three-Legs' belly was beginning to swell. Could the Mother have given her another young one? Once before, not long after she had disappeared the first time, she had given birth, but the calf had not been strong and had died within a few hours. Three-Legs had stood over it all day, as if mourning; then she had seemed to forget about it and had come back to Zena.

It seemed strange to Zena that each time a calf began to grow inside Three-Legs, she had recently run off to be with other gazelles. Could mating have something to do with it? The Mother had placed

a young one in her belly not long after she had first mated with
Lotan. But that did not make sense. How could mating be connected
to infants or calves?

Zena puzzled over the enigma, but no solution came to her, and
after a while she gave up thinking about it. Other, more immediate
concerns demanded her attention, as the land became drier, the way
more difficult. But her mind did not relinquish the question entirely.
The possibility that mating and young ones were somehow connected lingered just below the level of conscious awareness, as if
waiting for the time when she would fully understand.

II

For fifteen million years, tons of burning rock smoldered and shuddered deep within the earth's molten womb, until finally they
forced two great land masses to split apart. Thus was the Great Rift
Valley of Africa born. Longer and wider than any valley in the
world, it dominated the landscape, influenced all the life forms in
eastern Africa.

Hot beyond imagining, the viscous mass poured in triumph
through the giant trough it had so relentlessly labored to create.
The triumph was short-lived, for as it hit the air, the cooling lava
hardened and shrank, then cracked in pieces, so that more of the
molten stuff could squeeze through. Again, it cooled, again it
cracked. Over and over, the lava poured through and cooled and
cracked, until all the land was broken into massive, separate chunks.

As if sliced by a giant hand, some of the huge pieces tumbled
into gaping holes left by the escaping lava. Falling even below the
level of the sea, they formed vast deserts of unendurable heat. Over
the eons of time, oceans moved in to cover the places where the
land had sunk; then they slowly retreated. Wide stretches of gray-
white plains, and enormous salt formations that looked for all the
world like waves and foam that had been ossified and left to die,
lay exposed behind them. Brackish grasses shimmered in the heat,
and hot springs bubbled up, death to any that came mistakenly
to drink.

On either side of the baking plains, the red-hot rock pushed far
into the air to create high plateaus and jagged peaks, black as the
lava that had formed them. The rivers came then and poured between the plateaus, eroding their sides into escarpments so steep no
vegetation could take root. The erosion came faster, the escarpments
became steeper, until chasms thousands of feet deep prevented any
creature but a bird from traveling between them. But from the val-

ley floor, the plateaus were accessible. There, they sloped up gradually, and trees and grasses grew in abundance on their gentle hillsides, luring the unwary traveler. Their promise was deceptive, for the land soon split again and there was nothing to be seen below but another deep cleft, impossible to cross.

Above it all, the mountains loomed, dominating the landscape. Some were so high few animals could breathe with ease, if they managed to climb their summits. Others had bowl-shaped tops and belched out smoke and fire that shimmered in the heat-laden air. Once, the volcanoes had smoked and sputtered beneath seas that had long ago rubbed their peaks to smoothness. They smoldered still, and when the pressure of molten rock against hard crust was strong enough, they exploded. Earthquakes followed, and fires, and floods and droughts, leaving behind them piles of steaming rubble and tumbled boulders, or huge expanses of smooth black lava and endless sand, where nothing grew.

Sometimes, though, amidst the desolation and violence, there emerged places of unearthly beauty, places where plants and trees, even birds and animals, grew larger and more fruitful than they ever had before. One such place lay at the northern edge of the great valley Zena and her tribe traversed. But this northern oasis, like all the others, was hard to reach. Deserts and smoking mountains blocked the way, and always, there were the impassable chasms that sliced the fractured land.

Zena stared at such a chasm, and knew they could not go on. They had finally come to the high plateaus and smoking mountains she had seen in her vision. What her vision had not revealed was the desolation between the plateaus. There was no life anywhere in the baking gray-white valley below her, except for vultures that soared in endless circles. There was no water, either, only bubbling springs that smelled of rot, and brackish ponds with the same distinctive odor. Lotan had warned them away, remembering the two men who had died so cruelly.

To avoid the terrible heat and dryness, they had trudged up countless plateaus, trying to find a higher route, where there was water and food and above all, coolness. Unless they could walk up here, in the highlands, Zena did not think they could go on. But each time, they had ended up in a place like this, where the land dropped away on all sides, staring helplessly into an impenetrable chasm. Each time, they had returned the way they had come, steeling themselves to endure the searing air that would soon assault their faces, their feet, their lungs.

Wearily, Zena turned to retrace her steps once again. She moved slowly, for the infant within her was big now, and pressed against her legs. The others followed patiently, but she saw the exhaustion in their faces, heard the sighs and gasping breath they tried to conceal. For the first time, she wondered why she had brought them here, why she had undertaken the journey at all, and whether they would survive it. The savannah they had left seemed infinitely comforting.

Heat hit like a physical barrier the moment they stepped onto the pale earth of the sunken valley floor. It pressed against their skin, pulled every drop of moisture from their bodies. Zena saw a thin ribbon of shade beneath an overhanging escarpment, and led them to it. But even here, they could not escape the sun's blinding glare, its scorching heat on their shoulders. The air was so hot they had to pant in an effort to cool it before it reached their lungs.

Bushes ahead caught her eye. Perhaps there would be berries on their branches. They would be welcome for their moisture even more than as food.

The bushes began to move strangely. There was something behind them, she realized as she came closer, something that looked like the heads of others like themselves—only they were not like themselves. They had the slanted foreheads and heavy jaws of Big Ones, but they were smaller, much smaller. Dirt smeared their faces, and they were thin, undernourished.

They emerged from the bushes, each clutching a stick or rock. There were many of them, and the fierceness in their eyes frightened Zena. They moved toward her, staring hungrily at the baskets, the gourds, at Three-Legs, at the children too.

"Put the young ones behind," she ordered quietly. Perhaps these Fierce Ones meant no harm, but she did not think so. They moved as a leopard moved when it stalked its prey.

Alerted by their predatory stance, Three-Legs galloped away and scrambled up the side of the steep escarpment. Unencumbered by Clio, whose leg had healed well enough for her to walk some of the time at least, Three-Legs moved fast. She was out of sight before the Fierce Ones could sling rocks in her direction, and Zena was glad. They had no meat to trade this time.

"Sticks, and rocks. Quickly!" Bran's voice was firm, but there was terrifying urgency in it. His eyes were fixed on the face of the largest male.

The Fierce Ones came close and pointed to the basket Nyta carried. Grunting, one of them reached out to take it.

"Give them one?" Zena suggested, looking at Bran to see if he agreed. Bran nodded, and held out his basket. The biggest male snatched it and ran off, holding it tightly against his chest. The others did not follow, but crowded close and tried to snatch more baskets. One grabbed a gourd and shook it. Water splashed out and his eyes lit up with astonishment. The others grabbed at gourds too. They uttered guttural sounds of threat as they reached, and their hands were insistent, demanding.

Fear caught Zena so hard she was dizzy for a moment. The Fierce Ones would not be satisfied with one basket, even two. They wanted all the baskets, all the gourds. If they gave them up, her tribe would have no food, no water. They could not survive without the water.

One of the Fierce Ones pointed at Sima. He grabbed her arm and tried to pull her away from the group. Quickly, Zena thrust Sima behind her, protecting her with her body. The Fierce One reached for Clio instead. Kropor roared and lashed out with his stick. It hit the male squarely on the head, and he dropped. The others moved closer, growling.

"Run! Take the young ones and run!" Bran whirled as he spoke and swung his stick hard from side to side, to make the Fierce Ones back off so the others could escape. Kropor joined him, brandishing his bloodied stick, and Lotan stood just behind, ready to club any Fierce One that dared to move.

Zena obeyed unquestioningly. Pulling Sima with her, she tucked the screaming Clio under one arm and ran. The other women followed with the frightened children. As soon as they were out of sight of the Fierce Ones, Zena left them hiding in a dense clump of bushes and ran clumsily back to see what was happening with the men.

The sickening sound of sticks hitting flesh came to her even before she reached the scene. Suddenly, she smelled fire. There was an abrupt silence, then she heard a series of yells and the sound of running feet. Zena sprinted as fast as she could, desperate to know what had happened.

Coming closer, she saw that the bushes were burning. She stopped, perplexed. How had they caught fire? And the Fierce Ones were running, fleeing as if their lives depended on it. Gourds and baskets littered the ground behind them. Bran and the other men were watching them, open-mouthed with astonishment. Suddenly Bran turned to Lupe and hugged him.

"You have made them run!" he shouted excitedly. "It was the fire that made them run, not our sticks!"

Lupe hugged him back, thrilled at the praise. At eight, he was too small to fight the Fierce Ones, but he was also unwilling to run away with the other children. Instead, he had tried to think how he could help. All day, he had carried a burning stick despite the heat. When he saw that the Fierce Ones were hurting Bran, he had plunged it into the bushes, trying to create a distraction. Dry as tinder, they had blazed furiously. The Fierce Ones had stared at the fire, then at the stick that had caused such magic, and then they had run as fast as they could go.

"We must get away quickly, while they are afraid," Bran said, gathering up the baskets and gourds.

Zena nodded distractedly. Her mind was full of questions. Bran and the other men had looked so eager when they had faced the Fierce Ones, as if they relished the opportunity to fight. Women would fight, too, especially if the young ones were threatened, but she had never seen that eagerness on their faces, nor felt it herself. Why were the men so different?

Still pondering the question, she scrambled up the side of the escarpment to look for Three-Legs, and found her grazing peacefully on the lush grasses that grew in abundance on the plateaus. The others followed eagerly, glad to escape the oppressive heat as well as the Fierce Ones.

Unlike the other plateaus, this one seemed to run north, Zena noticed hopefully. Perhaps they would be able to travel up here. Her hopes were dashed when she saw the line of jagged cliffs that rose all along its northern edge, blocking the way. And even if they could negotiate the cliffs, the land behind them fell away into nothingness, as it always did, making travel impossible.

Too drained to absorb still another disappointment, she concentrated on finding a place to sleep. They might not be able to travel on the plateau, but they could at least spend the night. To shiver a little would be wonderful, after all the nights they had spent trying to endure the stultifying air.

Lotan spotted a pile of boulders under one of the steep, overhanging cliffs, with an open space in front for their fire. It was a good, secure place, and Zena was glad. They needed to feel safe, after their frightening adventure.

"I felt sorrow for the Fierce Ones," Sima said later, as they sat around the fire. "They looked very hungry, and the bones of the young ones had nothing on them. But they frightened me too. Their eyes were so hard."

"I wonder that they do not live up here, instead of remaining in the hot valley," Lotan commented.

"Perhaps they do not know how to change," Zena answered.

"The Mother may not have given all of us the ability to think of new ways to find food, new places to live.

"I, too, felt sorrow for them," she added, "especially the young ones. Still, they would have taken all our food and water, our tools, if Bran and Kropor and Lotan had not protected us so well. And Lupe, who frightened them away with fire.

"It was because of you, all of you," she said, looking into their eyes one at a time, "that we are safely here now. You were brave. To fight Fierce Ones like that takes great courage. I thank you, and the Mother thanks you."

"It is your job to lead us," Bran responded, "but it is my job to keep the tribe safe.

"It is good Kropor has returned," he added. "We might need to fight more Fierce Ones." He looked pleased at the thought and raised his fist, as if to deliver a blow.

Zena frowned, wondering how he could possibly look forward to another encounter. Then her eyes opened wide as understanding came. That was why the Mother had made males as She had. They needed to be aggressive so they would welcome a fight when fighting was necessary. Otherwise, a whole tribe could be killed. Their belligerence was bad only if there was too much of it, or it came out too easily. As Ralak had once said, some men had too much of the harsh earthforce in them. Kropor had been like that, until Ralak had helped him to change.

She sighed, glad to have this mystery finally resolved, but more than ever conscious of the responsibility she carried. A strong wise one made the difference, Kalar had often said, for then she could help the men to control their aggression so the tribe could live in peace. This she must never forget.

She lay down with the others to sleep, but her mind would not rest. A higher route must exist; in her visions, she had seen them traveling in a lush green valley, not a menacing, waterless desert. To find it was more important than ever now. Bran might not mind another confrontation with the Fierce Ones, but Zena had no intention of taking such a risk.

Zena opened her mind to the Mother, and listened as hard as she had ever listened. But no clear message came. She had only a terrible sense of unease, as if something were wrong, and beyond it, a feeling of hope. There would be wrongness, and then somehow, a solution. With that, she had to be content.

She woke later in the night, certain now that something was terribly wrong. The feeling was in the air, in the earth, in everything around her. Slipping from the shelter, she stared out at the moonlit

night. Nothing looked amiss. Stars littered the sky, and there was
no wind, no sign that a storm was coming. Only the clouds looked
different. Heavy and edged with black, they moved as if they
owned the sky. They were gathering with incredible speed; even as
she watched, they blotted out the whole firmament of stars she had
seen a moment ago. Soon, only the half-grown moon was visible
behind them. It shone through their mass, giving them an ominous,
unearthly glow.

Zena turned away, and as she turned she saw that one star still
remained, high above the cliffs. It was the brightest star of all, and
always pointed north. She stared at it, as if seeking confirmation
for the journey she had initiated. If the star was still there, guiding
her, perhaps they would be all right, despite the travails they had
endured, might still endure.

Another glow to the west caught her attention. She had been
watching the smoking mountain for days now, certain it would
soon explode. She thought they were too far away for it to harm
them, but still she worried. Now flames as well as smoke were
erupting from its bowl-shaped top. Probably, she realized, the impending explosion was the cause of her distress, but somehow that
did not feel quite right.

Fiery hunks of molten rock shot suddenly from the mountain and
soared in huge arcs before they hit the ground. Zena could not see
where they landed, but she was certain fires would break out there,
fires so hot and intense nothing could escape. She shivered convulsively, glad to be far away.

She whirled at a noise behind her. Three-Legs had burst from the
shelter and was galloping headlong down the hill. Clio sprang out
after her, but Zena did not think she had seen the gazelle, or saw
anything else. The wildness in the child's eyes was stronger than
Zena had ever seen it before.

A prickle of terror ran up her spine. Something *was* wrong. She
was not the only one who felt it. Three-Legs felt it, and Clio . . . .
Clio, who was so close to the earthforce.

Kropor appeared, rubbing his eyes. Behind him, an infant began
to wail, and then another started, and within moments, all of them
were crying. Kropor paid no attention. Grabbing Clio before she
could run, he tied a stout rope around her waist and followed as
she began to dance and leap. He always did this now, when the
moon attracted her, or when a storm came, so he could keep her
from hurting herself again. But the moon was not full, and there
was no storm.

A tremor shook the earth under Zena's feet. Another came, then another, and suddenly, she knew. This was the thing she had feared.

"Out!" she screamed. "Away from the rocks!" She charged toward the shelter. Already, Bran and Lotan and the others were pulling the children out.

"Down," Bran yelled. "Down to the fields below. It is safest there."

Within moments, all of them but Clio and Kropor were huddled close together in a small hollow, well below the cliffs. They were just in time, for another, stronger tremor shook the ground. Rocks crashed above them, and dust and debris rained down on their heads. The earth seemed to swell and then suddenly collapse, rolling them wildly in all directions. Zena was jostled forcefully against Toro, but when she reached for Sima, who had been nestled against her, she was gone. The heavy clouds had completely obscured the moon now, and she could see nothing.

She jumped up to look for Sima, but before she could take a step, still another tremor shook the earth and knocked her down again. Now she could not feel any of the others around her, except for Toro.

She yelled Sima's name and the names of each of the others. Crashing rocks and ominous rumblings drowned out her voice, but she kept calling anyway, hoping they would finally hear and find their way to her. Sima cried out from somewhere below; then Zena heard Nyta's voice, and soon the others answered. They crawled toward her, unable to stand, as the earth continued to heave and shake. She counted them off as they appeared. They were bruised and frightened, but no one was badly hurt.

Only Lotan was missing now. No. There was no sign of Metep either. Bran and Toro jumped up to look for them, while Zena stayed to guard the others. The tremors seemed to have stopped, but they could start again without warning.

The moon slid out from behind the bulky clouds, and at just that moment, Bran's voice sounded below her.

"I have found them. Metep is not moving, but the infant is all right, and Lotan, too."

Bran and Toro appeared, their figures ghostlike against the background of jumbled rock and thick dust that still hung in the air. They were carrying Metep, and Lotan limped beside them.

Bran laid Metep gently on the ground. Her eyes opened briefly and she moaned. Zena passed her fingers over the young woman's skull, trying to feel what she could not see. There was blood, still sticky, and a cut. Her shoulder was cut, too. Perhaps a rock had fallen on her?

"I cannot tell until morning," she said, "unless we make a fire. I think the earthquake is finished."

The appearance of Kropor carrying Clio, with Three-Legs trotting behind, seemed to confirm her words. If Clio had fallen asleep and Three-Legs had returned, the danger was probably over. Clio especially would feel the earthquake's vibrations if they still lingered beneath the ground.

Bran went to see if there were any burning sticks left from their fire. He returned quickly, carrying only a basket.

"The earthquake has swallowed our fire," he told them, his voice tremulous with awe. "It has swallowed the whole place, the fire, the clearing, even the cliffs."

Zena closed her eyes, trying to absorb the message. The earth had opened up where they had lain and swallowed everything. It could have swallowed them as well.

"Great Mother," she said simply, "we thank You with all our hearts for warning us."

The others murmured thanks, too, and all of them sat very still for a long moment, thinking of this miracle. Then they set about the practical task of making another fire. By its light, Zena could see that Metep's cuts were not deep.

"She will be all right; I am almost certain of it," she told Toro, who was peering anxiously over her shoulder.

They settled down to try to sleep while they waited for the light to come again. None but the children succeeded very well, and Zena was glad when a faint glow from the east told her the sun was almost up. She rose slowly and went out to see what had happened to the cliff.

No jagged peaks showed against the pale sky; instead, there was nothing but rubble. Zena climbed up on the tumbled boulders and looked longingly to the north, where she wanted so badly to go. She stared, looked away, then stared again. Tears began to pour down her cheeks, and she gasped in wonderment.

The route was there. The earthquake had carved it for her. The cliff was gone, and so was the chasm that had blocked their way. Where they had been were jumbled rocks, easy to cross, and then a long, gradual descent through rocky hillsides into a valley, a valley so lustrous and beautiful her heart leaped into her throat at the sight. A river wound through it, sparkling in the early morning sun; there were trees and grasses, and animals of all kinds. Far beyond, so far she had to squint to see, stretched a great body of water, so wide and vast it had no end.

Overcome with emotion, Zena fell to her knees. The cliffs had opened, so they could go through. The Mother had given them the way.

For a long time, she was too stunned to move or even speak. She looked up, as if seeking the Mother somewhere in the vastness above. The star was still there, faint now against the pale sky. She raised a hand to it in thanks, then she rose slowly to her feet.

Without volition, her arms opened wide to embrace the scene below. Her voice rang out, strong and powerful, as she thanked the Mother. The others heard, and came running, and when they saw what Zena had seen, they, too, spread their arms wide and chanted their thanks. Stronger and stronger their voices rose, until all the land reverberated with the sounds.

Then, when they were certain the Mother had heard them, and knew of the love and gratitude in their hearts, their voices died away. Gathering up the children, they began the descent into the paradise that awaited them below.

CHAPTER

18

Zena watched flamingos drop from the sky and settle in a rosy cloud on the water. Thousands upon thousands of them came, so many that the lake turned deep pink with their jostling bodies. Sweeping their heads from side to side in broad swaths, they skimmed up the blue-green algae that grew thickly in the salt-infested water. Any other bird or animal that ventured into this lake would die. Only the flamingos could tolerate its salinity. The long-legged birds seemed to know they were safe. They did not interrupt their feeding to watch for predators, nor did they bother to hide the nests they built on raised mounds above the shallow water. There was no need. No other creature could reach them.

At some unseen signal, the flamingos rose again and flapped over Zena's head, their wings flashing scarlet against the brilliant sky. Shading her eyes with one hand, she stared in wonderment. She had seen the spectacle of their flight many times before, but it still amazed her. Everything about the valley they had found amazed her, and she thanked the Mother constantly for bringing them to this wondrous place. All they needed, and far more, was here. Another lake with fresh, clear water harbored an abundance of fish and turtles and clams. Just as bountiful was the wide river that wound lazily through the center of the valley. Along its banks grew broad-leaved trees, their branches heavy with sumptuous fruit. Smaller trees nearby were laden with shiny black objects Zena had never seen before. Their taste was strange but delicious. Streams bubbled down from the hillsides, and clumps of bushes littered with berries decorated their banks. There were animals in abundance. Like the fruit, they were bigger and fatter than any Zena had ever seen. Even the lions and tigers they saw were larger than usual. At first Zena and the others had been alarmed, but the huge beasts paid no attention to them except to stare lazily from time to time, for their stomachs were easily filled with larger and tastier prey.

Beyond the valley was the huge body of water Zena had seen in her vision. A pale luminous green near the shore, it deepened into turquoise, then shades of blue and slate gray as it met the horizon. There was no end to it, at least no end that Zena could see. It stretched away from the long, curving coastline at the northern edge of the valley and disappeared into an unfathomable distance. Enormous fish leaped from its depths and twisted their sleek gray bodies in the air, then tumbled back with a mighty splash. The fine-grained earth was there, too, sparkling white in the sun, just as she had seen it in the vision. The cool, moist granules crumbled beneath their feet, and rustled softly as they slid back and forth with the surging water. A multitude of scurrying crabs and other tiny creatures hid beneath the porous surface. Bubbles twinkled above their fragile homes, making them easy to find. The children delighted in digging them out and watching them wave their miniature claws in defiance or scramble frantically toward the safety of the water. Sometimes they brought the crabs back as food, but Zena cautioned them over and over never to take more than they needed. The Mother had brought them to this paradise, and they must not abuse Her generosity.

She rose, anxious to resume her search. She was looking for a place to build a new circle of stones. Deep in her heart, she had always known she must build one when she arrived at her destination. Like the circle of stones by the river, it would be a place to give birth, but even more, this one would be a place to honor the Mother. Zena was determined to find exactly the right location. She wanted to create the feeling of peace and enclosure she remembered so well, but she also wanted to be able to look out upon the valley so that they would be constantly reminded of the abundance the Mother had provided.

For days, she had been scouring the area near the clearing where they had constructed their shelter, worried that her infant would be born before she had built the circle of stones. But so far, none of the places had felt right. Her chest tightened with anxiety lest she fail in her search and disappoint the Mother. Then she began to laugh at her stubbornness, at her slowness, still, to understand the Mother's ways. While she carried this burden of anxiety in her heart, she would never find what she sought. There was no need to struggle; she needed only to let the Mother guide her.

Zena relaxed and began to wander peacefully through the quiet woods, the fragrant fields, letting the Mother lead her as She would. And just as the sun reached the western horizon, she found it. As soon as she came to the secluded glen, she knew. This was the place. The Mother was here; Zena could feel Her presence strongly, and she felt the same sense of peace she remembered from the first circle of stones, where all her worries had seemed to melt away. She could see the valley, too, in all its splendor. Tall trees enclosed the little glen on three sides, but just as she had wanted, the fourth side was open to a magnificent view of the valley and the great water to the east.

She rested for a moment, savoring her find. Then she trudged off, heavy now with the unborn child, to find the others, so they could begin work right away. Already, they had located suitable stones. Together, they hauled them to the glen.

Zena picked up the first stone and laid it carefully against the fragrant earth. She bent to pick up another, and a strange confusion overcame her. She could not think for a moment who she was, or why she was placing stones in this way. It was as if another person had entered her body, were picking up one stone after another and arranging them carefully in a circle. Too absorbed in her movements to wonder at the strange feeling, she simply accepted it and continued the task. The others helped her, and soon the circle of stones was complete.

Zena shook her head, to clear it. Her confusion vanished, and she remembered what she wanted to do next.

"Help me bring this one now," she told Bran and Kropor, pointing to a flat slab of rock she had found earlier.

Together they dragged it to a clear space near the open end of the glen. The men helped her to balance the slab on two upstanding rocks, so that it formed a shelf. There she placed the first statue Lett had made, where all could see it when they came to speak to the Mother and listen for Her voice.

A few days later, the first contraction plunged through Zena's body. She smiled. This was as it should be. The circle of stones was ready, and the moon was full, to help draw the infant forth. Now her child could be born.

Another contraction came, and then another. Already, they were strong and close together. Zena sensed she would not have long to wait. She called to Nyta, to bring dry grasses and fresh water from the stream that bubbled nearby. Then she began to walk, around and around the circle, absorbing the Mother's peace, savoring her joy at being in this glorious place. Each time she came to the open end of the glen, she paused to look out at the valley, the glimmering water, and the beauty she saw there seemed to draw away her pain, give her the strength to walk some more.

Lotan came to her and shyly handed her a statue he had just finished. It was the best he had ever made. Polished to a high sheen, its dark wood seemed to pull in the last rays of the sun and reflect them back into Zena's body. She felt the warmth go into her, easing the tightness in her belly.

"I thank you, Lotan. It is beautiful. Already, I feel the Mother in this one."

Zena regarded the small figure gravely. Like the others, its belly and breasts were full and rounded, but it had a larger head, and its face had expression, as if it were aware that it was more than a wooden statue. Zena hugged it close to her heart and went to rest for a moment on the bed of fragrant grasses the other women had prepared. She had intended to get up again and resume her patient pacing, but the infant did not let her. As soon as she lay down, she felt its head between her legs.

The moon slid out from behind the trees. Zena smiled in welcome. Once, she remembered, the moon had made her uneasy. Now it gave her comfort, and she looked to it for guidance. The moon marked the passages of the seasons, gave order to their lives. It told them when the rains would come, and the dryness, when an infant was ready to emerge from its mother's womb, even helped to pull it forth.

"Pull," she said to the moon. "Pull while I push, so that the infant may be born."

She raised herself to a crouch and almost fell as the next contraction rocked her body. Toro and Nyta grasped her shoulders to steady her. Now the spasms came so fast and strong she had to gasp to breathe. Four more times, they tightened her belly. Then, without volition, Zena felt herself pushing down with all her strength.

"The little one comes fast," she heard Nyta say, and almost before the words were out of her mouth, Zena felt the baby slide out. Nyta reached down to catch it.

"Very fast," she amended, examining it carefully. Already, the child was squalling lustily.

"It is a male child," she said, handing the infant to Zena. "A good, strong one." Her eyes clouded as she thought of the maimed little creature she had borne, but she brightened quickly. A new baby always delighted Nyta.

Zena cradled her tiny son, feeling blessed. The infant was strong and the birth had been easy, for like Kalar, she had wide hips and a big, strong body. As soon as she could get up, she would go to the alcove where Lett's figure stood, and thank the Mother. Perhaps she would place the statue Lotan had made beside it, as a special gift of thanks.

She tickled the baby's cheek with her finger and laughed, as Cere had once laughed, at the prompt response. His tiny head turned immediately toward her finger and his mouth pursed, ready to suck. She placed him at her breast. He nursed for a moment, then fell asleep. He, too, had worked hard during the birth.

She would call him Kalet, she decided. The first sound would remind her of Kalar, the second of Lett. When others were born, as she was certain they would be, she would name them in similar ways. They would have their own names, but still remind her of the ones she loved who had returned to the Mother.

Zena regained her strength quickly. Within a week, she was able to gather food with the others, and by the time the moon was full again, she felt completely normal, at peace with the world.

Her peace was shattered abruptly the first time the baby opened his eyes fully and stared up at her. She had noticed the paleness of his eyes before and had told herself the color was a trick of light. This time she knew it was not so. His eyes were exactly like Lotan's, nut-brown and flecked with gold.

A stillness came over Zena. For a long time, she could not move. Shivers of fear ran up her spine and lodged in her heart. She could not understand why Kalet's unusual eyes should bring such terror, but she was wise enough now not to question the unexpected response. The Mother had not given her fear without a reason. When She was ready, She would divulge its purpose.

Lotan came to admire the baby. For a split second, Zena thought to mention his eyes, but her mouth closed so quickly, so tightly, that she felt as if a hand had been placed against her lips. A terrible feeling of wrongness invaded her, as if she had been about to commit an act that would harm them all. Disturbed by these strange reactions, she handed Kalet to Sima, who loved to hold him, and went to sit in the circle of stones. Perhaps there, an explanation would emerge. But for the first time in her life, Zena found no peace in the blessed place. There was only the feeling of wrongness, the sense that some tragedy would overtake them unless she prevented it, only she did not know what was wrong, or what she should do.

Too restless to sit still, she wandered aimlessly away from the circle of stones. The Mother would not speak to her in Her special place while she held such torment in her heart. When she felt calmer, she would return. Finally, a strong impulse drew her to a steep hill above the clearing. Trees with round red fruit grew here, and the smell of their sweetness permeated the area. She sat on a thick ledge and faced the thoughts that were racing through her agitated mind.

Kalet's eyes were like Lotan's, and Lotan had been her mate. He had been her only mate, for no other man had been in the tribe except for Bran, who was brother to her, and Kropor, and she had never thought of him as mate.

Somehow, Lotan's eyes had grown again in Kalet. Part of Lotan was there, in her tiny son. Had he passed something to the baby, when he had mated with her? But if mating, and men, played a role in making infants, why had they never noticed before?

Zena's lips compressed as understanding came. Few men had a distinctive trait like Lotan's eyes that would be noticed. And almost never did a woman have only one mate. Zena could not remember such a thing happening before.

There was Three-Legs too. Twice, she had given birth after she had mated. Her tiny calf had lived this time, and delighted all of them with its antics. Had the male gazelle, like Lotan, passed something to her, that helped the calf to grow? Was that why she had been so eager to mate, so she could get a young one?

Around and around the thoughts flew through Zena's head. She let them whirl, sensing that calmness would return only after her mind had ceased its struggle to understand.

She was right. After many hours had passed, and the sun had traveled far across the sky, Zena realized that it did not matter whether males and mating were connected to young ones. The Mother was still Life-Giver. Everything, all that they had, came from the Mother. Without Her, there would be no animals, no food, no beauty or wonderment or joy in each other and the world around them. Nor did it matter whether she understood how males might pass something of themselves to young ones. That was not important. What *was* important was to understand the fear that had come into her heart, the terrible feeling of wrongness she had felt after she had started to speak to Lotan. It was as if the Mother Herself had placed a hand over her lips, to stop her. If the Mother did not want her to speak, there was a reason.

Slowly, carefully, Zena stilled her racing thoughts and opened herself to the Mother. The others saw her sitting there and did not disturb her. They knew without asking that she was waiting for a message. Though she was not in the right place, her stillness, her total lack of awareness, told them that. When Kalet began to cry, Sima gave him to Metep to suckle.

All through the evening, Zena waited. For a long time, all she felt was the sense of wrongness. Slowly, it escalated into fear, and then horror. She did not shrink, but let it fill her. Her eyes closed, as if to help her hold the feelings within her despite her pain, and when she opened them again, the valley had disappeared. She was no longer sitting on the hill; instead, she was on the mountain, on the flat rock, and the snake was before her, swaying, as it had swayed before.

Zena looked deep into the serpent's fathomless eyes, eyes that held the Mother's wisdom. A small part of her understood that she was still in her valley, but her heart knew she had returned to the mountain. So real was her vision that she began to sway in rhythm with the snake. She saw the golden summit, smelled the fragrance of flowers on the mountainside, felt the soft warm air.

Words came to her, only they were not words but thoughts that had no need of words. She drew them in, heard them with her mind, her heart, and her body.

"All things you may know but this. Only this knowledge, of mating and males, is forbidden. Do not speak, for if you do, all that I have wrought will be destroyed. Those who come after you will struggle to wrest food from a land no longer fruitful, and their young will be born into a world of pain. Remember this and do not speak, lest the horror you have felt fill the earth."

The snake's thoughts pummeled Zena; she felt sick and weak with their power. But the serpent had not finished. Abruptly, it ceased to sway and reared high above Zena. Its black eyes stared into hers with such force she fell back in fear. It did not strike at her sudden movement, but only lowered itself over her and continued its malevolent stare. Anguish poured into her from its eyes, a terrible, bloated anguish that filled her heart, as if years upon years of suffering had gathered there, leaving no space for any other feeling. Joy was lost, and love and caring. Where they had been was only pain.

The snake pulled back and coiled itself, as if waiting for Zena to respond.

"Never shall I speak of this knowledge," she vowed. "I have heard Your message, felt the anguish in Your eyes. I shall not speak." Her voice was no more than a whisper, but her thought was strong and clear.

For another long moment, the snake looked deep into her eyes. Then it turned and slithered away.

Zena sat transfixed. Darkness came, but still she sat, unable to move. Her body felt battered, bruised all over, as if she had been physically assaulted by the anguish in her heart. Slowly, the terrible feelings faded, and after a long time, they disappeared, and she could not remember the agony she had felt. But her memory of the snake's message remained. She did not forget the terrifying words, and she did not forget the vow she had made. Never would she speak of the forbidden knowledge.

II

Zena kept her promise. All through her life, she told no one of her experience, and she never spoke of the connection between mating and young ones. Slowly, peace returned to her heart, a peace interrupted only occasionally by reminders of the knowledge she must never divulge. Once, Lotan commented on Kalet's unusual eyes. But since he had never seen his own eyes, Zena did not worry that he might compare them and wonder. It was harder with the others, when they noticed the similarity.

"The Mother gives us many colors," she told them, keeping her voice serene. "Look at the birds! Perhaps She will give us more of these beautiful eyes in other young ones."

No one challenged this explanation, but Zena was still careful to mate with other men as well as Lotan, so he would not give the gold-flecked eyes to all her young ones. That was not difficult, for a number of other tribes with whom they often interacted lived in the rocky hills at the western end of the valley. To have others with whom she could share this special pleasure was good, but Lotan remained her favorite. The passion they had inspired in each other the first time they had mated never dimmed, and she chose him as her mate as often as she could without neglecting the others.

About five moons after Kalet's birth, Zena noticed blood dribbling down her leg. At first, she was frightened and feared she might be dying, like Ralak. The other women never had the bleeding while they were still suckling an infant. But she felt no weakness, had no sense that there was anything wrong within her body. Instead, she felt healthy and strong, full of vigor. That would not be so, if she were dying. The Mother would not fool her. She ceased to worry, and after a few days, the bleeding tapered off and then stopped.

A few weeks later, it came again for a few days, then stopped
again. Soon, she realized that the bleeding came with the full moon.
The moon seemed to draw it forth, as it had drawn Kalet forth. If
the moon was involved, the blood must have special power. Zena
began to welcome it as a time when she felt especially strong and
close to the Mother. Often, she spent long hours communing with
Her in the circle of stones as the blood from deep within her body
seeped into the earth. It was indeed sacred, she realized, for unlike
other blood, that signified wounds and death, this blood gave life.
Where it had fallen, the earth was fertile, and flowers grew in
great abundance.

When one full moon and then another passed and no blood came,
Zena feared at first that she had displeased the Mother. But she felt
at peace, had no sense that she had wronged Her. Instead, she
began to suspect something else. Her body felt different, as it had
with Kalet, and she was almost certain the Mother had placed a
new life within her. That another infant should come so soon was
astonishing. No woman had ever begun another child until the first
was weaned, after four or five full cycles of the seasons. Still, she
was content. If the Mother wished to entrust her with another life
so soon after the first, she would welcome it. The other women
could help to feed Kalet if that was needed. Deep in her mind,
Zena knew the new life had come from one of the men as well as
the Mother, but she ignored the knowledge. Mating was a gift from
the Mother, and new life was a gift from the Mother. That was
enough.

This time, she grew so big she could hardly walk, and to her
surprise, two infants rather than one emerged. Both were males,
strong and healthy like their brother. After their birth, a year passed
before the bleeding came again. Zena welcomed it as a familiar
friend, and resumed her ritual of returning the sacred blood to the
earth. When once again two moons passed without the flow, she
did not worry but understood that still another infant was forming.
The blood did not emerge, she realized, when a new life grew, but
stayed within her to nourish the infant, as it nourished the earth.
To her delight, the baby was a female. Zena called her Ceralak,
after Cere and Ralak.

As the years passed, Zena continued to give birth at frequent
intervals. Three more daughters came next, then another son arrived, and much later, one last daughter was born. The other
women also gave birth during these years, though not as often as
Zena, for only to her did the Mother give the ability to start another
child before the first was weaned. Metep bore two more infants,

Toro one, and Sima and Filar each had four when they grew old enough to bear young. Nyta never bore another infant, but she helped to care for all the others. The Mother never gave an infant to Clio, either, and Zena was grateful. Clio would not have understood.

Each time an infant was born, Zena performed a special ritual in the circle of stones, to thank the Mother who had given it life. Holding the little one in her arms, she spoke its name and asked the Mother for Her love and protection for the fragile new life. Then she sprinkled earth and water on the baby's body, so the Mother would know how much they valued these precious gifts. She was certain the Mother heard her, for almost all the children survived the sicknesses that so often seemed to afflict little ones.

She performed the ritual for infants born in nearby tribes as well. She visited them often, and like Kalar before her, she spoke to the people of the Mother and taught them to follow Her ways. As others had before them, they embraced the Mother eagerly, as if She had long been within them and needed only Zena's words to emerge. Zena made sure that the children from the various tribes also understood the Mother's ways. Most important, she told them, was to live in harmony with the Mother's creatures, and with each other. If any of them did harm another child, or an animal, her anger was strong. No one was permitted to speak to the offender until the child had apologized to the Mother and to all in the tribe. At the same time, she loved them all without restraint. Kropor's story had taught her a valuable lesson. A child who was treated badly by adults was easily led to violence. Her formula seemed to work, for children grew up to be peaceful and loving.

Sima and Lupe organized games like the ones Zena had once created for them for the growing broods of children, as well as teaching them the ceremonies. There were many now, for death as well as birth, for the killing of an animal, though food was so plentiful that was seldom necessary, for the coming of the rains. The dance for rain was everyone's favorite. The ceremony had come to Zena one day as she communed with the Mother in the circle of stones. Her eyes had risen to the clouds that were heavy with impending rain, though so far no drops had fallen. Suddenly, the strange confusion she had felt when she had first created the circle of stones had overcome her again. Without volition, her feet had begun to move in rhythmic patterns, and she had heard herself calling words. She felt as if another person had stepped into her body, that this other, rather than herself, was moving and speaking. The others had come to join her, infected by the power of her words and movements. They had stamped in rhythm with Zena's stamping, had shouted the words until their voices were hoarse, though they did not know why.

Now, they performed the ceremony every year. As the rainy season approached, they gathered in the circle of stones and repeated the hypnotic movements. Over and over again, their feet stamped against the ground, their heads rose high toward the sky, then returned to the earth. Words came from them, the word for *Mother*, then the word for *rain*. At first, their voices were soft, the dance slow and relaxed. But soon the pace increased. Their feet stamped harder, faster, in an ever-increasing tempo, and their voices rang out in the dust-laden air, obscuring all other sounds. The women danced within the sacred circle, while the men danced just outside. Like Zena, they sensed the presence of others in their bodies as they moved, and they knew without thinking where they belonged.

If thunder roared and lightning flashed while they were dancing, the pace became still more frenetic, their excitement even more intense. The men grabbed sticks and waved them in the air or pounded them against the earth, to imitate the thunder and lightning, and the women danced in delirious circles until they sank to the ground in exhaustion, only to rise and dance again. At these times, especially, they felt truly a part of the earthforce, as they called its restless spirit back to the ground with their pounding feet, their swaying bodies and insistent voices, and held its awesome power within their hearts.

The wild abandon of the dance helped them to understand Clio's behavior during storms, and to accept her death when it came. To whirl and stamp, calling on the earthforce to release its rain, its thunder and lightning, was intoxicating. Clio had been born with the dancing in her, Zena thought, for she had always been one with the earthforce. And even though she grieved at Clio's early death, it seemed fitting that it was the lightning she adored that killed her; fitting, too, that Kropor died with her.

The storm that day was particularly violent. Clio charged out, with Kropor behind her, and ran to the top of the ridge. A huge old tree grew there, and she loved to leap and whirl beneath its curving branches. She had often danced there, but on this day, the lightning chose the tree as its conduit back to the earth. Thicker and brighter than any Zena had ever seen, the jagged streak tore through the gnarled old trunk and hit the ground, killing Clio and Kropor instantly.

"The Mother has been kind," Zena said softly, when the shock of their death had subsided a little. "To lose Clio is hard, but to have the earthforce claim her in this way would have pleased her. And that the Mother took Kropor with her . . .''

She did not have to speak further. No one wanted to imagine the agony Kropor would have suffered if Clio had been taken from him. It was best this way.

"See," Sima added, her voice shaking with sorrow. "See; Kropor still holds her hand, and her lips touch his face."

The others nodded. Clio and Kropor always slept close beside each other, with Clio's small fingers curled in Kropor's big palm, her soft lips close against his bristly cheek.

They buried them that way, in a shallow hole near the base of the tree. Increasingly, they had come to believe that those who returned to the Mother should be enclosed in Her earth, from whence all life sprang. Covering them with fragrant blossoms, they chanted words to tell the Mother of their love for these two unique beings She had wrought. They spoke of Clio's closeness to the earthforce, of her special ways of knowing, her sweetness and love for animals. And when they spoke of Kropor, they spoke of change, how one with violence in his heart could become so kind and tender, so happy to give all, even his life, for those he loved. Once difficult, they told the Mother, this beloved male had become more compassionate than almost any other.

When all had spoken, Zena commended Clio and Kropor to the Mother.

"These two whom we have loved can now return to Your all-encompassing heart," she said, her voice strong with emotion. "Keep them with You, for they have served You well. And if it is possible, I ask that Kropor, and Clio, too, may now be reunited with Ralak. Kropor loved her more than any other besides Clio, and his face would light up with joy to see her again.

"Great Mother, Giver of All Life, they are Yours again." Zena's last words hung for a moment in the air; then they began to fill the hole they had dug with moist, crumbling earth, to keep Clio and Kropor safe and warm.

Three more times, in the years that followed, they gathered to perform the death rituals for members of Zena's original group. Nyta died first, for she was old and frail; Toro followed soon after. Their deaths were hard, but for Zena, Bran's death was hardest. She found him one evening by the lake, where he had gone to fish. Nothing had happened, she thought, except that he had simply ceased to breathe. As she knelt by the familiar form, her heart contracted with a grief so strong she had to gasp for breath. Not since the stampede had she felt such an agony of sorrow. Bran had been her stalwart friend, ready always to support and defend her. She would miss him terribly.

Though her grief was strong, it did not linger. Lotan was still there to comfort her, and the tribe was growing so fast there was no time for sadness. More and more infants were born as the young ones grew up and had young of their own. Soon Zena's original group had swelled to more than a hundred, and even the fertile valley the Mother had provided could not sustain them all. Some would have to find new homes, Zena decided, and she began to train wise ones, so that each could lead a group into new territory. She had observed the young women carefully as they matured, and when they were old enough, she selected as wise ones those who had a special closeness to the Mother and a strong desire to learn Her ways. She taught them everything she knew, all she had learned from Kalar and Ralak, of the power of the earthforce, of men and why they were different, of the need to accept the Mother's wisdom even if it was hard to understand.

The practical teachings were easiest. A wise one needed to know the various plants for healing, how to treat wounds and illness, the words and procedures for rituals. After that, the lessons were harder, for Zena tried to speak of wisdom itself, of what it meant to be a wise one.

"To be strong within yourself, kind and just with those you lead, is most important," she told the initiates. "Always, the tribe needs a strong wise one. When there is no one who knows how to speak for the Mother, we forget how to behave, and then there is no peace in the tribe. I have seen this happen.

"That is why your most important task is to learn to listen to the Mother and accept Her messages. To hear the Mother's voice is more important than all the lessons I have given you, for She can guide you better than I. Come with me now to the circle of stones, and we will begin to practice."

For many moons after that, Zena brought the initiates with her each morning and evening as she listened for the Mother in the circle of stones. Patience was needed to hear Her voice, and the ability to still the mind. That had been hardest of all for Zena. But the ones she trained did not find it as difficult. They had watched Zena for many years, and had often tried to imitate her stillness, her openness, so they, too, could hear the Mother. Soon, many of them could hear the Mother's voice almost as well as she. Zena blessed them and sent them forth, for they were wise ones now. Some went west, into a great river valley that lay beyond the mountains. Others went north and east along the shoreline, or south into the plains.

Of all the potential wise ones, her youngest daughter was most intelligent, most clearly of the Mother. This last child had been born many years after Zena's other sons and daughters, when she had thought herself past the time to bear young. At first, she had doubted the familiar feeling in her body. But early one morning the infant had kicked, and she had realized with wonder that another new life truly was growing in her belly.

The child had lingered long in the womb, growing big and lusty, as her mother had. Zena carried her lovingly. All through the long months, she felt calm and serene, filled with the Mother's grace. The infant seemed to sense her mother's serenity, for when she finally emerged just as the sun slid over the horizon, she did not wail but calmly looked around her.

Zena smiled in amusement at the baby's serious face, and wondered what she would call this tiny female who seemed so wise already. But deep in her heart she must have known, for when the women asked her to name the newborn child, her lips formed words she had not thought to say.

"Mina. This one will be called Mina, for she is my mother born again."

As the child grew, Zena knew she had been right. Cere had spoken so many times of Mina, had told how even as a child she had the promise of wisdom upon her. Zena's small daughter was the same. From the beginning, she seemed to grasp the Mother's ways as if they had been born within her.

Perhaps, Zena thought, she had absorbed them in the womb, during that long, peaceful time, and she was glad that this precious child would never have to experience the pain and conflict she herself had felt so long ago.

Only once did Zena see her daughter agonize over the right course of action. Many times, she had watched Mina look first at Lotan's eyes and then at the eyes of her brother Kalet. Always before, she had asked questions when there was something she did not understand. This time she never asked. Each time her lips moved to frame the question, they closed again, as Zena's had.

She, too, had guessed at the connection between mating and young ones, Zena realized; she, too, knew intuitively that she must not express her suspicions aloud. Zena did not answer the unspoken query; instead, when she thought her daughter was ready, she sent her to the nearby hill where the snake had appeared. And when Mina returned, Zena knew the Mother had spoken. It was written in Mina's face, in the horror and shock that lingered there. Once again, the forbidden knowledge was safe.

Of them all, this daughter was also the hardest to lose. The bond between them was very strong. They knew each other's thoughts without speech, felt each other's pain or happiness as if it were their own. But when one day Mina came to her and spoke of a vision from the Mother, Zena hid her grief and hugged her daughter warmly.

"Beyond the great water, there is more land," Mina said, "land that the Mother has shown me. This is where I must go. The Mother awaits me there."

Her young face was alight with passion, with the joy of knowing the Mother had entrusted her with a vision, as She had long ago entrusted a vision to her mother.

Zena rejoiced with her, and helped her to gather the supplies she would need for the journey, despite the pain in her heart. When all was ready, she blessed Mina in the Mother's name and smiled encouragement as the small procession headed into the surrounding hills. Only when the new wise one turned away for the last time did she allow the tears to fall. She knew she would never see her again, this child who was the mother she had never known reborn. But she knew, too, that Mina was truly of the Mother and must follow her visions, as Zena had followed her own. Long ago, the Mother had led her to this magnificent valley, and Zena did not doubt that She would one day lead Mina to a paradise of her own.

She was right. Mina journeyed north and east for many seasons, until she came to the end of the great sea. There she discovered a place so bounteous it came to be called the fertile crescent, for the land was shaped like the crescent of the moon. Her tribe prospered, and when it grew too large, she trained wise ones to lead smaller groups into new lands, as her mother had. She taught them tolerance and peace, respect for the earth and all that lived upon it, for that was the way of the Mother. The new wise ones, in their turn, trained others to teach the Mother's ways, and so the knowledge spread.

Slowly, generations of these wise ones and their tribes dispersed across the earth. They traveled in all directions, to great continents and even islands where none had trod before. Everywhere they settled, they built circles of stone where they could worship the Mother. Some were so massive no one, still, can explain their creation. Others found caves to shelter them when ice began to creep across the plains, for caves, too, were circles of stone, built by the Mother Herself. Thousands of years later, their descendants gasped in awe when they beheld the magnificent drawings these explorers left on the cave walls, to thank the Mother for Her bounty.

Other tribes went west and east to found great cities in the valley of the Nile and in the vast reaches of the Orient. As the years passed, they spread farther still. Mountains did not stop them, nor did oceans, no matter how forbidding or tumultuous. They journeyed onward until all the earth was covered with their kind. And all of them, every one, were descendants of Zena's original tribe, the ones she had led across the savannah and the desert to her valley paradise on the shores of the Red Sea.

PART III

The Pyrenees between France
and Spain—fifty thousand
to thirty thousand years ago

CHAPTER

19

Zena eyed the young male doubtfully. Conar did not look promising. He was small and thin, with a downcast air, yet at the same time his body was harsh with tension. His eyes met hers, then he lowered them again. But in that moment, she saw something that made her frown in perplexity. His eyes were not like his body; they held an expression she could not fathom. Was it understanding of her situation, or caring, or perhaps hope?

Heartened, she took his hand. It was cool and clammy. A sigh escaped him at her touch, and some of the tension left his body. Zena smiled at him. Conar's lips twitched up in response, then widened into an infectious grin.

"Come," she said. "I will show you my place. I would like to share it with you."

He did not answer, but his hand tightened around hers, and he followed willingly. He had large hands, she noticed, larger than she would have expected for his size. She wondered why she had paid so little attention to him in the past. Probably it was because he kept to himself, always wandering off on some pursuit of his own instead of joining the others.

She stole another look at him. Unguarded, his face was eager, almost joyous. Zena quickened her pace, excited now at the prospect of mating with him. Conar might be small and quiet, but he was also interesting. Besides, desire had been building inside her for two days, and he was the only young male in the group with whom she had not yet mated.

The Great Mother and the wise woman who spoke for Her, her own mother as well, had made it clear from the time of her first bleeding that she should invite each of the men in her age group to mate with her, without showing favoritism. When none were neglected, jealousy did not spring up to cause trouble between the men. Zena was happy to comply. She loved mating. It was always a pleasurable experience, and always different.

The tribe had many words for mating, or Akat. There was Akate, or lustful mating, which was often quick, and Akato, which was playful, full of laughter. Akatale was tender, Akatelo, slow and sensuous, and there were many combinations in between. Best of all was Akatalelo. That was spiritual mating, or "with the Mother," when two people soared together. Zena had not yet experienced that kind. She was not likely to, either, with Conar. He was young and had little knowledge. Probably this would be plain Akat, mating that had no special flavor or was for teaching purposes, when a woman showed a less experienced male how to proceed.

Zena remembered her own training, at puberty. How the women had laughed! But there was serious purpose behind the merriment. Proper attention to mating helped to keep peace within the group. Without Akat, some of the men became aggressive, and that was bad for everyone. The women became quarrelsome, and then the young ones grew cranky. That was why the Mother had given them Akat. It was a special gift, one that should not be taken lightly.

Conar smiled shyly as Zena pulled him down beside her onto the soft moss in the enclosure she had chosen as her mating place. Shady and cool, the small meadow was protected by a circle of tall trees. Sometimes the earth was a bit damp, but usually the sun overhead dried it, so that she could lie with her lover in comfort. The smells and sounds were wonderful.

Zena sniffed appreciatively, taking in damp earth, and floral scents from the flowering bushes nearby. But then she forgot to notice the smells, or the bird calls that usually held her attention, for she had begun to stroke Conar's back gently, and was immediately aware of a vibrancy in him. Something tingled just beneath his skin, infecting her fingers, so that they flew faster and faster over his back and hips. The tingling was in his fingers as well. He ran his hands slowly down her spine, and now all the clamminess was gone from them. His touch was warm, and infinitely caressing.

Sighing with pleasure, Zena relaxed completely. Her hands slowed down, to match his. She stroked his buttocks in a lazy, compelling rhythm, felt his answering strokes turn her body into liquid that felt like fire.

She looked into Conar's eyes. This time he did not lower his lids but stared back at her, so she could see his feelings. It *was* caring in his eyes, she realized. Perhaps he had wanted very much to be with her?

The thought aroused tenderness, and she pulled him closer. In response, he wrapped his arms around her and hugged her hard. Then he unclasped her and reached down to stroke between her legs, up and down, and almost inside her, but not quite. There was nothing rushed about his movements, though she had felt his hardness against her stomach when he had held her. Some men became impatient when they grew big and hard, and tried to hurry the mating. But Conar's hands and lips moved sensuously, almost lazily, and he seemed intuitively to anticipate her desires, as if he understood her body as well as his own.

During her training, Zena remembered, her mother had told her that occasionally a man was naturally good at Akat, and needed little instruction. Conar seemed to be one of these. His whole manner had changed, become more confident, as if he sensed he was special in this way. Then she ceased to think at all as he began to suckle her breasts lightly, using his tongue as well as his lips. A tingling sensation ran straight from her nipple to a place deep inside her, and she groaned in ecstasy.

Excitement engulfed her, a sensual excitement more compelling than anything she had known before. She reached down to caress Conar's hips, his buttocks, and felt the excitement in him, as strong as her own. It leaped between them, gaining strength as it passed through their bodies. Passion was in her belly, her head, her fingertips, in his fingers, his loins, his very being. She could feel it coming toward her in waves.

She could not bear to wait any longer. She wanted him now, inside her. She pressed her hips against his and spread her legs wide, an unmistakable signal of readiness. He understood; she could feel him move his hips into position. But then he backed away for still another moment. His tongue passed lightly, then more strongly over the exquisitely sensitive lips of her vagina, and she cried out with pleasure, with the agony of waiting too. She clawed at his back, loving the tongue but wanting more. He groaned, a long, animal sound, and came inside her quickly, without hesitation. Once, twice, three times, he thrust at her, gently at first and then more roughly. She felt the tide rise in her, uncontrollable now. Within seconds, spasms rocked her body.

Conar slowed his thrusting. He moved in deeply, then pulled away. She cried out with fear that he might leave her entirely—that she could not bear. But he came back and stayed very deep inside her, moving in a slow, circular rhythm. The sensations were delicate, exquisite. The tide rose in her again, overwhelming in its intensity. Over and over, the spasms shook her. When they had slowed down, she wrapped her arms tightly around Conar, loving him for the joy he was giving her.

He began to move again, harder now, and she clung to him. But he escaped her arms; his back rose in the air, rigid with tension. He flung himself down again, rose once more, and then his body shook with such force that Zena was almost frightened. A scream escaped his clenched mouth as the spasms intensified, then diminished into a gentle shuddering.

He fell back onto her body with a final shudder. He was still inside her, but the strength had gone from his organ. Still, she felt the wildness begin to build up inside her once again. She let it have its way. This time the spasms were small but very piercing, a final explosion to pull any remaining tension from her. After that, she could not move at all.

Zena lay back, astonished. She had performed Akat many times since her first bleeding, but never had she experienced such intensity as this.

She studied Conar curiously. His eyes were closed, and his face was entirely peaceful. He looked vulnerable, and very young. Probably he had not mated much before. His lack of experience certainly did not show.

Perhaps, as one of the women had hinted, the men had started their own learning sessions, and that was why Conar was so skilled. But Zena found the rumor hard to believe. Akat was the women's province. More likely, as her mother had said, Conar did not need teaching.

Was he as sensitive and responsive with others? Perhaps she would ask her age-mates, very subtly. To ask a direct question would be rude. The women often discussed Akat among themselves, but they were careful not to compare one man to another. To do so might humiliate a man, and the Mother taught that humiliation was wrong. It was hard enough for the men being unable to create life, as the women could. Women were naturally more like the Mother, closer to Her, for She was Giver of All Life, and women givers of the tribe's life. Men had been given no role in the process. That was another reason why mating was so important for them. Only when they were enclosed within a woman's body could they experience oneness with the Mother. Still, men were strong and often very brave. Zena admired them for their courage.

She sighed. It must be sad for the men. But she herself was sad, for the Mother still had not given her a child. For two years, she had walked beneath the Mother's tree, circling below its fruitful branches. That alone often started a little one growing in a woman's belly. When nothing had happened, she had knelt before the sacred Goddess figures, with their huge bellies and swollen breasts, within the circle of stones. The images were special to the Mother, and she had been sure that would work. But still no child had come.

This year, surely, the Mother would grant her wish, Zena decided. She would ask Conar to make a special Goddess figure just for her, and keep it with her always. He made the best figures of all.

She rolled away from him so she could see him better. Her movement roused him, and he propped himself on an elbow and looked shyly into her face. She touched his genitals gently, her eyes teasing, for now the organ was so tiny and crumpled. The joy left Conar's countenance, and he turned miserably away from her. Zena bent over him, compassion in her heart. She had not meant to hurt him. Murmuring soothing words, she stroked him lovingly until he looked at her again.

"You gave me great pleasure," she told him earnestly. "Much, much pleasure."

Knowledge that she was speaking the truth showed in his face. He closed his eyes in relief.

"I have wanted to be with you, to please you," he told her. "I wanted that very much. But I have little experience."

"You do not need it. You are a wonderful lover," she answered frankly, certain that he would not use the flattery to boast to the other men. He was not that type.

His face lit up like a child's when one of the big males tossed it gently into the air.

"Thank you," he said simply. Then, as if still doubtful, he added, "I was afraid I would disappoint you."

Zena widened her eyes in mock horror. "If you had given me any more pleasure, I might have exploded."

He laughed impulsively, and Zena laughed with him. She stood and offered him her hand as she turned to leave.

"We will come back here soon again," she promised. But she knew, as he did, that they would have to wait at least a week, lest the other men sense favoritism. Still, she meant to keep her promise as soon as she could. He *was* her favorite, for a lover, even if she could not admit it publicly. His body might be small, but his ability to give pleasure was not.

They wandered back to the resting place, hand in hand, but as they came closer, Zena untangled her fingers from Conar's and went on ahead of him. It was best not to be too public about her affairs. She liked to handle them in private.

Languorously, she dropped onto a sun-drenched rock to rest. Sleep overcame her. She dreamed of a place she had never seen, far to the west where mountains rose high and white beyond craggy foothills. In her dream, she and Conar were walking in deep tunnels that twisted in labyrinthine patterns beneath the earth. They came to a narrow passage that went through the rocks, and although she had never seen beyond it, she knew it led to a large open space. Conar disappeared, but she went on alone, for she was about to discover something, something important that waited for her in the open space.

Voices woke her just before she went through the passage. Disappointed, she sat up, ready to protest. Her indignation, and all remnants of sleep, dropped from her as she listened. It was her mother speaking, and her tone was harsh, compelling.

"It cannot be that we allow this," she said. "All the tribe will suffer. He must be banished."

Banished. The word rang in Zena's ears. Who would be banished, and why? Banishment was a terrible punishment. To her knowledge, it had happened only once before, when a man called Kort had tried to force himself on a woman. He had not succeeded, for she had screamed and the others had stopped him, but even the attempt was an unthinkable act. Always, it was up to a woman to initiate Akat and to choose a mate, for only she knew when she was ready and willing. That a man should usurp the woman's prerogative was truly beyond understanding. Zena felt herself grow hot with indignation.

She shook herself. She had no knowledge of what had happened. And she should not listen without revealing her presence. She slid from the rock and went into the clearing.

"Greetings," she said to her mother, Lune. "I could not help but hear your words. What has happened?"

Before she answered, Lune looked questioningly at her sister, Menta, who was the tribe's wise woman. Menta and Lune had been born at the same time, but they were very different in temperament. Menta was slow and wise, while Lune was quick and passionate. That was why Menta, rather than Lune, had been chosen as wise woman when their mother had died. Besides, Lune was medicine woman, the one who knew how to heal. Healing was her natural talent, just as Menta's talent was visionary. She could see far beyond what others saw, into time that had not yet come, and time that had passed long before any in the tribe were born.

"Zena can be told," Menta assured Lune. "All will hear soon. All must express their feelings before we decide."

"It is Tron," Zena's mother explained, her voice still shaking with anger. "He has had Akat with Pila without her consent, and now she is crying and in pain. He thinks he can do such things because he is strong and kills many bison."

"But that is terrible!" Profoundly shocked, Zena sought for better words to express her feelings. "Pila is too small. I do not think she has had even one bleeding."

"No," Menta answered. "She was not ready." Compassion, and suffering, filled her voice.

Zena hugged her, understanding her pain as wise woman. It was Menta who felt most responsible for the welfare of the tribe, she who would have to make the final decision about banishment. Kort had been banished for only a few months; then he had been permitted to return. But his crime was not as great, and he had changed his ways. If Tron had really forced himself on Pila, he might be banished forever. That, too, seemed almost unthinkable. How would he live without the others?

Perhaps, though, the tribe would be better without him. Zena recoiled at the harsh thought. Still, there was truth in it. Tron was different from the other men. They sometimes became angry or fought among themselves, but they were also kind and loving. Tron was not. He did not seem to care for anyone. Even as a child, he had wanted to fight more than anything else, and he seemed almost to take pleasure in hurting others. All of them had tried hard to be kind to him so he would change, but it had not helped. Zena realized abruptly that she had never liked Tron. His face had a sullen, brooding expression, and when she had mated with him he had been rough and uncaring of her pleasure. She had thought at the time that he simply lacked knowledge. But perhaps it was not his nature to be kind.

Menta seemed to hear her thoughts. "Sometimes," she said quietly, "a man or woman is born who is not kind. There is no kindness in such a person, no matter how hard we try to find it with our own kindness to them. It just is not there. It may be that Tron is one of those. We will see what the others think."

She turned to Lune. "Summon the people," she instructed. "We must go into council before the sun sets." Everyone in the tribe was a member of the council, and all must be present at the meeting to help make a decision.

"Go to Pila and comfort her," she told Zena. "Have her tell you what happened, if she can do that."

Zena and Lune ran to do her bidding. Normally, Menta would not tell any other what to do, but when she assumed her role as wise woman, all of them obeyed her without question.

Zena found Pila weeping quietly in a corner near the cooking fire. Truly, she was little more than a child. Her mother, Bly, was crooning softly to her and soothing her small, bony shoulders with caressing hands.

"Menta has sent me," Zena explained. She knelt beside Pila. "The Mother has not forgotten you," she told her. "That is not what happened. You are still part of Her. It is Tron who is not part of Her. He has lost Her by this act."

Her words seemed to reach Pila, for she looked up with a grave face and reached for Zena's hand.

Zena was not certain why these were the words that had come to her, but she knew they were truthful, and that Pila needed to hear them. To be so violated must have damaged her good feelings about herself, as well as hurting her body. And without good feelings about herself, she could not feel close to the goodness of the Mother. It must be hard for Pila to understand that what had happened to her did not make her less good in the Mother's eyes, or in the eyes of anyone in the tribe.

"Can you be strong enough to tell us what happened?" Zena asked the question tenderly, hating to rush the child, but aware that Menta needed to know Pila's story as soon as possible.

Pila nodded bravely. "I was searching for mushrooms in the woods, and Tron came upon me there. He did not speak. He just pushed me over and went inside me, and it hurt terribly. Then he shook all over and got up and went away."

She looked up at her mother with dubious eyes. "Does Akat always hurt that badly?"

Bly hastened to reassure her. "No, Pila, there is no hurt when you are ready. Do not worry. It will not be like this again. When you choose it, Akat gives great pleasure."

Despite her firm words, there was no certainty in Bly's face. She looked up at Zena sadly. Zena could sense what she was thinking. Would Pila truly learn to enjoy Akat again, after this experience? Would she not always be a little afraid, so that the pleasure was dampened? Akat was the supreme gift of the Mother, the gift She had given to them so their lives would be filled with harmony and that special kind of joy. To take such a gift from Pila was surely a monstrous crime.

Zena felt herself grow hot again with anger. Determinedly, she forced it away. Anger must not guide her judgment. To help Menta decide what was best, she must think clearly. A good decision, she knew, would not harm anyone, but benefit them all, even Tron, if that was possible. She sighed deeply. At the moment, she could not imagine how that could be done. But if she listened hard, the Mother would surely show her the way.

II

The tribe gathered just before sunset in the sacred circle of stones. The big, rounded rocks had been placed there long ago by the ancient ones who had come before them. Year after year, they had spoken to the Mother and performed Her rituals within the circle, and now Her presence was very strong. Zena saw the knowledge on each face as the people filed into the glen. They bent their heads toward the ground, then raised them to the sky, to acknowledge the Goddess, the one they called Mother among themselves. Their shoulders straightened as their determination to live by Her ways, to make decisions as She would make them, was strengthened.

Thirty people were in the tribe, and finding all of them had not been easy. Many had been out gathering food, and Katli and a few men had gone hunting. Most women stopped hunting, at least for a time, when they had young ones. But Katli had never stopped. As soon as she recovered from each birth, she strode off with the men, leaving her infants with her sisters, who loved them dearly and always seemed to have breasts hanging heavy with milk. Katli knew as much about the movements and habits of animals as the most experienced hunters, and they welcomed her participation. The animals, too, seemed to welcome her, as if sensing her devotion. They did not run so fast, and died easily when Katli was there. Always, she blessed them and thanked them for giving their lives so graciously.

And of course, Zena thought, *they did not really die.* Like those who hunted them, the animals were a part of the Mother's unending cycle of life and death and renewal. One day, they would be born again, to run across the plains and eat of its rich harvest.

When they were all assembled, Menta stood to speak. She was a small woman with long, flowing black hair, but when she became the Mother's representative, she seemed larger than even the men.

"Great Goddess, Mother of all," she said gravely, "we fear a crime against You has brought bad feelings to this tribe. The bad feelings churn in all of us, and make us less able to know Your joy and goodness. We seek to resolve these feelings, for if we are to recognize Your way, we must have peace within us.

"Guide our thoughts as we seek truth, our judgment as we make a decision. Help us to keep love in our hearts even when they are heavy with pain, wisdom in our minds even as anger confuses us, for that is the way of the Mother."

The people nodded, agreeing that they would try to abide by the Mother's way as they came to a decision. They listened attentively as Menta told them the story, though most of them knew it already. The terrible news had traveled fast. Sadness replaced anger in many of their faces as Menta spoke, sadness that such a thing could happen among them. Tron had violated all of them, not just Pila.

Zena glanced at him. He looked furious, not contrite. When Menta told how he had crept up behind Pila and forced himself on her, he grunted harshly and leaped to his feet.

"She wanted that," he burst out in an aggrieved tone. "She was crouched there, waiting."

A low rumble of protest sprang from the crowd. Menta held up a hand for silence.

"She wanted that . . ." she murmured, as if to herself. Eyes narrowed, she asked Tron to explain.

He shrugged. "I saw it in her face, when she looked at me."

Menta stared at him, frowning. Then she turned toward Katli. "Tell me, Tron. What is in Katli's face right now?"

Tron shook his head angrily. "I cannot tell," he muttered. "Perhaps she is thinking of the hunt." In fact, Katli's face was suffused with disgust.

"Tell me, then, what is in Bly's face," Menta asked. Tron looked reluctantly at Bly. "She is angry," he retorted. But there was no anger in Bly's face, only grief.

The people began to murmur impatiently, eager to get on with making a decision. Surely Tron was not telling the truth, anyway. Everyone could read what was written in others' faces.

Menta persisted. "What do you see in Zena's face?"

"Oh, she is just paying no attention," Tron snapped. His eyes raked Zena's face, and he sneered contemptuously.

Menta's frown deepened. As the others had noted, Zena was listening to the proceedings with intense concentration. Menta stood perfectly still for many moments, her eyes focused on Tron, as if she were seeing deep within him.

Tron stared back furiously. *These people made too much fuss over the child*, he thought bitterly. She had looked ready enough to him. Besides, he had felt lust and she had been there. And there was nothing wrong with Akat. Menta told them that all the time. But she had always singled him out for punishment, made him feel wrong. All of them had, even when he was a child. He had tried to show the other boys how strong he was, how skilled even then at killing animals, to make them pay attention to him. They had avoided him instead, so he had hit them to show he did not care. He liked hurting them. It made him feel better. Now that he was grown, nothing had changed. The women took him to their places of Akat, but he knew they preferred others. Being rough with them gave him satisfaction. The men were no different. They still avoided him, even though he was the best hunter.

He shrugged, to let them know he still did not care what they thought of him, and turned away from Menta's probing eyes.

The others waited in silence for a time, sensing that Menta was seeking guidance. Then they began to mutter impatiently again. The sounds roused Menta from her trancelike state.

"It is time now to hear from everyone who wishes to speak," she told them gravely. "All must be part of this decision."

Bly stood courageously. "I do not want him here," she said simply. "I speak not in anger, but in fear. He could do this again, and there are others, younger girls. Always, they will be afraid, and so will we."

Heads nodded vigorously, and others stood to say similar words. One small girl, clutching her mother's hand, brought tears to many eyes.

"I wish to run and play in the woods," she told them. "Now I will not dare to follow the squirrels, and look for the tiny ones that live in the roots of trees. And I want to have my little sister with me."

Another child stood, a boy this time. "Tron is bad to do this," he said, his young voice filled with disgust. "Bad people cannot stay with us. The Mother does not want them. So he must be sent away."

The oldest man of the tribe, Bakan, was even more forceful. He was wise, and respected by all, so the people listened carefully. He glared at Tron as he spoke, and the strength of the glare made Tron lower his eyes.

"All of us who love the Mother, respect Her wisdom, find horror in this act. The women of our tribe represent the Mother, for their bodies create the Mother's new life. And it is through the bodies of our women that we, the men, feel our oneness with the Mother.

To violate a woman's body is to violate the Mother. A man who would commit such an act does not belong here.

"There is badness in Tron," he continued, speaking softly now. "We have known this before, but we have waited, hoping that he will change. He will not change. He must be banished, and he must never be allowed to return."

A younger man jumped up. "How can we know that he will leave us? He could lurk nearby and still do this terrible thing. I think we should kill him instead, so he cannot."

A babble of noises emerged from the tribe. To kill one of their own was the most terrible act they could imagine. Never before had this been suggested, and they did not like the idea. Even animals could not be killed without the need for food, and they had to be blessed before it was right.

Katli stood to speak. "Once, in a group of wolves," she said slowly, choosing her words with great care, "I saw one animal that was not right, and turned on others of its kind. The other wolves killed it. They did not eat it, but left it for the vultures. They did this not in anger, I think, but to save the group. If they had not killed it, others might have been born that were also bad. Though many will not believe me, I know that a bad animal can affect the young. I have seen it happen."

Everyone listened carefully to her explanation. They had great respect for her knowledge of animals, and they also admired wolves for their ability to live together harmoniously. If this was how the wolves solved a similar problem, it was possible that killing could be justified.

Lune rose to her feet. Unlike her sister's, her long hair was ashen, so pale it was nearly white. Menta had been born of the earth, the people said, while Lune had been born of the moon. Though she was not as wise and calm as Menta, the boldness of her thoughts was respected.

"Perhaps there is another solution," she said in her firm voice, "one that is safer than banishment, and not as terrible as killing. We all know that Akat helps to keep men from fighting among themselves, or causing trouble. This is not working with Tron."

Murmurs of assent came from the group. They understood that without Akat, men could become aggressive. But Tron had not been neglected, and still he could not control his temper, or his actions.

"I have wondered," Lune continued, "if Akat works because it draws fire from the place of mating in men. Perhaps the sacs there are the place where the desire to fight or hurt others lurks, and if they are not emptied, they cause trouble. In Tron, it is possible that these sacs should be removed so that the fire in him can be taken away. Then he will no longer wish to cause trouble, or force himself on those who have not chosen him.

"Krost could do this," Lune continued. "He has done it many times when animals are prepared for eating."

Eyebrows went up as the people digested her words. No one had ever considered such a possibility before. But Lune had deeper thoughts than most, especially concerning the workings of bodies, and she could be right.

Krost, a big, gentle man with craggy features, rose to respond. Torment showed on his face as he considered Lune's idea. He had hunted many times with Tron, and was as much his friend as any of them could be. But he was also fiercely loyal to the group, and would protect them with his life. To stand by silently and see them hurt would be wrong.

"Lune's suggestion is possible," he agreed, "but it seems cruel too. I would not wish to do it." He shook his shaggy head fiercely, seeking to control his feelings before he spoke again.

"Tron must tell us if he truly wishes to change. If he does, then we should watch him carefully to see if he means his words. If he does not change, then he must be banished. I myself will make him promise not to stay near us, and I will watch to see that he does not come back."

"I, too, will watch," a deep voice asserted. It was Tragar speaking. He was Krost's brother, born of the same mother. Although he spoke little, he was by far the strongest man among them. Tron would be wise not to return if Tragar was waiting.

Heads nodded everywhere as Krost and Tragar spoke. Most people thought that Tron should be given a chance, but that he would have to be banished forever in the end. They knew him well. He was unlikely to change.

Zena looked up in surprise as Conar stood. Like Tragar, he did not often speak. The resolve in his normally quiet tone was evident to all.

"I, too, will watch," he said firmly, "and my watching will be different, for I can move without sound."

Tron looked at him disdainfully, for Conar was small and weak compared to him, but there was wariness in his eyes as well. Conar could move as silently as an animal, though he never used this skill to hunt, as Tron did. Instead, he tried to scratch the forms of bison and other animals in the dirt and on rocks. It seemed to Tron a useless occupation.

Menta listened attentively as a few others stood to voice an opinion, or to comment on the options being considered. When all had finished, she turned to Zena.

"You have not spoken," she said gently. Usually Zena was one of the first to speak, and had strong opinions.

Zena sighed heavily. Something was bothering her, as if another clue existed that no one had addressed. She went to Tron and stood directly before him.

"Do you know how terrible was your act, Tron? Do you know how badly you have hurt Pila, and the Mother, and all of us?"

"Akat is not wrong," Tron muttered. "The girl would have been ready soon enough."

"Something is lacking in Tron," Zena said so quietly that few heard. "Will he ever gain what is needed?" Bewildered, she turned away.

"I have not yet decided," she told Menta in a stronger voice. "I must listen more for the Mother's guidance."

Some of the others grunted in disapproval. They wanted the matter settled, and Zena's reluctance to speak meant they must postpone a decision. But they did not challenge her. The name of Zena was given only to a few, those who would one day serve the Mother in some special way. Though she was still young, they valued her ideas and would wait until she was ready.

Menta, however, nodded approval. Zena seemed to sense what she herself felt—that there were questions still unasked, or solutions still not considered. The decision could not be made until these uncertainties were resolved.

"I, too, must consult with the Mother," she told the tribe. "I must go to the Kyrie, where she awaits me. Until we have decided, Krost and Tragar will watch Tron, Conar as well."

The Kyrie was the place high on a nearby hill where the wise woman listened for the Mother's guidance. No other person went there except a very young girl who brought food and water and then crept silently away. All the group knew that Menta might stay in the Kyrie for many hours, perhaps all through the night and into the next day, while she wrestled with a decision and waited for peace to return to her heart. Only then could she be certain she had found the Mother's way.

Resigning themselves to patience, they went off to perform their tasks or to sleep.

The wait was long. Two nights and most of the following day passed before Menta emerged from her vigil. Her face was drawn and weary when she finally reappeared in the clearing, for she had hardly slept. She had not eaten, either, only taken water. Hunger helped her thoughts to clear. She knew she had found the Mother's way, for she felt peace in her heart with what she was about to do. But agony still clouded her eyes. The Mother had given her a vision, a vision that had devastated her so badly she was still unable to quell the turmoil in her mind. Now she would have to relate this terrible vision to the others, and shatter them as she herself had been shattered.

Menta straightened her shoulders determinedly. They must do as the Mother asked. It was their only chance, the only way they could avoid the horrors her vision had foretold.

CHAPTER

20

Thunder rumbled ominously as the tribe gathered once again in the circle of stones. All day, black clouds had scurried across the sky, and now they had coalesced against the western horizon. Menta tilted her head back to watch them.

"The clouds are like the words I will say," she told the others soberly. "They are black and brooding, waiting to spill their wrath upon us, but in another way, they are different. When the storm decides to come, we cannot stop it. We can only wait until it exhausts its fury, but we may be able to stop the words I will speak from becoming real. If we follow the Mother's way, do what She has shown me, there is a chance."

She broke off as a thin spear of lightning crackled through the sky. The people watched her, their faces uneasy. Menta's words were ominous, her voice somber. That was not like her.

An unspoken message flashed between Zena and her mother. Something very unusual must have happened at the Kyrie.

Menta's next words confirmed their impression. "The Goddess has given me a vision," she told them, "a vision that alters our decision. It takes us far from this time and into another. In it are things I do not wish to relate, but I must, if you are to understand what the Mother has asked us to do."

She broke off again, and the agony on her face was hard to behold. When she continued, the intensity in her tone brought shivers to every listener. Still, they had to strain to hear her at times, for her voice rose and fell and rose again as the drama she had seen unfolded.

"I came to a place I have never seen, far to the west, below the place where the mountains loom," she began softly. "In this place were caves, deep and secure, that wound beneath the hills. People were there, people like ourselves. They lived and worked as we do, except perhaps they knew more. It was as if they had discovered something in the caves, something that came from the Mother and was sacred to Her."

Prickles of suspense ran up Zena's spine. Could this be the place she had seen in her dream? How was it possible that Menta should see the same place?

Menta's voice, slow and gentle now, as if she were re-experiencing her vision, cut into her thoughts.

"The people are sitting outside a cave, in the evening, talking quietly among themselves. There is firelight, and a sound I cannot name, a beautiful sound that seems to come from a reed one man holds. The sound stops abruptly, for the people have heard another noise, one that brings them to their feet in fear. It is the sound of weeping, terrible, wrenching weeping.

"Suddenly, a young girl bursts into the circle of firelight. She is tall and slender, and her hair is the color of sunlight. It is she who weeps so passionately. There is blood across her cheeks, blood running down her legs. One of the women pulls her close and holds her until the weeping abates and she can talk. A man, a stranger, had come up behind her in the woods and forced himself upon her, she tells them. He cut her with his sharp flint, on her face.

"The people are horrified. They have never known such a thing to happen. They do not know what to do. The men leap up to find the stranger and bring him before the council, but he has hidden himself so cleverly that they cannot see him. They try to sleep, but they are afraid. All night they listen for the sound of footsteps. They know the man is out there somewhere, waiting to hurt another. They can feel the hatred in his heart; it comes through the night to pound at their own hearts.

"In the morning, they can still feel it, and all through the day. But nothing happens, and they think the man has left. They do not watch so carefully. This time, two women are assaulted, and the man who tries to protect them is wounded. The stranger thrusts his flint into the man's arm, and binds the women with vines so they cannot struggle while he forces Akat upon them."

Exclamations of horror filled the clearing. Never, in all their lives, had any member of the tribe heard of behavior like this. It was almost impossible to believe that any man would act so cruelly toward others.

Menta held up her hand. "There is worse to come," she said quietly, and her voice was filled with an anguish so deep that Zena wanted to put her hands over her ears, to blot it out. She squeezed her eyes shut instead, as if to deny the ghastly images Menta had placed in her mind. Hot tears of rage, that any man should commit such atrocities, surged against her eyelids and careened down her cheeks.

Menta took a ragged breath, and when she spoke again, her voice came hard and strong.

"There are other men, men who have forgotten the Mother. They are young and ruthless, hunters from fierce tribes, and they admire those who kill without caring, without remorse. More of them come, many more. They roam the land, violating the women, killing the men, for they know no other way to behave.

"Together, these cruel men prey on other tribes. They creep up on the people as they sit around their fires at night, and jump upon them without warning. There is no way to stop them, for they have terrible, sharp flints, and they draw them across the throats of the men before they can defend themselves, and point them at the women's breasts as they recoil in horror. They tie the women, the young girls, and force them to come, and the children are left behind, screaming for their mothers."

Sounds of muffled weeping came from the people, but Menta did not hear. All her attention was focused inward, on the vision only she could see. She was straining now, her brow furrowed in concentration.

"Much time has passed," she said suddenly. "Much time, more than we can think of. Many things have changed. There are more people, and they live in different ways. Their shelters are big now, so big that whole tribes can live in them. There are fields, and strange tools. . . ."

Her brow cleared, as if the vision had suddenly come into focus, and her voice came louder and louder as she pushed out the words to describe what she was seeing.

"The men have something in their hands. They are like our flint knives, but they are longer, and sharper, and they gleam in the sunlight. I do not know what they are, but they are terrible things, used only to destroy.

"More than anything else, the men love these strange knives. They do not love the Mother, or even know Her. They love only the knives. Everywhere they go, they hold their knives before them, to kill and hurt and mutilate. And because they know no other pleasure than that which comes from their knives, their sexual organs become like knives to them. It is as if they have killed Akat with their knives. They violate women with their organs, even small girls, and then they use the threat of their glinting knives to hold the women captive, make them do the hard work for all and beat them if they are too slow. With their knives, they kill the men, and every time they come to a new place, they even kill—"

Menta's voice broke. She was almost shouting now, and despair was written on her face. For a moment, it seemed that she might not be able to go on. But then, with an immense effort of will, she thrust out the last words in a howl of anguish.

"They even kill the children," she exploded, pounding the air with her fists for emphasis. "They kill infants and small children. I have seen it, seen them die! It is as if they kill the Mother Herself when they kill the children. I can feel Her pain, hear Her weeping.

"This cannot come to pass!" Menta screamed. "We cannot let it happen!"

Menta's final scream lingered long in the air, and when it died away, the clearing was utterly still. No one could speak or even move. They could not absorb the words Menta had just spoken. They were too terrible, too unthinkable. Everything she had told them was unthinkable, but to kill infants and children was truly beyond their capacity to imagine. Children were gifts from the Mother, to be loved and cherished and cared for by all.

Minutes passed in silence. Then, one by one, the people stood and began to mill about, too upset to sit still. But Zena did not stir. She felt numb, as if all the strength had been drained from her body and would never return. Would she ever be the same again? It did not seem possible. Something inside her, some place of peace, had been shattered. She could feel it in there, like a broken jug that could not be repaired.

Abruptly, the shattered thing came together again, but in a completely different way. It was as if all her innards had only one purpose now. She must prevent these horrors from happening. If it was in her power, she must stop the vision, never let it turn into reality.

"To kill the children," She muttered the words to herself. Still they made no sense. If a little one was badly hurt and could not survive, they gave it herbs so it would go quickly back to the Mother, without feeling pain. But to kill for no reason? No. That simply was not possible.

An immense feeling of relief suddenly invaded her, and she almost laughed. Of course, no one would do the things Menta had described. Even Tron would not. The Mother must have given them the vision so they would remember how beautiful were their lives, how filled with joy.

Menta seemed to read her thoughts. "The terrible happenings I have described are hard to believe," she said quietly. "But the Mother has shown them to me, so they are true.

"I do not know if the first man, the stranger, is Tron," she continued, "but I believe it could be so. If we banish him, this is what he might do, so he cannot be banished. He cannot be killed, either, because then we will do what none has the right to do—kill in anger. There is no peace in killing a man like Tron. Always, his spirit will be there, infecting us, keeping the turmoil in our hearts, so that we cannot be one with the Mother. She has shown me that, too."

"What, then, can we do?" Bakan's voice betrayed no emotion, and his calmness quieted the group's agitation. Menta glanced at him gratefully.

"There is a way," she told him. "I cannot be certain it will work, but we must try. But the Mother has shown me only the first part of our task. After that, I do not know, except that the pattern will emerge as it must."

Zena looked up abruptly, feeling Menta's penetrating eyes upon her. There was compassion on the wise woman's face, and a terrible sadness. Chills ran up Zena's spine and into her scalp.

"What we must do will be hard," Menta told the waiting tribe. "But it will be especially hard on Zena. She is the one chosen by the Mother to accomplish this task, or to try.

"It is you, my child," she continued, addressing Zena directly, "who has been designated by the Mother to try to change Tron, for that is the only solution. But you must never feel you have failed if this cannot be done, or if the outcome is not as we desired. The Mother has shown me no further than this."

Zena bent her head to hide her fear. She did not want to be the one, yet she knew she must be, had felt it already in the strange broken feeling that had so quickly resolved itself into determination.

She compressed her lips to stop their shaking. "What is it I must do?" she asked bravely, but the tremor in her voice was audible to all.

Menta answered gently, reassuringly. "You alone cannot change the vision. For this, we will need more guidance. Your role is simpler, and perhaps not so hard. What the Mother asks of you is to try to teach Tron to see what is in people's faces, so he will learn what he should and should not do. He is grown, yet still he does not know these things. Even a child can see better than he when joy or grief suffuses a face. Especially, he does not know how to see the true signals for Akat. He sees desire where it does not exist, and fails to see it when it is there. I have observed this many times."

Zena nodded in immediate agreement. Menta was right. She had given a name to the thing that was lacking in Tron. For a moment, she was excited to have found the answer to a question that had puzzled her badly. But then apprehension, and a terrible sense of dread, suffused her. Her resolve vanished.

"How is it possible to teach such a thing?" she protested. "I do not think he will listen to me."

"The Mother will show you the way," Menta replied calmly. "And all of us will help you, even the children. They, too, are learning. There will always be someone watching Tron as well. You will not be alone."

Zena sighed. What the Mother asked of her, she would try to do. There was no other way. But it was hard to see how changing Tron would change the horror of the vision Menta had related. Still, as Menta said, they could only do as the Mother requested. Then, surely, She would guide them further.

Her apprehension dissipated a little, but another thought took its place. "Can we be sure he will act as he should when he has learned to read our faces?"

"This I cannot answer until we see if Tron changes. It is your job only to try to teach him. Then, if Tron still does not understand the true signals for Akat, Lune's solution may be needed. But we will wait and see."

Menta pointed abruptly at Tron "Remove the bindings from his head," she instructed.

Before she had started to tell of the vision, Menta had asked Krost and Tragar to pad Tron's ears with a thick wad of leaves bound with vines, so he could not hear. It had taken the combined strength of both men to accomplish the task. Zena had wondered at the request, but now she understood. Menta had not wanted Tron to hear, for her words might make him believe he should act in the way she had described.

Zena studied his face. She saw anger, a stubborn hardness, but was there hatred, the kind of intense hatred Menta had described in her vision? She did not think so. But as the men took the bindings from his ears, he glanced at Menta and a bitterness so strong it was almost hatred showed in his eyes. Menta did not flinch. Her gaze pierced him, seemed to see into the farthest recesses of his thoughts.

"Stand, Tron," she said. Grudgingly, he rose to his feet. Menta came close to him and spoke sternly.

"You have violated Pila. You have violated her mother, and all who live in this tribe. You have violated the Mother, and that will not be forgotten. None of these things will be forgotten. Most of the people here wish to see you banished, not just for a time, but for all the time that remains to you.

"The Mother has shown us a different way. She wishes you to learn better what is in our faces, so that you will know when Akat is appropriate and when it is not. But because you have violated Her, She forbids you Her supreme gift, the gift of Akat, until the time when you have learned Her ways, and can show us that you understand the women's wishes."

She stopped for a moment to see if Tron would speak. But his lips remained firmly clasped together, and his eyes were expressionless.

"If you learn willingly," Menta continued, "the time will be short. If you do not learn willingly, much time could pass. It is up to you. Tell me now if you agree to this."

Tron looked down at the ground, and now his face was sullen. Zena was certain, though, that he was very surprised, even if he did not let the surprise show. Surely, he had expected to be banished, at least for a time. Perhaps he had even begun to think what he would do, where he would go.

His comment showed her she was correct. "I will leave," he said stubbornly. "I have no wish to stay here."

"That way is not open to you. You must learn to read our faces, as the Mother has instructed." The authority in Menta's voice could not be challenged.

"How, then, should I learn these things?" Realizing he had no choice, Tron gave in, but his voice was contemptuous. He knew well enough already when women wanted Akat, even if they did not know it themselves.

"Zena will teach you," Menta replied.

Tron's eyes shot up at Menta's words and fastened on Zena. A flash of pure hatred blazed in his face, then he lowered his eyes again and shrugged.

A dark lump of the hatred she had seen lodged in Zena's belly. It was as if Tron had thrown it at her, forced it into her just as he had forced himself into Pila. She shivered violently. Tron was capable of hatred. She had seen it. And all of it was directed at her.

Tron looked up again. Now his eyes were blank. She sensed he had not meant to let her see that brief flash. And later, when he seemed to resent the lessons less strongly, he became cooperative, even friendly. Zena almost began to enjoy him. But some part of her remained wary, as if she knew deep inside herself that he was only biding his time.

II

Nevilar had watched the proceedings with an intensity that rivaled Zena's. She, too, had seen the flash of hatred in Tron's eyes, the blankness that followed, and had covered her lips with her hand to hide her smile. No one must know that his reaction gave her secret pleasure. Tron did not care for Zena, as she had feared. All the other young men liked Zena best and talked about her constantly, even when Nevilar took them to her own mating place. But Tron, at least, did not. The hatred in his eyes, the scathing tone he had used earlier made that clear.

She stared hard at Tron, trying to induce him to return her gaze. She wanted him to know that she, at least, cared for him, that she would support him. But he kept his eyes stubbornly fixed on the ground, and would not look at her.

If only he had not been denied Akat. That would be the best way to let him know of her caring. Already, she had mated with him many times. He was not a very good lover, for he was brash and forceful and too quick to leave her, but she still found him desirable. His strong, swarthy body appealed to her. So did his manner. His forcefulness was exciting in a way. None of the other men acted like that, pinning her to the ground, paying no attention to her movements. Always, they waited to see what she wanted. Tron seemed not to care. Nevilar felt hotness spread within her as she thought of him.

Had he really done what Pila had said? Perhaps the child had made up the story, to get attention. And Tron had said she was waiting for him in the woods. Nevilar knew that was not likely, for Pila was too young to think of Akat. She was also a shy child who did not like attention. Nevilar held on to the thought anyway. It seemed to her that none of the others truly understood Tron. Zena especially did not.

Nevilar's lips compressed. Everyone thought Zena was so special, not just the men. Every day, her mother told her that she ought to be more like Zena, so she would not do so many things wrong. No matter how hard she tried, she could never please her mother, but Zena always did. Zena was proud of herself as well. The Mother taught that pride was wrong, so why was she so admired?

If they would let me take charge of Tron, instead of Zena, Nevilar thought bitterly, *I am certain I could change him. I care for him, and Zena does not.*

She decided to follow him when the council was over, to tell him of her feelings. Sliding into step beside him as he walked away, she tried to match his long strides with her smaller legs.

"I am sorry for the things that are happening to you, Tron," she told him.

"Why should you care?" he snapped. His eyes were hard and angry, and his lips were set in a tight line.

Nevilar hesitated. She had expected him to be grateful for her sympathy. "The Mother teaches compassion," she finally said in a small voice. "All of us care."

"Compassion! Caring!" Tron snorted the words. "These things have no meaning. It is necessary to kill animals for food, to eat and drink and mate. That is all that has meaning."

Fearing another outburst, Nevilar did not reply. Instead, she came closer and placed a hand on Tron's arm. His expression changed immediately. She saw desire in his eyes, only it was not quite the same as desire. There was coldness in it as well.

He turned to face her and began to stroke her breasts, then her hips. His hands were rough against her smooth skin.

She backed away. "No, Tron. Akat is forbidden. And others may be watching."

"I do not care," he replied, pulling her toward him again. He placed his lips against hers in a long, bruising kiss.

Nevilar broke away again, terrified by his behavior. She wanted to help Tron, but they could not ignore the injunction!

"Menta has spoken," she whispered urgently. "The Mother Herself has forbidden Akat."

"Menta!" Tron spat out the name as he had spat out the word *compassion*. "I care not what Menta says." He grabbed her face with both hands and tried to kiss her again.

"But the Mother—" Nevilar's words were cut off as Tron shoved his lips against hers. The surge of hotness came again, and her knees trembled. She tasted blood. Tron had cut her with his teeth. Her trembling intensified.

Footsteps sounded in the gravel beside the river. Nevilar wrenched herself away from Tron, her heart thudding with fear. If anyone had seen them . . . To be found with Tron like this, after what had happened . . .

Bakan emerged from the bushes that lined the banks of the river. He stared at them, a puzzled frown on his weatherbeaten face. As always, his look was direct, full of authority. After a moment, he raised a hand in greeting and went on.

Nevilar's body went limp with relief. He had not seen. Before Tron could make a move toward her again, she whirled and ran for the clearing, but her knees were shaking too hard to maintain the pace. Besides, she did not want anyone to notice her distress. Then she would have to explain. She slowed down and walked as normally as possible.

Tron came up behind her. His breath was hot on the back of her neck. She flinched away from him, but he did not touch her.

"Tomorrow," he whispered. "As the sun goes down, in the place we have been before."

Nevilar did not respond, but only continued to walk. All the way to the clearing, she felt his eyes burning into her back.

She fought with herself all the next afternoon. She should not go, but if she did not, she would not be able to help Tron, show the others that she, not Zena, was the one who could change him. And once he had calmed down, Tron would surely realize that Akat was impossible, since the Mother had forbidden it.

In the end, she could not go, for her mother asked her to help with some skins she was stretching, and Nevilar could not refuse. Tron looked at her disdainfully the next morning and would not answer when she greeted him.

"I could not come. But tonight I will come," she gasped out, afraid of the words, but even more afraid of his disdain.

He walked away without responding, his face obstinate with anger. Nevilar followed miserably. She should have gone. Now Tron was angry at her, might never like her again. Then she saw Zena, waiting to start the lessons. Tron hated them; she was sure he did, and even more, he hated having Zena tell him what to do. Nevilar felt better. Probably it was Zena, not herself, who had made him angry.

Zena saw Tron's glowering face as he came toward her and winced. Yesterday had been difficult; today might be worse. She wondered what had happened to put him in such a towering rage.

The children were playing nearby and she called to them to join her. As Menta had said, they too were learning, and Tron might be more comfortable with others in the lessons.

She arranged her face in an expression of sadness, then of happiness. These Tron could see, but when she put longing in her face, Tron only said "sad" again. Zena kept trying, but after a while, she turned to the children, to let them guess.

"Longing," they called out without hesitation, and did their best to imitate the expression.

Zena tried another, then another, turning first to Tron and then to the children. Each time, the children answered.

Mortification spread across Tron's face, that the children could answer when he could not. He shouted angrily and bounded to his feet. Zena closed her eyes for a long moment, trying to control her own mortification that she had not realized, that she had embarrassed Tron even as she tried to help.

The children looked startled at his outburst and shuffled uneasily. Then one little girl imitated his angry face, pulling her eyelids and lips with her fingers until her small face was a mask of sneering rage. The others copied her, howling with laughter. Tron stalked away.

Zena glared at the children and ran after him. It was not going to be easy now to induce him to continue the lessons! She caught up to him and placed a hand on his arm.

"I am sorry for the children, Tron. I should not have called them. Truly, I am sorry. That was not a good idea."

He shook off her hand and kept on walking. "Stupid children!" she heard him mutter.

Zena ran to stand in front of him. "No, Tron," she told him, holding on to his arm to try to impress him with her sincerity. "The children are not stupid. You are not stupid either. The children do not know how to hunt as you do. You do not know faces as well as some. They will learn one day to follow the animals as you do. And you will learn too."

He only grunted, but he stopped walking so fast, and Zena knew she had caught his attention.

She pressed her advantage. "We will do this next time where the others are not watching," she promised him. "That will be easier for you."

Tron grunted, and Zena assumed it was a grunt of assent. "We will start tomorrow," she called after him, and let him go. They would accomplish no more today. Tomorrow, she would take him to a place she knew of in the woods, where they could work alone. Menta had told her that someone would always be watching, but surely that was not necessary. She would speak to Menta, assure her there was no need to watch. Tron would not harm her, and he would learn better if he knew no one was listening.

Nevilar had lingered near the lesson, hoping to speak to Tron again. Now she knew he was too angry. She did not blame him. It was horrible to be humiliated like that! Zena should not treat him like a child.

A rush of sympathy flooded her. With it came determination. She must meet Tron tonight. He would need her to comfort him.

Just before the sun went down, she sneaked away from the clearing. Tron was waiting when she arrived at the place she used for mating. She had discovered the tiny enclosure years ago, when she had wanted a special place to go where no one could find her. Hidden within thick clumps of bushes, her retreat was barely large enough for two people to lie down in. But it was totally private. Here, she did not fear prying eyes.

Without speaking, Tron pulled her to the ground. "Wait!" she cried out. "We must talk."

He paid no attention. He lowered himself over her, and she felt his organ hard against her stomach.

"Wait," she cried again, resisting the surge of desire building inside her. She pummeled at his back with her fists, to make him listen to her.

Tron answered with a quick look of scorn. Grabbing her wrists, he forced them backward as he tried to enter her.

Nevilar groaned. She did not want to do this. The Mother had forbidden Akat, but never had she felt such an agony of desire. It tore through her, painful in its intensity. It was fierce, uncontrollable, as Tron was fierce and uncontrollable.

She felt him struggling to open her legs wider. She gasped with the effort to restrain him, then suddenly she gave up, unable to resist any longer. She spread her legs for him, as wide as they would go. With a gasp of triumph, he plunged into her. Back and forth he went, harder and harder, and Nevilar rocked with him. Almost at once, the ecstasy came for both of them. They shuddered violently and lay still.

One moment passed, then another, before Tron raised his head. Then, in one quick movement, he was on his feet. Nevilar stared in astonishment; already, he was leaving. How could he leave so quickly?

Before she could collect herself to speak, he was gone. Nevilar lay still, biting her lips hard so she would not cry. Tron's passion had brought ecstasy, but his fierce thrusting had brought pain as well. She felt bruised, inside herself and everywhere else—but even worse was the hurt to her feelings. He had not even bothered to speak with her, had hardly noticed she was there, except for her body. He still did not know of her caring, had not realized she had come to comfort him.

Perhaps, though, he had been afraid to talk to her, lest someone hear them. Nevilar considered these thoughts, trying to believe them. After all, Menta had said someone would always be watching. Tron was acting wisely, perhaps, to leave so quickly.

Had someone been watching? Nevilar rose, all her senses suddenly alert. She scoured the bushes fearfully, listening intently for any betraying rustle. Horror at what she had done slowly encompassed her. She had disobeyed Menta, let Tron do what the Mother Herself had forbidden. To violate the Mother's command was terrible, horrible. Why had she done this thing? Why, why had she behaved like that?

Darkness had come. They would be wondering where she was. Her mother would be looking for her, fearing for her, alone in the woods at night. Nevilar rose and hurriedly cleaned herself with damp leaves. They must not know, must not smell Akat on her. And she must hurry, before they came looking.

She ran back to the clearing, still shaking with horror at her actions, with fear that someone had seen. If they looked at her accusingly, what would she say?

But when she slipped into her place by the fire, the others barely looked up. Her mother frowned and told her irritably that she should take more care, come back earlier. Bakan had seen the prints of tigers nearby. Did she want to be eaten by a tiger?

Relief flooded Nevilar. After all, no one had noticed. No one knew, and she would never, never do such a thing again. The Mother had been kind, to give her this chance.

Trying to sound as natural as she could, she assured her mother that she did not wish to be eaten by a tiger, though she did not believe a tiger was really in the area. Her mother was just saying that to make certain Nevilar knew she had displeased her again. Sometimes it seemed her mother never spoke at all except to criticize.

Tron was sitting across from her. She saw his eyes flit over her body with an expression that made her skin feel cold despite the warm fire. The look seemed to say that she was his now, to do with as he liked. It was similar to the look she had seen in the eyes of the fierce little cats that roamed the area, when they had caught a mouse or some other small creature. She looked the other way. Meeting Tron had not been as dangerous as she had feared, but Akat with him was still forbidden, and she would not do it again.

The next day he came up behind her as she sat by herself washing tubers in the river. He placed his hands on her breasts and murmured in her ear.

"No one watches anymore," he whispered. "No one will follow this time. Come to me again tonight. Even to see you brings up my passion."

Nevilar gasped. So she had been right. He had not spoken, had left so quickly because he was afraid of being discovered. And he did care for her; he had said so. Pleasure welled up in her at the thought. She turned to look into his eyes, to see if there was truth in them, but she could see only desire, perhaps a little of the expression she had seen last night. Now, the look seemed exciting.

"Not tonight—tomorrow," she replied hesitantly, playing for time. With Tron fondling her this way, she could not think, and she had to think, consider.

"Tonight!" His tone was authoritative. He pinched her breast sharply, to emphasize the word, then left without waiting for a response.

Nevilar dared not go that night, for she felt her mother's eyes on her, saw the puzzled look on her face. Perhaps, after all, she had noticed something. But the next evening, her mother and all the others were busy skinning an animal Katli and the men had caught, and no one noticed when she slipped away. This time, she would make Tron listen to her, tell him that Akat was impossible, but that she would be his friend.

Again, Tron was waiting. He cuffed the side of her face angrily. "You did not come."

Tears sprang into her eyes. "My mother was watching," she protested.

He shrugged and pulled her down to the ground. Nevilar started to resist, but Tron's face became so suffused with fury she dared not protest any further. She lay still, torn between guilt and the desire that was building in her. And then, in another moment, she did not want him to stop, could not have borne it if he had stopped.

Again, their union was fast and passionate; again, Tron left as soon as he had finished. This time, Nevilar did not weep. In this, he was right, she realized. They could not risk spending too much time together. And perhaps this was what he needed, she told herself, to have her love him without question. Perhaps that was why the Mother had kept them from being discovered.

After that, Nevilar met Tron as often as she could. Slowly, the sense that she was committing a forbidden act faded. Guilt still tormented her sometimes, but she pushed it aside. Tron seemed so much more relaxed now, and even if she seldom managed to speak to him, she was certain she was changing him, just by accepting him without question.

Often, he was rough with her. He hit her face or her stomach if she failed to come when he had expected her, or if he thought she had brought another of the young men to her mating place. But she soon learned to distract him from his anger by encouraging him to perform Akat in any way he pleased. She always wanted him so badly, so terribly badly. He seemed to know that, to be reassured by her need of him. He needed her just as much. Nevilar was certain of it. The secret knowledge made her feel important, just as important as Zena, and she was glad.

Zena, too, noticed the change in Tron. He was much more agreeable now that they were meeting alone, and he was improving rapidly. He could name all the expressions she could think of, although subtleties were still hard for him. But as the weeks went by, he became adept even at naming feelings like loneliness, or bemusement, that sense of half wonder, half amusement at some happening.

Zena was gratified, but something about his manner still bothered her. Months passed before she realized what it was. Tron could name feelings of many kinds, but she was not sure he understood what they were. She was not certain, either, that he cared that he had learned to name them. He was learning because he had to, but it seemed as if he had never really understood the reasons for the lessons, nor had he learned to feel the emotions he now described with such ease. He could identify them, but they still had no meaning in his heart.

If she wanted him to learn to feel as well as know, Zena realized, she would have to stop avoiding the Mother's mandate. So far, she had not tried to teach Tron the subtleties of Akat. The thought frightened her, for how was she to show different kinds of desire, or use the expressions that meant a woman was ready, when she had no intention of acting on the feelings she demonstrated? But to teach Tron to read a woman's face and heart with regard to Akat was the point of the lessons, and it was time she began. Surely, if he learned to feel the wondrous variety of emotions that accompanied Akat, like compassion and tenderness and joy and caring, Tron would change, and the horrors the Mother had portrayed in Menta's vision would never come to pass.

CHAPTER
21

Zena followed Nevilar into the woods. It was time for them to go to the women's special shelter, the Ekali. For three full cycles of the seasons after their first bleeding, the young women came here when the moon was no more than a sliver, about ten days after each time of bleeding began. Four days and nights passed before they returned to the others. Akat was not permitted during this time, and men could not come to the Ekali. Once, Zena had asked her mother why this was so. Lune had replied that the Mother wished it, but only the wise one knew the reason. It was forbidden for others to know. Zena did not press her further. Perhaps she would understand one day, if she became a wise one.

When the three years had passed, the young women were welcomed into the tribe as full adults. After the initiation, any of the women, both young and old, could come to the Ekali whenever they wished, and they often did, for they loved this place. It was theirs alone. Here, they could speak together in peace, without the teasing of the men and the clamor of the children, for only suckling infants were allowed.

Their favorite time to come was during their bleeding, when the moon was full. Usually, all the women bled at the same time. To come to the Ekali at the Life-Blood time, as they called it, was not required, but they came anyway if they could get away. The experience regenerated them. There was power in the blood that brought life instead of death, and when they were all together, the power was immense. It filled their bodies and spirits, gave them new strength, even as their Life-Blood seeped into the earth and made it fertile, as they themselves were fertile.

During this time, they did everything together, as if they were one great woman instead of many. They gathered food and prepared it together, making sure to help each other instead of performing the tasks separately, and ate from the same pieces of food. They nursed each other's babies, cleaned each other in the stream, made the fire and stoked it together at the end of the day. Then, when the flames had settled into a warm glow, they sat close beside each other and began the chant. Ten times, for all the days that had passed since they had first seen the moon begin to grow, the chant rose and fell, but after that, they let the silence fill them. Within its embrace, they truly felt themselves as one woman, for they could see each other's thoughts, feel each other's pain and happiness. They felt their oneness with the Mother as well. They felt closest to Her in this place where only women came, for She, too, was woman and mother, and could understand their special problems and joys.

Zena was glad to be coming again. Being in the Ekali always gave her strength, and she needed to feel strong right now, to accomplish the task she had undertaken. To be away from Tron for a few days would also be welcome. He had become more cooperative, but he was still exhausting because she always had to be on her guard. She had begun to speak of Akat, trying to show the looks of willingness, of love and caring as well as desire. The last one, he understood easily, though he did not seem to grasp the others very well. Whenever she put desire on her face, he moved toward her automatically, as if he had no control over his actions. His eyes frightened her. Mingled with the lust was a fierce coldness that made her shiver.

She pulled her fur garment closer around her shoulders. The season of snow would soon be upon them. Already, the beautiful red and orange and yellow leaves had left the trees, and their bare branches swung in the gusty winds. As the days grew colder, storms would come, and the tribe would settle in for the long, dark time of winter. Last year, so much snow had fallen that they had hardly been able to walk. Each year, the winters seemed to become longer and harder.

Nevilar was walking ahead of her, and Zena ran to catch up. Like herself, Nevilar had only one more year when she came to the Ekali at this time. After that, it was not required, and most of the women soon became too busy with infants anyway.

Zena frowned, wondering why that should be so. It did seem as if infants began to arrive only after they had ceased to come to the Ekali in the middle of the moon's cycle. Of course, they were older then. Perhaps the Mother was giving them time before they undertook such a grave responsibility. Children needed much care, much love and teaching.

She fell into step beside Nevilar. This year, there were no others besides themselves who came to the Ekali at this time, though Lune would join them later, and Zena hoped Nevilar would be friendly. They had been friends when they were younger, but she thought Nevilar had been avoiding her recently. This was a good opportunity to become close again.

"You are happy to be coming to the Ekali?" she asked.

"I do not wish to come anymore," Nevilar blurted out. "I would prefer to stay with the others."

Zena looked up, startled by her vehemence. Nevilar looked strange, almost bruised, she thought. There were dark splotches on her cheeks, more on her arms and chest.

"Have you hurt yourself, Nevilar?"

"I fell in the woods," Nevilar replied. "It does not hurt anymore."

"I will put herbs on the bruises for you. That will help, even if they are no longer hurting."

Zena's voice was full of concern, and Nevilar felt tears prickle behind her eyelids. No one had voiced concern for her for a long time. Perhaps Zena was not so bad after all. She looked the other way, lest Zena see and ask her why she cried.

It was true that she had not wanted to come, for it meant leaving Tron. He had been angry that she was leaving, and had hit her, told her he needed her to stay with him. But now that she was away from him, Nevilar found she was looking forward to this time alone. Tron frightened her sometimes. He struck her more often now, and even the promise of Akat did not always stop him. She knew he lashed out because he was so frustrated at not being able to hunt with the others, at having to do lessons with Zena instead. He also became angry if he suspected she had brought another man to her mating place. Nevilar tried not to tell him, but he pinched her breast or her arm so hard the pain forced her to speak. He hit her even harder if she confessed she had been with another. But she had to ask others; if she did not, there would be talk.

Nevilar sighed heavily. She was glad he cared for her so much that he did not want others to be with her, and she was proud to be the only one who truly understood his frustration. Still, it was hard also to be the only one with whom he became angry, because he could not show anger with anyone else.

Now, for four days, she would not have to worry about him. Her steps lightened, and she ran eagerly into the Ekali, unaware that even as she thought of him, Tron was staring at her from his hiding place in a tree that overlooked the enclosure.

Tron was not sure why he had followed Nevilar and Zena, except that he enjoyed tricking those who tried to watch him, and that he liked to do what no one wanted him to do. Menta no longer asked someone to watch during his lessons, but he was aware that Krost or Tragar often kept an eye on him anyway. Today, Tragar had been nearby, but he was slow in his thinking, even if he was strong, and Tron had easily managed to lose him. And to follow the two young women to the Ekali excited him. No men were permitted to be here. He, Tron, had come anyway.

He peered into the enclosure. He wanted to see what the women did in this place they thought was so special. Before, he had not dared to come, for he had been afraid the Mother would somehow know and punish him. Now he knew the Mother was not so powerful after all. He had disobeyed Her by having Akat with Nevilar, and nothing had happened. Menta was not as powerful as she thought, either, for she had not been able to stop him from doing what he wanted. She was only a woman, after all, and women were weak. He did not understand why they were considered so important. Just because they had young ones, they thought they were special—but most of them could not even kill the big animals. That was far more important.

Zena, especially, acted superior because one day she might become a wise one. His eyes hardened as he watched her enter the Ekali. He hated her, hated the lessons, hated the fact that she could tell him what to do. A woman should not be able to tell someone like him what to do. That was wrong. And the things she taught him had no meaning. They were only words. What else could they be? He had never felt these emotions she spoke of. He did not think anyone had. It was just the women's way of being important.

Except Akate. That he felt. Akate was lust, and that was all there was to Akat. Zena kept trying to tell him of other kinds of Akat, but he paid little attention. Tron felt himself grow hard as he watched her. She made him feel lust, and the more he came to resent her, the stronger it became. He had seen desire on her face, too, and it had inflamed him even further. She was teasing him with it, showing desire and then refusing to act on it. One day, he would have her anyway, whether she liked it or not. The thought was exciting.

He lowered himself into a crook between two branches and sat as still as one of the great cats as he watched the two young women. Much time must pass before darkness came, and until then, he would not move.

Zena, too, entered the Ekali eagerly. The familiar place seemed to welcome her, and immediately she felt more peaceful. It was good that she and Nevilar would have some time together here. Perhaps they could talk, and she could try to understand what was bothering her friend. That something was bothering her, Zena did not doubt. She had seen the rush of emotion in Nevilar's face when she had offered to help with the bruises. She could feel Nevilar's tension, too, and her unhappiness.

Zena set about making a fire, while Nevilar washed the berries and grains they had brought in the stream that flowed through the small enclosure. The strain left their faces as they worked. They felt completely safe here, even by themselves, for the Ekali was surrounded by a thick barrier of thorny brush. Branches were added every year, and now the wall was high and deep, strong enough to discourage even the most determined predator. There was nothing else to harm them, so they never worried. Still, Zena kept looking up uneasily. She had a tingling feeling in the middle of her back, as if she were being watched. But she had seen no tracks of lions or tigers, and even if one lurked nearby, it was unlikely to leap over the barrier, especially when there was a fire inside.

Probably it was just her imagination, she decided, or came from spending so much time on her guard with Tron. Even here, she could not seem to forget him completely. She was glad Lune was coming later. Then, she could truly relax, for with Lune, she always felt safe. She turned her back to the fire and felt its warmth pull away the tingling sensation. Perhaps, after all, she had just been cold.

Nevilar came to join her. She was shivering, Zena noticed, despite the garment that hung from her shoulders. The sun had hidden behind scurrying clouds, and the temperature was dropping. She pulled out an extra fur she had brought and wrapped it around Nevilar. Again, tears welled up in the young woman's eyes.

Zena pretended not to notice them. "The fire will keep us warm," she said, patting the ground beside her so that Nevilar would sit. "Soon we will need coverings for our feet as well. See, I have brought some fur so we can work together."

She brought out the fur, taken from long-eared animals that had feet for walking above the snow. In winter, they were white; in summer, brown. Zena loved to watch their long ears twitch, see them leap and twist as they ran, and she was always sorry when they were killed. Still, they would live again one day, and in the meantime, she would have warm feet.

Handing a needle made of bone and a piece of the strong, thin animal gut they used as thread to Nevilar, she began to work. They sat in silence for a long time.

"You are unhappy, I think, Nevilar," Zena said finally, when she thought her friend was relaxed enough not to mind her words. "I would like to help if I can."

Nevilar jumped. She had been deep in thought, and had not expected Zena to speak. In this place that was so filled with the Mother's presence, the guilt she was able to repress when she was with Tron weighed heavily on her heart. She had disobeyed Menta, violated the Mother's command. Here, she could not hide that fact, even from herself.

Without warning, tears began to splash onto the soft fur in her hands. She wanted desperately to answer Zena, to tell her of the secret liaisons with Tron, but she did not dare. If she did, the others would find out, and then they might banish her.

A sob escaped and became a hiccup as Nevilar tried to disguise it. Zena waited again for many minutes, then began to speak, very quietly.

"I, too, feel unhappiness right now. I feel it because of Tron. It is hard to teach feelings to one who seems not to know them. But if I do not, all will suffer. And sometimes I am afraid of him. I do not know why, but—"

"I, too," Nevilar said, interrupting without thinking. She clapped her hand to her mouth, horrified at her words.

"Tron has frightened you too?"

Nevilar's eyes, still round with horror at her mistake, met Zena's for the first time in many months. Slowly, her resentment crumbled. She saw compassion in Zena's eyes, and concern, but there was no hint of superiority or pride. Instead, she saw the same quiet strength she had come to expect from Menta, the same promise of wisdom, and she understood why Zena would one day be a wise one. The words began to pour out of her mouth.

"He comes to me, to my place of mating. He has come many times, and I have wanted him there . . . I have wanted him so badly. But sometimes he hurts me. It is because he cares for me; that is why he hits me, because he does not want me to be with others, but I must take others.

"It is because of you too. He hates those lessons. He hates them. And then he comes to me, and I . . ."

Nevilar gulped, as if she were trying to swallow the words even as they sprang from her lips. "I have Akat with him. I have Akat because I wanted to help him. He cares for me and I wanted to help, but now I am afraid. And Menta—I have disobeyed her, and I have disobeyed the Mother. . . ."

Nevilar gave in to the sobs that consumed her. Zena listened to the wrenching noises, and her lips tightened.

"It is Tron who has bruised you?"

Nevilar nodded. Zena leaned over and picked up the garment that had fallen from her friend's shoulders and wrapped it around her protectively. Nevilar grabbed her hand and held it.

"Will they send me away?"

"No, Nevilar. I do not think Menta will do that. But you must speak to her, tell her what you have told me, and you must speak to the Mother, ask Her forgiveness. The Mother forgives all things if you are sincere."

Uneasiness gripped Zena despite her calm words. Nevilar's confession had shocked her, not just because of what she had done, but because of Tron's cruelty. Never had she known a man to hurt a woman on purpose, as Tron had hurt Nevilar. He must have hit her very hard, pinched her viciously, to make such bruises. And if he could do that, even as he was coming to her with his face set in pleasant lines, hating the lessons, hating her, and hiding that hate . . .

It was not Tron she had been seeing. He was other than that, a person she could barely fathom.

Zena shivered convulsively. She had been right. Tron could name the feelings she had tried so hard to describe, but he did not know what they were.

"Something is lacking in Tron." The words she had spoken at the council came back to her, only now she knew her first understanding was wrong. Tron did not lack just the ability to read faces. As Menta had feared, he lacked the ability to feel love or kindness at all. They were not there inside him.

She felt afraid suddenly. Even here, in this special place, there was fear. She must go, take Nevilar with her and go back to the others. Zena knew it absolutely, and she stood, ready to stamp out the fire, so they could leave.

A slight sound behind her made her look up in relief. Lune must have decided to come early. They would be all right now. Lune had come.

She froze. It was not Lune. It was Tron. He stood, hands on hips, rolling on his toes a little, as if he were about to spring. He was staring at Nevilar. She had not seen him, for her head was buried in her hands. But Zena saw, and her heart shrank with fear. There was fury in his eyes, a terrible consuming fury.

Nevilar looked up and gasped in terror. Before she could move, Tron lunged at her and grabbed her hair with one hand. Grunting, he hit her across the face, over and over again. She screamed and tried to pull away. But he had her hair, and every time she moved, he jerked it as he hit her again.

"You have betrayed me," he snarled. "You have told!"

Nevilar pummeled his wrist, begging him to stop. Her actions only increased his rage. Savagely, he pulled his arm back, then shoved his fist into her mouth with all his strength. The crunching sound of the blow satisfied him. She deserved to be hit! He had warned her.

"Tron! Stop!" Zena hauled at his arms. She succeeded in holding the arm that was hitting Nevilar. Tron gave Nevilar's head a final wrenching twist and turned on Zena.

He stood for a moment, enjoying the fear in her eyes. She was the one he really wanted to hurt. Every day, he had been forced to listen to her, be with her, but he could not have her, even when he saw desire on her face. Then she had said it was not for him, but for the lesson. Well, he would show her who it was for. He would have her now, take her by force. That would hurt her most of all. She thought she could control him, control Akat, but he would make her do what he wanted, and she would not be able to stop him. Menta had not stopped him, the Mother had not stopped him, and Zena would not stop him.

Savagely, he bent her arm backward, then punched her hard in the face with his other hand. She gasped in pain.

Nevilar pounded on Tron's back. "No! I will come with you. No, Tron, you must not hurt Zena. I will come!"

Tron turned and hissed at her through his teeth as he wrestled Zena's arms behind her back. "I do not care for you. I cared only for Akat. That you have given me. Now I will have it elsewhere."

Nevilar's face crumpled and she turned away. But then Zena screamed as Tron shoved his knee in her belly and forced her to the ground. Grabbing a stick, Nevilar whacked at his thick shoulders. He turned quickly and slammed his fist into her chest. Her body sagged and she fell back.

Zena clenched her jaw and strained upward, trying to free her arms. But Tron was on top of her now and she could not move at all. He was trying to force her legs apart, pushing and shoving. She willed them closed. Quick as a cat, he brought one arm around and punched the side of her thigh. She gasped, and for an instant, her muscles relaxed. He shoved his legs between hers. And then, before she could even take another breath, he was inside her. Gasping heavily, he thrust in and out, then shook convulsively as he ejaculated. In that instant, Zena freed her arms. She pounded at him relentlessly, but he seemed not even to feel her blows. He lay there, satiated, triumphant.

Rage filled Zena, that he had done this terrible thing, that he had hurt her, hurt Nevilar. She twisted out from under his heavy body and stood over him, shaking with anger. He grabbed her arm and hauled her savagely back to the ground. Zena raised her other arm, to hit him, but at just that moment, a body came hurtling into the Ekali.

"Conar!" Zena only whispered his name, but Tron heard. He leaped to his feet. Conar ran straight into Tron's hard body and began to pummel him wildly with both fists. Tron staggered under the barrage of blows, but quickly recovered. He took a step backward and then lunged at the smaller male, grasping him around the waist with strong, clenching arms. Oblivious to the rain of blows landing on his back, he wrestled Conar to the ground and knelt on his chest. Conar reached up to tear at the hard face above him, but Tron only lowered his head and began to pound it against Conar's neck. Over and over he pounded. Conar jerked wildly, trying to escape, but Tron was much heavier and stronger, and he could not budge. He groaned in an agony of helplessness, but then the groaning ceased, for Tron had placed both hands around his neck and had begun to squeeze.

A croaking noise came from Conar. Zena heard it, and she moved. Grabbing one of the big rocks that surrounded the fire, she brought it down on Tron's head with all the strength, all the rage in her body. The movement satisfied her, and she raised the rock to hit him again. She wanted to hit him over and over, as many times as she could, until he could not hurt her or any of the others any more. But before she could lower her arms, Tron fell forward across Conar's chest, then slid to the ground in a crumpled heap.

Zena held the rock against her chest, paralyzed with horror. Tron's body jerked once convulsively, and a strange croak came from his throat. After that, he did not move again.

II

Menta looked up from her task, her eyes suddenly alert. Something was wrong. She could feel it, as if the terrible thing were happening in front of her. But she did not know what it was, or where it was happening.

"Lune!" Her voice was sharp as she called to her sister. Usually, both of them felt wrongness when it came.

Lune came running, alerted by the tone in Menta's voice. But she had felt it herself, even before that.

"I think it is Zena. We must go to the Ekali, quickly."

Calling to Bakan and Tragar, who were working nearby, they ran into the woods. Tragar caught up to them.

"I was watching Tron, but he hid from me."

Menta nodded, saving her breath for running. She had known; from the beginning she had known. Why had she let Zena talk her into leaving them alone? Except Tron could not be with her today. She and Nevilar were at the Ekali, and surely Tron would not go there.

"Where is Conar?" It was Lune's voice. She had watched Conar, had seen how he followed Tron everywhere, even though Tron never knew. He would know where Tron was.

Bakan shook his head. "I have not seen Conar."

Lune pressed her fingers against her mouth as she ran, to keep from crying out. She could feel it, feel that something had happened to Zena.

Her heart thudded with joy when she saw Zena standing by the fire. Then her eyes took in the whole scene, and she gasped in horror. Blood covered Zena's hands, and her face was swollen and bruised. Nevilar was worse. She was groaning, rocking herself back and forth in agony, and when she looked up, Lune saw that one of her eyes was swollen shut, and blood dribbled from her mouth. The scene on the ground was appalling. Conar lay still as death, his face gray. As she watched, he began to choke and spit, trying to breathe. Lune ran to him and raised his head, wondering why Zena had not come to him first. She was right beside him.

Something else was beside him. Lune glanced at the still form, and closed her eyes in agony. It was Tron—except it was not Tron anymore. He was dead; she was certain of it, for his skull was a mass of blood. She did not look again.

How had he died? Had Conar killed him? But that could not be. . . . Lune's thoughts raced, and then her eyes darted again to Zena. She had not moved. She stood there, as still as if she were made of stone. Menta was standing before her, with a look of absolute pity on her face.

"You must tell us what happened." Menta's voice was soft, compelling, but Zena did not answer. Her eyes were focused inward, and she did not seem to hear Menta's question, or even to notice that they had come.

Menta went to Nevilar and took her face in her hands, so that she would have to look up.

"It is my fault," Nevilar sobbed. "I have made these terrible things happen because I disobeyed the Mother. It is all my fault. You must send me away, banish me!"

Menta frowned, puzzled, then her eyes narrowed as she began to guess. She had wondered what was bothering Nevilar. The girl had been unhappy, nervous, as if she were doing something she should not do. She had been bruised too. Was it possible Tron had inflicted the bruises? With a shock of recognition as sharp as a physical blow, Menta realized it was true. She had not known such cruelty was possible, except in the visions.

Zena's voice, cold and hard, cut into her thoughts. "No, Nevilar. Yours is not the fault. It is mine. I have killed Tron, and that is a sin against the Mother far greater than yours. To kill another is forbidden, but to kill in anger is worse, and can never be forgiven. That is the worst sin of all, and that is what I have done."

Zena's words hung in the air. No one knew how to respond. Even Menta's voice was stilled, for she knew Zena spoke the truth. To kill in anger was violence, and that the Mother did not tolerate. All else but violence, She would forgive.

Menta's heart sank within her. This was the beginning. Because Tron was violent, because one single man was violent, they would all suffer. Zena would suffer most of all.

"No." Lune's voice was passionate, filled with courage. "That is not right. Zena may have killed in anger, but she has not killed for no reason. Tron was dangerous to all of us. Perhaps this is what the Mother intended her to do. Perhaps by killing Tron, Zena has saved us, and all who will come after, from the violence Menta has foreseen."

Lune moved forcefully toward Zena and stood before her. "You must think of this, too, that you have served the Mother by your actions. When violence comes, perhaps we must meet it with violence."

Menta felt the Mother's hand heavy on her heart. Lune's argument was persuasive, but she did not think it was right. No peace would come to them through Tron's death. Whatever the cause, violence only brought more violence.

Fear gripped her abruptly. For the first time in many years, she did not know what to do. Never before had one of them killed another. She shook her head, as if to throw off the burden of responsibility she carried. Then, just as quickly, she straightened her shoulders and forced the fear away. She was their wise one, and she would deal with the terror of this happening. The Mother would show her what to do.

"I must hear why this has happened," she said. "Before blame is cast, we must know. As Lune says, it may be that your action has kept the violence from coming. We must listen for the Mother if we hope to understand.

"Come. We will return to the clearing, where all can hear. Then we will decide."

Bakan and Tragar hoisted Tron into their arms. Menta put an arm around the still-sobbing Nevilar and led her away, and Lune supported Conar. His ragged breathing contrasted loudly with Nevilar's sobs. Zena followed, glad no one had come close enough to touch her. She did not want to be touched again. She was alone now, separate from the others in some strange way she could not identify. She must stay that way if she was to survive.

The knowledge remained with her all through the proceedings that evening, through the day that followed. She barely heard Lune's brave defense of her actions, a defense enthusiastically seconded by Katli and Bakan and the others. Zena might have killed in anger, but she had also killed to save Conar's life, perhaps her own and Nevilar's as well. Besides, Tron had violated her, as he had violated Pila, would no doubt have violated others. To abuse the gift of Akat in this way was a sin almost as great as killing. And as the Mother Herself had said, Tron threatened not just them, but many who had not yet been born. It was good that he was dead.

With Nevilar, the council was not so generous. To have disobeyed Menta and the Mother could be forgiven, if she was truly sorry, but to have permitted herself to be so abused by Tron would take longer to forgive. *There is no love, no caring, in such attention,* they told her. *In having so little respect for yourself, you show disrespect for the Mother as well. You are part of the Mother, and when you allow Tron to abuse you, to hit you and force Akat upon you, by frightening you, you also allow him to violate the Mother. Even if you desire it, Akat must never be done because of fear. For this, you must apologize, until you understand it in your heart.*

The council decided that she would be required to go to the Ekali with the other women at the time of bleeding, as well as in the middle of her cycle, for one full season of warmth and cold. Nevilar protested wildly, for she never wanted to go to the Ekali again, and now she must go twice as often. The council did not relent. Only in the Ekali with all the other women, they told her, could she learn how in caring for themselves and each other, they cared for the Mother. Nevilar finally agreed, but Menta wondered if she truly understood. Something was lacking in Nevilar, as it had been in Tron. He had been unable to care for others, but Nevilar seemed unable to care for herself, as if some internal core that should have told her she was worthy of respect was missing.

"Almost," she told Lune, "I worry about what is lacking in Nevilar as much as I worried about Tron's lack of caring. What if none of us felt worthy of respect and permitted those who were stronger to abuse us?"

Lune nodded, but she did not answer. Her mind was on Zena, not Nevilar. Another full day had passed since the council had decided no action should be taken against her, and still Zena had hardly spoken. Worse, she kept herself apart from everyone, as if she did not believe she was still one of the tribe. The others reassured themselves that she was still in a state of shock and just needed time to recover. Lune was not so sure.

Menta, too, knew this was not true, but she did not speak of her fears. The tragedy that was playing itself out was in the Mother's hands now, and Zena's, and she could only watch. Nor did she express her thoughts about Tron's death. She knew in her heart that to meet violence with violence was not the Mother's way, but she did not blame Zena for her act. Probably she would have acted in a similar way, had she been faced with Tron's cruelty. Instead, she felt a deep, burning sympathy for Zena. She would judge herself more harshly than any.

Menta was right. Zena had paid little attention to the council's verdict, for she had reached her own, and theirs was irrelevant. The tribe had not banished her, so she would banish herself. That was the Mother's will. She must be apart from others until the Mother decreed that she could return.

That night, when all the others were asleep, she slipped away. She went first to a place in the woods where she had hidden her tools and flints and an extra fur garment, wrapped in a bag of tough animal skin. Food and water she could find as she wandered, but the other items were essential to her survival, especially now that winter had almost come. Then she turned and headed west, toward the mountains she had seen in her dream. She was not sure why she went in that direction, except that the dream seemed to pull her.

Conar had been in the dream, but he would not be with her now. For the first time since Tron's death, tears came to Zena's eyes. Ever since their first mating, she had felt a special bond with Conar. He must have felt it as well, for he had tried to defend her, had risked his life and almost lost it for her.

She thrust him out of her mind. Of Lune and Menta and the others, of the desolation that would come to their faces when they saw that she had left, she dared not think at all. She must not, lest her resolve falter.

For a few hours, she was able to move quickly through the familiar woods, though the moon was still little more than a sliver. Then she began to stumble. Her legs were tiring, her steps uncertain, for she had come out of the area she knew into rough terrain of jumbled stones and rocky hillsides. Still, she dared not stop to rest. By the time the light came again, she had to be far enough away so the others could not find her.

She blundered on, falling often now from weariness. Her mind felt strange, far away. Since Tron's death, she had hardly slept and had eaten almost nothing. She had not felt hunger, and when she had tried to eat, the food had seemed to stick in her throat. Even when she moistened it with water, she could not make it go down. Words stuck there, too, as if her throat had closed with the horror of the act she had committed.

The sliver of moon slid behind a cloud and plunged her into total darkness just as she started down a steep hill. She tripped and fell heavily. Rocks bruised her arms and shoulders as she rolled over and over, unable to stop the fall. She landed with a thump in a shallow hole. Too tired now even to think of moving again, she wrapped herself in both furs and lay where she was, grateful for even this minimal shelter. Her fingers were numb with cold, but at least here the wind did not reach her.

She dozed fitfully until fingers of light began to creep across the sky. Now she could see that she had fallen into a hole left by the roots of a big overturned tree. Wearily, she rose to continue her journey.

Below her a wide valley stretched away to the west. She had never seen it before, though she was sure the river that rippled through it was the same river that wound almost all the way to their clearing. Huge herds of animals, reindeer and antelopes, and bison with rounded shoulders covered in thickly matted fur, grazed peacefully in the distance. Along the river were wide-branched trees festooned with late-ripening fruit and nuts.

Suddenly hungry, she ran down the slope. Her throat opened easily for the soft purple fruit, though the nuts were harder. She took some with her, for they traveled better than fruit, hoping she would be able to eat them later. Nuts gave strength, and she would need much strength for her journey.

All day, she followed the river upstream. She felt safer now, for she was far from the places her tribe usually roamed. They went south along the other branch of the river, or north into the treeless tundra, following the herds, instead of heading west toward the mountains as she was doing. There were more animals there, the hunters said, though Zena wondered if it was true. Surely, there were as many bison and reindeer here as in the places they usually hunted.

She could see the mountains clearly now. Their peaks were already covered with snow and glistened in the sunlight. Below them were craggy foothills, softened by a thin covering of green. It was these low hills, even more than the high mountains, that seemed to draw her. She stared at them, felt them pull at her, as if they expected her.

A band of horses galloped by, distracting her. She loved their flying manes and tails, their wondrous grace. Zena moved slowly after them, her senses lulled by the smell of trampled earth and fruit and ripened grains, her mind made drowsy by the sun on her shoulders, the feeling of fullness in her belly after days without food. She walked without thinking, hardly knowing where she went.

Abruptly, alertness returned. She had almost walked into the river, for it had turned sharply back upon itself, blocking her way. She peered ahead, trying to see if it would change course and go west again, but hills and trees obscured her view. She kept going for a time, but with every step she took in the wrong direction, the foothills seemed to pull her more strongly.

She would have to cross the river. There was no other way. Zena went back to the place where the river turned. It was broad and fast moving, but at least the water was low at this time of year. Timidly, she poked her toes in the swirling current. It was not so deep; she could see the bottom most of the way across. Pulling the fur from her shoulders, she stuffed it into her bag and waded in, holding the bag above her head. The cold numbed her legs, but the footing was all right. She took another step, then another, until the water reached her shoulders. Suddenly, there was nothing beneath her feet. Zena flailed wildly as the current caught her and dragged her back the way she had come, away from the mountains. Kicking furiously, she struggled against it. She could not let the river take her back.

The bag slipped from her fingers as she reached out to grab a branch floating beside her. She lunged after it, still holding the branch. The precious bag bobbed and dipped as it floated away. Zena watched, despairing. Without her tools and coverings, she could not survive.

Abruptly, the branch was jerked out of her hands and she went under. Over and over, the river dragged her down, then popped her up again. Gasping for breath, she kicked and flailed, trying to shove her body toward the opposite bank. Her foot hit a submerged rock; then she felt sand under her. She dug her toes into it with desperate strength. One foot held, then the other, and then she was able to wrench herself upright and stumble out of the river. Shivering with cold and shock, she began to run downstream. She had to find her bag. She would die if she had no flints to make fire, no furs to warm her.

Bramble-infested bushes lined the bank; she plunged into them, hardly aware of the scratches they inflicted on her numb legs and feet. For almost an hour, she kept going, scanning the river constantly for her bag as she pushed through the tangled mass. Finally, she realized she could not continue. The bushes had become impenetrable, and she could no longer even see the river. Besides, her bag would have gone too far by this time. She would never find it now. Weak with cold and despair, she turned and trudged back the way she had come.

Another thought made her gasp in dismay. The river could carry her bag almost all the way to the clearing. If the others found it, they would think she had drowned. Lune's desolate face, and Menta's, full of sorrow, came before her. She watched them grieve, and her heart twisted with the pain.

Zena crouched against the cold sand on the river bank and wept. She could not go back. The Mother's will was clear, but to have the others think she was dead seemed so cruel. How could the Mother allow such a thing to happen? Was it punishment, because she had failed at the task the Mother had set her, because she had killed Tron instead of helping him?

Hugging herself with her arms for comfort, Zena crouched lower still and sobbed until there were no more tears inside her. Then she forced herself to her feet and trudged slowly toward the mountains. At least she had crossed the river.

The sun had disappeared behind storm clouds, and the wind was rising. A thin, drizzling rain began to fall. Zena wrapped her arms around her body and trudged on as fast as her waning strength would allow. She tried not to think of the night to come, of the terrible cold that would grip her. Never had she spent a night without at least a covering. Even when they were hunting, they built a temporary shelter, had a fire.

She could do that; she could try to make a shelter of some sort. Perhaps she could even find some new flints, to make a fire. Buoyed by this hope, Zena scoured the rocky ridges of some nearby hills until the light had almost gone. But there were no flints, only the ordinary dark rock that did not make sparks. Shivering, she pulled branches off the thick bushes that grew on the hillsides and tried to make a shelter between two boulders. The branches helped a little, but the rain was harder now. There were bits of ice in it, and the wind blew steadily. She huddled against the cold earth, trying to decide what to do. If she stayed still, she would die from the cold. But she was too tired, too cold to walk, and the light was almost gone. She could not go on, but she must, or she would die.

Her chattering teeth were loud inside her head. The noise interrupted her thoughts, broke them into thousands of incoherent pieces. She forced the thoughts back. Once, twice, she imagined herself rising, walking on, and was surprised to find that she had not moved. She tried again, but still her body did not budge. Then her mind stopped working at all as the cold gripped her senses, made them useless. She did not know that she had finally risen and started to walk through the dark and freezing night, uncaring of the icy rain against her skin, the numbness of her body. She had no idea where she was going or why. She had forgotten. She simply moved forward, swaying with exhaustion, until she fell. Then she huddled against the ground for a time, not knowing she was there, until once more she rose.

For hours she went on that way, falling and rising again for no reason except that somewhere deep inside herself, in a place the cold could not reach, she knew she must keep moving—and even that deserted her from time to time. More than once, she huddled against the ground for so long her breathing turned shallow. But the will to survive was strong in Zena, as it had been in the Zenas who had come before her, and each time, she finally rose and stumbled on.

Pictures tumbled in and out of her mind, of Menta and Lune and the others. She saw Conar, and then, just a short distance ahead, she saw the fire. The others were sitting around it. Zena smiled and ran forward, eager to join them. Thinking she was there, she sat on the ground and spread out her hands to feel the warmth, but the fire had gone out. Sighing, she lay down to sleep anyway. The others must have gone to look for wood, so they could make another fire. They would be back soon; she was sure they would, and then she would be warm. Contentedly, she closed her eyes.

This time, she might have slept and never moved again but for a strong, coherent thought that suddenly penetrated her delirium: she had to stay alive so she could go to the place where the Mother waited.

That was it. The Mother waited in the foothills. That was why they beckoned her. She must go there. Zena sat abruptly and staggered to her feet. The darkness was complete now, but it did not bother her. She did not need to see, for she was looking at pictures that moved in and out of her mind, pictures of the place she had seen in her dream. She felt the Mother there. Her presence was strong and comforting. And Conar was there again. She saw him clearly. The others were there too, except they weren't there, they were here, walking with her. Menta was right next to her, and Lune was in front. Zena could see her pale hair gleaming in the moonlight.

She started to run, eager to catch her, but Lune kept disappearing. The others had disappeared too. Zena frowned, puzzled. Then she saw them again, right ahead of her, and her heart thumped with relief. They were lying on the ground; she could barely make out the dark shapes of their bodies, covered with thick, warm furs. She did not know why they would be lying there instead of in the shelter, but it did not matter. She had found them, and that was all she cared about. Joyously, she ran to them and lay down close to their warmth. They shuffled and moved restlessly, but she only nestled closer, so that her back and her stomach, even her feet, were pressed against them. They were so warm, so blessedly warm.

Zena slept on until the sun came over the horizon, aware of nothing, not even of the warmth that was slowly creeping back into her body.

CHAPTER

22

Conar slid to his feet in a fluid, soundless motion. Grabbing the bag of tools he took with him always, he followed Zena out of the shelter. Earlier, when all of them had prepared for sleep, he had noticed that she had positioned herself near the entrance and he had determined to stay awake to watch her. But even before that he had suspected she might leave. He cared for Zena more than any other, and because of his caring he could see better than others the thoughts that hid behind her closed face. He did not know exactly what Zena intended to do, but he did know she would find her own way to deal with Tron's death.

Menta knew too. He was certain she did. She seemed to know what was in all their minds, though even she had been unable to grasp the extent of Tron's capacity to do harm. He glanced back into the shelter and saw that she was awake, watching him. She stared into his eyes for a long moment, then nodded slowly. Her lips formed words, and Conar strained to see them.

"Watch Zena for us," Menta's mouth said, and her eyes moved toward the entrance, as if she were visualizing Zena's slender body sliding quietly through the dark night.

"Go with the Mother," she added, still without sound. Then she lowered her head again as Conar stepped away from the small circle of firelight into the darkness.

Zena was heading for the woods. Conar followed noiselessly as she gathered up her bag of tools and an extra covering and began to walk through the trees. He knew he must not let her see him. Ever since Tron's death, she had wanted to be alone. The posture of her body, the stillness of her face had told him that. She would want to be alone on this journey too. If she saw him, she would send him back. He would not go, of course, but it would be much harder to track her if she suspected his presence.

So far, she had not suspected. Ever since she had begun to teach Tron alone, Conar had been following her. He had always been nearby during the lessons, though neither Zena nor Tron had seen him. This, too, Menta had known, and Lune, but they had not spoken. Zena had asked for privacy and they had granted it, but they had not objected when one of the men had watched anyway. No one, though, could watch as quietly as he could. Tron had eluded the other men, but he had not eluded Conar. Once, Conar had even seen him near Nevilar's place of mating, but he had not gone closer. To spy on a woman's special place was wrong. Now he wished he had. If he had known how Tron abused Nevilar, he would have spoken, and then the terrible events that followed might never have happened.

Even more, he wished he had gone closer to the Ekali. Conar felt his throat tighten with rage as he remembered. He had seen Tron following Zena and Nevilar, and had trailed him, had watched him climb a tree and crouch motionless between two big branches. He had not known, though, that Tron was staring down into the Ekali. That any man would violate the women's sanctuary had not occurred to him. Then Tron had abruptly vanished. Now, Conar knew he had dropped from the tree directly into the Ekali, but at the time, he had wasted precious moments searching for Tron in the woods—until he had heard Zena scream.

Conar took a deep breath and forced the rage away. When his throat tightened like that, he could not breathe. He rubbed his neck gingerly. It was still sore, but at least his breath was not ragged anymore, and Zena would not hear him behind her.

The woods were denser now, and it was hard to spot her shadowy form among the trees. She disappeared from view, over the crest of a hill. Conar quickened his step, straining to see in the dim light. Then the moon slid behind a cloud and he could not see at all. He stood quietly, waiting for a sound, however tiny or indistinct, that would betray her presence, but the wind was blowing the wrong direction and he could hear nothing.

He tried to think which way she would go. If she continued to head west, she would come to rugged, rocky hills, unfamiliar to all of them. The tribe never traveled that way. But if she went south a little farther, she would come to the river, which wound in a long curve from the clearing before it separated into two branches. Probably, Conar thought, she would go toward the river. Traveling was easier there. He crept cautiously through the trees in that direction, but after a time, he was not sure which way he was going. There were no stars to guide him, and the night was utterly black. It was cold, too, and the wind was still rising. Each year, winter seemed to come sooner. Conar wrapped his extra garment around his shoulders and stumbled on, hoping the moon would reappear so he could see, or the wind would drop so he could hear. But neither happened, and he finally realized he could not go on. He would have to wait for the light to come again to find Zena.

He crouched in the meager shelter of an overhanging rock to wait for dawn. Impatience gripped him, that he should be sitting still instead of searching. What if she was hurt, or a predator had followed her? How had he lost her so soon?

Too restless to sit still, Conar got up to search some more, but the blackness was impenetrable, and he fell immediately. Reluctantly, he sat again. For hours, he strained his eyes and ears against the darkness, trying to see and hear, struggling desperately to stay awake, in case Zena should come this way. He slept anyway, despite the hard ground, the wind that chilled him even through the furs. For two nights now, he had forced himself to stay awake, so he would know if Zena left the shelter. On this third night, his body could resist no longer.

When he awoke, the light was already strong. Conar leaped up, furious at himself for sleeping so long. He ran quickly through the trees toward the river. The distance was greater than he had remembered, and the sun was already in the middle of the sky when he reached it. All the way, he had listened, even climbed trees to look for Zena, but he had seen nothing. Here, though, he was out of the trees, and he would surely find her. For hours, he scoured the riverbanks, climbed each hill that came before him, so he could see into the distance, but still there was no sign of her.

Conar trudged on, too dejected now to fight the despairing thoughts that crowded his mind. He had lost Zena, might never see her again. And Menta; he had failed Menta. She had trusted him to watch Zena, keep her safe. The Mother had trusted him too. He knew it was so because the Mother made it so easy for him to know Zena's thoughts, as if she were part of him. Always, since their first mating, Zena had been part of him. Surely, the Mother would help him now.

He saw it then, wedged between two rocks at the edge of the river. Zena's bag. Conar's heart leaped with joy, then fell abruptly as he realized what the bag meant. If Zena's bag was here, she must have been in the river, and if she had been in the river . . .

"No!" Conar said the word aloud, to the Mother, to the animals, to any that would hear. "No! She cannot be dead. That is impossible. It cannot be." Frantically, he picked up the bag and held it close to his heart, as if his possession of it would make Zena return. His eyes searched the water for any sign of her, for her garment perhaps. Then he realized both furs were in the bag. She must have removed the one she usually wore. But why would she do that?

They were heavy, water-logged. The bag could not have come far, for the weight would sink it after a while. Perhaps she had dropped it when she went to the river to drink, and was still searching for it somewhere upstream.

Conar plowed along the riverbank, calling Zena's name. He no longer cared if she heard him. This was a sign from the Mother, and it must mean he was supposed to find her, be with her. It meant she was still alive too. Surely, that was what it meant. Conar did not allow himself to think otherwise, even as his eyes scoured the river for the horror of her body. Zena could not have drowned. The Mother would not let such a thing happen, not to Zena. He clung to the thought, stubbornly ignoring any objections his mind tried to raise.

The sun was close to the western horizon when he reached the hill where Zena had stared down at the huge herds of animals, run to the wide-crowned trees to gather fruit and nuts. Conar's eyes were moist as he looked out at the herds. The view made him think of his small sister, Lilan. Next to Zena, he cared for her more than any other. Often, he had brought her to places like this, where there were many animals to watch. Like him, she loved to scratch in the earth with a sharp stick, trying to capture the fluid shapes and graceful movements of the big creatures.

A long time might pass now before he saw her again. Conar imagined her face twisting with sadness when she realized that he had disappeared, and wished he had been able to speak to her, but there had been no time.

The light changed suddenly as thick clouds blustered across the face of the sun. Conar glanced up, startled. In moments, storm clouds had poured out from behind the horizon and covered the sky. He hurried on. Zena had no tools, no flints, not even a fur. The night would be cold, too cold to survive. He had to find her by the end of the day.

A memory came to him suddenly. He stopped and stared at the mountains. The dream . . . the dream she had told him about, when they had been walking near the mountains, in long, twisting tunnels beneath the earth.

That was where she would go. He was sure of it suddenly. He had been there with her in the dream; she had told him that. He remembered her face, eager with the pleasure of her vision, amazed at the caves, the tunnels that wound between them, the open space beyond, where something waited.

Conar began to run. But now the river was going the wrong direction. He stopped, frustrated. Why had it suddenly changed course? Perhaps it would turn again, if he kept going.

Again, recognition came suddenly. She had taken off her fur to cross. He must do it too. Conar went back to the place where the river doubled back and stared down at the muddy bank. Her footprints were there. How had he missed them before? She had been there, not too long ago.

He pulled off his fur and waded in, holding both bags high over his head. Just a little taller than Zena, he was able to touch bottom all the way, but by the time he had reached the other side, he was so numb he could barely breathe. Wind laced with freezing rain hit his wet skin. Shaking uncontrollably, fearful that he might find nothing, he examined the bank for footprints. Relief flooded him when he saw that they were there. She had crossed; she had not drowned—but she would be cold, too cold.

Joy and fear mingled uneasily in his heart. He hurried on, stopping only long enough to drape a fur across his body. Over and over, he called Zena's name as he ran through the long, pale grasses. If he did not find her soon, she would surely freeze.

A huge herd of bison filled the valley ahead. Never had he seen so many. As he stared, the last glimmerings of light faded. Slowly, the animals lost their individual contours and merged into a single enormous brown blotch against the earth. Conar called again, but now the hope had gone from his voice. The lowing and stamping of the herd would make it impossible for Zena to hear him.

He plodded on, determined to keep searching even in the dark. Zena would not walk toward the bison. She must have crossed the valley behind them. Bison could be mean if they were disturbed. They were beautiful, though, with their massive heads and shoulders, their graceful, swinging gallop. For a brief moment, Conar forgot his distress as the wonder of their shape and movement caught his imagination. A sudden sharp blast of wind and a spatter of icy rain brought Zena back to the forefront of his thoughts.

Fire! That was it. Why had he not thought to make a fire before now? She would be able to see a fire for a long distance, or at least smell the smoke. Hurriedly, Conar pulled out his flint and a bundle of grass he had stuffed in his bag earlier. Sparks flew out and caught in the dry grass, but everything else around him was wet, and he could not keep the blaze going. Finally, on his third try, he found some dry wood in a crevice under a rock and managed to build a meager fire.

He crouched near the tiny blaze, his body slumped in discouragement. The fire was small, too small for Zena to see. It was not even big enough to keep him warm. Shivering convulsively, he pulled his extra fur around him, but the shivering did not stop. Should he use Zena's furs? He had dried them in the sun as he walked, but to use them would feel like a betrayal, as if he were stealing the warmth Zena should have.

The fire sputtered and went out as the rain turned to heavy, drenching sleet. Conar jumped up and down to keep warm, but as soon as he sat down again, the shivering resumed. Three more times, he forced himself to jump around, then the cold began to grip his body, numb his mind, and he could not make himself get up again. Soon, nothing had meaning for him except the desire to be warm. Slowly, he brought out Zena's furs and wrapped them around his head, his legs and feet. Tears dribbled down his cheeks, from the icy wind that chilled him despite the coverings, from his despair. He wiped them on the furs and felt the thin layer of moisture freeze against his face.

The hours passed; dumbly, he endured them, waiting for the night to end so he could search again. As soon as there was light enough to see, he jumped up and began to scour the valley. He called Zena's name endlessly, with increasing desperation, but there was no response. By nightfall, the rocky foothills loomed before him, and he felt a spurt of hope. Perhaps she had traveled faster than he had and was there already. She might even have found one of the caves she had described in her dream. There, the icy rain would not reach her, at least. One part of him knew such a thing was impossible. He had barely survived the night, even with many furs. She could not have survived. But another part of him was not yet ready to admit Zena was dead. This part of him insisted that if he could find a cave like the ones she had described, Zena would have to stay alive to see it with him. That was what she had dreamed, so it must be.

The thought crystallized in his mind. He must find a cave. Then she would surely appear. Conar pushed his worries aside, lest they distract him from his purpose, and set about locating the cave that would bring Zena to him. All that evening, all the following day, he searched the foothills. Just before sunset, when the rain had finally stopped, he found one, tucked beneath an overhanging ledge. He stepped cautiously through the entrance and stared in awe. The cave was huge, encompassing. Tumbled boulders littered the floor, giving it a forbidding aspect. The impression disappeared as he spotted patches of earth between the rocks, smelled the tiny white flowers that still bloomed there.

Entranced, he ventured further, and immediately felt warmer. The air was soft and moist, without the chill of the air outside. A small stream bubbled up from an invisible source and traversed the back of the cave, then emptied into a tiny pond. Around its edges were more flowers, pink this time. Conar knelt to examine them, and as he straightened, the last slanted rays of the sun entered the cave. He gasped in wonder, for in the shape of the curved rock he seemed to see the bison. There, in that bulbous outcropping, was the outline of a massive shoulder, below, the shape of a haunch. Avidly, he traced the lines, saw them taper into hoofs and horns, swell again into rounded backs. Then the sun sank below the horizon and the bison disappeared.

The images sustained him as he built a fire, prepared tubers and grains for eating. He had collected more than he needed. If he had food for her, Zena was more likely to come. He made a tonic, too, from herbs he had found. Some he drank himself; the rest he kept warm near the fire for Zena. But as the darkness gathered around him and the fire sent strange shadows leaping across the walls of the cave, the fear he had managed to keep at bay overwhelmed him. For four nights, Zena had been without fire or shelter or even a garment to warm her. Conar saw her pressed against the cold ground, weeping with the pain of her freezing toes and fingers, watched her slip into the merciful numbness that brought death, and grief bent him double. He shuddered with it, gasped until he could barely breathe. The anguish filled him so completely he could not see or hear or even think.

Hours seemed to pass before the spasms of grief diminished, and when they did, Conar felt only exhaustion. Tears still swelled behind his eyes, rained down his cheeks, but now he lacked the strength to gasp or even to eat the food he had so carefully prepared. Numbly, he reached out to put more branches on the dwindling fire. The flames shot up, casting fantastic shadows all around him. There were bison in the shadows; he could see them clearly in his imagination. They galloped across the walls and ceiling of the cave in strong, flowing movements. He watched them listlessly, too desolate now to take pleasure in their graceful forms. Another shadow joined them, a shadow that looked different.

Conar frowned and sat up straight. It looked like a person. The hands were upraised, the legs strained, bent sharply at the knee, as if the struggle to move forward were too great to bear. The shadow stopped abruptly, then sank down against the wall of the cave until it was only a small bundle on the floor.

Behind him, Conar heard a soft thump. He turned his head and stared.

II

The animal reached toward her with an exploratory tongue, puzzled by the strange smell. Zena felt the rough tongue pass across her arm, but she was too warm, too content, to wonder at it. The animal sniffed again, then closed its eyes, sensing no danger in the presence of this small creature. Another animal moved closer, pressing its woolly shoulders against Zena's back. She nestled into it gratefully. A little one followed and pushed up against her feet. All around her, the herd settled into a close bunch, embracing her with their warm bodies and thick fur. Zena slept on, unaware of their presence. Only when the lump beneath her moved suddenly as dawn broke did she open her eyes.

Fur was all around her, woolly, dark brown fur. Strange rumbling noises came from deep within the fur, and it had a strong smell, so strong she almost choked. A warm, moist nose nuzzled her. Zena lay perfectly still, trying to understand.

Vaguely, she remembered that Lune had been there, lying on the ground, and Menta, and all the others. But she did not think they were here now.

No. That was wrong. They could not have been here. She had left by herself, and they could not have followed her. Why, then, was she surrounded by fur?

Suddenly, there was movement all around her. Legs materialized where before there had been only fur and warm dark lumps. They were shaggy legs, festooned with matted hair. Zena began to shiver again. The warmth that had comforted her all night long had gone. Slowly, she rose to her feet and moved close to the animal next to her, so she could huddle against its bristly hide and be warm again. It glanced at her and resumed its grazing.

Another animal approached, eyeing her warily. Its horns made sweeping arcs as it tossed its head. Zena stood still, strangely unafraid. It grunted, a low deep rumble, and moved away. Others came to examine her. She did not move, but only stood there, leaning against the animal that had kept her warm all night. After a time, they ceased to notice her. Then, moving very slowly, she began to make her way through the throng of bodies.

She had slept all night among a herd of bison. The thought was strange, a little frightening. Never before had she been so close to the huge animals. Bakan and the others had told her they could be vicious, but she thought that was probably only when they were alarmed. Still, she was eager now to find her way out, but all she could see in every direction were dark, shaggy backs. They were too high to see over, too thickly clustered to give her a view in any direction. She spotted a tree with low branches and climbed up it to try to see where she was, which way she should go to escape the herd.

For a moment, terror gripped her. For as far as she could see in all directions, there were only bison. They stretched the whole width of the valley. She could not get out of the herd even if she walked for hours, and if she wanted to reach the foothills, she had no choice but to walk among them.

Zena looked down at the expanse of rounded backs, at the thousands of curved horns atop the lowered heads. All night, she had slept among them, and not a single animal had threatened her. There was no reason why they would threaten her now.

Slowly, calmness returned to her heart. These were the Mother's creatures, like all others. If the Mother had put her among them, she would not fear them. Instead, she would be grateful for their warmth. Plucking some fruit to eat as she walked, she climbed down from the tree and rejoined the herd.

All day, she traveled with the bison, occasionally climbing a tree for nuts and fruit, or gathering ripe grains to eat. She found a few muddy streams and one big pond, for water. They were well trampled by thousands of hoofs, but the water refreshed her anyway. When night came, she snuggled down among the warm bodies. The big animals sniffed her curiously when she nestled against them, and a few licked her with their scraping tongues, but none threatened her. When they rose again at dawn, she rose with them and proceeded slowly on her way.

The Mother was speaking to her through the bison, she realized.

All the materials she needed to keep her alive—her garments, her tools and flints, even the company of her own kind—had been taken from her. She had only the bison now, and the Mother. To place her life entirely in the Mother's hands was hard, but it was the only way to atone for the act she had committed. She had taken a life and she must offer up her own, must trust the Mother to help her find ways to stay alive if that was Her will. She must recognize the opportunities the Mother gave her, too, even such a strange solution as a herd of bison.

By the third day, Zena felt as if she had traveled with the huge animals forever. When their numbers began to thin, and she realized she was approaching the edge of the herd, she was sad. They gave her warmth and the solace of their company, and she did not want to leave them. Later, though, as evening approached, a strong feeling of restlessness suddenly rippled through the herd. One bison raised its head and tossed it sharply; the next one imitated the motion. Soon all the animals around her were tossing their heavy heads and stamping at the ground with their sharp hoofs.

For the first time since she had been among them, Zena was afraid. This, too, was a message. She was being warned, and she must listen. She sprinted toward a tree, to get out of the herd, but before she could reach it, the animals began to run. Zena ran with them. She had no choice. Briefly, she was able to keep up, for the bison were not moving very fast. Then dust from hundreds of thundering hoofs rose heavily to fill the air. The thick cloud blinded her, made it almost impossible to avoid the jostling, shoving animals, or even to breathe. The bison could no longer see her, either. Soon, they would trample her.

Desperately, Zena swerved toward another tree and scrambled onto a low branch. It was small, but at least she was above the herd. The mass of animals charged past her, seeming not even to see the tree. It swayed and cracked with the impact of their heavy bodies. One of them crashed directly into the trunk, and she felt the tree begin to topple. She did not wait to hit the ground, but launched herself onto the back of the nearest bison and clung with all her strength to its shaggy fur. The animal shuddered and twitched, trying to throw her off. Zena clung harder. Again, it shook itself, then the momentum of the herd forced it forward. Ignoring her, it galloped on.

Dust-laden wind tore through Zena's hair, into her eyes, blinding her completely. She pressed her head against the bison's shoulder and wrapped her thighs around its back. Only one thought had meaning for her now. She must hold on, must ride with the huge creature beneath her as if she were attached to it.

On and on the bison ran, in long, lunging strides. Slowly, Zena adjusted to its pace. She felt the ripple of its powerful shoulders beneath her thighs, felt her own body begin to flow in rhythm with the strong, graceful movements. Though her muscles were taut with the effort of holding on, within herself she was utterly relaxed. Truly, she was a part of the bison now, had become one with it, as if her body had merged into its body. They belonged together, she and the bison, as they charged across the valley.

All fear left Zena. She felt nothing but the splendor of the massive creature beneath her, the power of its thickly muscled body, the grace of its movements as it propelled them forward. The sensation was ecstatic, wondrous. She wanted never to stop, to ride like this forever.

Gradually, the herd slowed down. Zena clung harder, for unlike its gallop, the bison's trot was bumpy. Sadness filled her, that the ride was ending, that she might never again experience this ecstasy. Her euphoria disappeared abruptly as the animal beneath her began to snort and stamp, once again aware of its unexpected burden. The other bison had slowed to a walk, but they were still restless. She could feel their uneasiness, as if it flowed from their bodies into hers.

Something must have disturbed them badly to make them stampede like that, she realized. Lions could have attacked at one edge of the herd, perhaps, and spooked them all. Now any strange smell or sight, like herself, would set them off again. To walk among them would be dangerous.

Zena clung grimly to the agitated bison, hoping it would settle soon. Her whole body shook with exhaustion, now that the ride was over. Her thighs were trembling, her arms aching with the effort, and she knew she could not hold on much longer.

A wide patch of lush grass appeared ahead. One bison lowered its head to eat; another followed suit. Momentarily distracted, the animal she was riding began to graze.

This was her chance. Carefully, Zena lowered herself from the bison's back and crept toward a small group of boulders. Despite her caution, one of the animals charged her. She ran headlong into the protection of the rocks, grateful that her ride had taken her even closer to the edge of the herd. When she clambered on top of one of the boulders to get her bearings, she realized that the ride had carried her across the valley as well. Finally, she had reached the foothills.

Zena smiled, the first smile that had crossed her face since she had left. The smile vanished quickly as she considered her predicament. The bison had kept her warm for three nights. Now, she would be without them. The light was fading fast, and once again, clouds were gathering.

Wearily, she hauled herself up a rocky ledge and set off into the foothills. She tripped almost immediately. Her legs were quivering so hard she could barely stand, and she was still shaking all over from the shock of her experience. Soon, the cold reached her as well. Her shivering intensified until she had to pick up each leg with her hands and push it forward in order to walk. She forced herself on. Up here in the hills, she might find flints. Maybe she could even find a cave. There were caves, she knew that from the dream. Surely, if she could find one, she would survive the night.

Rain began to fall in icy slivers. Zena spotted some likely pieces of rock for flint. Hurriedly, she gathered leaves and bits of grass, anything she could find that was still dry. She struck one stone against another as hard as she could, over and over. On the third try, sparks flew out, but they did not land on the little bundle of leaves. The next time, though, the leaves caught and blazed. Quickly, Zena plied them with twigs. The small fire burned brightly for a moment, then the rain came down in torrents and it fizzled into nothing.

Zena poked helplessly at the embers, trying to summon the strength to go on, the will to believe she could stay alive. It was hard to trust in the Mother when she was so cold, when there seemed to be no possible way to survive the night. How could she find a cave when she could barely walk, find dry grasses and wood to burn when icy rain penetrated every crevice?

For a long time, she just sat with her knees drawn up to her chest, her shoulders hunched against the freezing onslaught. Pictures came to her, pictures of fire and warmth, the protection of a cave. She imagined herself there, warm and comfortable. Her eyes closed, and the pictures were transformed into dreams. She was sitting in a cave, where there was no rain, where a big fire radiated heat.

Zena snapped away from the dream. She must find a cave, had to make herself get up again and look until she had found one. That was what the Mother was trying to tell her. She forced herself to stand, but her legs collapsed under her. Again she tried, again they collapsed. She crawled instead, moving slowly along on her hands and knees, like an infant. Her palms began to bleed, but her hands were numb now and she did not notice. She felt the rocks scrape her knees, though. The pain was sharp and irritating. She did not want to hurt. She was tired of hurting, of struggling. It would be much easier just to give up, to let the Mother take her. Perhaps, after all, that was what She wanted.

Sighing, she pulled herself under a boulder so she could lie down where the slashing rain could not reach her. Unexpectedly, the rain stopped and sun broke through the heavy clouds. It blazed from the western horizon in a final brilliant burst of light. Zena crawled out to it and for a few blessed moments she felt its warmth against her skin. Then the sun vanished and darkness and cold descended.

Pain began to shoot into her hands, an almost intolerable pain. Her feet had the pain too. She bit her lips, trying to endure it, and after a while it went away. She felt peaceful then, ready to sleep. Lazily, she stretched out against the cold rock, only it was not cold now. It was warm, comforting. She was in the dream again, was in a cave, and there was a fire.

The dream encompassed Zena, drew the pain from her body, the despair from her thoughts. She wrapped herself in it, sealed away the cold dark night. There was nothing anymore but the warmth and comfort of the dream. When hands reached out and lifted her, she did not notice, except to wonder if one of the bison had come back. There were bristly hairs against her chest, and soft, grunting noises in her ear. She was moving again, too, but this time, she was being jostled, jiggled up and down, as if the bison were climbing. Grimacing, she nestled closer, to steady herself. She wanted to sleep quietly, not be jostled like this.

The hands were under her shoulders now, tight and rough. They were forcing her to stand. Zena frowned, confused. Bison did not have hands. She dismissed the puzzle and concentrated on resisting the hands as they pushed her forward, propped her up each time she tried to sink to the ground. She did not want to stand or walk. She wanted to sleep, but the hands would not stop pestering her, and finally she gave up. It would be easier to do what they wanted. Then she could lie down again. She took one step forward, then another.

Fire! She smelled fire. Zena raised her head sharply. The fire smelled different. It was a real fire, not the fire in her dream. But that was impossible. Could it be real?

Hope flared inside her, broke through her numb oblivion. Slowly, agonizingly, she forced her frozen body to move toward the smell. The darkness was impenetrable, and at first she could see nothing. Reaching out with her hands, she groped her way along. Then she saw a glow in front of her, a glow inside a deep black hole.

Zena stared at it, not daring to believe. There was a fire, a fire in a cave. She staggered toward it, hands upraised, as if to ward off a blow, the blow of finding that she was still in her dream, that the fire, the cave, the warmth she felt already, were not real after all.

Something moved suddenly behind the fire. It was a figure, a ghostly, unsubstantial figure in the flickering light, one she had never thought to see, not here in this place.

Conar. It was Conar—but Conar could not be here. He was with the others. She knew he was with the others, so she must still be in the dream. The fire, the cave, Conar, they were all a dream. None of it was real.

Disappointment rocked Zena, made her sway on her feet, clutch at her belly as if she had been hit there. She slumped heavily to the ground, unable to sustain this final pain. It was too much, too much to bear, to feel the promise of life and then have it taken away because it was only a dream.

A voice called her name, reached through the depths of her misery. She closed her ears, her eyes, so she would not have to see or hear this dream that tormented her with hope and then left her with nothing.

Someone was touching her, trying to carry her again. Zena moaned and tried to tell the person to go away.

"It is the Mother's will," the voice insisted. "If the Mother did not want me to be with you, She would not have shown me your bag. She has sent me here."

Zena frowned. What did the voice mean, about the Mother and the bag? Reluctantly, she opened her eyes. Conar's face was right next to hers. Tears were pouring down his cheeks. Were there tears in dreams?

She reached up to touch Conar's cheeks. Perhaps it was only the rain—but there was no rain now. She felt tears prickle behind her own eyelids, as if in response.

"You must come by the fire," Conar kept saying as he pulled at her shoulders. Zena did not respond. She was too tired to move, to try to figure out if Conar was real or not. She closed her eyes again, wanting only to sleep.

The tugging at her shoulders increased, then ceased abruptly. Suddenly, there were hands near her mouth.

"Drink!" Conar's voice was stern, sterner than she had ever heard it. Obediently, Zena opened her mouth. Liquid poured down her throat, a warm, bitter liquid that made her choke. The warmth went down into her belly, into her legs, even her toes.

She opened her eyes again. Conar's face was grim now. He was rubbing at her hands, her feet, chafing them furiously. Zena pulled sharply away as sensation began to return. Her hands felt as if the fire were burning them, and so did her feet.

"Good!" Conar sounded satisfied.

"It is not good, that I should hurt," Zena shot back, surprised at the sound of her own voice.

The rubbing stopped abruptly. Joy poured into Conar's face; Zena watched it flow in, wondered at it. A small portion of the joy pushed at her heart and tried to enter.

Conar took her into his arms and hugged her, kissed her face over and over again. The delicate touch of his lips, the warmth of his embrace mingled strangely with the pain in her hands and feet.

"You are truly here!" she said in surprise. "Are you here?" The question followed immediately. Still, she dared not believe.

Conar seemed to understand. "I am here. I have found you again—no, you have found me—or perhaps the Mother has let us find each other. You are here with me, in the cave I found so you would come."

Zena stared at him, and suddenly she knew it was true. This was not her dream. Conar was here. He was real. The cave was real, and the fire.

She shook with the relief of it, with the joy. Reaching up, she brought Conar's face close to her own, so she could feel his skin, taste his tears mingling with her own, know with her lips and tongue that he was truly real. Just as quickly, she pulled away, unwilling to take her eyes from his face, lest he disappear, become a dream again. His features blurred and she clutched at him frantically.

Conar kissed her eyes, wiped the tears away, and his face came into focus again. "You are here, with me," he repeated, and hugged her harder, so hard she had to gasp for breath.

"Now you know I am real," he told her, loosening his grip and grinning.

"I do not want to let you go again, ever," he added fervently.

Zena held on to him tightly, still trying to absorb. She was here, in a cave with Conar, and there was a fire, a wonderful, hot fire.

How had she come here? There had been hands. . . . She remembered the hands.

"Did you carry me here?"

Conar looked perplexed. "I waited here for you. I did not carry you; you came yourself."

Zena shook her head, confused. Something had carried her. If Conar had not . . .

Perhaps the hands had been part of her dream. They must have been, but she did not think so.

She gave up trying to understand. Tomorrow, she would try to find the answer. And in the end, however she had come, it was the Mother who had brought her here, had helped her to stay alive even when she had begun to doubt, to give up. Her heart filled with gratitude.

Thinking of the Mother brought another memory. "I have banished myself," she said doubtfully to Conar. "How can you be here when I must be alone?"

"The Mother has sent me," Conar replied firmly. He was sure it was true, but whether or not he was right, he wanted Zena to believe his words so she would not argue with him, try to send him away again.

Zena frowned, considering, but her mind was too confused to work properly, and she could not tell if Conar was right. This puzzle, too, would have to wait.

"How did you get here?" she asked curiously, then realized she did not need to know the answer. Conar was here; she was here, and that was enough.

His response, though, was simple. "I walked," he replied, smiling down at her.

Zena sighed and sank against the ground. She wanted to sleep now. "I feel cold," she told Conar.

"Then we will go to the fire, and I will wrap your furs around you," Conar answered.

He pulled her to her feet and supported her as she stumbled to the fire. The tingling in her toes was stronger, but at the same time her feet were numb, and she could not feel the ground beneath her. She felt the furs, though, that Conar wrapped tightly around her, and the warmth of his body against her own.

"You found my furs," she muttered drowsily.

"They kept me alive," he responded gravely. "Without your furs, I would not be here now.

"Why are you alive?" The question popped out of Conar's mouth before he could reconsider. But Zena did not seem to think it strange.

"The bison kept me alive," she replied. "The Mother sent me to the bison."

Conar looked up at the place where the bison had seemed to leap and run in the shadows of the dancing flames, their bodies formed by the contours of the rocks themselves. He did not know what

Zena meant, and he knew she was too weary now to explain. But if she said the bison had kept her alive, it must be true. Tomorrow, he would thank them. He would give them life, life that would last forever, by drawing their magnificent bodies where all could see them. Here, on the walls of the cave he had found for Zena, he would make the bison come alive.

CHAPTER

23

Tron crawled toward the bushes. They had left him for dead. That much he knew, for he had heard them talking, but he did not remember the rest. He had let them believe it, had lain perfectly still, hardly breathing. To feign death was not hard. He had done it often when he hunted, so the animals would not know he was near.

Almost, he *had* been dead. For a long time, he had been unable to move at all. His head still hurt badly. He touched it cautiously, and his fingers came away sticky with blood. It was dark blood, thick and congealed, and there was a lot of it—so he was wounded too. But how had the wound come to him? And how had he come here, to the place where they buried the dead?

He frowned, trying to remember. He had followed Zena and Nevilar to the Ekali and climbed the tree to watch them, but of what had happened after that, he had no memory at all. The events of the past months, though, the hateful lessons, the forbidding of Akat, the humiliating session with the council, flashed through his mind with perfect clarity. He had wanted to leave then, but Menta had refused.

Rage coursed through him. Now, he would leave, and no one would stop him. He never wanted to see any of them, ever again. But before he could travel, he must regain some strength, get food and water, and after that, some tools and furs for the trip. Perhaps he could steal them while the others slept.

Gingerly, he pulled himself to his feet. Dizziness overcame him and he sat abruptly. He would have to get help. But how?

Nevilar. He would make Nevilar bring him what he needed. She would do it if he threatened her. He crawled toward the river, knowing she came there every afternoon to get water for her mother, and concealed himself in the thick bushes.

When Nevilar came down the path and knelt to fill her jugs, he was waiting. She was pale, he saw. He would make her paler.

He called her name. She looked confused, and wary. He called again. This time she rose and came toward the sound. Just before she reached him, Tron dragged himself to his feet. She stared at him and went completely white. Her mouth opened wide to scream. Tron clapped his hand over her lips, so the sound could not emerge. The effort cost him dearly. He almost fell over, but managed to prop himself on her shoulder.

"Do not scream!" he ordered. "Do not scream and I will let you go."

She nodded, her eyes wide with terror, and he released her. He wanted desperately to sink to the ground again, but he knew he would be far more menacing if he stood over her instead.

"You are dead," she whispered. "You are dead."

"I am powerful," he hissed, "too powerful to die."

Whimpering in fear, she shrank away from him.

She believed him, believed he had come back from the dead! Despite his weakness, Tron wanted to laugh. He stopped himself. It was more important to make her do what he wanted. To manage that, he would have to frighten her even more. Arranging his face into a terrifying grimace, he glowered at her fiercely.

"Do not speak of this, that you have seen me. If you speak, you will die." Now her eyes were so wide with terror he thought they might pop out of her face. A snort of laughter escaped. He disguised it as a growl.

"Bring me food and water, to the place where we meet," he commanded. "Tonight, when the sun goes."

Nevilar's head shook back and forth in frantic denial. He grabbed her face with one hand and put his face close to hers.

"Do this or you will die!"

She nodded dumbly. Slowly, Tron turned away, using every ounce of his strength to stay on his feet.

Nevilar turned and ran back to the river, her face rigid with shock. Tron had come back from the dead. He had come back. Zena had killed him, but he had come back. The image of his grisly face, his skull covered with blood, blood raining down his cheeks, into his fur, would be forever stamped on her mind.

Weeping, she sank to the ground. He had said he would kill her if she spoke of seeing him, if she did not bring him what he wanted, but she could not go there, see him again, see the blood. But if she did not, he would kill her. He could kill her easily. If he was powerful enough to come back from the dead, he could kill her wherever she was, anywhere.

Nevilar's hands went to her face in horror, came away again covered in blood. She squealed, a small animal sound of pure panic. His blood, the blood of someone dead, was on her face.

Her mother's footsteps sounded on the path behind her. Quickly, Nevilar washed her face in the river, started to fill one of the jugs. Her hands were shaking, and the water spilled out as fast as it went in.

"You take so long," her mother scolded.

"I had to fix the strap of the jug," Nevilar lied.

"Look! You spill the water as fast as you collect it," her mother said in disgust. "What is the matter with you that you cannot even get water?" Still grumbling, she took the other jug and filled it herself, then trudged back along the path.

For once, Nevilar was unaffected by her mother's harsh words. She crouched where she was, bent double with the horror of her situation. She had to do as Tron said, or he would kill her. But the others always watched her now, especially Menta. How could she find food, sneak away with it?

She made her way slowly back to the clearing, carrying the jug she had filled. Perhaps if she hid it, told her mother she had dropped it in the river . . .

With a quick gesture, she shoved the water jug into a clump of bushes. Later, when no one was looking, she hid strips of cooked meat and some fruit she had gathered in the same place. But how was she to get it to Tron?

She was lucky. The whole group set off just before sunset to find honey. The bees had a big nest in the field nearby, and if they were approached properly, they were willing to share it. No one was surprised when Nevilar elected to stay behind. She was afraid of bees, and they seemed to sense her fear. They seldom stung anyone else, but they almost always stung her.

As soon as the others had disappeared, Nevilar sped to her small enclosure. Tron was stretched out on the hard ground, and he did not move as she approached.

Perhaps he had died again. Nevilar went closer. Still, he did not move. Relief washed over her, made her dizzy for a moment. He must be dead again, or he would have spoken.

Hastily, she placed the food and water beside him, for she could not think what else to do with it, and crept away. Just as she reached the edge of the glen, a hand grabbed her ankle. She fell headlong into the bushes.

She screamed, a thin shrill scream that stopped abruptly as fear paralyzed her throat. Tron was dragging her backward; he was going to kill her, choke her, as he had choked Conar.

Tron thrust his face close to hers. Blood and grime blackened his heavy features, made them into a terrifying mask. The gritty mixture coated his cheeks, his nose, even the inside of his mouth as he opened it to speak. He reeked of blood, of waste and urine.

"I need more food, tomorrow," he growled. "Furs and flints, too. And much meat."

Bile rose in Nevilar's mouth. She choked, unable to speak. Instead, she nodded frantically, so he would let her go. Tron twitched her ankle hard, then fell back against the ground.

Nevilar ran. Vomit came from her lips, dribbled down her chest. She would not come again, she could not!

All that night, she was tormented by dreams of Tron finding her, putting his hands around her neck, hitting her with rocks until she died. By morning, she was so terrified she knew she had to do as he said. Feigning sickness this time, she stayed in the shelter until the others were busy with their chores. Then she thrust some flints and as much meat as she could find, as well as her extra fur and one that belonged to her brother, into her bag. Just before sunset, she went into the woods on the pretext of finding herbs for her stomach, and made her way to the glen. This time, she did not go into it, but left the bag in the bushes nearby and ran back to the clearing as fast as her shaking legs would allow.

The next day, indecision tormented her almost as badly as the dreams of the night before. Tron had not told her to come again, but that was because she had not gone near him. Probably he was waiting for her, and if she did not go, he might kill her even if he had not spoken.

Furtively, she stuffed some meat in an old basket and hid it under her bedding. But when she rose later, saying she must find more herbs, Menta placed a restraining hand on her arm and looked closely into her face.

"You are not well, Nevilar," she said gently.

Nevilar nodded, her eyes on the ground.

Menta looked at her for a long moment, then raised Nevilar's chin so she could look into her eyes.

"You are frightened, Nevilar. For two days now you have been frightened. I would like to know what has frightened you."

"Nothing has frightened me," Nevilar muttered, but she could not keep the panic from her eyes. Tron would surely kill her if she spoke, but Menta could see everything. She would not be able to fool the wise woman much longer.

"That is not true," Menta answered calmly. She did not speak further, but waited, and the posture of her waiting spoke of infinite patience. She would wait all day beside Nevilar to learn the truth, if that was necessary.

Nevilar's mouth twisted painfully. Part of her wanted to speak Tron's name, but the other part was terrified to utter it, lest he kill her, right here, as she spoke.

Lune came up beside Menta. She regarded Nevilar gravely, but she, too, kept silent. The pressure of their combined gaze was too much for Nevilar. Her eyes darted frantically from one face to the other, and then her lips began to move.

"Tron," she gasped out. "Tron frightens me." She looked over her shoulder, as if expecting him to leap from the bushes.

Lune's eyes narrowed. "Tron frightens you still, though he is dead?"

"He is not dead. He has come back from the dead." Now that the words had started, Nevilar could not get them out fast enough. She babbled on and on in a steady stream.

"He is not dead; I have seen him. He said he would kill me if I spoke, and he can kill even when he is not here, for he is too powerful to die. He can kill whenever he wants, and I cannot stop him. He has made me bring him food and water, and I am afraid. . . . Tron will kill me. . . . He has come back, back from the dead!"

Menta did not wait to hear more. "Watch her," she said to Bly and Bakan, who were standing nearby. "Keep her close to you, in the shelter."

She thrust Nevilar into Bly's arms and ran toward the place where they buried the dead. That Tron had come back from the dead was impossible. But had he truly been dead? Had any of them looked at him closely, to remember and cherish, as they did with those they had loved?

Lune was already there when she arrived, staring grimly at the empty space where they had left Tron's body.

"He was not dead," she said dully. "It is my fault. I did not go close to him, or I would have known. I am the one who examines those who have died, tries to understand the reasons. But I did not want to see his face, after what he did to Zena, to our tribe."

"None of us wished to," Menta replied. "All were avoiding the task of washing him, preparing him for burial. More than the two days had passed."

The transition from life to death took time, they knew, so they did not bury the newly dead for two days, but left the person in peace to commune with the Mother and adjust to the change. Usually, though, someone stayed nearby to make sure the dead one was safe and comfortable. No one had visited Tron.

Lune and Menta looked at each other, hearing each other's thoughts without speaking. The sadness of being alone as Tron had been alone, in life as well as in the death that had not after all been death, was terrible. But so was the fear, the pain he had brought to them, could bring again. To believe he was dead had been comforting. Now, Tron's violence once again threatened the tribe. Worse, all that the vision had shown could still occur.

"Zena," Lune whispered suddenly, and Menta thought she had never heard such anguish in a voice. "We must find her, before Tron does."

"Let us look for Tron first," Menta urged. "He could not have gone far."

Lune nodded. They sped back to the clearing to question Nevilar and organize a group to search.

"Speak, Nevilar. Tell us where Tron rests. He is not at the place of the dead."

"In my place of mating," Nevilar whispered.

"Take us there," Lune told her in the same uncompromising tone. Menta signaled to Krost and Tragar and some of the others to come as well, to continue the search if necessary.

"Hurry. We must hurry," Lune prodded.

Reluctantly, Nevilar began to run, but when they arrived at her glen, it was empty. The remains of the food Tron had eaten, his sour smell and patches of blood were there, but there was no sign of him, even when they scoured the bushes thoroughly.

"The tracks tell me he left many hours ago," Krost told Menta, following signs that were almost invisible to those not trained in tracking. "We can try to find him, but it will not be easy, after the rains we have had."

He was right. Just before the darkness was complete, he and those who had searched with him returned without Tron.

"We will go again tomorrow," Krost assured Lune, glancing at her agonized face. "We could not find him. His tracks disappear, and we could not find them again. He travels faster than I had expected of one so wounded."

Menta shook her head. "We must look for Zena instead," she told him. "I have spoken with Lune, with Bakan and the others. Now it is most important to find Zena. Conar has followed her, but he alone cannot protect her from Tron if Tron wishes revenge. She must be warned, but she must also be told that she has not killed. This is important for her to know."

"How shall we find her?" It was Katli speaking, and her gruff voice was dubious. She, better than most, knew how vast was the land around them.

"All of us must think hard, of anything Zena has said that might tell us. We must call on the Mother, too, in this time of need, to help us, give us the feeling of where she might be."

A small voice interrupted. "She might go to the mountains, I think. Once, I heard her speak to Conar of her dream."

The voice stopped abruptly as Lilan, Conar's small sister, put a hand over her mouth in consternation. She had followed Zena and Conar that day, hoping they would include her, but they had gone to Zena's special place instead. Soon after, Lilan had left, ashamed to be listening when they did not know she was near.

"I did not mean to follow," she said, her lips trembling. "It was just that I wanted so badly to have them take me to see the animals, so I could draw them as Conar does."

She looked hesitantly at the expectant faces. Lune rose and came to sit beside her.

"Tell us of this dream, Lilan," she said gently. "It is not good to follow without telling others; that is true. But still it is good that you heard of Zena's dream, for you might truly help us to find her."

"It was in the mountains, over there," Lilan responded, pointing to the west. "She said there were caves in the hills, and long tunnels, and that something waited for her there."

Lune frowned. This dream sounded strangely like Menta's vision. Could Lilan have mixed them up? But it also sounded like something Zena would say.

"It is good that you have told us this," she assured Lilan, so she would not be afraid to tell them more.

Menta, too, was surprised to hear of the dream that was so like her vision. Zena had not spoken of it. Perhaps she had been keeping it to herself until she understood it better. Zena always liked to think hard before she spoke. That was good, a sign of wisdom. Still, it was also good that Lilan had heard. Her knowledge might save them much time and worry. Unless, of course, Tron also knew of the dream.

"Did she tell others, do you think?"

Lilan shook her head. "I do not think so," she said slowly, her small face grave with the responsibility of trying to remember. "I think she said it was their secret."

Her lips trembled again. The burden of hearing another's secrets had weighed on her, and she felt better now that she had spoken. Still, it was hard to admit she had listened.

"The Mother Herself put you there, I think," Menta told her. "As Lune says, it is not good to listen without others knowing, and you must be careful not to do it again. But in this case, I believe the Mother was helping all of us through you. You should be proud to be so chosen."

Lilan's face lit up with the unexpected honor. "I will be very careful," she promised.

Menta nodded, certain this was true. Lilan was a lovely child, pure and unspoiled. Her drawings were remarkable for one so young.

"Let me hear what each thinks," Menta told the others. "It is very possible that Zena has gone to the mountains. I myself feel that it is so."

"I, too," Lune said, satisfied now that Lilan spoke the truth. The others nodded, agreeing. To go to a place of which she had dreamed, where something waited for her, sounded like Zena.

"Then we will go find her," Menta said simply. "Tomorrow, as soon as the light comes. Tonight, we will get ready."

"That is good," Bakan agreed. "It is time anyway to follow the herds, procure our meat for the winter before the snows are too deep. We can hunt as we travel."

"What of Tron?" Bly's voice was sad as she looked at her daughter, Pila. While Tron was dead, she had ceased to worry. Now, she was frightened again.

"Tron's fate is in the Mother's hands now," Menta replied. "But I do not believe he will linger here. He wishes to be far away from this place. And somehow, I do not think he looks for Zena, either. I have felt Zena struggling, but now I believe she is safe."

"Will we find enough animals for our winter food if we go west?" Katli still was not certain about the new plan. It seemed to her that it would be best to find Tron, make certain he did not harm anyone again. She had admired Zena for killing him. Sometimes, it was necessary to kill for the benefit of all. Still, she trusted Menta's judgment and would do whatever the tribe decided.

"I have seen many animals turn west along the river into the big valley," Tragar volunteered. "Bison are there, and reindeer, though I do not know if there are as many as in the plains to the north."

"We will find enough," Menta assured them. "I feel the Mother's hands in these events. Perhaps it is not only Zena for whom something waits in the mountains. Perhaps it is the Mother Herself who waits for all of us there, and it is Zena who leads us to Her. We shall go there and see."

II

The huge man peered out at Zena from his hiding place behind a rock. Despite his thick, heavily muscled frame, he could move as quickly and silently as the lions and tigers with whom he competed. Like them, he stalked the reindeer, even the bison, crept up upon them so he could plunge his spear into their thick hides. The others helped him, even the children. They had to. Many were needed to take an animal, and few were left in his tribe. Most of the women had died in childbirth or been stolen by the fierce hunters from the north, where they had once lived. All the men save himself and one other had died trying to defend the tribe from these savage people. He had led his people south to escape them, to escape the ever-increasing cold and snow as well, but now hunting threatened to kill still more. To hunt with so few was dangerous. All of them bore the scars. Yet they had to hunt, if they were to live.

He should be hunting now, but he was unable to repress his fascination with the slender woman, the one who could ride the bison. He had taken her to the man in the big cave when he had found her, for he had sensed they belonged together. There was meaning in their coming, he suspected, though he still did not know what the meaning might be. The strangers did not seem strong enough to be of much help. The man was as thin and undernourished as the woman, and all he had done in the time they had been here was scratch at the rocks within the cave. Still, he had helped the woman when she was too cold. That was in his favor. But neither of them would be much good at the hunt, of that he was certain.

He would continue to watch them, see what they did. Now, he must join the others. Soundlessly, he scrambled up the cliff face and disappeared among the rocks.

Zena looked up, alerted not by a sound, but by the feeling of a presence. She had felt it often in the months she had been in this place. Oddly, the presence did not frighten her. It did not feel the same as when Tron had watched from the tree. This presence was curious, not dangerous.

"Do you feel it?"

Conar was drawing, so absorbed that he hardly heard her question. "Feel what?" he asked.

"Someone watches," Zena answered. "Perhaps it is the one who carried me."

Conar grunted and went back to work. He had been drawing ever since the day Zena had arrived. He used the colors in the rocks, mixed them with water to make brown and orange and black, sometimes a reddish shade, to outline the shapes of bison on the rocks. Zena could see them easily now, as he had seen them even before he had created their forms. They leaped and soared across the walls of the cave, as graceful and strong in Conar's representation as they were in life.

They were beautiful, Zena thought, a wondrous gift to the bison, to the Mother, for leading her to the huge animals. They could not, however, be eaten, and at the moment, she was worried about food. So far, they had been lucky. They had been here for more than two moons, and only one snow had come. It had turned to rain, wild, torrential rain that had sent the river careening over its banks, had made her glad to be in a secure cave. Next time, though, only snow would fall and then there would be no more late fruit, no juicy grains, not even tubers, for the ground would be frozen and they would be unable to dig beneath it. Then, they had to have meat, and to get it they had to kill animals. She did not like killing, and Conar hated it, but they would have to do it anyway or they would starve.

Determinedly, she pulled on her fur boots and went outside, leaving Conar to his work. The boots were all that was left of a rabbit she had taken. It had sat perfectly still in front of her, when she was very hungry and cold, as if the Mother had told it to help her. She had thrown a stone hard and killed it. To do such a thing was almost impossible, and made her certain the Mother had helped. But the Mother could not make animals sit still every time she was hungry. She would have to get better at catching them.

She spotted some tunnels just above the ground, where rodents burrowed, and crouched beside them. When the earth rippled, she plunged her sharp stone against it. She was too late with her movement and the animal disappeared. She watched again, struck again, without success. After the third try, she sighed and gave up. There were still some nuts and a few wrinkled berries farther up the slope, and the grains of certain grasses swelled when she put water on them. Heated, they made a nourishing gruel. That would have to do for the moment.

She and Conar were eating the gruel the next afternoon when a grunting noise that sounded almost like a gasp of surprise brought them to their feet. At the entrance to the cave was a huge, pale-haired man. His chest, his arms and legs were almost twice as thick as Conar's, though he was not much taller. He was staring up at Conar's drawing. His hands reached out toward the flowing bison, as if in supplication, and an expression of profound awe covered his face.

He turned to look at Conar and nodded his head up and down, over and over again. Then his eyes moved to Zena's face. She saw worry in them, and again the supplication. He reached out a hand toward her, then swept the hand backward and pointed out at the hillside, as if he were urging her to go that way.

Hesitantly, Zena rose. "He wants me to come," she told Conar. "I think this is the one who carried me."

"He is very big," Conar objected, worried that the male would want Zena to stay with him, perhaps as a mate.

"I do not think he will harm us," Zena said firmly. "There is kindness in his face. I must see what he wants."

"Then I will come too," Conar said.

Zena touched the big man gently and curved her arms into a carrying position, then pointed to herself, as they followed him up the hill. His wide lips stretched into a smile of recognition and he nodded. Then the worry returned to his eyes. He uttered a few nasal sounds that had no meaning to Zena and pointed to her thigh, forming his hands into a smaller shape, as if describing a child. His face twisted, to show pain.

"Child hurts?" she asked, wondering if that was what he meant. Perhaps one of their children had been injured.

That she had guessed correctly was evident the moment she entered the shallow cave where her rescuer sheltered. A young girl lay on the ground near the fire. She was utterly still, and her face was waxen. Zena thought her already dead until she saw her chest rise and fall in rapid, shallow movements. Her small fists were clenched in pain, but she did not make a sound.

As Zena bent over her, the child's eyes opened. They were blue, bluer even than the sky, and the thick hair that fanned out around her face was yellow, like fields of grain in summer. Startled, Zena looked at the others in the cave. Another man, younger than the one who had carried her, had entered, and there were two women beside him. The belly of one was distended in pregnancy; the other was barely adult. Hiding behind their knees were two small boys. An aged woman crouched by the fire.

All of them except the old woman, whose hair was like snow, had the yellow hair, the intensely blue eyes. Coloring like this was unusual. In her tribe, only Lune and one or two others had light hair. But Lune's hair was paler, her eyes too, and she was small and slender. These people were big, much thicker than any in her tribe. Even the child's body was wide and sturdy.

The blue eyes were fastened on Zena's face. The girl did not seem surprised at her presence but only stared imploringly, with perfect trust, as if certain Zena could relieve her pain.

Why would she think such a thing? Zena frowned, trying to understand. Then she saw the cause of the child's distress, and all other thoughts disappeared. A deep gash ran all the way from the front of her thigh into her buttock. Angry red lines spread from the gash into her back, her belly.

Zena's heart sank. The wound was bad, and it had begun to fester. She was not sure anyone could fix such an injury. Lune had trained her, had taught her about the plants and herbs that helped healing, had showed her how to concentrate her mind, her energies, so that she could draw pain and sickness from another's body. Never before, though, had she tried to do these things by herself, without Lune to help her. To heal in this way took enormous strength, and most were not able to do it at all. Healing was a gift from the Mother, given only to a few. Lune had told her that.

She looked up at the expectant faces around her. Surely, one in their tribe was skilled in healing? But if that was so, why had they not put yarrow, or other plants that drew out poisons, on the wound? Was it possible they did not have this knowledge?

The two women, as sturdy as the males, though shorter, came up to her, and their gestures told her she was right in this guess too. They spread their hands wide in helplessness, as if to say there was nothing they could do. They must have tried to help and had failed, and now they wanted her to try.

The big man came close and gestured toward the wound. He tossed his head, then pointed to Conar and made motions with his hands as if drawing.

The bison. That was what he was trying to tell them, that a bison had gored the girl. How had such a thing happened, that a child was so close to the bison? And why did all of them seem to think she could heal such a wound? That they did was obvious. In all the watching faces, Zena saw the same trust she had seen in the child's eyes.

She closed her eyes, trying to summon the strength to live up to their trust. The big man had saved her life, had carried her to Conar. Now he wanted her to save the life of this child. It seemed an impossible task, but she must try, at least.

She called to Conar, and asked him to go back to their cave and bring the special basket she had made to hold medicinal plants and herbs. One of her first tasks had been to collect them before the snows came, and now she was glad she had been so determined. She breathed a message of thanks to Lune, that she had shared her vast knowledge of plants and herbs so faithfully, had worked so hard to explain how a healer's power could help the herbs to work.

Would she ever see Lune again, be comforted by her firm voice, her energetic presence? Sadness pressed against Zena, softening her resolve, and for a moment she wanted only the release of tears. She pushed the sadness firmly away. Now, she must think of nothing but the child.

"Water," she called out, gesturing as if to drink so they would understand. Lune had told her that it was important always to remove dirt from her hands before touching one in pain. The water was brought in a stone dish, and Zena wondered at it as she washed her hands. A bowl like that would be very useful.

Conar came with the herbs, breathing hard. Zena selected one for pain, the yarrow and lichen to rid the body of poison, and ground them with some fresh water in another bowl. She put an arm around the child's shoulder and urged her to drink. The medicines must work inside her body as well as on the wound. When the bowl was empty, she mixed up a potent poultice and smeared it gently all across the vicious gash.

The big blond people came closer, to see what she was doing. Apologetically, Zena gestured for them to move a little away. What came next was hardest of all, and she needed space to breathe. To heal, Lune had explained, a medicine woman could not rely on the herbs to do their work alone. She must draw out the poisons with her mind and body, absorb them into herself, then scatter them into the winds where they could do no more harm. After that, even though her body was still weak from the effort of drawing in the poison and forcibly ridding herself of it, she must summon the strength to give of her life force to the sick one. She must provide energy, vitality, through the power of her hands, power that came from the Mother, but which still had to be summoned by the healer, given freely to the one who suffered.

Slowly, Zena calmed her mind, opened it to the knowledge Lune had given her, opened it to the Mother, for it was She who would help most of all. When the calmness had spread to her breathing, even her belly, she moved her hands slowly across the child's body. She did not touch her, but only passed her hands just above the wound, along its length, along the angry red lines that splintered from it. Now she ceased to see the people around her, ceased to see even the cave, or Conar. She saw only the wound, the poisons that had entered the child's body through the terrible gash. They were real now, tiny bits of harmful matter that would wreak destruction if they could. She must fight them, draw them into her hands, scatter them to the winds. She felt their resistance, felt their power as they battled the healing herbs, struggled against the force of her concentration. She fought back with her own power, her will to heal. Over and over again, she passed her hands above the wound in long, slow strokes, to ease the pain, to force the poisons to submit.

The child sighed, and her face began to relax. Zena sighed with her, let her face go loose in the same way. She matched the child's breathing, felt air enter her own body in exactly the same way, leave her lips with the same small sound. Soon the pain entered her as well, and the poisons, for she had become the child, was attached to the child. Without conscious volition, she had ceased her stroking and had clasped the child's fingers tightly in her own, so they would be separate no longer. Now the poisons must battle her body, too, must kill her as well as the child if they were to succeed.

Slowly, Zena's hands grew warm, then hot as the poisons attacked her. She pulled them in, refused to let them go, though the tingling was terrible now, made her hands and even her arms feel as if they were on fire. Still, she pulled them in, held them harshly in her hands. When she had taken all she could hold, she let go of the child and lurched outside, to shake the poisons away, glad that the wind had risen and the night was dark, so they would scatter easily, be lost in the blackness. Then she returned and clasped the child's hands again.

Many more times, Zena drew out the poisons and shook them from her hands into the night sky. Only when the child's face was free of pain and the burning heat had gone from her body did she stop. But still there was work to be done, work that could last for hours, even days. Now she must give the child some of her own life force, for only that would make her well again.

Zena bowed her head and called on the Mother for strength. Her body felt weak, depleted of all reserves. She began to shake uncontrollably. Someone handed her a bowl filled with liquid, and urged her to drink. It was Conar, she thought, but she could not be sure. Her eyes still seemed to see nothing but the child and the wound and the need to heal.

The liquid settled warmly inside her. Her shaking stopped, and Zena was grateful. It was hard to be strong when her body shook. She closed her eyes and listened to her mind. It spoke of warm air and grasses, of the smell of ripe fruit and grains, the languorous heat of the sun. She felt it sink into her body, restore its vitality. And after that, she saw the bison, running in long, graceful leaps, saw herself astride the one she had ridden. The exhilaration came back, and the ecstasy. They filled her, even more fiercely than before, as she lived the ride, became one with the bison again. Her legs were strong, her arms and hands filled with power as she clung tightly, swayed in rhythm with the animal's powerful gallop.

Zena smiled, feeling strength flow into her body and mind. She would fill the child with this new energy, with the joy that came to her as she remembered the Mother's gifts of food and sun, remembered the wondrous aliveness of the bison, the exhilaration of her ride. This, surely, would make her well.

She placed her palms against the child's palms and wrapped her fingers around the small wrists, so the life force could spread easily up the inside of the girl's arm and into the rest of her body. Settling herself as comfortably as she could in this position, Zena pushed the strength the Mother had given her into the child. Slowly, as she watched, color began to return to the small face. Or perhaps it was the warmth of the sun, the taste of the fruit that Zena was imagining, or the wind in her face as she rode the bison, that pushed the warm blood from her hands into the girl's body and thence to her cheeks.

For hours, Zena sat there, all her energies focused on pushing the life force back into the child. And when she finally collapsed, not knowing she had moved, the child was sleeping peacefully. If there was pain in her body, none could see it; if there were poisons, they no longer showed in angry lines on her leg or in the heat of her body.

Gently, the big man laid Zena on a warm fur, though he was careful not to remove her hands from the child's. He had seen how she had given up her strength, passed it on to the girl he loved so dearly, and he did not want to break the bond between them.

He looked down at the sleeping pair. He had been right. There was magic in this woman. He had suspected it when he had seen her riding the bison, and now he knew it was true. He had told the others what he had seen, and they had agreed. A woman who could ride the fearful bison would surely have the power to heal the child they had hurt.

Her magic must be very strong, he realized, to have fixed the little one so quickly. If she had that much power, she might also be able to help when the time came for his mate to give birth. Perhaps now, this mate would not die as so many others had, when their infants had refused to be born.

The thin male must have magic, too, since he had made the bison come alive on the walls of the cave. His scratchings had not been so useless after all. With one hand alone, he had made the animals run and leap where all could see. If he had the power to do that, he would surely be able to tell the bison, maybe even the reindeer, to give up their lives more easily, without harming those who needed their meat.

Relieved, the big man lay down beside Zena. For the first time in many seasons, his mind was at peace. Now, all would be well with those who remained in his tribe. The two strangers had come to help them, just as he had thought. In return for their help, he would give them meat. Since both of them had power over the bison, the animals he hunted would surely cooperate, and the hunt would be less dangerous. Besides, now that he had seen the strangers more closely, he was certain they would not be able to get meat for themselves. They might have magic, but they still looked too weak and thin to hunt.

Yawning hugely, he closed his eyes. Already, the night was almost gone.

For a few hours the cave was quiet save for an occasional grunt, or the crackling of flames as someone stirred the fire. Then a ray of sunlight penetrated its east-facing entrance and shone directly into Zena's eyes. She sat abruptly, astonished to find herself in this place. She remembered how she had come here, but she had not realized a whole night had passed.

The child! She was no longer holding her hands, giving her strength. She had fallen asleep instead. Zena bent over the girl, terrified that she would be worse. But breath still moved in and out of her lips, and her color was good. Seeming to sense Zena's worried gaze, she opened her eyes. A smile creased her lips, then she closed her eyes and slept again.

Shivers of awe ran up Zena's spine. The brilliant eyes were free of pain, free of fever too. And when she examined the wound, she saw that the red streaks on the child's thigh and back were nearly gone.

She stared down at her hands, almost frightened at what they had done. They had healed the child. The Mother had given her the power to heal.

"Thank you, Great Mother," she breathed into the silent room. For a long time, she sat quietly, trying to absorb the magnitude of this precious gift.

The child stirred in her sleep, bringing her thoughts to the present. Zena bent over her, then she rose quietly. The girl was much better, but now she must eat, not heavy food like meat, but gruel, perhaps some fruit. She would get the food from her own cave before the others woke.

The slanted light dazzled her eyes as she stepped outside. She turned away from the glare and stood for a moment, feeling the sun heat her shoulders, pour energy into her body. The night's work had drained her. Lazily, she squinted along the length of the brilliant shaft of light. It shone directly into a crevice on the cliff across from her, seemed to widen it strangely.

Zena stared. The dream. This was her dream. The sun had reached into a slit and widened it. She had forgotten. That was what she had seen, just before she had walked with Conar through the labyrinthine passages beneath the earth, had come to the narrow cleft that led to the open space where something waited.

The entrance to the passages was here, in front of her. Zena turned to call for Conar, but he was already beside her. She grabbed his hand and pointed. Together, they scrambled up the short cliff and slid through the narrow opening.

CHAPTER
24

A trickle of water penetrated a crack in a rocky hillside, dissolving an infinitesimal quantity of lime. Years passed, and the trickle became a stream, then a river. More lime dissolved, and the crack continued to expand. Once too small to be seen, it became finally a gaping hole, big enough to swallow all the water.

The river poured into the waiting hole and disappeared. Now it attacked limestone beneath the surface to create deep caves and long, winding tunnels. As the land dried out, the river sank still lower, excavating new passages under the ones it had carved long ago. The tunnels above crashed into the ones below and suddenly there were immense chambers whose height was twice what it had been before. If the cave was close to the surface, light sometimes penetrated through chinks in the ceiling. Then, startlingly, a thin stream of sunlight, perhaps moonlight, shone brilliantly into an underground world that had known only darkness for thousands of years.

In deeper caves, moisture came through the chinks, and stalactites formed. Each time a drop of water fell, a particle of calcite was left behind. Drop by drop, the calcite accumulated, until a shimmering curtain of needles hung suspended from the ceiling. Drips from each needle fell to the floor below, leaving another bit of calcite. Each particle slid over the one before it, making it a little larger, like dribbles of sand that finally make a castle. The bulky structures rose slowly toward the graceful needles that had given them birth, and sometimes, if many centuries had passed, they met. Pillars formed then, long, shining pillars whose fragile tops rested gratefully on the sturdy layers below. In the perpetual darkness, none could see their beauty, but if light did fall upon them, they shone in a brilliant display of white lashed with all the colors of the rainbow.

It was at formations like these that Zena stared in wonder. Thousands upon thousands of slender needles hung from the ceiling above her head, glowing with color in the light of her torch. All around her were structures for which she could find no names, few comparisons. Never before had she seen anything like them. Some rose from the floor of the cave in thick, tuberlike shapes; others were like sticks, except they curved as no stick could curve without breaking. A few looked almost like trees that had been squashed, or planted upside down. Even the sides of the cave were covered with the formations. They spilled over each other, looking as if they would keep on spilling until they poured across her feet, but when she touched them, they were hard and cold, covered with a glistening layer of moisture.

She turned to look for Conar. He was staring in awe at the shining needles, at the bulbous shapes that rose to meet them. His flickering torch threw strange, dancing shadows across the formations, and they seemed suddenly to move. As she watched, his flare sputtered and went out. She looked critically at her own. It would not last much longer either. They must have been here longer than she had thought.

She hurried over to Conar, and they turned toward the narrow passage through which they had entered. Reluctant to leave, she took a last look at the magnificent cavern. It was too closed in to be the open space of which she had dreamed, but it was still the most extraordinary cave she had ever seen.

Deftly, she wriggled into the tunnel. Conar slid in behind her. She had taken only two steps when her torch went out. Immediately, the blackness was absolute. She could see nothing, not even her hand as it moved automatically in front of her face, to ward off the unknown threats darkness seemed always to bring. She could not see Conar, or the walls of the passages, or the floor beneath her feet.

"Zena!" Conar's voice reverberated strangely in the tight space. He reached toward her, feeling for her hand, so they would be connected. She grabbed it, glad she was not alone. Silently, they groped their way along. They could not see, but they could hear and feel and smell. Without their eyes, all their other senses were magnified. For the first time, Zena heard the soft, steady dripping of water, smelled the dankness of constant humidity, the faintly abrasive scent of wet rock. Her fingers registered the strange combination of stone so covered with moisture that it would have been slimy, but for the tiny granules that came away with her hands. She thought she could feel the darkness, too, as if the vast blackness of the night sky had come deep into the ground to embrace her. It filled her eyes, her ears and mouth, muffled her voice when she spoke, clung to her arms and legs as she moved.

Hours seemed to pass as they felt their way along the walls, crawled and scrambled through the maze of tunnels, trying vainly to remember how many turns they had taken when they had come. In the total darkness, nothing could be distinguished, not even memories of where they had walked before. Zena felt as if the blackness were closing in on her, pressing against her body and confusing her mind with its relentless pressure. Finally, she could not fight it any longer. She sank down heavily against the walls of the tunnel they were negotiating.

"We are lost," she said bluntly. "And we cannot wait for light to come, for light never comes to this place."

Conar nodded, then realized she could not see him. "Yes. We are lost," he agreed. "But surely, if we keep going, we will find the way out. These tunnels cannot go forever."

"We must think as we go," Zena responded, trying to give herself courage by making a plan. "We must think what each place feels like, if it seems deeper beneath the earth, or if it is dryer, and perhaps nearer the surface. When we first came into the tunnels, it was not so wet. Then we went down, I think. Now we must try always to go up."

The proposal restored her dwindling confidence, gave her the will to get up again. Just as she rose, something slithered across her feet. She screamed. The sound came back to her ears, went away again, and then returned, over and over, becoming fainter with each repetition.

"There must be snakes here," she said apologetically. "They frighten me when I cannot see, but at least it did not bite."

"I saw the thing that crawls in the big room," Conar reassured her. "It was like a snake, but it was small and harmless, I think."

Zena groped her way forward, trying hard to control her shaking legs. They shook not just because of the creature that had crawled across them, but from exhaustion and hunger. She had hardly slept or eaten last night, and once she had discovered the entrance to the caves, she had been too excited to think of food. They had stopped only long enough for her to take gruel to the child, for Conar to prepare their torches. Now she was paying for her foolishness.

"We are going down, I think," Conar said. "It gets wetter. I hear water below too."

Zena headed in the opposite direction. To restore her spirits, she began to make sounds, so she could listen to them bounce back like her scream. At first, the sounds were slow to return. They seemed to spread out hollowly before meeting another wall that sent them back. Then, as they rounded a long passage that curved to the left, the sounds returned faster, in a series of quick repetitions, as if the walls were close.

"The sounds!" she said excitedly. "We can tell from the sounds if we are in a big space or a small one."

"Perhaps it is true, but I do not know what good that will do," Conar objected.

"No. You are right." The excitement left Zena and with it went the last of her strength. She sank to the ground, too dispirited to go on. Conar dropped down beside her. His skin felt clammy against her shoulder, as if there were no heat left in him. She shivered convulsively. Maybe they would never get out of the tunnels. They could go in circles, and they would never know it. Or perhaps the passages just kept going, winding endlessly beneath the earth. Maybe she would never again see the sky, the leaves on the trees, or even Conar's face.

The depressing thoughts wandered around and around in Zena's mind, as twisted and confusing as the passages themselves.

"No!" Zena propped herself up. Beside her, she felt Conar jump at the suddenness of her word.

"We must not give up," she told him, and the sternness in her tone was for herself as much as him. "That is not right. The Mother Herself showed me these tunnels, and She does not expect me to lose myself in them. I must find my way out, so I can look again for the open space where She waits."

She pushed herself up and went on, making noises as she went. Perhaps Conar was right, and they would not help, but she could not think of anything else.

"Hoo," she called out, imitating the noise owls made when they hunted at night. The blackness made her think of owls, with their huge, wide eyes that could see in the dark.

The sound reverberated around them. The walls must be very close. Zena reached out and realized she could barely extend her arms. As she went on the width of the passage became smaller and smaller until she could barely squeeze through. Panic assaulted her, that she would be crushed, would not be able to turn around, go back again. And then she suddenly realized something.

"It is dry," she exclaimed. "The walls are dry, like the walls when we first came in."

She forced herself to go on despite the claustrophobic sense that she might never extricate herself from the ever-tightening space. Behind her, she heard Conar's rapid breathing. He, too, must be very frightened.

"Hoo," she called again, to distract them from their fear.

"Hoo," came an answer. Zena stopped abruptly. That was not her voice coming back. It was not Conar's voice, either.

"Hoo," she called again.

"Hoo," came the answering call.

Zena made the sound many times in a row. The sounds came back in the same way.

Conar clutched her arm. "Someone is in here," he gasped. "We must find the person."

"Who is there?" he called out. This time the response was different. Instead of the owl sound, they heard laughter.

"The children!" Zena exclaimed. "It must be the children." She moved forward as rapidly as she could, calling as she went. There was no answer, but she thought she heard the clatter of rocks as someone scrambled down the cliff. And then, as she turned the corner, there was light, blessed, brilliant light. It dazzled her eyes, made her shout with joy. She ran into it, weeping with the wonder of seeing again. Rubbing the tears away, she stared at the world around her as if she had never before seen plants and trees, or clouds in the sky. They were beautiful, magnificent. Never would she forget how wonderful they were.

Conar's face was as rapturous as her own. "The big cave was beautiful," he said fervently, "but this is even better."

The two little boys were at the bottom of the cliff, staring at them with awestruck eyes. They must have been playing up here, Zena realized with immense gratitude. But for their laughter, their imitations of her sound, she and Conar might never have found their way out. Next time, they must have flares that would last longer.

The two boys turned suddenly and ran back to their shelter, calling excitedly. Zena and Conar followed, curious to know what they were saying.

The shallow cave was imbued with warm, brilliant light. That must be why the Big People had settled here instead of in the larger cave she and Conar inhabited. Here, the morning sun would give heat that would last almost all day.

The big man looked up in wonderment as Zena and Conar entered. Was it possible that they had power over the rocks as well as the bison? The boys had told him the two strangers had been inside the cliff, making noises like owls, had emerged as if the rocks had opened for them. He would go look at this place for himself, to see if such a thing could be.

He came over to Zena and touched her forehead gently in a gesture of thanks. The others followed, their eyes filled with reverence. The man was powerful, but the woman had even more power, for she had healed the child as well as riding the bison and walking through the rocks.

Zena and Conar regarded each other uneasily. To be viewed with such awe was disconcerting. Perhaps if they could talk with each other, some of the strangeness would disappear.

Zena spoke in a friendly tone. "I am Zena. This is Conar," she said, pointing to herself and then to Conar.

"Gunor," the big man responded, pointing to himself. He pointed to the child. "Pulot." His voice had the strangely nasal sound Zena had noticed before, and the way he made sounds was unusual. Still, she would get used to it.

She went over to the child. "You feel better now, Pulot." The child giggled at the sound of her voice and watched curiously as Zena examined her. The red streaks were almost gone—the fever too. There would be no need now to watch over her all day. Zena was relieved. After the long night, the frightening experience in the tunnels, she wanted only to sleep.

The next day Gunor appeared with strips of meat and laid them by the fire. "I feed you," he said, gesturing to the meat, then to their mouths. "I good hunt." He ran a few steps, wooden spear in hand, and thrust it toward the bison, to show how he hunted.

"Thank you, Gunor," Zena replied, thrilled by his offer. Conar repeated her words with even greater sincerity. He hated the thought of killing the animals he adored, but he, too, had realized they could not live through the winter without meat.

Gunor nodded, gratified by their obvious appreciation. Zena followed him to his cave to check on Pulot. She was recovering nicely, though it would still be many days before she walked. And even then, she would limp. One of the boys limped, too, she had noticed. Many of them had scars as well, or bones that had not healed properly.

A few days later, she discovered the reason. She and Conar had climbed a hill in search of a type of nut that came very late in the season. They could not be eaten until they had been pounded and mixed with water, but they had a delicious taste then. Below them spread the valley she had traveled with the bison. A herd of reindeer was grazing there now.

"Look!" Conar called to her. Zena turned and saw the whole group of Big People, all but Pulot and the old woman, creeping up on a herd of reindeer. They were stalking them from all directions, trying to separate one or two animals from the others. One of the reindeer, a big, heavily antlered creature, spotted a child and turned on him, tossing its antlers and stamping. The boy leaped nimbly away. The second boy came closer, waving his arms and a short wooden spear. The two women followed and charged at the animal, to drive it in the direction of the waiting men. The reindeer bolted, almost trampling one of the men. He shoved his spear toward its belly, but it kicked furiously and ran off. The group began to stalk again.

Zena's breath left her lungs with an audible sound. "So that is how Pulot was wounded," she said, her voice heavy with awe at the child's courage. "Except they stalked the bison then.

"It is not surprising so many are wounded," she added. "They have courage, great courage, to go so close."

"They do not throw the spear," Conar objected. "Why do they not throw the spear instead?"

"Perhaps they do not know how. Or perhaps the spears are not sharp enough, and they must be close."

"We must look more carefully at them." Conar frowned, sorry now that he had so little knowledge of hunting. If he knew more, he could help the Big People find a less dangerous method. He had not hunted himself, but he was sure the hunters from his own tribe threw their spears before they came close for the kill.

Zena's words reflected his thoughts. "I wish now the others were here, so they could show the Big People how they hunt. They make the spears differently, and they do not need to go so close to persuade an animal to be killed."

She sighed heavily. There was another reason why she wished the others were here. Each full moon since she had banished herself had passed without any bleeding. Now a third month had come and gone, and she was sure. Finally, the Mother had given her a child, but instead of the joy she had expected to feel, there was only a pervasive feeling of wrongness, a terrible sadness that she could not speak of this to Lune, to Menta, to the others. It did not seem right to have an infant without a tribe to greet it.

Yells from below interrupted her musings. The hunters had succeeded in separating a young reindeer from the group. Killing it quickly, they dragged it into the bushes and began to cut it apart.

But now another threat appeared: a lion that had crouched unob-
served in the underbrush charged toward the group. The men continued to slash hunks of flesh from the reindeer, while the others
yelled loudly and waved their spears. The lion backed off, snarling.
Another lion crept up beside it. For a moment, the two massive
predators watched, and then they charged. This time, Zena saw,
they would not be stopped.

The men kept cutting until the last moment, then threw the meat
as far as they could into the bushes and ran after it. The women
snatched up the children and followed. Miraculously, the whole
group escaped. A few moments later, they started up the hillside,
lugging the meat. The two boys scampered ahead, laughing, seem-
ingly unconcerned by the dangers they had faced.

No wonder they are so strong and sturdy, Zena thought. *They must
have to hunt like this almost every day to get enough to eat.*

The Big People seemed to depend almost entirely on meat, she
had noticed. She had never seen them eating grains and tubers,
only a few berries. She might not be able to help with the hunt,
but she *could* help by showing them some of the other foods that
were available. Even when snow covered the ground, there were
always a few berries, even edible twigs.

As soon as they returned, she and Conar put together a basket
of various foods they had collected and took it to the Big People.
They accepted it with gratitude, but they looked surprised at the
contents.

Gunor tried to explain. He used his hands as much as words,
and Zena was able to grasp his meaning. Waving his arms to the
north, he shivered violently, then pointed to the grains and shook
his head. They had come from the north, his gestures said, where
it was very cold and there were no grains. He blew then, imitating
the wind, and showed the depths of the snow.

They must have traveled south to this place, to escape the snows,
Zena realized. Perhaps that was why the cold did not seem to
bother them. She and Conar needed furs stuffed with grasses for
their feet, and they had stitched together other furs given to them
by Gunor, so that they covered most of their bodies. The Big People
wore only a small fur slung around their waists, perhaps their
shoulders.

She shivered. The air might not seem cold to them, but it did to
her. Already, the frozen ground was covered with a thin blanket of
snow, and soon there would be more.

Zena's thought was more accurate than she knew. That night, a
massive snowstorm began. The white flakes fell all through the dark

hours, all through the day that followed. At first, they dropped slowly, as if part of a beautiful dance. Then the wind came bustling in from the north and blew the icy drops straight into their faces with savage intensity. She tried to go out, to look at Pulot, but the wind drove her back. Later, during a brief lull in the storm, she tried again. She had reached the hill above the cave when a figure suddenly loomed below her, almost invisible through the driving snow. Thinking it must be Gunor, she struggled toward him.

"Zena!" The sound was muffled by the snow, carried aloft by the howling wind, and reached her only faintly. But it was a man's voice, she was sure of that. She went closer, surprised that Gunor was using her name. He had not said it before.

The figure waved his arms, and she stared in confusion. He was not wide enough for Gunor, or any of the big people. But he must be one of them, for Conar was inside.

"Zena!" the call was louder now, and there was desperation in the voice. The figure fell and did not rise again.

II

Zena ran. Someone who knew her name was out there. But who could it be? She dismissed the question and concentrated on shoving one foot, then the next, through the deep snow. The figure was moving now, trying to get to his feet. He was big, not wide like Gunor, but tall like Krost and Tragar. Tron, too, had been big like that.

Tragar! It was Tragar! But what was he doing here? Zena bent over him, tried to help him rise.

"The others," he gasped. "The others are out there. They will die. . . ."

Zena stood perfectly still, unable to believe. The others—they had come! She was dizzy for a moment with the relief of it. Then she charged into action.

"Stay there," she yelled at Tragar. "I will get help."

Tragar nodded and slumped back into the snow. Zena ran, shoving her feet in and out of the depths until she thought her legs would give out beneath her. She ran on anyway.

Gunor's cave was in front of her now. She burst into it, calling. "Help!" she said urgently. "I need help!"

The big man came close to her, intent on understanding. She pointed outside and grabbed his arm. He nodded, and reached for some odd-looking contrivances made of curved sticks and vines and furs. He attached the objects to his feet and shuffled after her, calling out instructions to the others as he went.

Conar appeared on the hill, worried at Zena's long absence. "Tragar," she screamed at him through the wind. "The others!"

Tears pounded behind her eyes at the thought of them buried in the snow, freezing. She wiped them savagely away. She needed to see, not weep.

Tragar was standing when they reached him. He pointed down into a hollow, near the place where the big people had hunted. Zena stared through the blinding snow, trying to make out the forms. Were they really there?

Gunor made a sound of recognition and leaped down the slope. He did not sink in, Zena saw with astonishment, but stayed on top of the snow. His tribemates appeared with similar contraptions on their feet and lunged down behind him.

Zena followed as quickly as she could. Tragar lurched unsteadily after her. Conar did not bother to run but curled himself in a ball and rolled, as he had when he was a child. The technique worked, for he arrived before them.

"Conar!" Zena heard the voice, unsteady with joy. It was Lilan; she could tell even from here.

Another voice came, gruff and low. Katli! It was Katli speaking. "Take the children first," she told Conar. "Then Menta. She is the coldest of all, for she went in the river after a child."

And then she heard Lune. "Where is Zena? Have you found Zena? Is she with you?"

Zena plunged down the slope and wrapped her arms around her mother. Now she could not stop the tears. They poured down her cheeks, warm and comforting beneath the icy snow.

"Zena," Lune whispered. "Zena."

"Hurry," she said, releasing her hold. "We must get the others warm. They are cold, too cold. Only a few can still walk."

Zena grabbed one of the little ones. "Those who can walk, come after me," she shouted. "We will carry the others."

Already, she noticed, Gunor and the other male had a child under each arm and were struggling up the slope toward her cave. By the time she was halfway up, they had returned for more. Finally, they were all inside. As soon as they had brought in the last of the children, the Big People disappeared. She had not even thanked them, Zena realized.

She looked around her. The cave was suddenly, wonderfully, full of people, her people. With thirty of them inside, it no longer looked so big! But why were they here?

Zena thrust the question from her mind. All of them were cold and wet and exhausted, and she must help them first. She began to crush herbs for a tonic as fast as her hands could move. Already, Conar had built up the fire with deft hands, so she could warm the potent brew. She gave some to each child, then turned to examine Menta. The wise woman's eyes were closed, her breathing shallow. Zena looked questioningly at Lune.

"It was the river," Lune told her, her eyes tragic with remembrance. "It flooded its banks one night, when we were sleeping. The water rose very fast. It took one of Katli's sisters and her child before we even knew what was happening. Only Menta saw, and she went after them. But it was too late. We pulled Menta out, but already she was almost dead. Then the cold came, and we could not get her warm again."

Her voice faded and Krost took up the tale. "We could not cross the river, to come here as we wanted. It was too high. Instead, we had to follow it far to the north before we found a place to cross so we could come back again. When we reached these cliffs, we smelled your fire. But then the snow came, and for a long time, we could not find you. Only Tragar had the strength to keep searching."

"We have been traveling now for many moons," Bakan added. "More than two, I think. We did not mean to be so long." His words were sad but his furrowed face was wreathed in smiles that they were here, safely in a cave with Zena.

"But how did you know to come here?" Zena had not thought of this before, and there was such astonishment in her voice that some of the children began to laugh. The sound was wonderful to her ears.

Conar grinned and hugged his sister. "Lilan was the one who knew where to look," he reported proudly. "She heard you speak of your dream."

Lilan had not taken her eyes from Conar's face since she had entered the cave, but now she turned to Zena and spoke with great seriousness.

"I am sorry, Zena, to have listened. I meant no wrong."

"You have brought the others to us, Lilan," Zena replied fervently. "For that, I am grateful. All of us are grateful—the Mother too."

Menta gasped suddenly, and Zena's heart thudded with fear that she might be worse. Then she saw that the wise woman's eyes were open and she was staring up in wonder.

The bison. She was lying on her back, and the first thing she had seen were the bison on the ceiling.

The others followed her eyes, and they, too, gasped in astonishment. In the flickering firelight, the bison seemed to move across the cave walls in slow, measured leaps.

"Conar has made them," Zena explained, "to thank the bison. They saved my life, for I had lost my tools and furs in the river, and the bison kept me warm. After that, the big male saved me. He carried me to Conar, here in this cave."

A babble of excited questions broke out. Zena let Conar answer and concentrated on Menta. She rubbed her hands and feet as Conar had rubbed hers, and was gratified to see a spasm of pain cross Menta's face as sensation began to return. Her breathing seemed a little better too.

"The bison were in my dream," Menta said faintly, "but I did not know why. Surely," she added, and now her voice had more strength, "the Mother's ways can be strange—but always they are good. She has saved Zena, brought us to her."

"Tron has not come here?" Katli's gruff voice broke the momentary silence.

"Tron?" Zena frowned, not understanding. "Tron is dead."

"No, Zena. Tron is not dead." Lune came closer to look into Zena's eyes. "That is one reason we came. You did not kill Tron. He lives, though he is wounded. Nevilar saw him and then he disappeared. We feared he would try to find you. And it is important that you know you have not killed."

Relief flooded Zena. She felt it swell inside her, fill a place that had ached with remorse ever since Tron had dropped to the ground. She had not killed—after all, she had not killed.

The relief evaporated as quickly as it had come. In its place came a terrible feeling of responsibility. If Tron was still alive, he could still do harm. She had failed to teach him as the Mother had asked, and he had not changed. She was certain of it. There was a violence in Tron that could not be stopped. And that meant Menta's vision could still come true.

The pictures came back to her, as fresh and cruel as when Menta had related them, and she shuddered. Somehow, she must find another way to stop the violence.

The others were quiet, seeing the conflict on her face. There was little they could do to help. Then Lilan came up to Zena and patted her hand.

"I am glad, Zena, that Tron is not dead, because then we could come to be with you and Conar again."

"All of us are glad to be with you again," Nevilar said shyly. Nevilar's mother put a comforting hand on her arm as she spoke, Zena noticed. Perhaps her daughter's troubles had made her kinder.

"I am very glad, more glad than anyone could know, to see all of you," Zena replied softly, smiling at Nevilar. "And Lilan is right. It is good at least that all of us are together again. That is most important."

As always, she realized, she would have to digest the news about Tron slowly. In time, with the Mother's help, she would understand what she must do.

As soon as the storm was over, Bakan and Katli and the other hunters went to find Gunor, to show him their spears. They were eager to help the man who had saved Zena's life. She had told them how the Big People hunted, how Pulot had been wounded, and they wanted to prevent further injuries to the people in his tribe.

Gunor watched intently as they showed him how to throw the spear from the special launchers they made. He practiced for many days and could soon throw the spear farther than any of the others, for he was very broad and strong. In return, he showed them how to make the devices that kept him from sinking in the snow. Soon, everyone was using them. The two tribes began to hunt together, and as the weeks passed, their combined efforts became ever more successful. There were new furs for all from the many reindeer they took, and a good supply of meat was placed in a deep hole in the snow, where it would freeze. They celebrated together as well, to thank the Mother for Her generosity.

Best of all, Zena thought, the children no longer had to participate in the hunt. At first, the two boys had seemed to miss the excitement. Then they began to play with the other children, making balls of snow and throwing them at each other, sliding down the hills on old pieces of hide, and the restless look on their faces had disappeared.

Zena smiled contentedly. Now her only worry was Menta. Her feet had been badly frozen, and Zena wondered if she would ever recover fully or walk properly again. But if the terrible cold had damaged Menta's body, it had not damaged her spirit. She was indomitable still, eager to know all that had happened to Zena and Conar. Especially, she wanted to hear about the tunnels and caves beneath the earth. Zena tried to describe the magnificent cavern with needles, the darkness of the tunnels and the need for better light. She spoke, too, of her frustration that she still had not found the open place where the Mother waited.

"I, too, feel that the Mother waits for us in the caves," Menta told her. "When the time is right, She will show us the way. Until then, you must be patient."

Gunor appeared at the entrance to the cave, looking for Bakan and the other hunters. Zena jumped up to greet him.

"Bring Gunor to me," Menta asked Zena. "I would like to thank him again for all he and his tribe have done for you, for all of us, now that he can understand my words."

The two tribes had spent many hours in the past months learning each other's words so they could speak together. Now, they understood each other well, although Gunor and the others in his tribe still had trouble pronouncing some of their words.

Menta watched Gunor carefully as he came close. As Zena had said, there was great kindness in his face, but there was something else as well, a sadness, almost as if he was watching someone or something die.

"Your tribe has made it possible for us to hunt with less danger," Gunor replied when Menta had expressed her gratitude. "And Zena has saved the child. There is magic in her. Perhaps she can save my mate too."

"What is wrong with her?" Lune had overheard and was, as always, eager to understand anything that went wrong in a person.

Gunor tried to explain. "The infants cannot be born," he said sorrowfully. "They do not emerge, and the women die. Almost all have died."

Lune frowned. "How many moons until the infant comes?"

"It comes soon," Gunor answered. "Many moons have passed already, more than one full cycle of the seasons, I think."

Lune and Zena exchanged glances. That was a very long time for an infant to remain in the womb.

"I will try to help," Zena promised him. "Lune too. She knows far more of healing, especially of birth, than I do."

Gunor looked relieved and went off to join the others. But in the end, they could not help very much, except to relieve the young woman's pain when she struggled to give birth a few days later. By the time the infant finally emerged, her body had been battered beyond endurance. Blood flowed freely from a place deep inside her, and nothing would stop it. Before the baby had taken its first breath, she was dead.

At least the child will live, Zena thought. He seemed strong and healthy, and he was very big. Perhaps Bly could feed him. She had a baby almost ready to wean.

The arduous birth had not damaged his skull, as sometimes happened, she saw, examining the baby's head carefully. It was big and very hard, and the soft places that made birth easier were almost closed. If all the infants of the Big People had heads like that, it was not surprising they could not be born.

"There is a story of a time long ago," Lune told her, "far beyond the time of our memory, when many women died in childbirth. The infants lingered too long in the womb, and their skulls were big and thick, like this one. I did not believe the story, but perhaps it was true, and Gunor's people are still like this."

"That might be the reason why so many of their women have died," Zena agreed sadly. "Gunor said more than one full cycle of the seasons had passed. It must be very hard for him."

"We could not help," she told him miserably when he came to see what had happened, "except to ease her pain. I am sorry. But the baby lives at least."

He nodded and turned away hopelessly. No one could help with this, not even one like Zena, with magic in her hands. Something was wrong with the people of his tribe, that their babies could not be born, and no one could fix it. Soon, there would be no more of them, for how could a tribe live when all the women were dead? Without women, there could be no new life.

Strangely, it was Nevilar who comforted him. She had changed, Zena realized. Her time in the Ekali with the other women seemed to have softened her, but it had also given her a new kind of strength, as if for the first time she felt secure enough to give to others without taking from herself. Perhaps, too, she felt better about herself because her mother had become less critical.

Nevilar did not speak to Gunor, but instead placed her hand gently on his arm and sat with him for a long time. The big, sad man appealed to her, and she did not want to leave him alone in his misery. She helped him gather branches filled with withered berries, for there were no flowers, to place over the dead woman's body. It was their custom, he said, to bury their dead ones nearby, covered with blossoms. Now a hole in the snow and branches would have to do.

In the weeks that followed, Zena saw Nevilar walking with Gunor many times. When Nevilar confided that she had mated with him, Zena was not surprised. It seemed a good solution. There was only one other woman in Gunor's tribe, and she was hardly old enough to think of mating.

Zena sighed. She herself had never thought to mate with Gunor. But then, she seldom felt the desire for Akat now. Even with Conar, she did not enjoy it as she had before. Ever since Tron had forced himself on her, she had felt wrong somehow, as if her body were not her own. To describe how she felt was hard. She had tried to tell Conar, and he had been wonderfully gentle and caring, but she was not sure that anyone could truly understand, even one like Conar.

Perhaps it was because of Tron's attack that she still felt no joy about the infant within her, why she still had not spoken to Lune and Menta. She had thought to feel a flood of delight when she could finally tell them the Mother had given her a child, but instead the strange sense of wrongness was stronger than ever. It was as if Tron had left something of his violence deep within her belly, where the child also grew, that made her feel sadness about the new life instead of joy.

When she finally gathered her courage and spoke to Lune and Menta, she began to understand. No one else was in the cave, for it was a bright day, with clear sunshine. Many were hunting, the others were outside, enjoying the rare warmth.

Trying to sound cheerful and relaxed, Zena patted her belly. "The Mother has given me a little one," she said.

Lune and Menta traded glances, as they so often did. Their faces were apprehensive, not excited as Zena had expected. A flutter of fear passed through her chest.

"How many moons have passed?" her mother asked sharply.

"Five now, at least," Zena replied. "I suspected this soon after I arrived here, but now I am certain. I can feel the child."

Lune took a deep breath. "She must be told," she said to Menta. "We cannot keep the knowledge from her."

"Yes. You are right." Menta's face turned haggard as she spoke. It was an expression that came to her only when she was confronted by a grave problem, one that was hard even for her to resolve.

"What is this knowledge?" Zena asked hesitantly. There was a feeling inside her, deep and sure, that told her she did not want to know. She braced herself, as if for a blow.

It was Lune who explained. Seating herself across from Zena, she spoke slowly, choosing her words with care.

"Many years ago," she began, "I came across the knowledge as I watched the animals. I saw that the females only became swollen with young after they had mated, and then I understood that the males had given something of the life within to the females. I also saw, among the people, that some of the children took on the look of a particular man, just as part of its mother often shows in a child's features. Akat makes this possible, I realized, for during Akat the man passes something of himself to the woman who bears the child. I did not speak of this knowledge, for it seemed wrong to do so, though I did not understand why that should be.

"Menta saw these things, too, but in a different way. She saw the knowledge through her visions. She did not speak of it either, for the visions warned of great agony among the people if she broke her silence. The knowledge was forbidden, the Mother told her, because there were some who would abuse it, and all would suffer grievously as a result. But Menta saw the knowledge in my mind, as I saw it in hers. Always, we see this way, as you know. And so we spoke together, to think what we should do."

Lune stopped for a moment to gather her thoughts. Zena waited dumbly for the next words. She knew already what they would be. The knowledge had been in her for a long time, though she had not recognized it.

"As I watched over many years," Lune continued, "I saw that new life began more easily when Akat occurred midway between one bleeding and the next. That is why Menta and I brought the young women, like you and Nevilar, to the Ekali when the moon was only a sliver. We wished to give you more time, so you would be stronger, more able to bear a child and care for it."

A spasm of pain crossed Lune's face. To speak of the knowledge was easy, but to speak of what it meant to Zena was not. She had to force the next words from her throat.

"It was at this time that Tron stole into the Ekali and violated you," she finally whispered. "That is why I feared for you, and now what we feared has happened."

She could not go on, and Menta finished her words. "That is why you must have the knowledge, Zena, even when it brings pain. You must know what to expect."

Zena did not speak, could not speak. She felt as if someone had punched her hard in the chest, knocked all the air from her body. Of course these things were true. It was not the tree, the sacred figures, that made infants come, as she had persuaded herself. It was Akat, the Mother's gift, that made infants. And it was Tron who had made this one.

All of it made sense now, the feeling of wrongness, the sadness. She had been right. Tron had indeed left something of himself inside her, and now she must nurture it, struggle to bear it, help it to take its first breath. She must suckle it at her breast, watch it grow, be reminded, every day of her life, that Tron had violated her, that his violence had become part of her, that she would never rid herself of it.

Anger suffused her, broke through the wall of pain in her chest.

"No!" she screamed. "No! I will not have his child. Why should Tron be the one? I do not want anything of Tron in my body, in my child."

"All children are the Mother's," Menta reminded her gently. "That is why She fears this knowledge, because there will be some who will speak of a child as theirs, think that they, not the Mother, have given life. Then they will think they do not need the Mother. They will want Her power for themselves."

Zena did not wait to hear more. Ignoring Lune's restraining arm, she fled from the cave. She did not want to hear of the Mother, who had allowed this terrible thing to happen. She did not want to hear anything, except that the Mother would somehow take this burden from her.

Menta and Lune watched her go, their faces drawn with sorrow. "It does not seem fair," Lune said. "Always, it is Zena who suffers."

"Zena is strong," Menta replied somberly. "That is why the Mother chooses her. And perhaps through this challenge Zena will find a way to help us. Soon, all will have the knowledge, for it cannot be hidden forever. Most men will use it well, for to know that they also help to create new life will bring them closer to the Mother. But a few will not. These men will come to believe that they, not the Mother, own the earth and all that grows upon it. Then, the suffering will begin, and it is women who will suffer most of all."

CHAPTER
25

Tron closed his eyes and listened. He had found that if he pretended to sleep, the women talked as if he were not there. He had learned many things in this way. Still, there was much he did not know, though he had been in this place for almost three moons. At first, he had understood nothing, for the people who had found him had different words. But then, very slowly, their talk had begun to make sense. The children had helped, pointing out objects and people they had named, then testing Tron to see if he remembered. Tron had hidden his impatience at having to take lessons once again from children. He knew he had to learn the tribe's words if he wanted to understand the mystery involving Akat the women kept talking about. Besides, he liked the ways of this tribe, and he might want to stay among them.

Zena's lessons had been useful after all. These people had accepted him easily, for he knew how to make his face pleasant whenever he wanted. No one seemed to guess that beneath the façade, anger still boiled within him at Zena, at Menta and the others in his tribe who had wronged him. He had begun to wonder, though, if it was necessary to hide his anger. Everyone here seemed to admire violence. The men fought with each other, and shouted at the women, even hit them sometimes, in front of all the others. The first time he had seen this behavior, Tron had been astonished. But no one appeared to mind except one very old woman, and the men paid no attention to her remonstrations.

Still, he was wary of showing his true feelings until he knew more. The ways of this tribe were completely different than his own. Here, the man who was most strong and fierce, who was called Dagon, was clearly the leader. All the others listened carefully when he spoke and dared not disobey him. There was no talk of a wise one, no woman who could heal. These people did not even speak of the Mother, the Life-Giver. Tron had thought at first that they called Her Goddess, as those in his tribe sometimes did, but then he had realized they were instead speaking of one who was male. He was fierce, a good hunter, just as Dagon was fierce and a good hunter. The thought of a male god was strange to Tron, but he liked the idea, just as he liked the fact that the one who led the tribe was a man. Most appealing of all was the fact that the men, not the women, were in charge of Akat.

It was lucky these people, not others, had found him after the lion had attacked. He would rather be dead than live again in a tribe like his own. To be alone, though, was even better. Many changes of the seasons, ten at least, he thought, had passed since he had left the others, and for all that time he had traveled by himself, with only the animals for company. At first, he had barely survived. Someone had wounded him badly, though he still did not remember who it was, and he had been terribly weak. But he had made traps for small animals, had taken birds and eggs. As soon as he was strong enough, he had headed north, following the herds. He liked the bleakness of the northern tundra, liked the challenge of trying to kill a big animal by himself. Often, he could not, but there were always the traps if he failed.

He would have stayed alone but for the lion. For two full days, he had tracked a reindeer he had wounded. He was about to plunge his spear into its chest when the lion decided to claim it. After that, he remembered little until he had found himself lying in this hut, made of the skins and bones of animals. Dagon had told Tron they had rescued him only because he had battled the lion so fiercely, trying to defend his prize. The men had also admired his courage and his skill as a hunter, to take a reindeer by himself. Otherwise, they would have let the lion have him, for he was intruding on their territory. The meaning of this word, like many others, remained a mystery to Tron.

The men returned from the hunt. Immediately, the women stopped their chattering and went to serve them with food and water. One woman did not move fast enough for Dagon. He grasped her roughly by the arm.

"I am hungry, woman," he growled. "Remember that it is I who feed you. If you do not move faster, we will leave nothing for you."

The woman did not speak, but scurried off as fast as she could. She was old, Tron saw, and walking was hard for her.

Another woman, young and supple, came up to Dagon. To Tron's surprise, she sat down beside the fierce leader and took some of his food. Dagon did not object as Tron had expected, but instead put an affectionate arm around the girl.

He looked teasingly at Tron. "This one you shall have, Tron, when you are strong enough. You will need strength to handle her. She comes from my loins, and were she a boy, would follow me, for there is fierceness in her. But she is not, and so you shall have her, for I have seen that you are willing even to fight a lion."

Tron was confused. What could Dagon mean, that this girl had come from him? How could a man give life? He did not let his confusion show, but answered simply. He had discovered that if he said very little, the people here thought him wise and strong, and he could also hide all that he did not know.

"I thank you, Dagon," he said. "That will be good."

The other hunters, he noticed, did not look pleased at the fact that the girl, Veeta, would be given to him. Some of them glared at him openly. This, at least, he did understand, for he had witnessed the giving of a young woman twice already. Each man who had killed a big animal by himself was given a woman, as long as one was available. Some men had many women; others had only one, or none at all. To kill an animal alone took courage and skill.

It was Dagon who gave the women. He asked the man which one he desired, and if Dagon was in agreement, the woman was given. Her wishes were ignored. One girl, hardly old enough for Akat, had sobbed bitterly, Tron remembered. Some of the women had tried to comfort her, but the men had laughed at her misery, saying she would soon learn to enjoy what a man could give her.

"You may have to fight for this daughter of mine!" Dagon exclaimed, looking at the angry faces of the other men. He chuckled and cuffed the young woman lightly on the cheek.

Tron's confusion deepened. Women, not men, had daughters. He did not respond but only stared at the biggest of the other men until he dropped his eyes. Dagon watched approvingly.

"Get away from me now, Veeta," he said, cuffing her again. "You take too much of my meat. Go work with the other women, as you should."

"I do not wish to," Veeta pouted, but she rose obediently. As she passed Tron, she gave him a quick look of unconcealed ardor that made him grow hard with desire. Until now, he had been too weak to think seriously of Akat, for the lion had wounded him badly. Veeta had changed that. He would have her soon, even if he had to fight the other men.

The thought was exciting. Once a woman was given to a man, she had to obey him in all things, for he owned her. The idea had puzzled Tron at first, but he had come to understand that it meant the woman belonged to the man, as a spear did, or a fur, and he could do as he liked with her. Especially in Akat, she had to obey him, and he could force her if she refused to do as he asked.

From the look she had given him, force would not be needed with Veeta, and Tron was a little disappointed. Compelling a woman to have Akat satisfied a deep urge within him. To take a woman completely by surprise was even more exciting. He had done this many times as he traveled. Whenever he stayed near a tribe, he had watched and waited until one of the women was alone. Then he had crept up on her from behind and put a hand across her mouth, so her screams would not be heard, before pushing her to the ground. Some women were too terrified to scream anyway, but others were fighters. He liked them best.

Perhaps, when he was stronger, he would force one of the other women in Dagon's tribe. He had learned enough to know that while the women were not supposed to have Akat with any man except the one to whom they had been given, the men were admired for having Akat with many. A woman was beaten if she was discovered, but a man was seldom punished, even if he had taken another man's woman, or had used force. Tron grinned to himself. It was a strange system, but one that would suit him well.

Dagon came to him a few days later and asked if he was strong enough to fight. Tron saw the other men watching him, and he stood immediately, spear in hand. But it was not these men Dagon wanted him to fight. It was men from another tribe, who were killing reindeer in the area where Dagon and his tribe hunted.

This was the meaning of *territory*, Tron realized as he listened to the men speak of the battle to come. Part of the land around them seemed to belong to Dagon's tribe, just as a woman belonged to a man. If other men tried to hunt there, they must be killed.

The fight was short and unexciting, for the other hunters spotted them and fled. Dagon plunged his spear into the chest of a man who had been wounded and could not run fast, but the others escaped. They chased them for a time, but then snow began to fall and Dagon signaled that they should return.

Disappointed, the men began to boast of battles they had won in the past. Tron listened carefully, eager to understand these new ideas. Whenever they killed enough men from the other tribe, he gathered, they raided their dwelling place. Sometimes they killed the old people and any remaining men, but they did not kill the women. Instead, they forced Akat on them, then brought them back to join Dagon's tribe. There was always a need for new women, to be given to the hunters.

The fighting, the stealing of women, appealed to Tron. But most appealing of all was the idea of territory. Always, he had believed the land belonged to the Mother, that She had given it to all to use freely. Now he saw that men, not the Mother, owned the land, just as they owned women. The thought gladdened his heart, even as his anger grew. Menta and Zena and the others had lied to him about this, as they had lied about all else. There was no power in this Mother they spoke of so fervently. He had always suspected this was true, but now he was certain. Here, She did not even exist. To Tron, that was the greatest puzzle of all. If there was no Mother, how was it that the clearing teemed with young ones? Where did they come from, if there was no Mother to give them life?

Perhaps the god they spoke of was life-giver. But that seemed impossible. How could a male god give life? Only women could bear young. Akat was involved; that he knew from listening to the women. Tonight, Tron decided, he would get the answer. He would claim Veeta and mate with her. It would be easy enough to make her speak.

As darkness fell, he grabbed Veeta's arm and tried to pull her into the hut where he slept. She did not submit as he had expected. Instead, she shrieked and called loudly for Dagon.

"This stranger does not know how to proceed," she said angrily. "He cannot just drag me into a hut! No man can have a woman until she has been given. And I am your daughter, who deserves better treatment!"

Dagon strode toward them. "If you were not a stranger, I would kill you for this," he shouted at Tron. "I, the leader of this tribe, will tell you when you may have Veeta. She is my daughter, and better than the other women."

"I do not know your ways," Tron answered, keeping his voice pleasant. "Tell me what I must do. I would like to claim Veeta, and you have said I could have her."

"That is true," Dagon agreed, in a more conciliatory tone. "After the next hunt, when you prove again that you can kill a big animal, you may have her."

Tron waited impatiently for Dagon to announce a hunt. He would have liked to stalk an animal by himself, but Dagon said each man must make his kill while others watched, so no one could pretend by claiming an animal killed by a predator. In this, too, the big leader's word was law. The thought irritated Tron. He would prefer to be the one who made such decisions. One day, he decided, he would be.

Finally, Dagon announced that the time was right. Tron saw two of the other men watching him suspiciously as he prepared for the hunt. Dagon saw their looks too.

"These two will not fight you for Veeta," he told Tron jovially, "for they are her brothers. But should you wrong her, they will not forget."

Tron strode ahead, ignoring the looks. He would show them that he, Tron, was a better hunter than any, even Dagon. Within moments of reaching the herds, he had spotted a likely animal. An old male with massive antlers, it was feeding a little apart from the others. It had been weakened, he thought, in fights with other males.

He stole up on the old bull, making his breathing so quiet not even an animal could hear. Taken by surprise, the reindeer leaped in the wrong direction, and Tron was able to throw his spear into its neck. It staggered away, but Tron knew he had dealt it a mortal blow. He would not have to track this one for very long. When he caught up with it, the wounded animal struck out viciously with its feet and antlers. Tron waited until the worst of its thrashing had subsided, then he leaped in daringly and thrust his short spear into its chest. One of the hoofs caught him a glancing blow, but otherwise he was not injured.

"This Tron is indeed a good hunter," Dagon said admiringly. "To such a man, I willingly give my only daughter."

When they returned to the huts, he made his announcement to the tribe. "Tron the stranger may now have my daughter, Veeta," he told them.

"Let no other man have access to her," he instructed Tron, "so that she will bear your sons, and they can learn to hunt as you do."

He turned to Veeta. "It is time you had a man, and this will be a good one for you. Obey him in all things. That is my command. Take him now to your hut."

He turned away and called for food. Tron would have liked some food, too, for he was hungry after his battle with the reindeer, but he dared not disobey Dagon. And when he entered Veeta's hut, he saw that she had food and drink ready for him. She even had water, to bathe him.

Gently, she removed his furs and rubbed his body with a soft skin dipped in water. She handed him a drinking vessel cleverly made of an antler, and pieces of meat that had been cooked to tenderness on the fire.

"Is it all to your liking?" Veeta's eyes were teasing, but he saw that her hands were shaking a little. Perhaps Akat was new to her. Tron found that hard to believe, for she was surely old enough, but in this tribe, he supposed it was possible.

The thought excited him. He drew her against his body and kissed her lips, then her breasts. She moaned, and tried to pull away. He drew her closer instead, and when she struggled, he did not let her go. His movements seemed to excite her, even as she resisted. Slowly, he forced her to the floor of the cave. He saw her eyes then, eyes like a cat wanting a mate, but determined to struggle too. Pinning her arms over her head, he straddled her. She thrust her body up, trying to wriggle from his grasp. He pulled one of her hands down and placed it on his organ. It was rigid, rocklike, and she shuddered. He made her hand stroke it as he forced her legs apart with his knees.

She gasped and then, suddenly, her resistance disappeared. Her hands came around his back to pull him against her, and she thrust her hips at him urgently. Tron entered her, feeling the moistness, the tightness. She was good, this one, full of fire, like another he had taken, a long time ago, except that one had fought him fiercely. . . .

He shook his head to push the memory away. So often, it had started to become clear, then disappeared. He did not want it now.

Veeta's body began to shake, and she cried out. He watched her contorted face and smiled. He would be able to make her do whatever he wanted, as Nevilar had, for the pleasure he could give her. But this one was not soft and yielding like Nevilar. She was a fighter, and he liked that. He thrust into her hard and fast. Her eyes opened wide, her mouth too. She screamed, a shrill scream of pleasure that turned to a whimper of pain as Tron went deeper still. The sound pushed him over the brink of his passion and he exploded inside her.

Moments passed, then Veeta moved beneath him. "You are as fierce in mating as you are fierce in hunting," she said.

"You have mated many times?"

She shook her head indignantly. "I have not. I have waited for the one I wish to be the father of my child."

Tron tensed. This was the thing he wanted to know, but at the same time, he did not want to betray his ignorance.

"Tell me of this," he said cautiously, hoping to make her speak further.

"Well," she replied, "everyone knows that it is during mating that the man gives a child to the woman. But if a woman has many mates, no one can tell. Some of the women do that. But I will not," she concluded virtuously. "I will have only your child, for I will not mate with another."

Tron did not reply. Emotions and thoughts were whirling so fast he had hardly heard the rest of Veeta's words. Only the first had stuck in his head. The man gives a child to the woman. He, Tron, was giver of life, not the Mother. How they had fooled him, made fun of him!

He stared at Veeta. He could do anything he liked with her, with any woman, for he, not they, gave life. They were not better as they had always made him think. They were nothing without him. Rage filled him, that he had been fooled for so long. Well, he would get his own back now. He would be sure to give this one a life. He would mate with her over and over again until she could not move. The thought aroused him as he had never been aroused before. He felt his organ grow hard again, hard and long and angry.

Before Veeta could speak further, Tron flipped her over onto her belly and pulled her buttocks up so he could enter her from the back. This he preferred to any other form of Akat, for it was what the animals did. Veeta croaked with surprise, but he was inside her before she could move. In and out he went, as hard as he could, enjoying the fact that she was helpless, could not resist his heavy thrusting, which shoved her breasts, her face into the dirt. Then the pressure became too great, and after one final, lunging thrust, he exploded and fell across her body.

Veeta pulled away from him. She was shaking with rage, he saw, and he was surprised. Perhaps here, they did not perform Akat in that fashion. Nevilar had never minded. She had seemed to enjoy it. But Veeta was clearly very angry. Still, she belonged to him now and he could do as he wished.

"That is like the animals," Veeta hissed. "You cannot do that to me, the daughter of Dagon. Some other woman, perhaps, who has no place, can be treated as if she were no better than an animal, but no man can do that to me! My brothers will hear of this! My father too!"

"I can do as I like with you," Tron replied lazily, closing his eyes against her furious face.

A rustling sound made him open them again. Veeta stood above him clutching a rock. He grabbed her wrist, to prevent her from bringing it down on him, and as he made the gesture, he saw the memory again. But this time, instead of eluding him, it came clearly into focus: Zena—it had been Zena, the one who had fought so fiercely. He had forced himself on her in the Ekali, to get back at her, and then she had stood over him, as Veeta was standing over him.

It was Zena who had wounded him. The thought amazed Tron, that a woman could have inflicted such damage. But there was another recognition, one that grew and grew until even his hatred for Zena, his anger that Menta and the others had abused him, had told him lies, receded before it. Now there was only one thought in his mind. Zena could have his child—his child, not hers. It was his, and he would have it.

Tron paid little attention to the furious barrage of Veeta's words, to her threats. She would get her brothers to beat him, she screamed, for he had abused her, treated her as if she were an animal. She was not an animal. She was Veeta, Dagon's daughter, and she would not tolerate such abuse. He realized what she had said only when she ran from the hut and he heard excited voices outside. Then he moved fast. Stuffing some meat into his bag, he grabbed his furs and spears and crept silently toward a sparse growth of trees beyond the clearing. No one saw him enter the woods. It was fully dark now, and all the others were sitting around the fire deciding what they should do.

"Tron must be punished for this," he heard one of the men say. "To violate Dagon's daughter means revenge must be taken."

"I will gladly kill him," another man replied. "Tron may be a good hunter, but he does not belong in this tribe. He is not one of us."

The last voice came from one of Veeta's brothers, Tron thought. To kill a man for having Akal in that fashion seemed foolish to him, and he could not believe the man meant his words. But maybe a woman who was the leader's daughter was different. Perhaps he was not permitted to treat her like other women. Or perhaps they did not want a stranger in the tribe and would use this as an excuse to kill him. Well, he did not want to remain with these people anyway, nor did he want Veeta. She would bring nothing but trouble, and to be ruled by Dagon had become more irritating every day.

Silent as an animal, Tron slid through the dark trees. He did not think they would follow him for very long, but still, he would be careful to hide his tracks. He did not intend to let anyone kill him, not right now. He had something far more important to do. He had to find Zena. If she had his child, he would take it from her. It belonged to him, and he would have it, for he was the one who had given it life.

II

The child, Rofal, struck out sharply at his small sister as she jumped from a rock and stumbled into him by mistake. Zena took his hand and placed it firmly between her own.

"Look at me, Rofal," she commanded. The boy raised his eyes reluctantly.

"To hit is wrong," Zena told him. "To hit your own sister is doubly wrong. You should help to care for her, not hit her. She needs you to help her learn how to jump safely."

"I do not want to help her," the boy said stubbornly, and pulled his hand away.

Zena sighed and let him go. That this child had something of Tron in him had been obvious from the beginning. Ten summers had come and gone since his birth, and still he hit out at other children. Nothing she said or did seemed to help. Still, she must keep trying. She had failed to teach Tron how to care for others, but she was determined to teach Rofal. The Mother depended on her to succeed.

Only one child escaped his temper. Rofal never hit Sarila, the daughter of Nevilar and Gunor. She was a beautiful child, tall and slender, with long hair the color of sunlight. Young as he was, Rofal often stared at her with longing in his eyes, and if any other child tried to harm her, he rushed to her defense. She seemed to care for him as well, and often reached for his hand. Then he sighed with pleasure, as if his world were suddenly right, and his violent manner dropped away.

There was hope in his feeling for Sarila, Zena realized. He did know how to care. If she could help him to care for others in the same way, the part of him that had come from Tron would surely diminish over time.

She picked up her daughter, to comfort her. The child was staring at her brother with sad eyes, eyes that were remarkably wise for one so young. Even in infancy, the look of wisdom had been present. Menta had noticed it first. When the time for the naming ceremony had come, she had glanced back and forth between Zena and her baby daughter, momentarily puzzled, then her gaze had abruptly settled on Zena's face.

"We will call the child Zena, like yourself," she had announced, "for I feel the Mother within her."

Conar was in her too, Zena thought, looking at the child's dark curls, the small, lithe body that were so like his. Perhaps it was because of the deep love between herself and Conar that their daughter was so clearly of the Mother.

Everyone in the tribe now knew that men as well as women helped to create new life, for Menta had called a council soon after she and Lune had spoken to Zena. The knowledge could no longer be hidden, the Goddess had told her, for the time when all Her people would know was fast approaching.

Some had been surprised, but others had guessed already. Bakan had only smiled when Menta had spoken, and when Lune had asked him why, he had pointed to her pale hair, then to his own, to their light blue eyes that were exactly alike.

"I have known this for many years," he told them, "but I kept silent, fearing that some men might try to keep a woman for themselves, so that no other could be the one to pass on a part of himself to her young. Then we would forget that the purpose of Akat is pleasure, and to keep peace within the tribe."

"I knew this as well," Katli confided, "from watching the animals. Among the wolves, I can sometimes see the look of one male in the cubs. This is the male chosen by the female who is the leader of the pack. The other males accept her decision, and do not fight among themselves. Instead, they help to raise the young. But among the reindeer, the males fight constantly to mate with the females and keep them. I knew we did not wish to live that way, so I did not speak."

"This must not happen, that the men fight among themselves to be the one to mate," Krost added in his deep voice. "Akat must remain as it is, with the women deciding. But the women must be even more careful than before to include each man, lest the others become restless. Then there will be trouble even in a tribe as peaceful as this."

"It is best if we act as we always have before until we receive more guidance from the Mother," Menta agreed. "The knowledge itself is not bad, She has told me, but only the fact that some men could abuse it, like the men from the north Cunor has described."

Gunor nodded. "The people there do not know the Mother," he told them. "The men believe that they are the ones who make new life within the women, and they fight each other to keep a woman for themselves. They treat the women harshly, force Akat upon them and even beat them sometimes. It is not a good way to be."

Tron was a man like that, Zena realized suddenly. If he knew that Akat helped to create new life, he would fight others to be the one to mate, would force himself on women even more brutally than before. He might even come to believe that the young belonged to him, not to the Mother.

His face came before her, brutal and filled with satisfaction, as it had been after he had attacked her in the Ekali. She flinched and thrust the picture away. Tron could not hurt them now. More than ten cycles of the seasons had passed since he had left. Probably he was far away, perhaps even dead. But there were many like him, as Gunor said, men who knew nothing of love or compassion, who worshiped one as violent as themselves, who encouraged the men to rape and kill.

Images crowded into her mind, so fast and sudden she almost ceased to breathe. She saw men, savage men, forcing themselves on women, even young girls, over and over again. They would not stop no matter how the women cried out in pain. Zena watched in horror as the women's bellies grew big with young. They swelled before her eyes, and then, one by one, the women gave birth and cradled the infants tenderly in their arms. But as soon as the babies could walk, the men snatched them up and carried them screaming into the distance as the mothers wept in desperation. She heard the men shout words she could not understand, but still she knew their meaning.

"Mine!" they shouted. "The child is mine!"

Tears streamed down Zena's face. She shook her head hard, to rid herself of the images. They were horrifying beyond belief, and she did not want to see them.

Rofal was looking at her curiously, a worried frown on his face. Zena reached out and hugged him to her, and for once he did not object. She pulled the young Zena close as well. The child's round face was suffused with sorrow. Always, she had felt her mother's distress as if it were her own. It was as if they were one, she and her daughter.

Zena tried to smile, to reassure the children. It was not good for them to see her so upset. Perhaps she would take them to the caves, to distract them. They loved to creep among the tunnels, clinging always to her legs, lest they lose themselves in the maze. The caves would distract her as well, drive the terrifying images from her mind.

"How would you like to go into the caves, to see if we can find Conar and Lilan?" she asked them.

The children nodded eagerly, their unhappiness forgotten at the thought of such a treat. Zena grabbed some lamps and led them through the labyrinth of tunnels to the cave where Conar and Lilan were painting. Gunor had shown her how to make lamps of animal fat, with a wick of moss, in the stone bowls she had noticed so long ago, when Pulot was wounded. The lamps burned very slowly and lasted much longer than the flares they had used before. With them, they had been able to explore many of the dark passages and caverns that wound beneath the craggy cliffs.

The lamps also allowed Conar and Lilan to paint even in the darkest caves. Already, the drawings Conar had made in the big cave where they lived had begun to fade. If the bison were to live forever, as he had promised, Conar knew he must create their vivid forms in caverns deep within the earth, where neither sun nor rain nor smoke from fires could erase the flowing lines. In these protected places, water from above hardly penetrated, and the temperature never varied, even on the coldest days.

Zena watched as Conar and Lilan pressed the children's hands against the cave wall, then sprayed color around them through a thin reed, leaving a perfect handprint. The children adored this game, and wanted to cover every empty spot. Even Rofal was quiet and happy, and did not need her attention.

Taking advantage of her momentary freedom, Zena took a lamp and crawled through the narrow passage that led to the next cave. This was the Mother's home, and to be here for even a moment would help restore peace to her heart.

She and Conar had found the lofty cavern soon after the arrival of the rest of the tribe, as if the Mother had been delaying the discovery until that moment. The power of the magnificent chamber had leaped out at them as soon as they had entered, as strong and compelling as lightning from the sky. And when they had seen that the cave was shaped like a perfect circle of stones, they had known Menta was right. It was not only Zena for whom the Mother waited in the foothills. Here, in this sacred place, She waited for them all.

They had run to get the others. Zena smiled, remembering. Krost and Tragar had carried Menta as far as the narrow passage, for it was still hard for her to walk. Then Zena had led her, crawling, through the tunnel, had watched tears form in the wise woman's eyes when she had raised them to survey the wondrous chamber. For Menta, such a show of emotion was rare.

"This is the Mother's home, the place where She was born," she had said, her voice shaking with awe. "She honors us to bring us here."

She pointed to a smaller circle of rocks on one side of the cavernous space that Zena had not yet noticed.

"The Mother Herself has placed them there," Menta told her, and Zena saw that she was right. The big rocks were too large for any man or woman to move, and it did seem as if they had been placed there on purpose. The flat expanse of sandy soil they enclosed was just big enough to hold all the members of the tribe. Light from a narrow opening high in the rocks on the other side of the cave shone on the circular space, as if assuring them they were welcome there. The light sparkled on a small stream that ran through the middle of the cavern, shimmered across the opaque surface of a deep black pool that lay still as glass on the opposite side.

The others had entered after Menta, instinctively bowing their heads, then raising them to the arched ceiling, as they always did when they entered a circle of stones. This circle was especially sacred, for the Mother Herself had created it. In this place She was Goddess, full of power and energy, as well as Mother, with Her infinite compassion, and they came reverently into Her presence.

Zena sat quietly and felt the Mother's spirit fill her body and mind, erasing the terrifying images that had distressed her earlier. There was truth in them, she knew, but here in the Mother's home she was aware of nothing but the wondrous mystery of Her presence. Always, the spirit of the Goddess had been stronger in this place than any other, and now it was stronger still. Here, in the blessed circle of stones the Mother had created for them, Menta held the councils, performed the ceremonies for birth and death, for the killing of an animal or the coming of rain. As the rituals were performed over and over again, the voices raised, the minds opened to the Mother's ways, the power of the place had grown, until even the smallest child could feel its energy, like a vibrating pulse that rose from the sacred stone to enter their bodies. It seemed to attach them to the Goddess Herself as they spoke to Her and listened for Her voice.

Zena sighed. To have found this place, so filled with the Mother's spirit, was wonderful, but she still had not found the open space of her dream. Surely, one of the passages must lead to it, open onto the cliffs.

Voices interrupted Zena's absorption. Conar and Lilan were calling to say they would take the children with them when they went for food and water. Zena was glad. To have this opportunity to commune with the Mother was good. It was good, too, that she could once again feel joy in the Mother's presence. For a long time after she had discovered that Tron had helped to make the child within her, she had felt only the sense of wrongness, and a terrible restlessness that had made it almost impossible for her to listen to the Mother. Now, there was joy in her heart once again, and it was Conar who had helped her to get it back.

Warmth filled her as she remembered. One day, as she had grieved over the child not yet born, Conar had taken her hand and brought her with him to another place deep inside the earth, just beyond the huge cave filled with needles they had first found.

He had drawn her down beside him on a moss-covered patch of earth. There he had pulled all the wrongness from her body with his gentle, loving hands, had caressed her over and over until she felt herself flooded with life and joy. They had lingered so long that the stone lamps had sputtered and gone out, so that once again, they had to find their way through the tunnels in darkness. But by then, they had traversed them many times, and knew them so well they could laugh at their dilemma.

The pleasure of remembrance made Zena's body tingle. Akat in all its forms was surely the Mother's finest gift. And that day, they had experienced every form she could imagine, except perhaps Akate. But if lust was not there, all else was. At first, she had felt mostly Akatale in the tenderness of Conar's embrace. Slowly, this feeling had merged into the slow sensuousness of Akatelo, a sensuousness that grew until it was so intense they could hardly bear it, just as the glowing embers of a fire grew redder and redder until they burst into flames. Later, after they had rested, the sensations had swelled into the perfect ecstasy of Akatelelo, Akat so spiritual, so totally encompassing that anyone who had experienced it never forgot. Then, they had felt truly one with the Mother. And in the end, as they had laughed together in the darkness, there had been Akato, full of play and childlike wonder.

After that time, she had begun to live fully again, to trust that the Mother would show her the way. Conar had made this possible, Zena knew, but it was also Akat, especially Akatelelo, that had defeated the pain inside her, for then the Mother had entered her body, replacing the pain with joy.

The joy was still there. Zena felt it strong and warm, deep in her belly. It was as if the Mother had entered her again as she thought of her time with Conar. Never before had Zena felt Her presence so strongly. The Mother, the Goddess, was inside her, all around her. . . .

Zena stiffened. The Mother had something to tell her. Soon, She would speak, but this time She would not speak of violence. She wanted to speak of Akat, except it was not quite Akat, but something more than Akat, something even greater.

That was it! The Mother wished to speak of the new life that could come with Akat, if She willed it. She wanted Zena to think of this, to focus her mind on the miracle that brought new life to the tribe.

Zena settled her mind. There were many steps, all perfect and precise, in this act of creation. First, a man entered a woman through the strong, narrow passage she held so secretly between her legs. If a child should form, it lived for many moons in the dark comfort of its mother's womb. Zena saw it there, floating serenely in its watery home, listening to the sound of its mother's heartbeat, but seeing nothing except the darkness. She watched it grow; each day it was bigger, stronger, until finally it was too big, and it kicked and twisted, trying to find comfort in the confining space. Another moon passed, and now the infant was so big it could barely move at all. Only when its head was down, pressed against the mother's bones, could it fit in its cramped enclosure. It pushed and shoved against the hard bones that blocked its passage, as if aware that finally it must emerge.

She saw the infant begin to struggle, ready now to escape the warm, enclosing womb and emerge into the unknown world that lay beyond, but the passage was narrow, too narrow. The baby's head was squeezed and pummeled, but still it pushed, for there was no safety within any longer. The turmoil increased as the mother's body sought finally to expel the beloved burden. Contractions tore through the swollen belly; the mother writhed and twisted and moaned, desperate now to get the infant out, to hold it in her arms, feel it there, alive and warm against her breast.

Pain floated around the laboring mother, darted inside and made her scream. It churned deep in her belly, in the bones, the skin that had to stretch too far, but she pushed it away from her mind, just as she pushed the infant away from her body. If ever she let herself hold the pain, remember it, she would suffer always. She was woman, and the Mother had entrusted her with this task, the hard, compelling task of bringing an infant forth. It was fraught with danger, but she was woman, and she would do it. And when all went well and the infant emerged, strong and healthy, she knew she would feel a joy, an utter serenity, that came no other way. There was power, too, in this blessed act of creation, power that only a woman could know. Formed in the image of the Mother Herself, only woman could nurture new life within her body, feel an infant grow there and struggle to be born, know that it was her strength as well as the Mother's that allowed it to open its eyes for the first time to the light.

Zena looked up at the light streaming into the cave. It seemed to beckon her, as light must beckon a newborn babe. Her eyes traced the shimmering beam to the opening high in the rocks from whence it came. No member of the tribe had gone there, for there was no way to reach that side of the cave except through the deep black pool. This, they did not wish to touch. The pool was sacred, for it was the womb that had nurtured the Mother Herself. To disturb its dark serenity seemed a violation.

The light was shining on the center of the pool. Zena watched, entranced. It seemed to dance on the opaque surface, illuminating nothing beneath, only spreading out in a wide, luminous circle. She rose and went closer, mesmerized by the hazy, dancing light, by the softly glistening water. Perhaps, after all, the Mother wanted her to touch it, to feel its womblike fluidity. She knelt and placed her hand gently against the velvety blackness. Ripples formed where her fingers met the water. They shimmered away from her to the center of the pool, where the light waited.

She must go toward it, toward the light. Zena was sure of it now. The Mother wanted her to enter the sacred womb from which She Herself had emerged, wanted Zena to feel the power, the joy of the birth that had brought the Mother to them so long ago.

Gently, she put a foot into the black water. It was soft and warm, and smelled faintly of something familiar that she could not name. She placed her other foot beside the first. The ripples moved farther this time, drifting lazily toward the opposite side of the pool, toward the narrow shaft of brilliance that came from the outer world. It was a signal, she thought. The answer she wanted was there, beyond the pool, where the light came through.

She took another step, then another. Slowly, the water deepened around her. She felt no fear, only a kind of ecstasy. The dark water seemed to embrace her, as if it had been waiting for her. She smiled, loving the sensation of softness and comfort. Now she knew the smell. It was the scent of her own body, the fluids that came from her when she embraced a man in Akat.

The pool was the Mother's creation as well as Her womb, she realized suddenly. The Mother had been born of Herself, for She was all there was. She had created the deep black water even as it had nourished Her, had created the sacred chamber that was Her home. She had created everything they knew, the earth and skies and all that lay within them, even as they had given Her birth. Now she, Zena, must experience that birth. Like a child too big for its mother's body, she must struggle through the dark water, find her way out to the light. The Mother would speak through the light, and she must go there to hear Her voice.

The water lapped gently at her belly, her breasts. She went farther. Abruptly, there was nothing beneath her feet. For a moment, her mind flashed back to the time when she had crossed the river, and fear stiffened her limbs. But then she felt the water holding her, as if she were no more than a leaf that had dropped on its surface. She lay quietly and waited. Slowly, the water moved her into the center of the pool. The light bathed her face, made her blink in its brilliance. It seemed to examine her, ask if she were ready. And then it disappeared.

Suddenly, there was turbulence all around her. Ominous rumblings sounded deep within the pool, and an explosion of movement shoved her rudely in one direction, then another, as the water shifted and tumbled, oblivious to her presence. She was helpless against it. Now she was being squeezed, so that her limbs, her head, ached with the pressure. Slowly, relentlessly, the pool drew itself around her in an ever tighter embrace. It seemed not to be water now but to be solid, like the rocks.

She drew in a huge breath as the squeezing water that was as heavy as the rocks pulled her down, whirled her body over itself so that her head was facing toward the bottom of the pool. Down she went, down and down and down.

There was darkness, only darkness, smooth and black. It smothered her, but then she seemed gradually to spread out in it, so that she was huge, as encompassing as the darkness itself. A pinpoint of light appeared in the middle of the blackness and slowly expanded until the pool was saturated with strong, glowing light. The light entered her body, filled the cave, seemed to fill the whole earth.

And then she knew. She knew everything that had ever been known, everything that had ever been thought by those who had come before her, those who would come after. All of it was here, in the deep pool that was both dark and light, both water and rock, that held her gently and pummeled her into its depths. This sacred place that was the Mother's womb, the Mother's creation, was more even than that, just as the Mother Herself was more than life. The pool was wisdom, a vast reservoir of wisdom, deep and unending, like the Mother Herself.

She saw the earth, the waters, the moon and stars, the sun, the precious sun, moving in their spheres. They were one, even as they were separate; they moved together in endless rhythms that ordered the days, the nights, the storms and times of calm. Every leaf that ever fell, each massive tree or tiny insect or hungry animal was connected to the sun, the moon, the waters. Each star that lit the sky, each drop of rain that dampened the ground knew each other intimately, for they were one. Even the opposites were one: women and men, darkness and light, fluid and solid, the calm and the storm; they were all one, for they were nothing but movement, unceasing movement that was perfectly still even as it soared and swayed and danced.

The wisdom came to Zena through her eyes, her ears, her skin, and she drew it lovingly into her body, her heart and mind. It was hers now, an integral part of her being, and she knew it would never leave her. Complex and mysterious, it was infinitely simple in its oneness. Chaos—all was chaos even as it was as ordered as the movements of the sun. It was perfect; all was perfect.

As abruptly as it had seized her, the water let her go. It thrust her up in a great churning movement; she felt herself propelled across the pool, feared she would hit her head on the rocks beyond. Her hands reached out to soften the blow. They felt the rock, clung to it, as the water dropped her gently on a boulder. Light streamed into the cave again, the water was as still and dark as if nothing had ever happened.

Zena took a deep, calming breath. The light was above her now, directly above her. She was almost there.

Slowly, she pulled herself up the steeply layered rocks until she had reached the narrow opening that led to the outer world. She passed through it, hardly daring to look out. And then she could not look, for sunlight dazzled her eyes and she had to close them. When she opened them again, she gasped in recognition. Before her lay the open space high in the cliffs, the place where something waited. Finally, the Mother had shown her the way.

CHAPTER
26

Pulot burst into the clearing, her blue eyes gleaming with excitement. She had discovered something truly special for the children. They clustered around her, chattering excitedly.

Full-grown now, Pulot had young ones of her own, but she still loved to play like a child, and could keep the children entertained for hours at a time. She was a wonderful help, Zena thought to herself, responsible and caring, but so lively and eager too.

A wide grin split Pulot's flushed face. She stood still, struggling to bring her mouth back to its normal position. When the grin had disappeared, she lifted a slender reed to her lips and blew. A thin, breathy sound emerged. She blew harder, and a stronger sound pierced the air. The children clapped and jumped up and down, begging for a turn.

Delighted at their enthusiastic response, Pulot began to strut around the clearing, piping as she went. She did not see the look of horror that had suddenly crossed Menta's face, but Zena saw it and frowned. Why should Pulot's new game cause Menta such distress?

Lune rose and went to sit beside Menta. The fear was on her face, too, Zena saw. And then she remembered. It was the vision, Menta's vision, so long ago. She had almost forgotten. In the vision, there were people, people like themselves, sitting around a fire, and one of them was blowing on a reed, making a sound like the one Pulot was making. And after that had come the screams. . . .

Surely, though, the fact that Pulot had found a new way to entertain the children did not mean that Menta's vision would come
true. There had been no violence now in all the years since Tron
had left. Zena had to remind herself constantly of the mission the
Mother had entrusted to her, to keep the violence from coming. It
was hard to know how to do such a thing when there was no one
around who wished to harm them.

Lune voiced Zena's thoughts. "The reeds do not mean your vision
will come," she assured Menta. "It cannot be the same. The sound
you heard was beautiful. I remember you said so. This sound is
not beautiful."

That is certainly true, Zena thought, relieved that the shrill piping
was fading as Pulot led the children down the hill toward the
marshes where she had found the reed. But they quickly returned,
each holding one for themselves, and soon the clearing resounded
with piercing, discordant noises. Zena shooed them away and went
to join Menta and Lune.

"I have not seen any of Menta's vision on the cliffs," she told
them, trying to reassure herself as well as them. The fear in their
faces had startled her, forced her to confront the sense of uneasiness
that had plagued her recently. The feeling was so nebulous she
managed to ignore it most of the time, but it never disappeared
entirely.

"The Mother shows me many things there, but she has not spoken of violence," she added, almost defiantly. "She speaks instead
of the earth and its creatures, of the sky and sun and moon, shows
me how they are connected, how intricate is the web of Her
creation."

She had told Menta and Lune, and the others as well, of her
discovery of the open space. No one else had tried to go there.
Some were fearful of the black water, but they also believed that the
Mother meant only Zena to enter Her sacred womb. And perhaps it
was true, she reflected, for now the pool seemed to welcome her.
Never again had it buffeted her with its dark power. Instead, an
almost imperceptible current swept her across the glistening water
to the other side, so she could climb the steep rocks to the opening
that led to the light.

"The wisdom of the circles," Menta said, smiling faintly. "That
is what you have discovered, Zena. Always I have called it that,
for the Mother's thoughts can come from anywhere, from what has
passed long ago, from what happens each day, even from what has
never been. They are like a circle that has no beginning and no end,
but always the circle expands as all that happens, all the knowing

that comes from the Mother to our bodies and minds, gathers in the deep black pool of wisdom. It lies there, still and dark, waiting for us to seek its understanding. You will go there many times, and still there will be more to know.

"You are a wise one now, Zena," she added somberly. "The Goddess has made you a wise one by showing you the way to the open space, your Kyrie, where you will receive Her visions. Always, this must be a high place, so that if there is pain or violence in the Mother's revelations they cannot reach the earth but instead spew into the sky."

Zena sighed. "The visions can be hard," she said sadly. "Already, the Mother has sent one, though it was before I found the open space. In it, the men snatched children from their mothers' arms, and carried them away. There was pain in all their faces, and I did not see how I could help."

"You help by seeing what the Mother shows you," Menta replied. "A wise one helps her tribe and those who come after her when she opens herself to the visions and absorbs the pain. Only in that way can she hope to change what will come to pass.

"I am glad it is your turn now to be our wise one," she continued, "for I can no longer go as you do to a Kyrie to accept the visions and listen to the wisdom of the circles. My spirit stays strong, but my body grows weak, and even all Lune's powers of healing, and your own, cannot make me well."

The old woman's voice was pensive, and a frisson of fear skidded up Zena's spine. Perhaps Menta's health was the source of her feeling that something was wrong. How would any of them manage without Menta to guide them?

As if sensing Zena's fear, Lune grasped her sister's hand and held it tightly. "You may be weak in your legs, Menta," she stated firmly, "but as healer I can tell you that many seasons, still, will pass before you go again to the Mother."

Zena smiled, reassured by Lune's comment. Menta was far stronger than she looked. Still, her uneasiness persisted, became stronger than ever as spring turned into summer. To hold fear in her heart when the earth was so bountiful, the faces of those around her so tranquil, seemed wrong to Zena, and she often berated herself for failing to enjoy the Mother's abundance, Her time of special joy. The air was sweet and fragrant, wildflowers grew on the hillsides, and berries and fruits were plump and ripe, but the pervasive sense of impending wrongness did not go away.

Partly, she thought, it was Rofal who caused it. And that was truly strange, for Rofal was more at peace with himself than he had ever been. Fourteen summers had passed now since his birth, and there were few signs of the violent nature that had marred his earlier years. Akat, Zena realized, was responsible for some of the change. Rofal disappeared very often with Sarila, the daughter of Nevilar and Gunor, and Zena was sure they were mating. She did not ask; their private activities were not her concern, but she smiled inwardly, glad for both of them.

Akat, though, was not the only cause of Rofal's inner peace. The other cause was Pulot's discovery: the reeds that made piping noises. Unexpectedly, Rofal had adored the pipes from the first time he had heard them. He spent hours making holes in the reeds to create a variety of notes, then blowing into them, always with an expression of profound absorption on his face. The sounds he made were beautiful, so beautiful that everyone sat entranced as he played. That was why she worried.

As the days passed, her uneasiness escalated into a strong sense that something terrible was about to happen. She could hardly sleep or eat. Menta felt it, too, and Lune, but they did not speak of it. There was nothing they could do except wait.

Over and over again, Zena went to the Kyrie, seeking a message from the Goddess, but all that came to her was a feeling of wrongness, similar to the feeling she had had when she carried Rofal within her, but much stronger and sharper. She felt it like a wound in her belly, as if Rofal had been torn from her instead of coming forth in birth.

When the attack came, she was not surprised, though the horror of it still turned her heart to stone. That the events unfolded almost exactly as Menta had seen them did not surprise her either. She and Menta and Lune and a few others were sitting one evening around the fire, listening as Rofal played his reed. Most of the others were still in the valley below, gathering food, for in early summer the sun lingered long above the horizon. Rofal's beautiful sounds floated in the quiet air, soothing those who listened.

Suddenly, another sound pierced the air. A thin, high scream rang out and then there was the sound of weeping, low, anguished weeping. Sarila burst into the firelight and ran sobbing to her mother. Her long hair, the color of sunlight, was matted with dirt and twigs. Blood dripped from her face, ran down her legs.

Nevilar clasped her in her arms as recognition came slowly to her face. She had heard of this before, long ago: a young woman, tall and slender, had burst into the circle of firelight, weeping passionately.

"No," she breathed. "It cannot be."

Rofal sprang to his feet, his face abruptly drained of color. Someone had harmed Sarila, the one he cared for more than any other. Why had he not been there to protect her?

"What has happened, Sarila? What has hurt you?" He ran to her, tried to look into her face, but she buried it against her mother's chest.

"No," she cried out. "No one must touch me, not even you. He has frightened me, and I cannot bear it!"

Zena made her voice calm despite her pounding heart. "You must tell us, Sarila, so that we can help." She knew already what Sarila would say, but she must make sure.

Sarila shuddered. "I was near the path that leads to the Ekali," she blurted out, "when a man, a stranger, came up behind me and shoved me to the ground. He forced himself on me, and I could not get away. He cut my face with his flint knife—"

Her voice broke off as the sobs resumed. Zena met Nevilar's eyes, saw the horror in her own reflected there.

"I will kill him for this!" Rofal's voice, still light and youthful, was thick with rage.

Zena turned sharply, terrified by the change that had come over her son. Every vestige of the serenity that had marked his face only a moment ago had gone. Anger, harsh and uncompromising, had taken its place, but at the same time, he looked so young, so terribly vulnerable and untried. Soft, downy hairs showed above the lips that had curved so sweetly around his reed all summer long, and his youthful body looked fragile, not yet broadened into its full strength. Now the lips were taut and harsh, the body stiff with fury.

"I will kill him for this," Rofal repeated, and a deadly certainty invaded his tone. He ran toward the place where Sarila had emerged from the trees.

"No! You must not go alone," Zena shouted. "We must find the other men." But Rofal did not stop.

Lune grabbed the reed Rofal had been playing and blew into it with all her strength. A long, shrill whistle emerged.

"The others might hear," she explained. She ran to the top of the hill that overlooked the valley and blew again and again, long, discordant notes of alarm.

Her tactic worked, for in a few moments, the others began to lumber up the hill toward the clearing. Gunor arrived first, his face filled with apprehension. Conar and Krost were right behind him, after them came Katli and Pulot. The rest of the tribe straggled behind.

"Find the other women, especially the young ones," Zena instructed Katli and Pulot. "Someone has attacked Sarila.

"Go after Rofal," she said to the men. "Please, do not let Rofal find this man alone."

They understood immediately. Everyone knew of Rofal's devotion to Sarila, his desire to protect her from any hurt.

The men searched far into the night and most of the following day. Rofal insisted on going with them, but Zena asked Conar and Gunor to stay near him, so he would not find the intruder alone. But the man had hidden himself well, and they saw no sign of him. Perhaps, they reassured themselves, he had left the area, fearful of being discovered. Zena hoped this was true, but in her heart, she knew it was not.

"What can we do?" she asked Menta, desperate to prevent further agony.

Menta considered. To Zena's surprise, Menta had seemed to grow stronger, more determined, now that her vision was upon them. Zena had expected her to be devastated.

"Perhaps we can use my vision to our own ends," she answered, "instead of sitting here letting this man frighten us. While all of you were looking, Lune and I have been devising a plan."

She called Nevilar and Pulot to her. "Do you remember," she asked Nevilar, "how in my vision, two women were attacked next?"

Nevilar nodded. "You shall be one of them," Menta told her, "and Pulot will be the other. We wish to trap this man, and so we will leave two women alone, to see if he comes—but the men will be hidden nearby, to catch him. Are you willing to help us trap the man who violated Sarila?"

"In this, I will gladly help," Nevilar said firmly. She considered for a moment. "I will do it most eagerly if Gunor is not far away," she added, and now her voice trembled a little. "He is the strongest of all, and he cares for me more than any."

Pulot, too, was eager to help. Lune told her of Menta's vision and what they expected to occur. The thought of being attacked did not disconcert Pulot.

"If this man tries to violate me, he will be surprised," she stated, her bright blue eyes flashing. Despite her fear, Zena wanted to laugh. Almost as wide as she was tall, Pulot was a match for any man.

The next day, Pulot and Nevilar set off along the path Sarila had used when she was attacked. Pulot chattered cheerfully in her nasal voice even as her alert eyes took note of every movement in the shrubbery. Nevilar looked frightened but purposeful.

When they came to a small glen surrounded by bushes thick with berries, Pulot gestured that they should stop. It seemed a good place for a man to spring upon them from the concealing bushes, and there was a thick clump of trees nearby where Gunor and the other men could hide. The two women lingered there as the sun climbed slowly toward the middle of the sky, picking the juicy red berries and filling their baskets. Nevilar tried to eat some, but she was so nervous she found it hard to swallow.

She had bent over to catch a berry that had rolled to the ground when the man came up behind her. So quietly did he move that even Pulot did not hear him. His hand came over Nevilar's mouth and he forced her to the ground. Pressing her face hard against the earth, he pulled her arms behind her and began to tie her wrists together with a vine.

Pulot saw his movements then and sprang on his back, clawing and tearing at his skin like an angry cat. He turned, surprised, and Nevilar was able to twist from his grasp.

A cry of disbelief sprang from her lips. "Tron! You are Tron!"

Startled, Pulot stopped beating at him. Perhaps this was someone Nevilar knew, not the one who had attacked Sarila. But why, then, had he shoved Nevilar to the ground? She resumed her pummeling, but Tron knocked her away with a mighty heave. Pulot crouched, ready to spring again, but before she could move, Gunor charged from the trees and launched himself on Tron. He pulled the strange male away from Nevilar and slammed a massive fist into his face. Snarling, Tron lashed out with his flint knife. The knife tore a great slash in Gunor's arm. Momentarily stunned, he dropped to his knees.

The other men sprang forward. Holding his knife in front of him, Tron stepped back toward the trees. His eyes were fastened on the approaching men, and he did not see the slight figure hurtling toward him from behind. But Zena saw, and she gasped in horror. It was Rofal.

"You have violated Sarila, and I will kill you for that," Rofal screamed, slashing at Tron with a sharpened stone.

Then, all was confusion. Everyone sprinted toward the fighting pair. Zena ran with them, terror in her heart. Rofal was not supposed to be here; they had not told him of their plan, lest he try to fulfill his vow. And now the man was Tron!

Rofal jabbed wildly. Zena could see the fury in his face, the answering fury in Tron's. Tron would kill him, kill the child who had come from him! Already he had knocked the stone from Rofal's grasp, and his big, unforgiving hands were reaching for Rofal's throat.

"It is your son!" she screamed at Tron. "He is your son!"

Tron whirled at the sound of her voice, and as he turned, Rofal retrieved the sharp stone and plunged it deep into the big male's chest. Tron screamed and fell to the ground.

Gunor grabbed Rofal with his good arm and thrust him toward Pulot. Rofal was shivering now, stiff with shock at what he had done. Pulot held him tightly, so he could not escape, but still her arms were comforting.

Zena bent over Tron. His eyes were open, but there was a filmy glaze across them. He stared into her face.

"He is mine!" he said hoarsely. "He is mine, for I gave him life. I came to take him from you. I will take him from you still. . . ."

But Zena knew it was not true. Flecks of blood had appeared around Tron's lips, and already his skin was waxen. This time, he would not recover.

She called for water, a cool poultice for his brow. At least they could give him comfort as he died. She began to tell him of the son he had never known. Perhaps to know Rofal would have gentled him, pulled some of the violence from him, for then he would have seen the helplessness of a tiny child, seen how even a young man-child needed help. Perhaps it would have been so. She thought it must be true, for when Tron looked at her again, the challenge had left his eyes. He looked confused now, as if he could not understand.

"He has killed me," he said, so quietly only Zena heard. "I thought to take him with me, teach him how to hunt, how to . . ."

His voice faded. He sighed, a deep sigh that seemed to emerge from a place inside himself he had never known, just as he had never known his son. Zena held the big, hairy head in her arms and watched her tears fall on his dirt-streaked face. He had looked so brutal once, she thought. Now he only looked lost, lost and empty, as if nothing were left inside him.

II

They buried Tron with great care, as if to make up for their earlier neglect. Zena herself saw to the washing of his body, massaged his limbs with lavender and other soothing herbs, to bring him peace during his journey to the Mother. The others brought fragrant flowers and placed them gently across his big frame, covering the jagged scars left by tearing horns and sharp hoofs. Tron had killed many animals, but the creatures he had killed had left their marks upon him.

When they had laid him deep within the Mother's earth, they went to the circle of stones, to remember him and commend him to the Goddess, as they always did for one who had died. Each person tried hard to think of something good to say of Tron, hoping the Mother would take him back to Her heart and thereby change him, so the violence that had seemed to rule his life would die with him.

"Tron was braver than any in the hunt," Krost said. "He did not hesitate to come to my rescue when an animal had turned on me, or any of the others. Once, he saved Bakan when a bison charged him, by thrusting his spear into its chest."

The others were silent for a moment, thinking of Bakan, who had returned to the Mother a few years ago. He had been the oldest and most respected man in the tribe, and they missed his wise and patient presence.

"Perhaps we should have spoken more to Tron of our admiration for his hunting skills," Zena said finally. "Maybe then he would have felt better with himself."

"I think Tron never understood why he was not liked," Conar said quietly. "He tried to make us like him by acting strong, by becoming a good hunter, but all he did was make us afraid. We went away from him instead of coming closer."

"He liked to hurt, though," Lune said. "I could see it in his face. We must not make him better than he was because he is dead. Instead, we must try to understand why he acted as he did."

"It is true that Tron liked to hurt," Nevilar agreed, placing a protective arm around Sarila's shoulders. "Perhaps he learned that when I permitted him to hurt me."

"The desire to hurt was there already," Menta told her. "It was part of him from the very beginning, so you must not blame yourself. Nor is it Zena's fault that she could not change him. The badness was deeply ingrained in Tron long before she began. Even the Mother could not make it right."

"Perhaps he was born with this badness, just as an animal is sometimes born with the urge to kill others of its kind," Katli remarked. She opened her mouth to speak again, and closed it abruptly. Rofal was sitting across from her, his head bowed on his knees, and she did not wish to say what she believed, that animals born with this murderous urge sometimes passed the urge to the young they helped to create.

"The brutal men Gunor speaks of in the north cannot all be born with the desire to hurt," Tragar objected. "Some, at least, must learn it."

"Perhaps some are born with it, but many others must learn," Zena answered. "It is easy to imagine how that can happen in a tribe where those who fight are admired. Then, there is no one to teach the children that hurting others is wrong."

The others nodded, thinking of Rofal. Zena had insisted that each time he fought with another child, one of the adults must take him aside and speak of the need for kindness and caring between those who lived together. Their efforts had seemed useless then, for Rofal had just looked stubborn, but in the end, he had changed. The violence in him had seemed to disappear until the attack on Tron, and that they could understand.

Now, it had disappeared again. He was limp, without energy, and so withdrawn Zena wondered if he would ever speak again. She watched him carefully, lest he banish himself as she had so many years ago. But she did not think he had the strength. It was almost as if he had done the thing he had been born to do, and now all the vitality had drained from his body.

Was that, perhaps, the Mother's way? Perhaps those who forced Akat on a woman were doomed to die at the hands of the children whose lives resulted from their violence.

It was not over, she thought sadly. There was more violence to come. Even without Menta's vision, she knew it in her bones, her belly, in the feeling of wrongness that had not left her when Tron had died, but only dimmed a little.

The feeling diminished still more as the seasons passed with no sign of the violence she feared, though it never left her completely. Then, almost five years after Tron's death, it began to escalate again. One day, a white-haired woman stumbled into the clearing, a baby on each hip. A group of hungry children trailed behind her. Their tribe had been raided by a band of men, she told Zena. They had killed the men and the old ones, stolen the women. She and the children had been in the forest and had managed to escape. For many days, they had been walking, looking for another tribe with whom they could live.

Zena took them in gladly, but her heart was heavy with the news. It was only the beginning, she knew. More of the bands of men would come, then more, as Menta's vision had foreseen.

Gunor knew who they were. "These are the fierce hunters from the north who killed so many in my tribe," he warned Zena. "I know it is so, because that is how they act. They kill without thought, all but the women they want for their hunters."

"They come because of the cold," Katli added. "The animals they hunt are leaving and they follow. Gunor and I saw this when we tried to go north to hunt."

She was right. Slowly, inexorably, the cold had extended its grip. Blankets of ice that never melted covered what had once been tundra; vast stretches of forest had become barren snow fields where the wind howled and only stunted bushes could grow. As the air grew ever more frigid, the ice thicker, the huge herds of reindeer and bison traveled slowly south, seeking forage. With them came the tribes that preyed on them, the fierce hunters Gunor had known so long ago. They sought fertile valleys where game was plentiful, warm caves for the long winters, women for their hunters. The home beneath the craggy cliffs Zena and Conar had discovered so long ago had everything they needed.

Anger boiled in Zena's chest at the thought that these savage men, who knew nothing of the Goddess, might desecrate Her home, the sacred circle She Herself had built. She would keep it from them, she vowed, for as long as she possibly could.

The anger dissipated as quickly as it had come. They could not defend the caves against men like this. As Menta's vision had shown, they were brutal beyond belief. They were young, some hardly more than boys, for the hunters sent the young men ahead to scout for new homes for their tribes. Alone and leaderless, they were more savage even than the men who spawned them. Killing was no more than a game to them, Akat only a way to hurt.

They might not be able to fight them, Zena decided, but they could hide from them. The Mother had given them the caves, and they would make good use of Her gift. One day, perhaps, they would have to leave, but she was not ready to give up yet.

"We must be ready, in case the men should ever come here," she told the others. "To fight them is impossible, but the Mother has given us the caves in which to hide. There, we will be safe, but we must learn to enter without being seen, learn to go through the passages without light, so the men cannot follow."

They covered the cleft that led to the caves with brush and rock, so that no one who did not know it was there could find it. Each day for many weeks, they practiced darting unseen through the trees to the tunnels, gliding silently through the dark, winding passages until they came to the Mother's chamber, where finally they could see. Soon, every child, even the smallest, knew the way. After that, they collected food, as well as extra furs and tools, to keep in the chamber in case they were needed.

Conar became their scout. Sometimes he was gone for many weeks as he tracked the roving bands of men—the men with knives, they called them, for their flints were long and sharp. Each time he left, Zena suffered agonies of fear lest he be killed. But Conar could move like an animal, without ever being seen, and he always returned.

"The men with knives are heading north to join their tribes for the winter," he reported with satisfaction when he came to join them in the Mother's chamber after his latest foray. "There will be no more raids now."

"They will come back when the snow melts," Zena replied grimly. "Then the killing will begin again."

The young Zena came to stand before her mother. "Why must the men kill?" she asked, her eyes filled with bewilderment. "Surely the Mother provides enough food and caves for all. The men do not need to kill to get them."

Anguish showed in Zena's face as she tried to find words to answer her daughter's question. To speak of violence to one so innocent seemed a desecration. Only six years had passed since the young Zena's birth, and until the men with knives had come south, she had known nothing but peace and kindness.

The child looked up, waiting for an answer. Her face was grave, her eyes wise beyond her years. Zena's courage returned. As Menta had seen, this daughter was of the Mother. Almost as soon as she had words, visions had begun to come to her. And if she was to survive in the years to come, she must understand.

"It may be that they kill because they have come to love violence in the same way we love the Mother," she began slowly. "That sounds impossible, I know, but it can be true when people have forgotten the Goddess. You see, my child, there lurks in some of us a terrible capacity for violence, which only the Mother and the wise ones can control. Young men especially can fall prey to it. There is a fluid inside them that makes it so. When people like this worship one who encourages violence, they come to believe it is right. Then all is lost, for children who have never known kindness are capable of great brutality when they are grown. We have seen that in the men with knives."

Zena knelt and looked deeply into her daughter's eyes. "Remember what I have told you, my child, for one day you will take my place. It is the sacred task of all those who bear the name of Zena to serve the Goddess and teach Her ways."

The young Zena nodded. "I will not forget," she promised.

"I am certain you will not," Zena responded, hugging her warmly. "One day, when you are older, I will bring you with me to the Kyrie, so that the Goddess Herself may teach you. But now I must go by myself, to learn if there is more we can do to keep the violence from coming."

Slowly, she rose and approached the ledge where they kept the big figure of the Goddess. Conar and Lilan had carved it of stone, so that neither time nor weather could destroy it.

Zena spoke directly to Her. "Great Goddess, the men with knives have brought such pain to so many people. Unless they can be stopped, they will cause untold suffering. It is to me, Great Mother, that You entrusted the task of preventing the violence that threatens to overwhelm us. Show me now how this can be done."

Zena bowed her head, waiting. The Mother's presence was all around her, warm and encompassing. The others felt Her, too, and they sat quietly. For a long time, the cave was utterly silent, save for a baby's cry. Its mother put it to her breast and silence came again.

Light tickled Zena's eyes. She raised them and saw that the sun shone straight on the face of the Goddess, making Her seem to come alive. That was the signal. She knew it absolutely. Once again, the Goddess waited for her in the open space.

The others watched, mesmerized, as she approached the pool and stepped into the dark water. It seemed to pull around her as she floated slowly to the other side, then it released her onto the rocks. She climbed higher and higher, until she disappeared. They sighed, a long, collective sigh of hope.

III

The space opened out before Zena, vast and beautiful. She clung for a moment to the opening that led to the circle of stones, seeking its reassurance. Then she stepped forward and let her eyes rove over the vastness of the Mother's earth. She saw the cave where they lived, no bigger than a dark hole from her precipitous perch, and the valley where the bison had carried her to Conar. They were back again now, their shaggy bodies transformed into tiny moving dots that showed black against the lush green of the valley. Beyond were the mountains, their snow-covered peaks gleaming in the sunlight. Zena thought sometimes she could see all the way to the end of the Mother's earth from her Kyrie, for in the far distance there was only space, as if the land had given way to nothingness.

She was utterly protected here. One side of the crescent-shaped ledge on which she stood was enclosed in the curve of the hill, but the other sides dropped away in sheer, overhanging cliffs, impossible to climb. Above her, too, were impassable peaks that rose straight up as far as she could see. The goats could come, though. Their hoofs seemed to stick even to the most precipitous rocks. Zena reached out a hand to the one that clattered toward her. it was white as snow, and had elegant curving horns. The goat tossed them gently, then nuzzled her hand. Many times before, it had come to greet her when she stood upon the ledge. She welcomed its presence, for it seemed to her that the goat held the Mother's wisdom in its deep black eyes. They were like the pool, opaque and fathomless. When she stared into them, the visions unfolded before her.

Even before she was ready, before she had steadied her mind and body, the visions came hurtling toward her. There was no slow unfolding this time, but instead a barrage of images, full of turbulence and confusion. She saw an ant scurrying along the forest floor. She seemed to shrink, enter its body, so that she was the ant. A bird swooped down from the sky and grabbed the ant in its sharp beak. The movement was so fast she felt no fear. There was an instant of searing pain, gone almost before she registered its presence, then a strange sense of peace. She was part of the bird now, and as she perched on a limb, a shadow passed above her. Talons enclosed her flesh; again there was the instant of pain and then the peace.

Faster and faster the images came; she felt herself growing, stretching, galloping across the plains, kicking up her heels at the joy of being there. The lion came, and she ran and ran, but soon she felt the claws, the tearing teeth and then again the peace, and understanding flooded her body. They were all one, the ant and the birds, prey and predator. They were the cycle, the Mother's cycle of life.

The animals became themselves again, each distinct and separate. Zena saw them on a web now, a huge, circular web with many strands. It was colored like a rainbow, so beautiful to gaze upon that tears came to her eyes. Animals grazed and ran within it, birds flew and insects crawled; there were trees and plants and fish as well, and people wandering slowly through the meadows and forests. Sunlight shone down upon the web, then moonlight, so that the brilliant strands turned pale. But then clouds began to form; they grew huge and black and forbidding. A storm battered the web, and Zena thought it must break in the fierce winds, the blinding rains, for the strands seemed thin as gossamer. But like spider's silk, the web was stronger than it looked. It stretched and swayed and stretched again, but it did not break.

A hand reached out, the hand of a man. The hand formed a fist. Zena gasped in horror, for the fist was moving toward the center of the web.

The fist hit, and a dull sound reverberated through the air. The web pulled back in a great arc, farther and farther, and then, slowly, it returned to its former shape. One strand had broken, Zena saw, but the others were intact, and she breathed a sigh of relief. But then she gasped again in horror, for the fist was not satisfied, and it hit again and again and again, and soon there were broken strands hanging from all sides of the brilliant web. They were covered with blood and fur and feathers and mutilated bodies. Zena shrank from the sight.

"That is the difference," she heard the Goddess tell her, and Her voice came from everywhere. It was in the air, in the rocks, the trees below, in Zena's body. The voice rose and fell, rose and fell again. Sometimes it came to Zena's ears as harshly as winter winds shrieking around the protesting cliffs; sometimes it was as soft as the whispering cadence of misty rain on grasses and leaves.

"There is no violence in taking food as it is needed," the Goddess began, "for that is the Mother's way. But to kill for no reason cannot be forgiven. Only that can pull the web to pieces, the beautiful, vital web of My creation. Over and over again, the earth, the waters and the skies can cleanse themselves, renew themselves, but in the end, the web of their intertwined lives will die, as everything dies, if its wounds are too great. Then, even I, Goddess and Mother, cannot make it well.

"That is what I have come to tell you. You, and all those who live by the Mother's ways, must become the guardians of My world. Long ago, all people knew the Mother, but many now have forgotten. Their numbers are growing; soon, they will spread across the earth, and with them will come violence, untold violence. Strength cannot stop them, nor even sharp knives, for their violence will be directed not just at others but at the web of life itself. Just as they believe that they, not the Mother, create life within the women, and own that life, so they will come to believe that they own the land and all that lives upon it, that they may do as they like with the Mother's creatures, with the earth itself."

The voice faded. Zena huddled against the earth, afraid and vulnerable. She did not want to hear more. But the words came again, low and intense, and Zena felt her body tremble against the impact of the thoughts they expressed.

"There will come a time of imbalance, when the dark will blot out the light, when the strong will brutalize the weak, when men will rule over women, force Akat upon them and make them bear young they cannot feed. In all that I have created, there has been a balance, between strength and weakness, between predator and prey, between that which is female and male, between the coming of new life and the resources to nurture that life, between the joy of birth and the release of death. But when the Mother's ways are lost, the balance will die with them. So terrible will be the imbalance that the earth will no longer be able to renew itself but will strangle in its own decay. All of you to whom I have given life will be trapped in a chaos of your own making."

Zena was weeping now, and the voice seemed to soften. It soothed her like the murmur of a stream, or the whir of a dragonfly's wings. As she listened, some of the agony left her body, for she saw that despite the violence, there was hope.

"All that I have shown you will come to pass," the Goddess told her, "but there is much you can do to prepare. You cannot keep the violence from coming, but you can still help to save the Mother's world. Listen now as I tell you how this can be done.

"Once before, I asked you to try to teach the Mother's ways, the ways of love and compassion, to one with violence in his heart. Now your task is far greater: to keep the Mother's ways alive as violence spreads across the earth. The time will come when you can no longer speak freely of the Mother, for the name of the Goddess will be forbidden. Then, the wisdom of the circles will be no more than a distant memory, and no one will remember that I, the Goddess, gave Akat to the women, that once My people lived in peace. But you will remember; even in death you will remember. That is your sacred task, the sacred task of all those who come after you who bear the name of Zena: to hold My secrets, all that I have taught you, so close in your heart that even death cannot dislodge them.

"The task will be long and harsh, and none will blame you and those who follow if you falter. Year after year, even when you are shunned and persecuted and killed, you must pass the knowledge from mother to daughter, over and over again. Sometimes you will not even know that the one you worship is called Mother. You will know only that a deep and fervent love for something you cannot name lies deep within you, that it is wrong to despoil the land, the waters, to take from those who are weak and watch some starve while others feast. For your beliefs, your courageous acts, you will be persecuted anew, but no matter how painful the torture, how great your agony to be alone, cast out of human groups or condemned never to see the light of day again, you will know you cannot be other than you are.''

Zena bent low to the ground, her body heavy with anguish, but the Goddess gave her no relief, and the words continued inexorably.

''There is more. To keep the Mother's ways alive has little meaning if Her earth should be destroyed. That is why I have made you healer as well as wise one, for just as you heal a wound, so you can heal the land. Each of the ones called Zena will be a healer, for you will teach your daughter, she will teach the one who comes after her, she will teach the next, and so the healing will continue even as the earth is ravaged. To draw the poisons from the terrible wounds that lie open and sore, filled with putrid wastes, deep within the earth and the waters, to pull the hurt from the aching gashes that scar the valleys, the forests and hillsides, will take all the strength, the courage and vitality you possess. And after that, the poisons, the pain, must be absorbed into your own bodies and sent reeling into the vastness of the skies.

''But even then you will not be finished. For just as a healer gives her strength to the one she heals, so you must give the Mother's wisdom, the wisdom of the circles, back to the earth. You must fill the gaping wounds, the livid scars that remain, with the caring in your hearts, with the ways of love, the Mother's ways. Though only a few will notice, the wisdom, the caring, will grow and spread until one day they are strong enough to emerge. There will be people then who will remember that once we lived in harmony with the earth and all its creatures, and they will speak. Some will argue, refuse to listen. But others will hear the message, will know in their hearts that those who seek to protect the earth speak truth. Their numbers will swell and slowly, very slowly, the web of life will be restored.''

Silence came, a long, deep silence that seemed to wrap itself around Zena, soothing the turmoil in her heart. And when the Goddess spoke again, her voice was gentle and caring.

''It is you, Zena, who will begin the healing.'' Zena felt the words like the tender touch of an old woman's fingers on her brow. The fingers seemed to draw her upward, and she stood, opening her arms to the sky.

Once more the Goddess spoke, and now Her voice was as powerful as thunder, filled with authority. Zena pulled the words into her mind and heart so she would never forget.

"Go, now, and tell those who wait for you that I have spoken. Do not lose courage. The Mother will be with you for many years to come. And when the time of violence is over, She will return to the minds of all the people. Because you and all those who bear your name have held Her safely in your hearts, the world of the Goddess, the Mother of all life, will one day be reborn."

CHAPTER
27

Menace hung in the air. Zena could smell it, taste it, like a physical presence. Four years had passed since the Goddess had warned them, and each summer the invaders came closer in their yearly raids. This time, they must be very close.

Her eyes darted around the clearing. They were all here, except for Conar.

He sprang suddenly from the trees. "Into the tunnels! Quick!" The urgency in his voice was unmistakable.

The others responded immediately. Their movements were fast and practiced, for they had done this many times. Each of the adults picked up a child, grabbed another by the hand, and sprinted for the tunnels. One at a time, they slid through the narrow opening and made their way to the Mother's chamber. There, they would be safe, this time at least.

So far, the men had not discovered the caves, but one day, Zena thought grimly, they would. Before that time came, she must take the young Zena away. Her daughter was the next guardian of the sacred knowledge, and she must keep her safe.

The sharp sound of pebbles hitting the ground brought terror to her heart. Was it possible that this time the men had found the entrance to the tunnels?

She strained her ears, listening, afraid. But there were no more sounds. Perhaps some small rocks had fallen in the adjoining chamber.

For a long time, the group sat in complete silence. Even the children knew they must make no noise at all. After a while, Zena handed them some berries to eat, to make the waiting less arduous. They always kept food and water in the chamber now, for times like this. Finally, when the light that came through the opening high above told them many hours had passed, Conar rose.

"I will see if they are gone," he whispered. Zena nodded and watched him slip away, silent as a shadow. The familiar agony invaded her heart, but this time it was worse because she knew the men were nearby. They could be hiding in the woods, behind the rocks, where they could spot Conar as he left the tunnels.

The young Zena reached for her mother's hand. Her small face was clouded with worry. She, too, suffered when Conar left. Zena held the child's palm against her cheek, tried to smile in reassurance.

"Protect Conar for us, Great Goddess," she prayed silently. "Keep him safe, for we love him and we need him to warn us."

The agony did not dissipate. It would not leave her until Conar returned; she knew that from experience. To distract herself, she began to think of the ones who had already left, to search for a new home in a place where the violence had not yet come. Zena had sent them east, always east toward the sun, for that was what the Goddess had shown her.

Lilan, now a wise one herself, had led the group. Pulot and Nevilar and Gunor had gone with her, taking Rofal and Sarila and their tiny infant, and many others in the tribe as well. Even Katli had gone, for Zena had persuaded her that one who knew the animals so well would be needed on the journey. To lose them had been hard, but Zena was certain that one day they would all be reunited.

Probably she and Conar and the young Zena should have gone, too, Zena thought, watching her daughter's anxious face. But it had seemed to her that only here, in the place where the Mother had been born, could the young Zena learn all she would need to know to speak for the Goddess in the years to come. To leave Menta and Lune had seemed unbearable as well. In the last years, both of them had become old and frail. Menta especially had been too weak to travel, and Zena had known that Lune would never leave her sister—and so she had stayed.

She glanced at the fresh dirt at one edge of the circle of stones. Menta and Lune were there now, buried side by side in the Mother's chamber, as they had wished.

"When we return to the Mother, you must bury us here," they

had said. "It is a good place to be, for part of us will be here always, in the sacred circle built by the Mother Herself."

They had died within days of each other, as connected in death as they had been in life. A sickness that had affected many in the tribe had carried Menta away first. Seeming then to lose all strength, Lune had followed. Zena had offered them herbs, thought of trying to heal them, but they had waved her away. "It is time for us to return to the Mother," they had agreed. "She awaits us."

Sadness overcame Zena again as she remembered, but she knew, too, that this could be a signal from the Goddess that the time to leave had come.

Conar was suddenly by her side. Relief flooded her, and she pulled him close. He pressed against her, and she felt his heart thud harshly against her chest.

"They have gone," he told her softly. A sigh passed through the chamber as the others relaxed. Some of the children began to chatter, their voices quiet as if they were not quite certain yet that talking was safe. They understood the meaning of danger, Zena thought sadly, for they were children she had brought to the caves after their tribes had been raided. They had watched as the men they loved were slaughtered, had seen their mothers and sisters raped and taken away. For this reason, too, she was glad she had stayed. At least she had been able to save some of the children by bringing them here.

The young Zena came to greet Conar, and he reached down to enfold her in his arms. Ten years had passed now since her birth, but she was still small enough to hold. Still, she was strong, in her mind as well as her body, Zena knew.

Conar looked at Zena over the child's head, then his eyes returned to the child, and then they traveled once again to Zena's face. She understood his unspoken warning. To keep the young Zena here was no longer safe. She must hurry, to finish the training.

"I need one more day, only one more," she told Conar, her eyes anxious. "Can you tell if the men will return?"

"They follow the bison tonight," Conar replied, "tomorrow as well. But they will be back. I know many of their words now, and I heard them speak of caves. It is possible they know of this place." The warning look returned to his eyes.

"I will be ready tomorrow," Zena promised. "After I have taken the young Zena with me to greet the Goddess, we will leave."

Conar nodded and slid through the tunnel to resume his watching. Zena breathed another prayer for his safety, then she led her daughter into a quiet corner of the cavern.

"Tomorrow," she said, trying to keep her voice steady, "we must leave, to go to the other caves, the ones Conar spoke of. To stay here is no longer safe."

Three days' journey to the east, Conar had discovered a smaller group of caves. They would go there first; then, when they were certain the danger was past, they would begin the search for Lilan and her group.

"I wish to stay here." The young Zena's face was stubborn.

"That cannot be," Zena replied sadly. "The men with knives are coming closer. One day, they might find the entrance to the caves, and then all of us could be killed."

"But who will protect the Mother's home if we are gone?"

"We must trust that the Goddess Herself will protect it," Zena answered.

The young Zena's face was a mask of sadness as she absorbed these words.

"Taggart and Lipa are at the other caves already, waiting for us," Zena told her gently. "They went ahead to make sure the way was safe if we needed to come."

Taggart and Lipa were Pulot's oldest son and daughter, and were two of the people Zena had chosen to help her guard the young Zena on their journey. Both were strong and fearless, and they loved the young Zena dearly, would give their lives for her if that was needed.

The child's eyes lit up at the thought of seeing two of her favorite people again, then grew sober once more as she remembered what the journey meant.

"Now you must eat and drink," Zena continued, "for a special task awaits us, one that may take many hours. As soon as you are ready, we will go together to the Kyrie. The Goddess Herself wishes to teach you now, through Her visions. Only in that way can you absorb the remaining lessons in the time that is left to us.

"I will stay with you," she added, seeing her daughter's eyes widen in apprehension, or perhaps it was awe.

When they had eaten, she led her daughter to the deep black pool and held her close as the dark water closed around them. The child pressed against her but made no sound as the almost imperceptible current slid them gently toward the rocks on the far side of the chamber. No turbulence, no whirling vortex assaulted them, as it had when she had first entered the pool, and Zena was grateful. There was so much already for the child to absorb, so very much for one so young.

Pain sliced through her chest as they clambered up the steep path to the cliff. It was not shortness of breath that caused her pain, or even fear, only the knowledge that she would never again climb these rocks with the beloved daughter who clung so tightly to her hand. She had thought to bring her here many times, to sit with her and listen to her thoughts, watch her grow in the Mother's wisdom, and now she would not.

Zena stopped for a moment, steeling herself. To teach the young Zena and keep her safe was most important, and she must not let sadness deter her from her purpose. Even if all of them were killed, even if she herself died, the young Zena would have the sacred knowledge, and the Mother's ways would not be forgotten.

They came to the opening high on the cliff. Zena led her daughter out upon the ledge and stood, arms upraised, to greet the Goddess. The young Zena watched, still and silent.

"Great Goddess, I bring You my daughter, who is destined to serve You, for she, too, bears the name of Zena. Help her as she learns Your ways; walk within her as she journeys through her life. Send her Your knowledge, Your wisdom; guide her heart and mind as she leads our people in the years to come. Blessed Mother, we reach now for Your strength."

Zena waited until she felt the Goddess within her, deep and secure, before she turned to speak to her daughter. The young Zena listened carefully, for she knew she must never forget what she learned this day in the sacred place.

"For many years, more than any can remember," Zena told her, "we have lived in harmony with each other and with the life around us. That is because we have followed the ways of the Mother, the ways of peace and caring. In each tribe, there was a wise woman who taught the Mother's ways to her daughter, or her sister's daughter; she, too, passed on her knowledge, and so it has been, until now, for all the years of our existence.

"Some of these wise ones were called Zena, like ourselves. To us, the Mother entrusts her most arduous tasks. The first one lived long ago, before the time of our people's memory. Still, her love for her people, her suffering when they were hungry or in pain, was no different than our own. The next Zena could see far more with her mind than any other, and she changed our world in many ways. Because of her, all people came to know the Mother, so that all could live in peace.

"The one who came after her was myself, and already you know something of my story. But now you must know all; you must journey into my heart and mind, into the hearts and minds of the others who bore the name of Zena, for we are one even as we are separate. Here, as we wait on the cliff, the Goddess will bring you our lives, in Her visions. You will feel our joy and suffering, know our thoughts, our fear and wonder, see and hear all that we have seen and heard, until you have become us. Only in this way can you fulfill the destiny entrusted to you by the Goddess: to keep the Mother's ways alive in the time of trial to come.

"Come with me now, child, come with me to greet the Goddess, for She calls us. Pull Her wisdom into your heart, Her strength into your body, Her love into your heart. Feel Her deep within you as She takes you back to the beginning, to the one who was first called Zena. She will teach you, as each of us will teach you. Fill yourself with our lives, our knowledge and visions, all that we have experienced, until we have become a part of you, a part of all the Zenas yet to come, so that the ways of the Mother will never be forgotten."

Hours passed, hours that encompassed days and months, then years beyond counting. The sun vanished in an explosion of orange and red, and darkness crept across the land, became black as the pool below. Not until the moon was high in the night sky did the young Zena finally slump to the ground. Tenderly, Zena carried her down the steep rocks, through the deep pool, and into the circle of stones. There the child slept for many hours. And when she opened her eyes again, Zena knew her daughter had fulfilled her mission. The visions were hers now, never to be forgotten. When the time came, she would pass them to the next Zena; she would pass them to the next, and so it would be without end. Thus would the Goddess live.

II

The vast chamber was dark save for a faint glimmer of early light that filtered through the opening high in the cliffs. Zena sat stolidly within the circle of stones, her body heavy with anguish. To leave the home she had lived in for so long seemed more than she could bear.

"We go now." Her voice was barely audible in the cavernous space, but the others heard. One at a time, they came to kneel before the Goddess, then made their way through the narrow passages to the entrance to the caves.

Zena rose and went to stand before the image of the Goddess.

"Great Mother," she prayed, "we grieve that we can no longer guard the sacred chamber that is Your home. Keep it safe for us, so that we can hope one day to return. Protect myself and Conar, the young Zena who will one day serve You, and all those who come with us, as we search for a new home where we may live by Your ways. Great Mother, we go now, from this place where You were born. May we keep it always in our hearts."

Slowly, she turned away. Conar came to take her hand; the young Zena went ahead, her small body straight and purposeful. They bent to crawl through the narrow passage that led from the Mother's chamber, and emerged into the room Conar and Lilan had painted. The bison and reindeer and all the other animals stared down at them, as if they, too, were bidding them farewell. Through the winding tunnels they went, to the magnificent chamber with its hanging needles and massive upright pillars. The formations glimmered softly in the dim light of Conar's flare. The walls of the tunnel pressed in on them then, as they had so many years ago when Conar and Zena had first entered the caves. Then, with startling suddenness, they were outside.

The sun had not yet breached the mountains, but a thin shaft of light from behind the horizon slid softly between two low hills to the east. It seemed to Zena to form a path for them.

For the last time, she gazed at the ledge high on the cliff where she had spoken so often to the Goddess. The goat was perched there, its body silhouetted against the sky. Zena raised a hand in greeting, then she turned and walked into the light.

AUTHOR'S NOTES

PART I: The first Zena was a late *Homo habilis*, or early *Homo erectus*, human ancestors who lived about one million years ago and had a brain size of about 900 cc. (Human brains range from 1,000 to 1,400 cc.) They were distinctly humanlike, but probably did not have extensive speech.

Tope's death in a flash flood was inspired by "Lucy," a remarkably complete fossil skeleton of an earlier prehuman type, who is thought by some anthropologists to have died in just that fashion. The scene in which Zena steps in Dak's footprints was inspired by anthropologist Mary Leakey's discovery of early human footprints, in which a smaller person inexplicably walked inside the prints of another, larger companion.

Inspiration also came from the discovery of a two-million-year-old circle of stones in the Olduvai Gorge in Africa. The space within the stones had obviously been used, but it contained few of the bone and stone fragments associated with living sites. Instead, it may be the first circle of stones built by our ancestors for spiritual or ceremonial purposes.

Infanticide is common among primates, and probably existed among our early ancestors as well. Males are generally protective of infants born to females in the troop, but will often try to kill infants of strange females, females with whom they have not mated. The female then becomes sexually receptive so the male can mate with her and get his genes into circulation. For this reason, and

403

because mating brings special favors, female primates are careful to mate with all the males in the troop. I believe our early ancestors had similar mating habits. For females especially, monogamy had no rewards.

PART II: The second Zena belonged to a tribe of people who were in transition from late *Homo erectus*, with a brain size of about 1,100 cc, to *Homo sapiens*. The transition began about half a million years ago and resulted not just in increased brain size, but also in extensive brain reorganization. The frontal lobes, especially, became larger, permitting greater language and cognitive facility. The forehead became higher and more rounded, the skull larger. Birth was undoubtedly difficult during this period. The pelvic girdle cannot expand beyond a certain point in animals that walk upright without making it impossible to do anything but waddle—a dangerously slow gait in a world filled with fast and efficient predators. Natural selection finally forged a solution: accelerated birth. Human infants began to be born earlier in the developmental process and lived outside the womb for many months before they reached the stage of maturity typical of other primates at birth. Skulls became lighter and somewhat smaller, and were probably more easily compressed during birth because fontanels, unfused areas in the skull, were larger than in the past. But before these adaptations were perfected, many women must have died trying to deliver babies who had remained longer than usual in the womb while gaining the maturity to be viable at birth, and whose heads, especially, were too large to fit through the birth canal, and many infants born at the normal time must have died because they were not developed enough to live outside the womb.

Zena herself was *Homo sapiens*, born before this balance was achieved. Her brain capacity was probably greater than that of people today, and she could be thought of as an early genius. Zena was unusual in another way: she was the first woman to develop the ability to conceive before an existing child was weaned. Like other primates and hunter-gatherer women today, our female ancestors normally gave birth every four or five years. About ten thousand years ago, probably due to increased body fat and decreased mobility, the capacity to give birth at more frequent intervals spread through the population, with profound consequences for human fertility.

The Big Ones Zena and her tribe encountered are a remnant population of a prehuman type called *Australopithecus boisei*, a large, omnivorous creature that eventually died out.

The Fierce Ones are another remnant population, called *Australopithecus africanus*, which also died out.

PART III: The third Zena was *Homo sapiens*, often known at this stage as Cro-Magnon, and lived between 50,000 and 35,000 years ago. She and all the others in her tribe would have been indistinguishable from ourselves. Cro-Magnon artists created the magnificent painting on the cave walls in France and Spain.

Gunor and his tribe were Neanderthals, who lived at the same time. I have made them blond, rather than swarthy as they are often pictured, because they lived in the north, where light skin was adaptive because it absorbs more sun. Neanderthals were short and stocky and unusually strong. Scientists believe they were intelligent and capable of speech, although they may have had trouble pronouncing certain vowels. One of evolution's great mysteries is why Neanderthals disappear from the fossil record about 30,000 years ago. One possible answer is that they died out not because they were killed off by *Homo sapiens*, as is often suggested, but because they never developed the adaptations to the enlarging brain that saved *Homo sapiens* from extinction. Neanderthal skulls were larger and heavier than our own; if they continued to grow without the life-saving adaptations of accelerated birth and lighter bones, birth may eventually have become almost impossible.

The figure Kalar asked Lett to carve was the first example of the large-breasted, big-hipped "Venus" figures that abound in archeological sites in early Europe. Their purpose was not pornographic, as some suggest, but was instead spiritual, a way of thanking the Goddess, or asking for Her help.

Similarly, Conar's painting of the bison that saved Zena was the first of the many superb cave paintings discovered in France and Spain. No one knows what inspired the paintings, though many believe they were related to hunting activities. I believe they were, instead, gifts to the Mother that expressed a profound appreciation for the wondrous abundance of life She had created. The fact that there are few paintings of the animals most often hunted seems to support this theory, as does the fact that many of the paintings are found deep underground, not where people lived but in special chambers where storms and extremes of temperature did not affect them. As gifts to the Goddess, they were meant to last. Handprints are often found on the cave walls. These, I believe, were made not for some profound purpose, but for fun, to entertain the children while their parents painted.

The fierce hunters from the north are based on prehistorical evidence showing that bands of invaders periodically came from the north to devastate the peace-loving, Goddess-worshiping people who lived in southern Europe. The raids continued for thousands of years and ultimately destroyed the Goddess. Why the northern hunters were so violent, in contrast to Goddess-worshiping societies, is a question with profound significance today. Zena and her people understood intuitively what science is now beginning to confirm: that people who have been bullied or abused as children are at risk of becoming violent adults, and that only intensive remedial efforts can repair the damage. In scientific terms, the damage is real—repeated abuse leads to changes in the brain circuitry for two neurotransmitters that regulate aggression. Zena's people also believed what cross-cultural studies and contemporary experience confirm: that children who are raised in a violent culture will tend to become violent themselves, that young men, especially, are at risk of becoming violent, *and* that an occasional individual may be inately violent and incapable of empathy, and cannot be changed. Tron was one of these.